SACRED STRUGGLE

A DRAGON RIDER FANTASY ROMANCE

TALES OF THE VANIR
BOOK I

I0769660

Cover Design by 100 Covers
Formatted with Atticus

Thanks to the beta readers and editors who helped make this a better book:
Cindy Ray Hale and Keele Publishing
Kaitlin Slowik
Keeya Marquez
Gemma Poulton

And perpetual thanks to my alpha reader, Cynthia Davis

Dedication

To everyone who wants to ride a dragon ...
and the dragon rider.
This one's for you.

Astarot's song is *Way Down We Go* by Kaleo

Content Warning

This book is intended for adults only, and contains subject matter that may be difficult or disturbing for some readers.

Sensitive material includes, but is not limited to: frequent profanity, violence, graphic torture and killing of people and dragons (but not the cat; nobody messes with Thor), sexual assault (but not between the main characters), emotional abuse, socio-economic power imbalances, frequent mentions of blood, and genocide (of elves).

Sacred Struggle also contains explicit, open-door sexual content that will escalate over the course of the series.

Reader discretion is advised.

CONTENTS

Glossary

Ætt: Clan/Fhord's people

Dragon's-Length: Unit of measure; sixty feet

Draikana: Female of a mated dragon pair

Drake: Male of a mated dragon pair

Draugr: Undead

Drott: Chief/leader

Dróttning: Queen

Kastali: Castle

Konungr: King

Male's-Height: Unit of measure; six feet

Meistara: Lady

Meistari: Lord

Seiðr: Ability to predict the future

Thunder: Group of dragons

Valkyrie: Shield maiden/female warrior

Vekter: Guards/police

Viku: Unit of measure; one mile

MAP

TALES OF THE VANIR
NJORDHEIM
BARRIER
TRAINING GROUNDS
NORTHERN NEST
VANATIA
REVALLE
SOUTHERN NEST
TRAINING GROUNDS

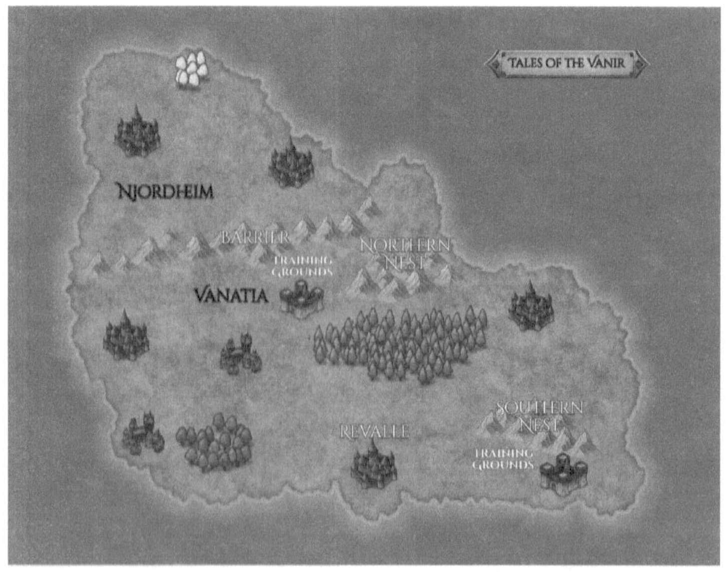

CHAPTER ONE

SIFA

THE TIME IS NEAR

"**Y**OU'RE TOO BEAUTIFUL TO be a shield maiden." The voice that spears at me from down the hall is loud, full of bluster.

Got him.

Even in a land filled with Valkyrie, some men can only see us as bedmates.

It makes them very predictable.

Which comes in handy in my job.

Turning, I give the male, Thrym, a smile instead of the smirk he deserves for being so easy to snare. He's one of the tavern's wealthier patrons, an older male who may have been handsome in his youth. The drinks that flow freely in Vanatia—and an ugly demeanor—probably stripped him of his looks years ago. Thrym's known to bed any woman who'll have him. He's not nearly careful enough for a man with his wealth and appetites.

"Can I help you, Meistari?" I force my tone to be flirty, although I want nothing more than to sneer my disdain at his advance. Instead, I saunter toward him, my hips swaying in a rhythm that can mean seduction or swagger. I let the rest of my body tell him which.

"Maybe I can help you," he responds as he closes the distance between us and reaches out to caress my shoulder with his sweaty fingers.

It takes all my strength to resist the urge to wipe off his touch. Even after all these years, my skin still crawls whenever someone touches me that way, as if my body is theirs to abuse. I don't know if that angst and anger will ever go away.

But I don't let him see that side of me. I can't. I'm finally starting to get jobs from Bevin, the most important overseer in the town. Thrym's got information Bevin wants. If I don't get it from him, I may not get another chance. And if I can deliver, Bevin will trust me with his more sensitive work, bringing me closer to the country's ruler, Konungr Beron.

More importantly, I'll be a single step away from the Konungr's wife, Dróttning Nerthus, the true source of power and knowledge in this land. Even the dragons bow to her, heeding her call before the calls of their riders. She controls the information I need.

If I can get to her, I might be able to find my way home at last.

I need to get Thrym alone. So I reel him in. "And what do I need help with?" My voice is low, sultry.

"I could help you find my room." His face shifts to an expression he probably thinks is attractive. I hold back the groan that wants to come out. "Make sure you never have to work again."

"What if I like what I do?"

"You'll like my money more. I'll make it worth your while."

I let my gaze track down his body, pausing at the growing lump in his pants. It's not much to brag about, and I'd wager good money it's all he has to offer.

"Yes, I bet you would," I whisper before looking back up at his face. Holding the smile I know will keep him hooked, I rest a slender hand on his arm. "Maybe I could use a little extra coin this week."

He nods and reaches behind me, placing a palm on my ass as he pushes me forward. It's all I can do to stop myself from grabbing a blade and taking that hand from him. Instead, I hold my tongue as I let him guide me down the hall, my dark curly hair bouncing on my shoulders with each step. There'll be plenty of time for knives when we get into his room. I can't very well leave a bloody path for just anyone to follow.

Thrym directs me to one of the tavern's better rooms, but I'd have been surprised if he stayed anyplace else. This mark likes to flaunt his wealth. The problem is he'll do anything—betray anyone—to replace what he throws away. He hasn't gotten punished for that yet.

Today his luck changes.

Bolting the door behind us, my lusty suitor leans against the wood and loosens the cord around his waist, his gaze landing on my tits and never straying. As soon as his pants are loose, a clumsy paw reaches inside to squeeze what he finds there.

"Strip," he snarls, all hints of the seductive tone he'd feigned in the hall gone.

Well, that's not gonna happen.

Sauntering toward him, my fingers tugging on the belt hugging my hips, I drop my skirt just as I get close enough to touch him. It's black leather, perfect for hiding the knives on my thighs while giving me easy access to them. Before he can move, I've got one against his neck. He isn't staring at my tits now.

"What the fuck is this?"

From the corner of my eye, I see a hand reaching down, so I grab another blade and shove it through his palm, driving it into the wood. His eyes bulge so hard I almost laugh, and then he squeals like my cat, Thor, when Toffer pisses him off.

I put just enough pressure on the knife at his neck to draw blood.

"You will stop screaming, or I'll slice your throat and find what I need myself."

His howl shuts off instantly. I always draw blood early in a job. I hated it at first. Weeks of living with the stench of my own blood haunted me long after I escaped from the dragon Nest. But violence is part of daily life in Vanatia. I was a shit spy before I started using my blades because nobody took me seriously unless I caused them pain. That's why I'm not too worried about his screams. The tavern's nearly empty this time of day, but most people will ignore us anyway. It's never safe to stick your nose into someone else's business in this gods-forsaken place.

After I reach down for the knife on his leg and toss it aside, I look him over quickly. "Any more blades on you?"

He shakes his head, but I can hear his heart accelerate just a bit as he does. I dig the tip at his throat deeper as I *tsk* at him. "You'll lose more blood than you can afford if you lie to me," I snarl. "Where is it?"

His gaze drops, but he stays silent. I bite back the moan as I realize this is going to take longer than I'd like. *Gah! I'm tired and I want to go home. And Thor's probably hungry. Toffer refuses to feed him, stubborn troll that he is.* Reaching around Thrym, I run my hands down his back, finding the sheath at his waist.

"Is this the only one?"

This time, Thrym's responding grunt rings true. I'll watch him until he's tied up, but I don't think he has another weapon.

"I'm going to free your hand, and you're going to sit in the chair by the fireplace. If you try anything, I'll take a finger. Or maybe a thumb. Understand?"

His eyes are burning into mine—it's almost funny how angry he is—but he dips his chin once. Wrenching the knife free, I step back and wave him forward. But he's not ready to comply yet. He lunges for me, his shoulder aiming for my gut.

Idiot.

Stepping backwards, I bring the knife's hilt down on the back of his head, dropping him like a sack of coal. As he groans,

I *tsk* again and straddle his back, a blade again at his throat. "That won't do," I whisper in his ear as I stretch my other knife forward and remove his right pinkie.

While he's shrieking, I pull a strip of fabric from my belt and gag him. Can't let him scream too long. That might draw unwanted attention if someone's trying to sleep in a nearby room. And I can already tell this guy's gonna be stubborn. We'll be here a while if he forces me to rummage through his brain myself.

"You'll soon learn that I always keep my promises," I mutter as I bind his wrists. Standing, I yank him to his knees and then his feet. He's a bit more complacent now, with so much of his blood decorating the floor. They always are after I take the first finger. I don't untie him when I plant him in the chair, just strapping his arms to the back. The rope might be a little tighter than necessary, but he's pissed me off.

"I'd hoped to make this easy on you," I explain as I pull up another chair and drop into it in front of him, "but that's up to you. You took information from the Kastali." His eyes widen at that declaration. He probably thinks I work for the Dróttning. That could come in handy so I let him believe whatever he wants. "I'm going to take off the gag and you'll tell me where it is."

"Fuck you."

His first words don't help his cause, so I stand to saunter behind him. Shoving the gag back into his mouth to stifle his next shriek, I reach for his left hand and pull apart the fingers he's trying to clench together. He's fighting me with everything he has, but he won't win this battle. They never do. When I've freed his left pinkie, I place my lips close to his ear and *tsk* at him while I slice it off. Then I head back to my seat and watch him writhe.

"Maybe you don't realize what's about to happen." Squaring my shoulders, I shift into the facade that helped me convince Bevin I'm one of the best spies in the country. Over his shoulder, I catch a glimpse of myself in the mirror: full lips, dark as the copper decorating the room, set in a thin line; warm, umber skin; bright brown eyes, narrowed for emphasis; high cheekbones and a well-defined jaw, clenched tight. My don't-fuck-with-me face.

"I'm going to get what I need from you," I purr. "If you give it to me willingly, I'll let you live. You'll have lost a couple of fingers in this reminder about what happens to people who take something that belongs to the Dróttning, but you'll leave with your life."

I've got his attention now. He's sputtering, but I'm not yet ready to hear whatever he wants to say.

"If you don't cooperate, I'll spend an hour or so trying to convince you. That'll involve more fingers ... and other parts," I add with a glance down at his paltry penis, "before I give up and take what I need. If you make me do that, I'll kill you for my trouble."

I don't tell him the real reason I'd kill him. Other than the Dróttning herself, only elves like me and a few of the Dróttning's most trusted soldiers—who she's somehow managed to imbue with her own powerful magic—can walk through people's thoughts. It gives me talents most don't possess. I can find information and convince Bevin's marks to do things they'd rather not.

But I can't rely on that skill too much and risk revealing myself. Nobody can know I'm an elf. The Dróttning had every elf in Vanatia imprisoned when she took power centuries ago. Other than dragons, she and her hand-picked clique of soldiers are the only beings in this land allowed to possess and wield magic. The Dróttning controls all of them, dragons and soldiers alike. I'm free only because I grew up in a different world and somehow got sucked into this one. If anyone discovers what I am, I'll end up in one of the elven prison camps.

Luckily, elves can hide amongst humans. I'm sure others walk this world, but I've never gotten close enough to any to gain the trust they'd need to share that secret with me. As long as I maintain control over my body—never let my pointed ears appear—and hide the mind magic all elves possess, only those with their own magic could recognize me. And that's only if my shields can't keep them out.

Thrym has no magic. And Bevin wants what he has, so I'm going to get it. One way or another.

"Do we understand each other?" I ask after giving Thrym a moment to consider how the next hour might go.

He nods, his eyes wide and much duller than they were a few minutes ago. Maybe this'll be easier than I thought.

I point my knife toward his mouth. "You won't scream again if I take this off, will you?"

He shakes his head, quick, jerky movements.

Releasing his gag, I poise my knife over his groin. A reminder of what's at stake.

"Where is it?"

"Aksell has it," he spits out, eager to comply now. "He knew I had business in the Kastali, paid me well to get a satchel one of the maids held and bring it to him."

"When did you give it to him?"

"Just this morning. It should still be in his house."

"Anything else I need to know?"

"Nothing. I swear."

I watch and listen for a moment, testing his words. They ring true, no signs of deception appearing in his eyes or heart rate. "Thanks for your help." I give him the smirk I've been holding back since the hallway as I flick my knife up and smack its hilt against his temple. His head whips to the side, eyes rolling back in his skull, and I breathe out a sigh of relief.

I've been doing Bevin's dirty work for months, walking a thin line the entire time. I risk being exposed if I get too close to powerful people like the Dróttning. But I need information they alone possess if I'm ever going to find my way home. I've seen enough hints to convince me that the Dróttning's libraries hold answers I've been seeking for ten years. And I'd risk just about anything to go home again. So I'm relying on my shields, which can hide me from all but the most powerful, and working my way toward the Dróttning's inner circle. Little by little.

Now I have to get the satchel from Aksell, but reaching him should be easy. He's even more reckless than this idiot. I'll go there in the morning, well before the sun rises. He may need a bit more convincing—he'll know the Dróttning didn't send me—but he deserves whatever fate may bring him. He's not a good male.

Although a hungry cat no doubt awaits me, I don't race home. After stopping by the tavern's kitchen to grab the bag they have waiting for me, I start walking. My route takes me along the water, and I find a peace here that I sometimes need. Revalle—Vanatia's biggest town, its stronghold in the south—spreads out around me.

Because the Konungr and Dróttning have a home here, some parts are opulent and picturesque: paved roads lined with manicured shrubs and bushes; large shops and homes painted in bright reds and oranges and yellows; fruit trees that bear succulent, delicious harvests, yet somehow never seem to litter the ground below. Grass and flowers and benches fill parks the wealthy stroll at night.

Those aren't the places that bring me peace.

My path home takes me through the poorer parts of Revalle. I wander along a shorefront teeming with storehouses and fishing boats. And then the road leads inland, through the homes and shops of the less favored members of this harsh place. They have little and must scramble for all of it, but they find joy in their lives. Their rulers don't always make it easy. Still, in house after house, I hear the happy chattering of children, unrestrained laughter, and animated conversations.

Here I find the peace I need.

The strength to keep searching for my path home.

Already, the day's stress is whispering out of my bones, letting go of me for another twelve hours.

I feel the tension fully leave my shoulders when I catch sight of Halla's long silver hair as she sits on the stairs waiting for me. She's small for a ten-year-old and wears a dress that's so threadbare, it's a wonder it hasn't fallen apart yet. This one offers no protection from the elements—necessary in the evenings, even in this warm climate—but Halla doesn't have many to choose from. Despite their limited means, Halla's always clean, her hair combed and tied back with a faded ribbon. Her dark eyes are bright and reflect a wisdom beyond her age.

I found Halla two years ago when she tried to take a bag I'd set down next to me for a moment. Only eight years old at the time, I soon learned why she had to steal to survive. And then I met her mother, Sagga, and learned much more about Halla. Now, I bring food and she occasionally relays words from Sagga, who claims to possess seiðr, the ability to predict the future. She's only ever foreseen simple and unsurprising events for me—a new person I might meet, a difficult day at work—but Halla says Sagga feels better providing something in return. We all like this arrangement more than Halla's reluctant thievery.

I'm never sure if she'll make it to meet me. Sometimes Sagga asks her to stay home and she does, even though they both desperately need the food I bring them.

"Hello, Halla," I say as I sit down next to her.

"Hi, Ms. Sifa!" Her exuberant response always draws a smile. It took a while to break through the distrust she'd developed toward all adults except her mother. I'm grateful I did.

"They served roasted boar at the tavern today," I share as I hand her the bag with tonight's dinner and enough extra to get them through tomorrow.

Her eyes light up in response. She loves boar. "Mama will be happy," she responds. But then her grin drops away and she casts her gaze down. She doesn't like the words she's been asked to share with me today, I can tell.

"It's okay," I assure her. "Tell me what your mother said."

She nods slowly, not yet looking up. When she does, she stares at me with the most intense focus I've ever seen, her sapphire eyes bright and wide. "The time is near," she says in a voice I've never heard her use. "Your enemy approaches, but he is not your enemy. Take a risk when you know you shouldn't, and we all will prevail."

"That's more cryptic than normal." I can't hold back an uncertain laugh at her words. I have no idea what to make of them.

"Mama said you'll know when the time comes. And if you listen to her words, you'll change everything. For everyone." She grimaces and lifts her shoulders in a helpless shrug. She seems as confused as me.

"Well then, it's great advice. Thank you." I watch as she stands and takes a step down, holding the full bag with both hands.

"Mama asked me to come home soon tonight," she explains as she turns to look at me again. "But there's one more thing I need to tell you." Halla pauses, looking away before her gaze finally returns to mine. "I understand this one, and it makes me sad." She looks down for the briefest moment as a pair of tears tries to break free.

I reach out to cup her cheek. "It'll be okay, whatever it is."

She bobs her head again before taking a big breath. "Mama said you'll be going away soon and you'll be gone for a long time. She wants you to know we'll be fine. We'll be here waiting for you when you get back."

"Well, I'm sure that one's wrong," I respond with another laugh. "I don't know where I would go, and I would miss you too much if I did." I grin, making sure it reaches my eyes. She needs to know I'm here to stay for the foreseeable future. I've been searching long enough to know I won't find my way back home anytime soon.

"I'll miss you too. But Mama said you need to go when the time comes. And you shouldn't worry about us."

"Tell your mama thank you," I tell her. "I'll try."

Halla returns my smile and reaches out for a quick hug before turning away. I watch until she rounds a corner, wondering what would happen to them if I disappeared. I need to make arrangements for someone else to bring food to them and Toffer if I ever have to leave. Mikkael and Johan will help. They've been working for Bevin for a long time, but they're good males. Good friends.

Shaking my head, I start to walk home. I'm going to meet an enemy who isn't an enemy? My actions will change everything? And I'm leaving for a journey soon? None of Sagga's words make much sense, although the last one was more specific than normal. It makes me nervous, even if I don't want to admit it.

I'm lost in those thoughts when I sense something unnerving—a power unlike any I've encountered before in Vanatia, that I'm drawn to in a way I could never have anticipated. My heart beats more erratically, my hands clenching, as the strange magic ripples around me, poking at my shields. I stiffen my spine and push up my chin. Whatever or whoever this is, I won't let them see the effect they have on me.

It's not an elf, I can tell right away, although I grasp hints of magic similar to mine emanating from this being. Elven mind magic *feels* different than the raw power it emits. Maybe it's one of the Dróttning's trusted few, but that doesn't seem right either. I've felt their abilities once or twice. It's an echo of the Dróttning's power, and has never been this primitive or strong. I've also never felt connected to that magic the way I do this. My power is humming inside me, demanding release, as if it wants to dance with this stranger's essence.

Pausing, my breath hitching in my throat, I stop walking and spin to search for its source.

And I find the most stunning, terrifying man I've ever seen.

A sharp jaw and cheekbones, along with bright green eyes, are framed by a tousle of thick hair, dark against his lightly tanned skin. His full lips are set in a thin line, as if he's angry to have crossed my path. He's tall—probably a full head bigger than me—with a firm, lithe body. If I look, I'm sure I'll find only muscle beneath his tunic and leggings.

I'm drawn to and also completely repelled by this unexpected, magnificent male.

And I can't ever let myself get near him.

I have no idea how I know it, but every part of me screams that he is the most dangerous thing in this world to me. Still, it takes every ounce of will I possess to stand there and watch him turn and stride away. Because as positive as I am that I have to get away from him, I want him more than I've ever wanted anything.

These warring emotions he's inexplicably stirred in me make even less sense than Sagga's nonsensical warnings.

I take my time walking home after that, not ready to face a life that suddenly holds many more questions than answers.

CHAPTER TWO

SIFA

AM I DONE HERE?

MORNING SEX. AKSELL'S PALE, flabby ass is bouncing up and down while his consort, a female I know named Liv, stares at the ceiling above and tries to keep from yawning. If I had any idea I'd find him like this, I'd have dawdled a little getting here. This isn't the image I need to start my day.

I woke way too early this morning so I could sneak in and out of Aksell's house before the staff gets up. He should have been asleep, maybe in his wife's arms. Instead, he's on top of Liv. His moans and the smack of flesh against flesh, like fish being tossed onto the pile at the harbor, fill the room. Ick.

Maybe I should turn around and come back in a few minutes—probably more than enough time for a man like Aksell. But I'm here. May as well get it over with. At times like this, I'm grateful the underside of Revalle is a small place. Liv works for Bevin too. She's pretty, with straight blonde hair, eyes the color of the sea and an hourglass shape, everything perfectly proportioned. Bevin must have decided to assign two of us to this job, although I have no idea how Liv knows Aksell has the satchel. I'll worry about that later.

If Liv's here fucking Aksell—and there's no denying it, much as I wish I'd never seen this—she hasn't yet gotten what Bevin wants from him. We'll try my way. Stepping forward, I raise my finger to my lips as Liv's eyes grow wide. She holds her tongue while I slide my blade between them and position it at Aksell's neck. He goes still, even the pathetic thrusts of a moment ago coming to an abrupt halt. My other hand wraps around his mouth to make sure he doesn't call for anyone.

Tugging him off to the side, I let out an involuntary laugh as his manhood flops to rest on his thigh. Or should I say boyhood? Aksell's a hefty guy, but his pride and joy apparently stopped growing at a young age.

"You're here for that?" I whisper to Liv, who still looks like she may never blink again. "No wonder you were bored to tears." Turning again to inspect Aksell's still exposed crotch, I smile. "You should cover that up. I'm tempted to relieve you of your misery. It must be such a disappointment when you pull that thing out."

"What do you want?" His voice is more respectable than his dick. But that's not saying much.

"Thrym sends his regards," I whisper, leaning forward to rest the knife's tip on his collapsed cock.

Aksell's eyes grow wide as he realizes why I'm here. But he's not ready to give in yet. "I don't know what you're talking about," he sputters, little bits of spittle erupting to land on his face and chest.

I dig my blade in just enough to draw blood, triggering a whimper as a few drops trickle down Aksell's leg to fall like crimson tears onto the sheet.

"Aksell, please. We both know that's a lie. I usually start with fingers but this ... pitiful penis ... is sitting here just begging for attention. I'll start there. Unless you tell me in ten seconds where to find the satchel Thrym gave you."

Aksell's lips set in a thin line, while mine grow into a wide grin. I'm gonna enjoy this.

"Ten, nine, eight ..."

"You wouldn't dare." His voice is shrill, desperate.

"Seven, six, five, four ..."

"I'm a powerful man."

"Three, two ..."

"Fine, stop." His tone is angry now, defiant. "It's in that closet, on the left side at the back." His chin is pointing to a set of doors on one side of his room but his gaze never leaves me.

"Wise move." Pulling ropes from my pack, I bind him to the bed as Liv pulls a skintight dress over her head and shrugs it around her curves. When I'm done, I step back to double-check the view I'm leaving for his maid, then stride over to the closet to find Bevin's package. It's exactly where Aksell said it would be.

Smiling my thanks, I capture Aksell's gaze. "I'm taking this to Bevin. He'll be very angry if you tell anyone I was here."

That should keep him quiet; few people in this town are willing to risk Bevin's wrath. "You asked her to do this," I warn as I gesture at the ropes, "so she did. Now be a good boy and stay quiet while we leave." Pausing, I glance over at Liv. May as well help protect her cover while I'm here. "Oh, and I'm gonna take her with me."

"I can't go to Bevin. He'll hurt me." Liv's voice barely reaches my ears. She's a good actress. Aksell tenses, a sneer teasing at his lips as his gaze bounces between Liv and me. He probably believes she's terrified.

"Not if you come without a fight. Bevin will just want to talk. Make sure you understand why you can't say anything about what just happened." I turn to Aksell. "He still might hurt you for getting involved in this," I say as I wave the satchel at him, adding a threatening laugh that always makes my marks nervous. "Or he might not. That's up to Bevin."

"You won't get away with this." His voice warbles with anger. I've made a dangerous enemy today. Thankfully, Bevin's more dangerous.

"I work for Bevin," I remind him as I shove a gag into his mouth and lift his head to tie it. "He decides who gets away with what. If you have a problem with me taking this," I add as I grab the satchel, "talk to him. But if you're a smart man. You'll let this go."

Grasping Liv's hand, I drag her toward the door and down the hall. We barely make it out of the house unnoticed. Twice, we're forced to scramble around a corner to avoid one of the cooks walking toward the kitchen. But we find our way out without being caught and are heading to Bevin's home before the sun starts to lift over the horizon. Bevin will be up—he doesn't sleep much—but it's too early for him to be in his office.

"Why did Bevin send you to Aksell?" I ask once we're a half-viku or so away from Aksell's home. "I only found out last night that he had the satchel and I hadn't reported that yet."

"I wasn't there for the satchel," Liv explains as she strides along beside me. "Bevin's still got me working for Ulfhild. She sent me to Aksell."

"Why?" Ulfhild runs the most exclusive—and expensive—brothel in Revalle, which means she's well connected. I've been watching her for a while.

Liv turns to me, eyebrows rising into her forehead. "Come on, Sifa. I can't tell you. If Bevin wants you to have that information, he'll give it to you."

I know but it never hurts to ask. We're quiet as we stroll to Bevin's home, not familiar enough with each other to make small talk. The morning is beautiful, still holding the overnight cool. Revalle's days can be unbearably hot this time of year. Although we arrive at Bevin's house early, a maid ushers us in without hesitation. Bevin's always available for business.

"I didn't expect to see you two together." Bevin's voice carries a hint of surprise as we walk through his sitting room door.

I realized shortly after I met Bevin that he's old, maybe even older than me, but he looks like a man in his forties. His black hair and beard have a spattering of gray running through them, like streams across the desert on a bright night. His flawless sunbaked skin, sharp chin, and silver eyes combine with a thick, muscle-bound physique to lend an overall look of cold cruelty. If we were close enough, I'd ask if he's an elf, but we are not close. I work for him. Nothing more.

"We were just as surprised as you." I choose the seat closest to Bevin as Liv nods her agreement and drops into an adjacent chair.

"And you were successful?" His gaze lands on the satchel at my feet for a moment and then shifts up. It moves more slowly than I'd like, lingering too long at my chest, but I'm used to that with Bevin.

"As requested." I lift the satchel and hand it to him. "I tracked this to a man named Thrym." Bevin's eyes widen for a moment and then narrow again, but he doesn't interrupt me. "Thrym had picked it up at Aksell's request and gave it to him yesterday before I had a chance to get it from him. I went to Aksell this morning and found Liv there."

Bevin nods, his long, dark beard shifting up and down with the slow movement. "Good work, Sifa."

"Thank you. Am I done here?" Bevin holds information close to his vest. He can't want me around for whatever Liv plans to tell him.

"No." Bevin's response is sharp. "I've been considering sending you with Liv. Perhaps the gods are giving me a nudge. Let's see what she has to say." His gaze finds Liv's. "Is Aksell more than a client to Ulfhild?" His voice is now a harsh rasp.

"Much more." Her hand drops to rub her thigh—a gesture Bevin notices, his eyes narrowing—and I wonder how she feels about continuing to work for Ulfhild. She'd been a bedmate for months before Bevin started giving her jobs. Perhaps she's ready to spend less time on her back and more on her feet.

"Aksell's become frustrated in recent months with his wife's limit on his spending. He's started making money in less legal ways. Ulfhild wonders how loyal he is to the Dróttning—or if he's started to sell parts of himself to others. She wants me to find out how deep he's gotten into whoever or whatever's funding him."

I'm not surprised. Aksell loves money and status, and rumors are he had none in his youth. He found an heiress to marry and clawed his way into the overseers' numbers through her wealth and means. If he's not getting what he wants from his wife, he'll find it elsewhere.

"And why is Ulfhild so concerned about who's loyal to the Dróttning, and who's not?" Bevin's voice drops further, a dangerous note entering it. This is important.

"I know your suspicions. I haven't been able to confirm them. I'll report to you as soon as I do."

"You've been helpful, but you're a bedmate. Not trained to find things you shouldn't." I have to hold back a grimace at his words. If Bevin had to fuck someone like Aksell, he'd have a bit more respect for what Liv's willing to do to get the information he demands.

Bevin's gaze shifts to me. "Sifa is exceptionally good at finding things. Perhaps she can help."

His eyes lift to the ceiling for a moment and then he nods to himself, looking back at Liv. "Take Sifa to Ulfhild. Introduce her as a friend who needs work and can handle a blade." Turning back to me, he adds, "You'll work at her house—as a shield maiden if she'll give you that job, a bedmate if she won't. Or even a maid. I don't give a fuck. Just get in and stay in. I must know what Ulfhild is playing at."

I nod, even as my stomach turns, because I can't do anything else. If I refuse Bevin's demand, he'll stop asking. But I sure as fuck won't sell myself to any man, even for him. Not after what happened in the dragon Nest when I landed in this place a decade ago. I'll need to make sure Ulfhild sees me for my skills, not my looks.

"Now we're done," Bevin adds, his tone terse. Nodding again, Liv and I stand and spin to leave. "Don't disappoint me, girls." Bevin's warning when we step into the hall echoes in my mind. I turn to catch his gaze and dip my chin in a quick acknowledgment, then close the door behind us.

Liv's face is cast toward the ground as we stride down Bevin's long hall. "This must be important, if he wants two of us working on Ulfhild," I point out. "What do I need to know?"

She turns toward me with a sigh, shadows in her pretty blue eyes. "Ulfhild has no love for Bevin," she mutters. "She can't know you work for him."

I know that much but I don't tell Liv. Ulfhild may not recognize me—we've never met in person—but I've learned much about her over the years.

"I understand," I assure her. "Why is Bevin so interested in Ulfhild?"

Liv doesn't answer right away. I realize she's deciding whether she needs to tell me everything. Finally, she shrugs, as if part of her just capitulated in an argument she had with herself, and turns toward me.

"Bevin suspects Ulfhild uses the brothel to help the rebellion, going places she wouldn't otherwise be welcome. We need to find out if that's true. If it is, Bevin wants to know her contacts. And anything else that's important." She's silent for a moment, adding in a more speculative tone as wrinkles form on her brow, "Whatever it is they're doing, Ulfhild is terrified of Bevin learning about it. Or worse, the Konungr and Dróttning."

"I'll be careful." Liv doesn't offer anything else so I move on. "We need to know a little about each other if we're going to convince Ulfhild. How long have you lived in Revalle? Where were you before?"

"I've been here seven moons," Liv explains. "I'm from the North, west of the largest dragon training grounds. I stayed out too late one night, after curfew, and accidentally saw them in formation, going through drills just outside my village. One of the riders realized I was there and I barely got away. I came here to avoid the death I would face there."

"You're lucky they didn't catch you." For reasons I've never understood, dragon training is shrouded in secrecy. The areas around the grounds have strict curfews, and the Dróttning has ordered that all deviants be put to death.

"I am," she agrees. "I can't go back or even tell anyone where I'm from. They're probably searching for me. I couldn't get a job in a household without a sponsor, so I went to work for Ulfhild."

"What did you do before you came here?"

Liv laughs, releasing some of the morning's tension. "I cared for the overseer's children. A far cry from my work here."

"Very far cry," I echo. "How did you start working for Bevin?"

She glances at me, her eyes speculative. "That's a story I don't share often," she says after a few moments. Turning, she gestures toward a large house. "That's us. But I don't know why you're here looking for work. What should I tell Ulfhild?"

"If she asks, tell her I killed a man who tried to rape a slave girl in a distant village," I suggest, my voice firm. "We met at the Shaking Boots, when you were getting a drink and saw me asking for work. We started talking, and you decided to bring me to her."

She nods as we walk slowly toward the door. "I'll introduce you, but you'll need to convince her to give you a job."

"This is what I do," I tell her with a smile. "I am whatever I need to be to get what I want."

"If you say so," Liv murmurs with a shrug, her eyebrows rising as her head tilts to the side.

She's skeptical—and I'm not as confident as I sound—but I'm not lying. I've thrived in this land, even more so than in my worlds, by knowing instinctively what I need to do and say in every situation. It's my special skill.

Ulfhild swings open the door, to my surprise. I've seen her from a distance but she's even more stunning than I recall, with light brown skin and dark mahogany eyes, the silver hair that comes from age, and a spattering of wrinkles. Her lithe body, dressed in a simple but stunning red gown that hugs her curves, is stronger than it looks, if my information is correct. It's her eyes that draw me in, though. Sharp and focused, they tell me I'm dealing with an unusually smart female. She'll either be a valuable ally or a worthy foe.

"Meistari Aksell's maid visited this morning, Liv." Ulfhild's shoulders are tight, her lips set in a thin line. She spins and leads us into the house, her long skirt swinging behind her as her hips sway with her steps. "Why did you tie him up before you left?" she asks without turning around.

"He asked me to," Liv responds with a shrug of her shoulders. "I think he wanted to shock his staff."

"He's a foolish man." Ulfhild's tone still holds a hint of disapproval, but she glances back to reveal one side of her mouth ticking up just a touch. "Did he not think to relieve himself before his odd request?"

"Now that you mention it, he didn't. Did he ... have an accident?"

"The poor woman who found him said his pathetic penis was not the most embarrassing thing for the Meistari." Ulfhild's smile is broad and genuine as she pauses to gesture us into a large room, full of bookshelves and plush furniture in warm, soothing colors. "While she enjoyed the laugh, it wasn't worth the mess she had to clean up. She asks you to send him to the privy before you tie him up next time."

"I'll do that," Liv assures her, her own grin emerging as she settles into a chair by the fire. "And I'll apologize to the poor woman."

"Please do. Her goodwill is as important as the Meistari's."

"Yes, Meistara Ulfhild."

Ulfhild chooses a chair next to the wall—the room and both its entrances within her sight—and drops into it with ethereal grace. She watches me with a question in her eyes as I sit across from her. "Have you brought me another bedmate?" She looks me up and down. "She's a rare beauty. We could make space for her."

"I'm Sifa," I explain in a tight voice, the shard of ice that speared down my spine turning my words cold and brittle, "and I'm no bedmate."

"Then why are you here? The kitchen is fully staffed and I don't think you've come to buy what we have to sell."

Releasing the breath that's caught in my throat, I relax my shoulders. *Calm confidence*, I remind myself. "My talents differ," I explain with a little tilt of my lips. "I can wield a sword like no other, and with or without blades, I win every fight, even against males much larger than me."

"I don't need warriors." Ulfhild narrows her eyes, suspicion growing. "And I don't trust you enough to place my girls' lives in your hands. Why would I?"

In the next moment, two of the blades I keep on my belt are in my hands and flipping through the air, each landing a hair's breadth from Ulfhild's ears. Her smile widens as she holds my gaze. Next to manipulating minds, which I can't risk with someone as astute as Ulfhild, my skill with knives is my most useful tool.

"Nice trick," she says in a firm voice, "but unless your knife pierces the heart of one of my men, the fact remains I don't need another warrior. I ask again, why would I trust you enough to hire you?"

Now I smirk, letting her see my devious side. This is where being a spy comes in handy.

Watching her as I stroll over to pluck my knives from the wall, I move to the chair closest to her and lower my voice. "I've been keeping your secrets for a long time, Meistara Ulfhild."

"What secrets could you hold, girl?" The laugh that accompanies these words is forced. She wonders if I'm telling the truth.

"Two moons ago, a man drowned north of the town." I hold my smile as I watch Ulfhild's drop away. "He'd been drinking—he liked his mead—so the vekter believed he'd fallen in. But we know differently, don't we Ulfhild?" My gaze hasn't left hers.

She opens her mouth to speak but apparently thinks better of it, clicking her jaws shut after a moment. "He had stolen from you, and he took too much joy in causing pain to the females he bedded. Vanatia lost nothing when the sea claimed him. So I held my tongue."

Ulfhild nods. She understands my unspoken threat, which is why I make it my business to gather tidbits of information about powerful people in Revalle.

"Perhaps it would be good to have a shield maiden who can pass as one of my girls," she concedes after a moment. "You can join them when they're called to one of the estates, or to the Kastali to entertain the Konungr and Dróttning and their guests." She lifts a hand, rubbing her thumb along her jaw as another smile emerges. "Yes, you'll do well."

"Understand, though, that I'm not a bedmate. Ever. You'll make sure nobody chooses me." I don't tell her why—that I couldn't protect myself in the Nest, and swore I'd never be touched by unwanted hands again.

"I'll do my best. If you catch the eye of someone powerful, it may be hard."

"I don't care. I'll kill anybody who tries to bed me. Make sure it never happens."

Ulfhild stares at me for nearly a minute. "I can send you with something that will repel most suitors," she says at last. "It's powerful but if any are interested enough in you to ignore it, you'll also have a sedative you can give them. Just make sure they drink enough to believe it was the ale, and nothing else. We can't have people suspecting we drug our clients."

"That will work," I agree. "I'll return tomorrow. You'll have a place for me?"

"I will. I trust I can rely on your discretion in all matters?"

I spin my knives in my hands a few times, never looking down at them, and then dip my chin. "I've kept your secrets, Meistara. I won't stop now."

I make it home within an hour, ready to become myself again. Sagga has no new words for me today, thankfully, and Halla is delightful without the weight of her mother's premonitions. We laugh and chat about her day and how much she'll enjoy the chicken on tonight's menu. And then she skips off, leaving me to wander away lighter than when I met her.

Toffer looks up when I open the door, a broad smile taking over his crooked face. He's the perfect embodiment of trolls from stories told in my worlds. Short enough for me to rest my chin on his shaggy yellow hair when we hug—which we do often—he's stocky and surprisingly strong. With a broad, round face, an absurdly-wide nose, and a beard hanging halfway down his chest, Toffer looks exactly like Midgard children imagined when they pictured trolls.

He stays home most of the time because very few trolls exist in Vanatia. When he ventures out, he causes a stir. People gawk and talk about his unlikely existence in animated whispers. And that attention always—every single time—triggers his innate need to kill. I've had to stop him more than once. Since I've managed to convince him he should try not to kill people who don't deserve it, he doesn't often leave the house without me these days. He's learned to lean on my presence to control his most base urges.

"Sif, my Sif," Toffer yells as he launches himself from the couch and picks me up in a huge hug—the response I get every time I come home, like a dog ecstatic at its owner's return. "I thought you'd never get back."

"Toff, I won't leave you. You know that," I assure him as I return his hug and pat his back a few times.

"You tell me that, but you're always gone so long. It feels like forever." His huge eyes don't stray from mine as he sets me down and then reaches up to touch my face. "I don't like being home alone."

"You're not alone, Toff," I remind him. "Why don't you chat with Thor?" I gesture toward our cat, who stares at me as if I've condemned him to death. His gold eyes are bright against his black fur, which is disturbed only by a bolt of white, like lightning, on his forehead. He always looks like he'd throttle both of us if he could.

"He doesn't like me," Toffer complains as he glances toward the cat. "And it's very hard to stop myself from killing him when he looks at me like that." He turns to me again. "I know you love him. I don't know why, but I know you do. I stop myself. For you."

"Have you tried talking to him?"

Toffer, like most trolls, can speak to animals. He's my permanent sidekick because we somehow got sucked into Vanatia together. Turns out, he was imprisoned in Midgard by the same man who was holding—and torturing—me. I know why Jonathan captured me, the bastard. Toffer had no idea why he'd been targeted. Maybe just because Jonathan was a psychopath.

I push that asshole out of my thoughts. I might despise him even more than the Dróttning, and I refuse to give him any space in my mind. He's worlds away and I'll worry about him if we ever make it back home.

Toffer and I got yanked from Jonathan's dungeon at the same time, landing in Vanatia together. We still don't know how or why. We dropped into a cell beneath the northern dragon Nest. Convenient, since that's where we'd have been sent anyway. Once we got here, we were tortured some more. Ten years later, I can think about those days—and sometimes talk about them—without collapsing into a fetal position. But it took a while.

Toffer and I weren't alone and the Dróttning's people knew it, although they couldn't figure out what I was hiding. Luckily, she disappeared before Toffer snapped out of the daze he'd been in when we arrived. I still have no gods-damned idea why she came with us or how she escaped the Nest, but it doesn't matter. The weeks of the Dróttning's torture weren't enough to drag that secret from me, but Toffer might not have held out. If they knew about her, we'd have no hope. I don't know exactly how we'll need her, but I know we will when the time comes.

I couldn't leave Toffer when I escaped, so I broke him out too. Now he's sworn to me until he pays back the life debt. Since he hardly ever leaves the house, afraid he'll accidentally murder someone, he'll be mine for as long as he lives.

Which won't be long enough. He's aging here much more quickly than me. In our worlds, time passes slowly for elves and trolls. I looked like a teenager when I landed here, although I've been alive nearly three hundred years. Now, only ten years later, most people think I'm in my mid-twenties. Toffer is racing through his life even faster. If we don't get back to our worlds soon, Vanatia will suck him dry. And then me.

Toffer's not thinking about that right now, though. His head spins so he can throw death rays at the cat, who yowls in response. "He told me to fuck off. Again. Even though I've told him I hate that word." He turns to me and smiles. "He's hungry, but he refuses to be nice to me. He knows he doesn't get food unless he's nice to me."

Exhaling, I step away from Toffer to pick up Thor. He starts to purr and snuggles into my arms. Dinner is coming soon, he knows. "Maybe if you fed him without threats he'd be nice to you. You could try."

"Nope. He has to try first. Stupid cat." Toffer turns toward the kitchen. "You, though, I'll feed. Even if you don't give me many options. Tonight, the cooler held pork. Nothing else. I added a few beans and that's what you get. Pork and pintos for my pretty princess."

He grins at his alliteration. For some reason, he loves word-play. When he's nervous or anxious about something, he falls into that pattern, a coping mechanism from our time beneath the Nest, I think. It makes it easier to keep a murderous troll around the house.

"A queen's quota from my quazy quiller," I respond with a smile. "First I need to change," I add as I head into the bedroom. I wear black when I work—usually a leather skirt or pants along with a fitted corset—because it helps me blend into my surroundings. But I don't like it. Big, bold colors always make me feel better. I grab the shirt on top of the stack in my drawer, a bright pink number with loose sleeves and buttons down the front, then add baggy blue pants and furry slippers. A sigh escapes as I become me again.

As usual, Toffer's meal is divine. He's lived long enough to learn to cook, and seems to enjoy it. Which I love. In my hundreds of years, I've figured out how to make food I can eat, but I've never liked cooking. Another reason I'm happy Toffer's around.

After dinner we settle down on the balcony with tonight's drink, a blend of fruit juices and the mead that's popular in Vanatia. Talking to Toffer helps me think through my day and my searches for a path home.

"Why worry, woman?" he asks, his lips lifting as he savors his word choice.

"I have a new job," I tell him. "I've joined Ulfhild's girls. As a shield maiden, not a bedmate," I clarify when I see him frown.

"Well, that's good," he says with a carefree expression he probably hopes will lighten a subject that would weigh us both down if we let it. "Because your bed's barren. Bounceless and bereft. You'd be out of practice. You're pretty enough, but I don't think they'd pay much for someone who hasn't"—he pauses as his wrinkled cheeks bloom like a summer rose and then glances at the ground before finishing—"pleasured a man for years."

"Do you think I've forgotten?" I ask with a laugh. As his eyebrows shoot up, I add, "It hasn't been that long." *It really has, but Toffer doesn't need to know that.* "Besides, when it comes down to it, one dick is much like another. They all like to be sucked and pulled and maybe bitten a bit."

"Bitten?" Toffer demands, his eyes wide. "Why would you bite it? Remind me to never let you anywhere near my trollpikken," he adds.

"Your pikken is safe," I assure him. "You're my friend. We'll keep our parts to ourselves."

"Yes, we will," he declares, his hand moving to protect his crotch from me. He narrows his eyes and then takes a gulp from his drink.

Smiling, I settle into my chair and look up into the night sky. Ulfhild's brothel is connected. I'm happy Bevin sent me to her. Maybe I'll finally start getting the information I need to get Toffer and me back home.

CHAPTER THREE

SIFA

AND YET HERE I AM

"WE'RE GOING WHERE?" I glare at Ulfhild, astounded at what she's asking of her girls. And me.

Already, a rock has dropped into my stomach, filling me with dread. I force my face back into the mask I wear with clients and throw back my shoulders. Ulfhild can't see my fear.

"He pays well," Ulfhild explains, as if that's all the answer I need. "And I know a safe route."

Another madam who cares more about money than her girls. Looks like Ulfhild will be a foe.

"There's no safe route," I insist. "The last time you sent a harem, three were caught. You paid dearly to retrieve them and even then, two nearly lost their lives. If they catch us this time, we'll all be dead. The penalty allows no exceptions. You know that."

Ulfhild's eyes widen in surprise at the knowledge she didn't know I possess. And then she smiles, her face settling into a look of cold calculation.

"You'll be there to help make sure everyone is safe."

I stare at her for a moment, evaluating her resolve. Finally, I dip my chin. She isn't going to change her mind. Bevin wants me here, so I have no choice but to go where Ulfhild sends me.

This is not *the northern Nest*, I remind myself. *I don't have any reason to fear this place.* And as much as I dread it, I need to go to Vanatia's forbidden areas. The training grounds should have a library I can search. I've never had an opportunity like this.

I just wish my stomach agreed.

"Who's going?"

"Liv will join this time. She knows well the rules to follow when dragons may be doing drills nearby."

I spin my head to look at the woman who somehow feels like an ally, though we barely know each other. It's unsettling. I have few friends and didn't want another. Still, I feel strangely connected to her. She's pale, holding her chin high but unable to hide its slight tremble as she wipes her hands down her skirt. Liv is just as terrified as me of sneaking into the outskirts of the southern training grounds, but she has no more choice than I do.

"Frida will be in charge," Ulfhild continues. "She's led this trip before. Ten other girls will join you, along with a few guards."

"When do we leave?" I ask at last.

"Tomorrow morning. Bring clothes for a week." Ulfhild pauses before asking, her voice skeptical, "Do you have dresses you can wear?"

"I will be exactly who I need to be," I assure her as I leave.

I show up in the morning ready for travel—my extremely revealing gowns packed away where they belong for as long as possible—only to find all the girls looking like they plan to find extra jobs along the way.

"Why would they be dressed like this already?" I ask Ulfhild as I gesture toward the skin on display.

"We have a reputation to maintain," she explains in her most peremptory tone. "Whenever we leave the house for work, we dress for the occasion."

"And do you expect me to bare everything for this two-day trip? Where would I hide my knives?"

"You'll need to get creative. I have great faith in you."

Ulfhild spins and strides away, leaving me wondering why in the nine worlds I agreed to do this. I knew I'd need to conceal a dozen knives in odd places once we got there but didn't expect I'd have to travel for two days with them hidden beneath a courtesan's dress.

But if I need to look the part now, that's what I'll do. I spend the next fifteen minutes in the bathroom finding places for all my blades under one of the ridiculous outfits I brought with me. Finally, when I feel like I can sit down without spreading wide for all to see, I emerge and join the harem.

Within an hour after climbing into the small, rickety carriage, I need to pull the knives from my thighs. I can't move with the sheaths constantly rubbing against my most sensitive parts, a pair of cocks poised to pick me apart from the inside out. Soon, the knives under my arms come off. And then the three along my back.

Liv and the others watch with increasing laughter as I give up one blade after another, stowing a few next to me and the rest in my bag. I hate feeling unprotected, especially if I'm stuck inside and can't watch my surroundings.

We reach the inn after sunset, gratefully stepping out of the trap that held us. Next time, I'll insist on a horse. I'll dress as a man for the trip if I need to. That would be better than this ridiculous dress.

Dinner is good, at least. It helps tamp down the anxiety that's been building in me all day, as we get closer to the training grounds. And it gives me a chance to watch everyone—the girls and their guards. Most seem comfortable, eager even, despite the destination. They've been before and know that usually the trip there and back is safe. The guards aren't nearly attentive enough. Other guests watch us with interest. It wouldn't take much to overwhelm the sentries in the food hall.

We pair up for the evening and I insist on sharing a room with Liv. I need to learn what she knows about dragon training grounds.

"Not much," she insists, a shrug lifting her shoulders. "You know how secretive they are. At home, we'd see them sometimes during the day, when the senior riders take their dragons on security runs. We never saw anything else. Children's lessons all include the importance of training secrecy. It's drilled into us."

"You don't know why?

"I have absolutely no idea. It's always seemed so strange to me. Why do they care so much that they'll kill anyone who sees a dragon run drills, or even exercise. But they do. We lost my uncle to the penalty." Liv looks down now, her back curving as her shoulders droop forward.

And I hate the Dróttning even more. She's destroyed so many lives for so little cause.

"What do you know about our contact?" I ask after a moment.

"His name's Knut and he's part of the rider guard," Liv explains as her gaze finds mine again. "His job is to serve the leaders of the training facility. He never asks us for anything. I think he wishes we brought some males with us, other than as guards," she adds with a grin. "He arranges the entertainment for others. Ulfhild's girls go every few months, but I've only been once before."

"Did you learn anything helpful?"

"I wasn't working for Bevin yet. This is my first time since then."

"If it's for the leaders, why do we have to sneak in and out? And why did some of the girls get caught on the last trip?"

"Oh, it's not approved. The Konungr and Dróttning would have us all served to the Thunder if they knew." She shivers, her gaze dropping to her lap. "The thought of being eaten by a dragon," she adds under her breath before shaking her head and looking at me again. "The men are stuck there for months. Some spend time with other trainers, or maybe students, but most prefer our company. Men always do," she says with a wink. "Knut makes sure Ulfhild's girls come often enough to keep them happy with him."

"What happened last time?" I ask, a tremble rolling down my spine at the reminder that we're risking much by traveling to the training grounds without the Kastali's consent. "How were the women caught?"

"They went for a birthday party. Someone important. It wasn't the best time. The Dróttning's guards were scheduled to visit a week later, and Knut didn't want to bring the girls. He wasn't given a choice. The birthday boy wanted entertainment. Then the guards showed up sooner than anyone expected."

"How did they get away?"

"I don't know for sure," Liv tells me, "but I think Ulfhild paid off a guard. She may have killed another, who wouldn't take coin for his silence."

"Does Knut always bring in Ulfhild's girls? Or does he use other houses sometimes?"

"It's always us. I saw Frida and Knut together when I was there, and I'm sure they're friends. They acted like they were close."

I pause as a shiver rolls down my spine then expands out, filling me with the restlessness and unease that wrapped around me two days ago. The male I encountered in Revalle is here. I'm overwhelmed by a compulsion to find him that's so strong,

I have no choice but to follow it. But then it's paired with the most intense repulsion I've ever felt, a blanket that would smother the pull toward him if I let it. A bitter taste erupts in my mouth as bile rises in my throat.

I've never experienced such discordant and overwhelming emotions, triggered by the same person.

"Is everything okay?" Liv's question draws my gaze back to her, and I realize I'm staring at the door as if I might see the stranger if I focused hard enough. One eyebrow is raised, wrinkling her brow.

"Yes," I murmur. "I just need to find something. Get some rest," I add as I stand, swallowing a few times to stop myself from spewing all over her. "And thanks. I appreciate the information."

"We're in this together. Anything you need, just ask."

"I still appreciate it," I tell her, dropping one hand onto her shoulder with a light squeeze.

He's moving away more quickly than I'd hoped. Grabbing a cloak, I open the door and check the hall. The rumble of patrons drinking—and everything else—floats toward me but I ignore it. The only sense that matters now is the one that will lead me toward his unexpected presence. My heart rate is increasing with my need to see him again.

I step out, my feet light enough to be hidden by the noise below, and follow my senses. I'm struggling to keep him within my grasp while I jog downstairs and toward the kitchen, my legs moving faster as I try to catch up. I feel a hint of his emotions—the anger that's driving him. A desperation to get away from something.

Me.

The simple answer strikes me like a hammer.

He can sense me too.

He knows we're connected.

And he wants to get away from me.

So now I must find him.

But he doesn't want to be found. Within a few minutes, he disappears. And my heart drops to my stomach. I've been here a decade and never felt a power like that. One so tied to me. Suddenly, though, he's dropped into my life twice in the span of a few days. It must mean something.

I wander the grounds for nearly an hour, finding nothing. Finally, I trudge back upstairs and fall into bed, exhausted. Tomorrow. I'll search more tomorrow.

I don't have time. The harem is scheduled to leave the inn at first light so I'm up early with the other girls, scarfing down the simple breakfast offered. Before the sun reaches the horizon, we're on the road again.

Today is so much worse. We were able to stick with roads and well-trodden paths yesterday. Now, we're too close to the training grounds for that. Hours before our arrival, our carriages leave the road behind, bouncing us along a little-used trail like balls in a cage.

By the gods, I hate traveling in this peculiar world.

After *hours* of struggling to hold down my breakfast, the carriage starts to slow, and then stops completely. I can hear whispers around us tinged in fear. My heart responds, quickening as it prepares to fight or flee. I start to stow my knives on various body parts again because I *do not* flee.

And then the presence appears again, moving in our direction at a snail's pace. I'm not sure if he's hesitant or taunting us. I'll know soon enough. He's no longer trying to avoid me.

"I can't stay here," I whisper to the girls in the carriage. I manage to keep the hint of desperation out of my tone, stating my intent in a matter-of-fact way that doesn't reveal my *need* to see him again. "Something's here that I have to understand, so I can help protect you and the other girls."

"You're supposed to stay with us," Liv reminds me. "You'll be safer if you just pretend to be a bedmate, don't let them see that you can fight."

"I'll be safer out in the open, where I can do whatever's necessary to protect you." I reach toward the door but then pause for a moment to turn toward Liv. "I promised to keep you all safe. This is how I keep that promise."

Her gaze holds mine for a moment but she finally nods. "Be careful," she says as I open the door and step out into the cool afternoon.

We've journeyed far inland and are surrounded by trees, the paltry path we're following a haphazard ribbon tossed between them with no discernible purpose. The guards stand around the carriages, hands on the hilts of their swords as their gazes scan the forest, searching for whatever approaches.

And then we see them. They wear the clothes and colors of the royal house—thick black breeches tucked into boots that are even darker, tunics in the blood red the Dróttning loves with sable straps across their chests for the swords on their backs. But this group seems less disciplined somehow. It's as if they're the candidates who didn't make it through soldier school.

Approaching us with an informality the Dróttning would despise, the apparent leader steps forward. But I don't make the mistake of confusing her nonchalance with weakness. She's a warrior, fierce and strong, with short brown hair and piercing hazel eyes.

"Why do you travel these roads?" The woman's voice is firm, demanding.

A girl I don't know well—Frida, I think—steps forward. I sense no fear. Ulfhild chose her for a reason.

"Thank the gods you've found us," she says in a tone rich with relief. "We found ourselves on this miserable road this morning." She raises a peremptory finger to point at one of the drivers. "He swore he knew the route, but here we are. Will you lead us back to the road?"

"You're lost?" the leader asks, her lip quirking with her skepticism. "You ask us to believe you've trekked more than two vikus away from the main road by accident?"

Frida turns to sneer at her chosen scapegoat—*she's playing the aggrieved traveler to perfection*—then looks again at the woman whose soldiers bar our path.

"He's so stubborn," she explains, her voice dripping with frustration. "I told him we were going the wrong way, but he insisted on taking us down this rut of a path. Our Madam will be so angry with him."

"He's led you toward a place you may not be. This land belongs to the Kastali. The punishment for entry is death. Perhaps we should take him to the Konungr and Dróttning for drawing you down such a dangerous path." The woman's lips still twist. She knows Frida's lying, but we haven't entered the training grounds yet—I think—so she's not quite ready to condemn us all.

"Our Madam would be even angrier if we lost him," Frida explains, her voice taking on a plaintive note. "He's her brother, so she cares for him, tries to make him feel useful when she can. Perhaps you know of her? Meistara Ulfhild."

The woman smiles. It doesn't reach her eyes. "Of course we know of Meistara Ulfhild. All do. But that does not give her leave to send her bedmates into forbidden lands. There still must be a punishment."

Before Frida can respond, the woman's chin lifts and her gaze turns to the nearby forest. The presence that seems to be following me is racing straight toward us now. And I'm torn, my gut clenching with a dread I can't explain. I'll finally get to talk to the male who has run from me twice. I need to be here, to understand how we're connected, but my instincts scream at me to get away. Fast. My stupid stomach has twisted for no reason at all.

I stomp down those frantic parts of me. I'm not going anywhere.

Everyone's quiet, watching the woman in charge as she waits. Long seconds drag by.

When he emerges from the forest, my breath catches in my throat. He's every bit as magnificent as I remembered—tall and strong and dangerous. Now that he's closer, I can see the tattoos that were too far away to notice in Revalle. Hints of them appear on his hands and neck, but the rest are hidden. An irrational, reckless part of me suddenly wants nothing more than to take off any piece of clothing necessary to follow those lines and swirls wherever they lead. Preferably with my tongue.

I don't know what's gotten into me.

His gaze should be focused on our guards. It's not. Instead, he stares directly at me as his horse carries him into our midst—eyes sparkling emeralds sitting in beds of dark lush lashes. Not once does he look away.

And then he sneers.

He knows it too. We could destroy each other if we let ourselves get too close.

Finally, he turns to the woman. "Let them go," he commands, his horse pawing at the ground and prancing, as if it needs nothing more than to run.

"But they are forbidden to be here," she responds, her voice surprised.

"I don't give a fuck. Let them go."

My heart beats a dozen times while she watches him, confusion in her eyes. And then she bobs her chin and turns to the rest of the warriors. "Retreat," she tells them.

They all bow slightly and spin their horses around. Within a minute they've disappeared into the forest.

He shifts in his saddle to again hold my gaze.

"You shouldn't be here," he tells me. His ominous tone sparks an emotion I barely recognize, a mix of anticipation and anguish.

"And yet, here I am." Foolish, I know, but I can't back down from him. Not now. Not ever.

"I've given you a chance to disappear. Take it."

And then he tugs the reins and nudges the horse with his heels. It doesn't need a second request. Leaping forward, it launches itself after his soldiers. They head away from the training grounds, leaving our path open if we decide to take it.

Nearly a minute passes before anybody moves or speaks. And then Liv opens the carriage's window to look at me, one brow lifting as she grins widely. "What was that about?"

I take a deep breath, finally getting control of a heart that's been racing since I saw him. "I don't know." It's true. I have absolutely no idea what just happened between me and that male.

"He never looked away from you. Not once."

"He glanced at me and knew I'm no bedmate," I deflect, rolling my eyes as I force a smile.

"Sure," Liv responds, her voice dripping with sarcasm as she looks me up and down. "Really, what was that about?"

"I honestly don't know, Liv," I insist, focusing on my hands, which seem determined to fidget. *I always control every part of my body*, I remind myself. *This body does not fidget.* "I've never met him before today," I add after a moment, ignoring our first encounter. "You know exactly as much as I do."

"Well, whatever it was," Frida interjects, "it was a gift from the gods. That woman didn't believe us. He gave us a chance to get away—one that we should take. We can still make it by the end of the day if we go fast."

Her words seem to unlock an urgency with the rest of the group. As one, we race to our carriages and horses. Within a few minutes, we're bouncing along toward the one place in this part of the country that we are forbidden to go.

SIFA

I'M SEARCHING

THE REST OF THE day does not go smoothly on the bumpy trail we're following, but at least we're not bound and headed to prison.

We are, though, still traveling toward the training grounds. We've got hours left. I'm stuck in the carriage again, and my thoughts keep replaying our stop. Drawing up his face, examining every scar, the cut of his chin, the shape of his eyes. My mind's eye imagines the markings that lead up chiseled arms to a broad chest, and then down to parts I can't stop thinking about. Fantasizing about.

Even now, my veins throb with repugnance, so strong it threatens to tie me up in knots, mixed with a fervor I haven't felt in the centuries I've been alive.

By the gods, I need to do everything I can to stay away from that man.

At least it keeps my mind off my fear of getting too close to a Nest. Of being captured again.

We finally make it to the mansion I'm told always houses the bedmates when they come. It's vast, capable of holding a hundred people or more. I've witnessed a lot of opulence in my life, but this is one of the most lavish estates I've ever seen. More than anything else in this land, it highlights the fortune that smiles on dragon riders here. Reportedly chosen by the Dróttning because they already possess power—and spurning the bonds that would naturally form between dragons and the riders the fates chose for them—dragon riders have many rights and few responsibilities.

In principle, they're obligated to protect Vanatia from threats but there are none. The Dróttning controls her land with an iron fist, and no one has challenged her in the decade I've been here. Although I hear talk of a rebellion, it's impotent, so far as I can tell. Some dragon riders work in one of the Nests and others serve by punishing any who stray from the Dróttning's firm grip—which those riders and dragons are rumored to enjoy a bit too much. But many dragons are simply toys of the elite, with no job beyond ferrying their riders around.

As I inspect the estate, I'm relieved to see it's different enough from the northern Nest to not remind me of my time there. It's not what I expected. Where the Nest is dark—caves and cells hidden deep underground—this is bright and open.

Knut also isn't what I expected.

He meets us at the door, gregarious and welcoming. He's the least soldier-like soldier I've ever met, with a slim build that appears to hold very little muscle, a wide grin, and wild hair.

His appearance reveals his allegiance to the Dróttning only because he wears her uniform. His demeanor is carefree—a contrast to others who don her colors—but shadows hide in his bright eyes. Knut is not all that he seems.

Still, I like him right away, and even more when he escorts us each to our own suite, where we find hot baths waiting. He tells us to take our time, and that he's arranged a hearty meal for us in the dining room. With plenty of mead and wine.

Yes, I like Knut a lot.

I inspect the room, which holds many places for a hole or even a person to hide, then strip off the ridiculous dress I've worn the last two days. It feels so good to sink into the water. I don't move for a long time, letting the heat soak into me and work out all the stress that built up on the trip. Finally, as the water is turning cold, I wash with the orange and mint soap and shampoo provided. Stepping out of the tub, I grab one of the plush towels from the cupboard and wrap it around myself.

The bedroom is large and just as luxurious as the rest of the house. A massive bed sits against the only solid wall. Windows line both sides, providing a surprising view of the nearby fields and mountains in the distance. This area is supposed to be secret. Why would Knut give us rooms that would put any nearby training activity on display?

I don't have long to ponder it. A knock on the door drags me from my reverie. When I open it a crack, a woman dressed in a maid's smock tells me dinner will be served in ten minutes.

Choosing a simpler dress than the one I wore here—nobody's working tonight—I follow my nose to the meal. It is decadent. Pork roast with sage gravy, two different kinds of potatoes, melt-in-your-mouth butter rolls, and a surprising selection of vegetables. And the wine. Oh, my gods, the wine. It alone is almost worth the trip we took to get here. Almost.

Knut's an entertaining host. He spends the evening regaling us with tales of the men and women stationed in the Nest. But despite the number of words that spill from his mouth, not a single one reveals the Kastali's secrets. Dragons are part of every life here, yet he barely mentions them. When he does, the references are vague, lacking any details beyond what every Vanatian knows.

Knut is very good at what he does.

As the meal winds down, I realize Frida's role here is more than just a bedmate. I watch as her eyes meet Knut's for the briefest moment. His eyebrows lift slightly, and she responds with the smallest dip of her chin. I guess I know what I'll be doing tonight.

After dessert—three different options, all of them scrumptious—I join the group for coffee in the library.

"Your patrons will arrive tomorrow afternoon, an hour or so before dinner," Knut explains when we're all settled on chairs and couches. He looks at me quickly, then casts his gaze around the room.

"We'll have a few dozen riders for you. Those of you who've been here before know what to expect. Who will want what, who may be more difficult, and who to send my way so I can drug them into oblivion if they're chasing something you don't sell." Knut glances at me again. "You'll watch out for the new girl?" he asks as he turns to Frida.

"We'll make sure Sifa knows all she needs to do her work here," Frida assures him.

"And you can stay for three nights?"

"We're at your service for three nights, Meistari," Frida responds with the barest bow, dropping her chin to hide the lips that tip up at the ends. I can feel her laugh from here.

There's so much more to this arrangement than Ulfhild told me. I wish I could dig into their minds to find answers to the many questions bouncing around mine, but I'd be a fool to use my power to search for the secrets they're not sharing. Knut runs a mansion important enough to the Dróttning to warrant imbuing him with some of her magic. I can't risk being caught if he's able to sense me rooting around in his brain. So I'll spend my time here doing what any human would—following them around like a stalker. Tonight should be revealing.

Finally, everyone starts to wander to their rooms. I do the same but circle back when my hallway empties. After trekking through the corridors without success, my search takes me outside. I try my best to appear casual, but I can't risk missing whatever they have planned.

At last, I find them in the last place I'd expect because it's so close to the manor. As I approach the stables, I hear a whispered conversation. Lightening my steps, I make my way to the closed door and find a hole I can peek through. I'm closer to them than I should be—a male's-height at the most—so I make sure my breaths are light and silent.

I don't have to wait long to learn why they're here. "Ulfhild needs more than that to do her part," Frida insists stridently. "You ask much of her but give her little to work with."

"It's all we have," Knut responds, frustration warbling his words. "We know about Aksell's work. We still can't figure out who's supporting or directing him. We need your girls to get that for us."

"Aksell must suspect us," Frida declares. "He's very careful when my girls are around. Or perhaps they booted him out. He's not the strategist he once was. I think the mead addled his brain."

"He's still connected to them. We've seen him with others within the last fortnight."

"Then he knows about us, and he's hiding his secrets when my girls are there. I can't risk them going to him again." Frida pauses a moment, her next words hesitant and even more of a whisper. "Take me to Troels," she urges. "Let me talk to him."

"He'll give you the same answer." The authority in Knut's voice surprises me. He's a different male now than he was at dinner. "This remains our best way into Aksell's home."

"Then my answer is the same. My girls will not return to Aksell. Find another way."

Silence fills the air. I can almost see Knut's face as he considers her demand and his response. His grunt comes a full minute later.

"Tomorrow, after the guests leave, join me here. I'll ask him to meet us."

I can't risk staying any longer. I've learned all I can for tonight and slink into the nearby forest for cover. Just in time. The door swings open, and Frida strides away as I find a large tree to hide behind. Knut doesn't follow immediately. When he emerges, he looks around as if he suspects someone's been eavesdropping. He finally shakes his head and follows Frida into the house.

Everyone but me sleeps in the next morning. Our work happens at night so there's no reason to wake anyone early. But I have limited time here and much to learn. I'll sleep when I get home.

I'm searching for Bevin—Knut has secrets he'll want—but more for me. I haven't been this close to one of the dragons' lairs for a decade, and my only goal then was escape. I've suspected since Toffer and I landed here that the magic that drew us into this world is bound to the dragons. I don't understand exactly how, which is why I need access to the Dróttning's libraries.

I can't squander this chance to hunt for answers to questions I've been asking since I landed here.

Stepping outside for a moment, I turn toward the rising sun. I still haven't seen a dragon, which surprises me. I assumed they'd be regularly flying above this close to the training grounds. Maybe they avoid this area when they know guests use the estate, which would explain why we have rooms with views and can wander the place.

For now, I'll focus on the home and then its surrounding buildings. I decide the library's the best place to start as I walk back into the house and look around. A manor this large must have one, probably better than most. And I won't rouse any suspicions browsing bookshelves.

It takes longer than it should to find it. I'm nearly ready to give up and head to the second floor when I round a corner and see a set of double doors in front of me. They're unlocked and when they swing open, I'm stunned by the size of the room. Floor-to-ceiling rows of books appear. There must be thousands of them. I'll never have enough time to look through everything, but if they're well organized, I should be able to find areas to focus on.

They're not. An anarchist must have shelved these books. I can see no rhyme or reason to the order. It's as if they were simply set into place whenever they were acquired, without any attempt to categorize them as they came in. I scan the titles of a hundred books, maybe more, and find nothing helpful.

The grumble in my stomach could be frustration, but it's probably hunger. Maybe I'll have thoughts on how to approach this search with some food in my belly. I turn to leave for the kitchen, and my mouth drops. Snapping it shut, I tip my head toward Knut, standing in the doorway. But this isn't the kind, welcoming soldier I first met. His lips are set in a thin line, eyebrows drawn together, and back straight. Even his hands appear angry, clenched into tight fists.

Now he looks like one of the Dróttning's soldiers.

I don't like this version of Knut, without the mask he normally wears. It's good to see the real him, though.

"We do not often find bedmates in this room," he announces in a flat tone. "Perhaps you are lost."

"Apologies. I enjoy reading and don't have many options in Revalle. The libraries aren't nearly as expansive as this one. I thought I might find a novel to pass my days."

"This room does not hold fables," he tells me, his voice devoid of the gaiety and charm he displayed at dinner. "Ask the chef. She learned to read in her youth and may have books to share."

"I also like history. Some of it feels more fanciful than the tales writers spin. Perhaps you can point me toward the legends of this land."

"Perhaps not. Our stories are written for those familiar with dragon society." He turns his head toward the door and then looks at me again. "You will find breakfast in the kitchen," he says.

"And just in time. My searches have made me hungry. Thank you for your help." I tip my head again—although he probably expected a bow—and stroll into the hallway. The door slams behind me, and a lock quickly spins.

Such a strange place.

I definitely need to spend more time in the library while I'm here.

Breakfast is hearty and quick. I'm relieved because I have more ground to cover. I won't try the library again—that'll be my overnight entertainment—but there's a lot to see.

I head to the stables, another place I might be expected to visit without a purpose.

And it's worth the trip.

A dragon and its rider have come to join the festivities. I saw plenty of dragons in my worlds, but none this close since I came here. This one is every bit as magnificent as the dragons I knew before. Like them, it appears to be sixty or seventy feet from its nose to the tip of its tail. With wings that probably would span to nearly that length, it exudes power. Its yellow gaze catches mine, eyes narrowing as it spits a small flame from its mouth.

It's covered in feathers like birds, similar to my worlds' dragons and the others I've seen here. It's not nearly as nice, though. I never feared any of the Thunder at home. Zaria and Signe—Lia and Freyr's dragons—even carried me occasionally, spinning me in the air so I could join them in the joy of flight. This creature looks like it would sooner eat me than give me a ride. It emphasizes that disdain with a snort and another burst of fire.

The rider notices and strides over, casting his gaze up and down as he examines me.

"You are one of the bedmates sent by Ulfhild?" He almost sounds bored, as if he'd rather be anyplace but here.

"I'm one of Ulfhild's girls," I tell him in the most non-committal voice I can muster. I don't want to pique anyone's interest. Especially him.

He scans his eyes over me one more time, pausing at each curve.

He likes the prestige, the power he gets from his dragon, I realize. He's probably quite cruel in bed. I'll warn the girls to avoid him if they can.

"You're a rare beauty. I'll consider you."

I tip my head, loath to let him see the glare his words inspired, and watch his boots stride away. Good riddance.

The dragon and its rider turn out to be the highlight of my day. If there are secrets here, they're well hidden. I can find nothing of any interest other than the library. Frustration grows as the sun treks through the sky, reaching its zenith and then dropping toward the horizon.

Worse, as the day begins to merge into night, I find myself less and less able to concentrate. It's been ten years since I escaped the Nest. Those long weeks—the things they did to me—haunt my nights more often than I care to admit. I don't like being so close to forbidden grounds.

As I sit in my bathing chamber adding makeup to my lashes, working to prevent the tremble that seems determined to emerge, I wonder how I'll respond if I'm forced to enter a room alone with a man I don't know. What if he tries to force himself on me? Will I lose control? Will he survive it?

Ulfhild better keep her promise.

She does. In the most revolting way possible.

Literally revolting.

Frida knocks on my door just as I'm finishing my make-up. She enters with a smile, anticipating whatever's planned. "Ulfhild told me we need to make sure you're left alone," she tells me.

"That's right," I agree, growing nervous about whatever she has planned. She's enjoying this way too much.

"This'll do the trick," she assures me, handing me a small metal vial. "But let me leave the room first." Reaching for a second vial, this one glass, she adds, "Use this if the first one doesn't keep them away."

"What have you brought me?" I shake them, listening to the slosh of liquid inside.

"Treat the first one like a perfume and then plan to stay in the corner all night. We'll have a couch for you there. Nobody will notice it if they don't get close to you. I've warned the girls to keep away. It will repel anyone who gets within a few feet. The men will detect a smell and attribute it to that. But it's more than just a scent. I'm told it's quite effective. The second one goes on your lips. You'll need to kiss him ... or her ... but it'll act quickly after that. Just wipe it from your mouth as soon as you're done so you don't pass out too."

Smart. I've heard of these elixirs but never tried one. It's probably exactly what I need. Frida smirks just like Thor when he's taunting Toffer, then opens the door to escape.

I expect a repulsive smell when I uncork the first vial, but I'm still surprised by how my senses react. My nose goes first, triggering a series of gags as it rebels against the attack. My other response is more interesting. The elixir wriggles into my thoughts to find whatever repels me and amplify it. I get a touch of déjà vu as the magic hints at a subtle memory but it passes quickly, the elixir gaining full control of my senses. I feel as if I'm eating bugs, their crunchy bodies and mushy centers sliding down my throat. Now I'm really fighting to stop myself from vomiting.

Thankfully, that feeling passes after a minute or so. And I'm left with the smell. Even that isn't a problem for long, as my senses dull to it too. Perhaps five minutes after I painted the liquid onto my pulse points, I'm ready to join the crowd.

I finish quickly and head down the hall, letting the rising noise lead me to the ballroom where everyone will gather.

It's enormous and dripping with displayed wealth, gold and silver threads highlighting the purples and reds that adorn the walls and ceiling. Men and women dressed in serving clothes wander through the room, balancing trays of drinks and appetizers they offer to all the guests.

Two hundred people could fit in here easily. The fifty or so that are here would make it feel empty were it not for the dozen couches positioned strategically through the space—one for each of the girls. Mine sits in the corner, as Frida said it would. Half the bedmates have arrived and they're holding court on the recliners they chose. Already, each has a group forming around them, staking their claim to time that night. The others trickle in over the next ten minutes or so.

The elixir works better than I could have hoped. I make my way to my spot in the room, getting a wide berth from anyone I can't avoid. And then I watch. It's a fascinating dance tonight. The women hold court, but there's no doubt who holds power. Their suitors seem to instinctively order themselves according to rank. Each of the bedmates has someone sharing her couch and every single one ripples with strength and domination. The others all give them the space and privacy they clearly expect.

Three times, someone in the crowd notices me and wanders in my direction. The first man wears a seductive smile, probably convinced he's scored a quick pass to the front of the line. As he gets closer, though, his lips start to shift, slowly dropping into a confused frown. And then he's fully engulfed by my scent. His eyes widen in surprise as he takes a step back, then another. Mouthing his apology, he finally turns to flee.

I've never enjoyed a rejection so much. It almost makes the smell worthwhile.

The other two have similar reactions. And then nobody else tries. I've earned my solitude. Now I can relax and observe.

Within a half hour, the first bedmate rises to her feet. She extends a hand to welcome her companion to join her and strolls across the room toward the hallway. She must be the signal to the others for the evening's festivities to begin. One by one, they follow suit, leaving me as the sole bedmate in the room while the rest of the suitors chat and drink, waiting their turn.

For four hours, I sit by myself and inspect the men and women trusted enough to live in this forbidden place. None are very remarkable. In my worlds, dragons choose their riders, often based on their strength of body or character. Not here, it seems. These people are soft, their wealth denying them the lessons of a hard life. Arrogance and egos dripping with entitlement are the strongest emotions I sense from them.

The night finally ends just after midnight. Everyone has been sated, and the girls are dismissed to go find their beds. I join them, making sure I'm seen heading down the hall toward my room. But my night has just begun.

Tonight, I'll do the first reckless thing I've done since arriving here.

CHAPTER FIVE

SIFA

I TOLD YOU TO LEAVE

KNUT AND FRIDA AREN'T nearly careful enough.

I follow Frida out to the stables and then both of them to a nearby clearing. It takes us barely thirty minutes to reach it—far too close for a meeting they hope to be secret. And then they're louder than they should be. Like they want to announce what they're doing. Or they're too arrogant and reckless to suspect they'd be followed. Whatever the reason, I'm happy to be able to get close enough to see and hear them well.

Troels doesn't keep them waiting long. Within a few minutes of their arrival, a large man emerges from the trees. He stalks toward them, boots kicking branches out of his way as he glares with narrowed eyes at the pair. Maybe he doesn't like being summoned to a meeting in the middle of the night.

"Why am I here?" he demands as soon as he gets close enough.

"We need to make other arrangements," Frida explains, her generous chest thrusting out as she throws her shoulders back.

"No, we do not." Troels stops only when he's inches from Frida, his nose nearly close enough to touch hers. His lips are pressed together in a thin line. "You and Ulfhild will do what we ask of you. Whatever we ask."

Frida doesn't back down. Her chin holds firm as her gaze battles with his. "You want more than we can give without risking ourselves. Aksell must suspect something. Our girls are in danger every time they go to him."

I'm not surprised to hear Aksell's name. He'll do anything—betray anyone—for money or power.

"It's a risk we must take." He pauses, inhaling deeply before he speaks again. This time, his voice is more measured, less demanding. "They plan something. If they succeed, it will destroy everything we've done. All that we've fought to achieve. We must find out what they're doing and when."

"But why us?" Frida probes, her tone less strident. "You must have someone else who can get this information. I think he suspects us. If one of my girls gets caught, you'll lose all of us. And all our connections."

"I don't like it any more than you do." He reaches out a hand to place it on Frida's cheek, holding it there until she lifts her own hand to rest it on his. "I wouldn't ask if it weren't important. This is important."

They stand like that for a long time, staring at each other. I see the moment she resigns herself to his request. Her shoulders slump a bit as she looks toward the ground. She holds that position for a few seconds, her chest moving in and out slowly. And then she looks up and smiles.

"You'll owe us. So, so much."

"We already owe you so much, Frida," he says softly. "Should we send more men to guard the women?"

"We have enough. And if they do know, no amount of protection will save us. But we're committed. We'll do what we must."

The briefest smile passes across his lips as he leans down to give her a gentle kiss. She responds with passion, one hand moving to entwine itself in his hair and pull him in closer. He doesn't resist.

There's such an interesting story here. I wish I could ask her about it.

"Thank you, Frida," Troels says as he draws away from her.

"I never could resist you," she responds. Stepping back, she squares her shoulders and glances at Knut. "You'll tell us if you hear anything? Warn us if you learn we're in danger?"

"Always." Knut agrees. "You'll be the first to hear of any threat to your girls."

"I must return," Troels interjects. "They suspect anyone who strays at night. And Fhord's people are there, putting everyone on edge." For the briefest moment, the tendons stand out on Troels's neck, a pulse spiking in his veins. Then the mask returns.

"What games does he play now?" Frida asks, the tips of her lips curving up.

"The same ones as always," Troels tells her. "He walks a fine line between the Kastali and the rest of us. I never know whose side he's really on."

"Not ours," Frida says with a huff. "That's all we need to know."

"Never ours." Troels glances at Knut. And then he turns and stalks back into the forest.

"Do you still trust him?" Knut's whisper barely reaches my ears.

Frida turns to Knut with a sigh. "I don't know. We played together as children. I sometimes think I know him better than myself. But the longer he spends in that place, the more I wonder if he still stands with us."

"You'll do as he asks, though?" Knut's words emerge as a plea.

"Yes," Frida's laugh is light. Resigned. "We'll keep trying with Aksell. And the others. We know how much it matters."

"Good." Knut turns to look in the direction of the house. "We should go."

Frida nods, and they turn to walk back, more quickly than they came. I give them a few minutes before following. But I don't go to my room. The library awaits. Hopefully it's not still locked.

It is, but not with anything effective. A few flicks of my tools and the door opens. I walk in with a plan because I don't have enough time to do a thorough search. I've realized the chaos may be intentional.

If I wanted to hide secrets—and Vanatia has lots of those—I'd do it exactly like this. Stacks of books with no apparent order. Only those who know where to look could find the texts that really matter. They would be high up, mixed with others that appear irrelevant. Out of reach to the casual reader.

I climb the rungs of the ladder and take a few minutes to inspect the books within reach. None are interesting but that's no surprise. Nothing's ever so easy. Dropping to the floor, I tug on the ladder, which squeaks when I pull it over. My fingers freeze as my stomach flips. Pausing, I wait for someone to appear at the unexpected noise. Nobody does.

The next time, I move as slowly as I can. It takes nearly a minute to shift the ladder a half-dozen feet. It was worth it, I see as I reach the top shelf, and my gaze lands on the first helpful book I've found—but not for Bevin or Ulfhild. This one's for me. It's about elves and maybe will finally explain why I'd be imprisoned if anyone learned what I am.

My steps are even lighter now than before. Breaking in here was bad enough. If anyone finds me reading this book, I'll be killed even if they attribute it to curiosity. If I could, I'd sink into a chair in a corner, hide in the shadows. But I need light to read, so I choose the most visible spot in the library, right where the moon's glow falls through the window. I feel exposed, like I've lifted my skirts to bare myself to anyone who happens in.

My heart pounds the entire time I sit there, but I finally get some answers. I've wondered since I arrived if my power here was unique, or perhaps part of the explanation for the elves' banishment. And now I know. If this text is true to history, elves once lived freely in this land. They sat on the ruling council and played important roles in governing. Because they were powerful, like me.

I skim through the hundred or so pages, reading stories of elves who helped build this country. Males and females found their spots in Vanatia's history, many for their relationships with dragons. They seemed to be closer to those massive beasts than others. Whoever penned these stories believed elves were more attuned to hatchlings and that they'd been key to earning the Thunder's trust.

My stomach sinks as I reach the end without any news of what happened. Why elves became enemies to Vanatia's leaders. Why so few elves have been born since they all were imprisoned. Why they spend their lives in labor camps, never allowed to know or see anything else.

If I can answer those questions, maybe I'll figure out what drew me here, and how Toffer and I can get back home.

Sighing, I tiptoe toward the ladder to return the book. Before I can, though, I feel him. The strange male that triggers intense emotions is in this estate, stalking closer. My stomach flips as fate seems to tower in front of me, drawing us together for the third time in less than a week. It feels intentional, like the gods have intervened to ignite this weird connection.

The knob twists, and the door swings open. He's dressed nearly the same as before—a dark tunic with black leggings tucked into leather boots, also black. But he's left a few of the buttons on his shirt undone, revealing part of what looks to be a golden dragon etched on his broad chest. It takes all my willpower to drag my gaze up to his face. Green eyes stare at me, bright with an anger that looks ready to rip out of him.

"Why are you here?" His voice is low, dangerous.

"Why are you here? Are you following me?" I force my tone to be as threatening as his. I won't let him think he can intimidate me.

He scoffs, his gaze flitting down my body and then back up. "You have nothing that interests me." His words are cold, dripping with spite, even as his pupils expand, exposing his lie. "This room is forbidden. If they find you here, they'll feed you to the dragons. The Thunder isn't allowed humans nearly as much as they'd like. You'd be a tasty treat."

"Or perhaps it's you they'll feed to those beasts."

Now he sneers, his lips quirking his disdain. "My dragon wouldn't tolerate it." He shifts to the side, extending his arm toward the hall. "Leave this place. You're not safe here, and you're a fool for not realizing it. Don't come back."

"I'm exactly where I should be," I snarl at him. "I'll leave when I'm ready."

He stands in silence, arm still pointing my way out, thin lips and a straight back exuding frustration. I hate to give in, but the longer we stand here, the more likely we are to be found. Finally, I realize I have no choice and stalk toward him.

"Leave me alone," I warn as I step through the doorway.

"Stay the fuck away from me and I will." His words are clipped, angry. "The book," he adds as I turn away.

Gah. He has me so flustered, I didn't even realize I still had it. "Fine," I respond, spinning around to shove it into his hands.

I shouldn't let him know I was reading *this book*, but I have no choice. And for some inexplicable reason, I'm sure he won't expose me. Spinning again, I set my shoulders and stride away. I never look back. Even though I desperately want to.

After tossing and turning most of the night—my dreams taking me back to the cave I found myself in when I came to Vanatia and the weeks that followed trapped in the dungeons below the northern Nest—I give up on sleep just after dawn. Even if I can't go back to the library, this house holds other possibilities. Maybe the chef's a gossip.

She isn't. She's happy for the company as she starts fires and begins to pull out ingredients for bread. She's even willing to put me to work and chat while we knead dough together. The conversation, though, never strays far from the benign and meaningless. We talk about the weather, the fruits and vegetables available now, and those she misses the most. She shares stories of her children and asks if I have a lover.

That's it. Never once does this talkative woman stray into forbidden subjects. And maybe that's why she's here. In a place that values secrecy above all else, those who can keep secrets have tremendous value.

That's what I find with everyone today. Not a single person gives me a bit of useful information. By the end of the day, I'm frustrated and grumpy. And ready to go home. This has been a wasted trip.

After bathing and dressing quickly, I sit down to prepare myself for the repellant Frida gave me last night. I know what to expect when I remove the cork from the elixir, but I'm still startled. I sit still, breathing slowly as I let my senses work through the onslaught. Finally, long minutes after applying it to my neck and wrists, I'm ready to join the festivities.

Tonight feels much like last night. Many of the same people appear, most choosing different bedmates to circle. As they did yesterday, the truly powerful people in the room share couches with Ulfhild's girls. They drink and enjoy a passing bite of food while they wait. And then the same bedmate rises to draw her consort away. Others stand and do the same. Nobody comes near me.

Until he arrives. I sense him as he approaches the front door, my emotions waffling between anxiety and excitement at his presence. I force them to settle down. It'll require all my concentration to understand what's going on. Taking a deep breath, I release the firm hold I always keep on my mind.

I learned to control my wandering psyche within a few weeks of landing here. At first, I welcomed the escape. It let me slip away from the room they kept me in, the things they did to me. It let me see into people in a way I couldn't in my worlds. It's what eventually helped me escape.

Too often, though, I came back to a body barely clinging to life. When I wasn't there, I couldn't use what little power I possessed in those caves to intimidate and repel my tormentors. I realized I needed to be present and interact with them, or they would go too far. So I forced myself to stay put. Endure the pain. Until I found a way out.

In the years that followed, I taught myself how to send out my thoughts and call them back reliably. I even discovered how to maintain the barest hold on my physical form, alerting me if I needed to return quickly. I can do this without much risk now. So I do.

It isn't hard to find him. His presence calls to me like a beacon. My mind goes directly to the front door where he stands. I'm breathless, even as my heart decides it's running a marathon.

But that's as far as I can go. For the first time since I started reaching out to other people, my spirit hits a wall. I feel his presence but nothing else. I can't see into him at all or sense a single emotion. Not even the hint of a thought.

That's never happened before. Always, I can at least grasp the vibrations that every being emits. It lets me understand them, catch hints of what they're feeling and thinking. Even with him once before, I knew he was angry when he approached in the forest. Not tonight. He's an enigma. Impenetrable.

Reeling my mind back in, I take another deep breath and wait. He's coming this way. He'll find me.

Once again, his gaze lands on mine almost immediately. I can see his smirk from across the room. He's amused by my solitary presence in a corner. The room parts for him as he strides directly toward me. And I struggle to control my beating heart, the breathing that grows faster with every step he takes.

He seems to feel it too. Even from here, I can see his pupils dilate as he approaches me. But he can't avoid the elixir any more than the others. He slows as he gets closer, drawing to a complete stop a few feet away. The arrogance in his face drops away, replaced by confusion.

"Why do you," he pauses as his nose wrinkles, his lips twisting into a look of disgust, "stink?"

"Girl problems," I tell him with the most saccharine smile I can muster. "You wouldn't understand."

He watches me for a moment, his eyes watering a bit from the aroma he can't avoid. Finally, he speaks again. "I told you to leave."

"It may have slipped your notice, but we do not stand in a forest. Or a library. I left. But not because you told me to."

"You know what I meant. You shouldn't be in the Nest."

"Next time, be more precise. Or better yet, don't say anything. I'm not yours to command."

He snarls at me—literally snarls—his eyes somehow growing even more narrow. Still, I can see the fire in them. I incite the same emotions in him that he does in me.

"You'd be wise to listen to me, but maybe you're as foolish as you seem." He takes one step toward me, lowering his voice. "You don't belong here. They'll catch you if you stay."

I sigh, forcing my tongue to drip boredom. "Perhaps you could use a distraction." Lifting my arm, I wave toward a few of the couches. "They may be able to give you the attention you seem to need. Go bother one of them." And then I smile, my eyes twinkling. "But they go by rank here. You could be waiting a while for your turn."

His hands clench as his jaw tightens. I can almost hear teeth grinding. "So fucking dangerous," he breathes, almost to himself. He inhales again and then exhales slowly before biting out his next words. "I will not tell you again. The Dróttning comes. She'll detect your presence, and she'll kill all of you. The others will die for bringing you here. If you somehow manage to escape, you'll never know peace again. Once she realizes you live in Revalle, she won't rest until you're found and captured."

The strange man snarls one more time, as if for good measure, and then turns on his heel. He stalks out, a handful of soldiers gathering behind him to follow.

I ignore the intense emotions vibrating through me—a heady desire combined with an aversion so deep it seems unnatural. As if fate is fucking with me.

None of that matters. The Dróttning is coming. We can't be here when she arrives.

It takes nearly ten minutes to find Frida. She's in the furthest room, entertaining a woman whose squeals should have drawn me here in the first place. I don't bother knocking—nobody cares who sees what—and almost laugh out loud at the scene.

Frida's partner is thin as a reed. I can't see a bit of fat on her body. Even her tits are tiny, as if the gods had little material left when they made her. It's good she isn't standing, I think, because her legs appear incapable of holding her up.

But her pussy has swallowed the biggest dildo I've ever seen.

It's fully inserted when the door swings open and—because they're too distracted to notice me—I watch in amazement as Frida pulls it out, her tongue reaching in to take its place for a few seconds, and then shoves it back in. The woman squeals again, legs that are thinner than the beast in Frida's hand lifting her ass as she tries to take in more of it.

This girl is very happy with her chosen bedmate. I hate to interrupt her pleasure, but we need to go.

"Frida," I whisper as I stride forward.

The woman's eyes widen, but she doesn't move at all. Her butt is still suspended a foot above the bed, the dildo stuck in place. "Oooh, a surprise." She licks her lips as she looks down at Frida, who's gone still. "You don't need to stop. She can join us. Maybe I can watch you two when we're done."

"I'm not here to play," I respond with a smile, "although it looks like you're having fun."

"So, so much fun," she agrees, wiggling her hips a little to get Frida's attention, or maybe just to restore the friction she was enjoying a moment ago. "And we're not done. If you're not here to strip naked and drop onto this bed, go away." Now I can see the soldier in her. She's accustomed to people following her commands.

"She needs to come with me," I explain as I stride forward and reach out for Frida.

Before I can touch her, a hand snakes out and takes my wrist. And then she smells me.

Her lips twist, the ends dropping like rocks, as her eyes start to water. She spins her head to glare at Frida and then turns that haughty, hateful stare on me.

"You're making a mistake. I've taken lives for less. Get the fuck out of this room, or your scent will be the least repulsive thing about you."

"Let me finish, Sifa," Frida urges, her eyes pleading with me, even as she tries to hold back her own tears. "I won't be long."

"You'll be as long as I need you to be," the woman demands.

I nod once and turn to return to the hall. In almost no time, the woman's shrieking again, her cries escalating quickly. She ends with a few moans and then a whimper, whispering something I can't catch when she's done. Less than a minute later, she stomps out the door, glaring at me as one hand rises to cover her nose.

"Frida promises she didn't, but I know she rushed me. You're lucky she gave me such a good orgasm. I've killed people for less."

I watch as she marches away, fully a soldier again.

"You are lucky, you know," Frida murmurs. "She's very powerful. You'd be dead if she ordered it."

"I'm sorry to interrupt. I saw the man from the forest. I think he came to warn us. The Dróttning is coming here. We need to leave."

"You're wrong," Frida insists, resting her hands on her hips. "Knut would have told me if she was coming."

"I only know what he told me. I don't think he's lying."

"I'll check with Knut, but if you're right, we need to go. Get the others. Tell them to be ready. I'll have our mounts prepared if Knut thinks it's possible."

I glance down the hall and then back at Frida, a question in my eyes.

"Start there," she relents with a sigh, pointing to a door. "He probably came in the first few minutes and is spending the rest of his time cuddling. She can help you gather the girls."

"Good. We'll pack and meet you at the stables."

Frida's afraid. Leaving at night will be dangerous.

But not as dangerous as staying if the Dróttning comes.

SIFA

YOU CAN'T WIN

"**W**E CAN'T LEAVE THE way we came," Frida says as she and Knut round the corner toward the stables. "We'll never make it in the dark."

"It's safer than the road," Knut insists. "If the Dróttning comes, you'll cross paths. She'll kill you."

"How far do we have to go to be safe?" Frida's eyeing the carriages, her mouth set in a tight line.

Knut pauses as he looks toward the little trail we'll follow to escape. "In half a viku," he says at last, "you'll reach a turn with boulders on either side. It's too far from the road and the house for the Dróttning to sense your presence. Wait there. I'll send word when they arrive so you know you can leave at first light."

"Yes, that'll work." Turning, Frida gestures at the girls. "Get in. Let's go." And then she turns to me. "Not you, at least not until that scent wears off. Knut has a horse for you."

Thank the gods. I was dreading being trapped in a carriage again. I'd much rather be on a horse with a sword on my hip and knives ready to fling.

This horse, though, leaves much to be desired. She must be the worst mount in the stables, a nag Knut can lose without much concern. I wonder if she'll have the strength to carry a rider. Her back droops nearly as much as her eyes.

She's pissed about all of it. She doesn't want a bit in her mouth. She definitely doesn't want a rider. And she absolutely doesn't want to leave her warm stall in the middle of the night.

It takes two men to saddle her. Both lose bits of flesh in the process. I would laugh if I wasn't the one destined to suffer her spite. I wonder if I'll be able to avoid her teeth as I try to get on her back. I'll need to take a minute to get to know her first.

"What's her name?" I ask Knut as he walks to my side. His nose wrinkles, but he doesn't back off. I wonder what he wants from me.

"Hilde. It means 'ready for battle'. She lived up to it for most of her life. She was the best of the war horses."

"What treats does she like?"

"She's partial to apples," he tells me. "She didn't like being ignored and forgotten," he adds after a moment. "But once she accepted it, she decided she didn't want to go anywhere. Maybe you can help her find the adventurous soul she had in her youth."

"I'll try." I walk over to find an apple, cutting it up for better bribes, and then I approach Hilde. Slowly.

She watches me warily, her eyes narrow. When she catches the scent of the apples, she brightens a bit, her front hoof pawing at the ground as she lets me approach her and takes the slice of apple I offer.

Placing my hands on her cheeks, I capture her gaze and hold her stare for long seconds. Her emotions whirl around, the anger melting a bit as she lets interest take its place. She's been bored for so long. She convinced herself she'd never leave again and finally accepted it. But she wants to leave. I help her find that longing.

Finally, her eyes let go of the distrust she'd held in place for so many moons. She lets them fill with hope.

We spend another minute eating the rest of the apple, all of my fingers intact when we're done.

"You're good with animals," Knut observes as he walks up to stand by my side, braving my smell yet again. I get the sense he's measuring me, evaluating whether he can trust me. After a few moments he nods to himself and leans toward me.

"I know your secret," he whispers, his gaze holding mine. I force my expression to stay flat—although my mind is scrambling for some response—as he continues. "I also know you followed us last night, heard our meeting with Troels. We're involved in something important here," he tells me. "We need people we can trust. You should talk to Frida and Ulfhild about our work."

I watch him for a moment, struggling to keep my expression neutral. Bevin will be pleased if I get access to this group. And if Knut does know my secret, I need to tread carefully. "We all have secrets," I respond vaguely, "but I'll think about it." He nods, one side of his lips tipping up just a touch as I turn back to the horse. I can't lose the tenuous bond we've forged. "I'm going to ride you, Hilde," I say. "Together we'll find some fun."

She watches, motionless, as I take the reins and lift my foot into the saddle. Shuffling a bit, she seems to ponder whether she'll let me mount her. And then she pauses, standing still for me.

"Thank you, Hilde." I stroke her neck for a moment and then lift my other leg to get settled on her back. She accepts her new rider without complaint.

"Send word as soon as you know anything," Frida urges Knut as she motions to the guards to lead us away.

As one, we turn to follow them. Hilde is surprisingly compliant. Maybe she's already realized she'd rather be on this bumpy road than stuck in her stall.

I'm grateful to be on the back of a horse again. To not be trapped in a carriage, relying on other senses because I can't see anything. Even in the middle of the night, the stars unwilling to provide any light, I'm at peace. If we're attacked, I'll fight.

Twice along the way, I catch hints of a presence nearby. Maybe it's the strange man who seems to have been following me. Or the Dróttning. Whoever it is, if I can sense them, they can sense me. I nudge Hilde to move faster until we're far enough away to lose them, as I urge my heart to calm down and the butterflies in my stomach to still. Hopefully, their senses aren't better than mine, and they lose me when I lose them.

It takes more than an hour to reach the boulders. And then we wait. In some ways, this is worse than fighting. If they were here, I'd know what to expect. Whether we can win. Instead, I'm stuck wondering about all of it.

When I feel the presence approaching again—realize it's coming toward us—my stomach flips, sending my heart rate soaring.

I was wrong, I know now. Fighting is worse than waiting. We have too many people to protect and too few warriors to do it. If it's the Kastali and they send more than a handful of people to capture us, we'll be doomed.

But there's nothing I can do. We'll never outrun them. If we try, we'll just appear guilty. So we wait. Again.

When I see him, I'm not sure if it's relief or fright I feel. He'll let us go. But only after I'm forced to talk to him. Part of me can't wait. Another part—the instinct that kicks in when he's near me—tries its damnedest to get me to flee. I squash it down. Like it or not, I need to hear whatever he has to say.

I'm not surprised when his eyes focus on me and his horse makes a beeline in my direction. When he's a few feet away, he points his chin toward a teeny path into the forest. "We must talk. Follow me."

"Please." My tone is low, insistent.

"What?" he demands, his eyebrows pulling together to create one large caterpillar. I almost laugh. He looks so befuddled.

"Please follow me. I'm sure that's what you meant to say."

His mouth actually drops open as he stares at me.

Now I do laugh. He needs someone to tell him no every once in a while. He snaps it shut when my guffaw escapes, his jaw twitching. "Please," he spits out before turning his steed to lead me into the forest.

We ride for nearly a quarter viku before he stops, spinning to look at me.

"I don't know why you had to call me out here," I mutter before he can speak. "They can hear anything you have to say to me."

"You shouldn't have come to these grounds," he growls, urging his horse to close the distance between us. "Listen to me and listen well. *Do not* ask Ulfhild or Frida about Knut's work. *Do not* tell anyone—especially not Bevin—anything you've learned here. Leave Ulfhild's house and don't return. You're playing a game you don't understand. A dangerous game, that you can't win. I won't be able to help you much longer."

I reel back, anger blossoming from my chest to fill every part of me. "I don't answer to you," I remind him. "And I don't want your help. I'll go wherever I must to survive. If I need to talk about what I've seen here, what I've learned, that's what I'll do."

And then I lean forward, holding his gaze as I fill my eyes with the intimidation that always forces humans to back down. This male, though, doesn't respond like anyone else. He glares at me, his bright green eyes sparking with his own anger. He speaks before I can.

"I won't tell you again. You've already cost me too much time. I've taken too many chances to protect you from yourself. Let go of what you're pursuing. They'll find you. They always do."

"Then they'll find me," I respond. "But I have no choice. I can't stop what I'm doing."

I can almost see the anger roiling inside of him. He looks like he wants to throttle me, settling instead for gripping his reins like they're snakes he's struggling to subdue. At last, he gets control over his emotions. His face settles into something like resignation.

"You're a foolish female," he snarls at me. "So fucking dangerous. I won't interfere again."

He yanks on a rein and kicks his heels, racing away from me at a reckless speed.

Good riddance, I assure myself, the anger he's able to ignite in me bubbling to the surface. I'm always in control of my emotions. They've never reacted to anyone the way they do to him. I don't understand it, but I'm filled again with the certainty that I must stay away from him. He is more dangerous to me than anyone I've ever encountered.

Liv watches as I ride back toward the carriages, a gloating grin on her face.

"You've got the wrong idea, Liv," I hiss at her. "Sorry," I add after a moment. "That male really pisses me off."

"We can see the sparks flying from here." Liv's all smiles again, enjoying whatever she's decided to believe about him and me. But she *is* wrong. I don't even know his name. And I don't want to.

"Will we be chased from here?" Frida asks, all business.

"I don't think so. He didn't say anything about the Dróttning." I sigh to myself. I can't believe I didn't even ask him the obvious questions. I'm a lousy spy when he's around. Another reason he never can be.

The rest of the trip is unremarkable. We stay at the same inn and get back to Ulfhild's before night falls. She asks a few questions but not nearly as many as I'd expected. She probably expects to get whatever she needs from Frida. After offering me a day off—which I gratefully accept—she asks me to return at dusk in two days. She even says she'll stable the horse for me, prompting a grateful smile. I've grown fond of the old girl.

But I can't go home yet. I should check in with Halla, make sure she and Sagga have enough food. Then report to Bevin. Which I'm dreading for some reason.

Halla's grin when she sees me lifts my spirits. We chat for ten or fifteen minutes before she needs to get home. She's been bothered by the long trip I'm supposed to take soon but also wants to make sure I know they'll be fine without me. I think she's reminding herself as much as me.

Bevin doesn't waste any time when I make it to his favorite tavern. Within a few minutes, I'm shown into a back office he claimed years ago. He doesn't rise or wave me to a seat as I enter.

Instead, he gets straight to the point. "What did you find?" he demands as soon as we're alone together.

"What makes you think I found anything?"

"You're a spy. And you were on the outskirts of the training grounds. Of course you found something."

My job is to tell him everything. It's what I must do to stay in his good graces. To continue working my way into his organization, and eventually get close enough to the Konungr and Dróttning to get access to information that can help me find my way home. I've spent ten years getting to this point. I can't squander it now.

But for reasons I'll never be able to explain, the strange man's face appears in my mind. His words echo.

And I decide not to report all that I learned to Bevin.

"They are the most secretive group of people I've ever encountered," I tell him instead. "I spent hours talking to the staff one day and learned about their families and pets but nothing more. I think they're chosen for their discretion."

"And what of your searches?"

Even sitting down, his power over me is intimidating. I struggle to stay neutral, to hide my deception from him. "What searches?" I ask in the most bland tone I can muster.

Bevin doesn't move. At all. Eventually, his pupils constrict, as if light just flooded the dim room.

"Don't do this, Sifa," he warns me in a flat voice. "We both know you searched while you were there. What did you find?"

"Nothing," I assure him. That much is mostly true. "I went into the library twice but I was found and berated both times. They made it clear I'd be punished if I tried again. I didn't find any other interesting rooms, and nothing on the grounds gave a hint as to what Ulfhild is involved with. Or Aksell."

"And the dragons? What did you learn about the training grounds while you were there?"

"Even less. I saw a single dragon when its rider came to entertain himself. But we see that around here all the time. I didn't see any training runs or even any dragons in flight. The riders knew we were coming. They must have held back on working the dragons while we were there."

Bevin leans back and watches me in silence. I don't let my gaze stray. He hates weakness. A minute or more passes as we stare at each other. At last, he sighs. "I don't believe you. You're keeping information from me."

"Why would I do that?" I demand, letting frustration seep into my words. "I have earned your trust, Bevin. Have you ever known me to be untrustworthy?"

"Never," he concedes. "But that means nothing now. Loyalty often can turn on the flip of a coin."

"You're trusting me now because you know you can. My loyalty isn't so flimsy. I'm sworn to you. You have no reason to doubt me."

"Maybe so. Maybe not. Know, though, that I'll be watching you."

"Good. Watch me closely. You'll see that my fealty is to you."

"We shall see," Bevin responds after a few more moments. He stands, his body as graceful as a cat, and strides to open the door where his man waits. "Sifa will join Fhord tomorrow," he says. "Get a message to him to meet us here an hour after dawn.

He should be prepared to travel. He'll take the trip we've been planning."

"I'm to return to Ulfhild in two days," I interject. I don't know who this Fhord person is, but I don't want to work with him. I'm better alone.

"I'm displeased with your work for Ulfhild. You won't be returning to her. Make an excuse so you can go back if I need it. For now, you'll assist Fhord. You'll be gone for two weeks."

"I'd rather not," I insist. "I don't do well with partners."

Bevin spins and strides forward, erasing the distance between us. When he speaks, spittle sprays at me, little flecks of disdain. "Did I ask your opinion?" I've never before heard such anger in his voice.

Much as I want to move away from him, I don't. It'll be worse if he sees my fear. "No," I respond simply.

"Why would you presume to give it, then?" His nostrils flare as he stands tall to glare down at me.

I do the same, making sure I never look away. "You want me at my best. I'm not as effective when I must work with someone else. But if you want me to partner with this person, I will."

"Yes, you will. Know, though, that he's not your partner. You'll assist him. He'll tell you what I need from you. Make sure you don't fail me again." Dismissing me with a wave of his hand, he steps around his desk and sits. When he looks up to find me still standing there, a single brow lifts. "What?"

"You want me to work *for* him?" I can hardly believe my ears.

"Was I not clear?" Bevin's patience has nearly run out.

This is what he asks. It's what I need to do.

I drop my chin, hiding the anger in my eyes. "Apologies, Bevin. I'll do as you request."

"Yes, you will."

Bevin looks down toward some papers on his desk. He doesn't say another word as I stride out the door.

My spirits drop as I walk home after arranging for Mikkael and Johan to check in on Toffer and give Halla food while I'm gone. Even the troll's excitement at my return—and Thor's perfunctory meow in hello—don't pierce the gloom that sits all around me. Toffer gives me space, sharing a silent dinner together before nudging me with his elbow shortly after we sit down on the balcony with glasses of wine.

"What's wrong, my Sifa?"

"I think I fucked it all up," I tell him, fighting to hold back the tears I can't let him, or anyone else, see.

He doesn't chastise me for my language. He must be really worried.

"Tell me, Sif-Sif," Toffer urges. "You'll feel better if you talk about it."

"I don't even know where to start." I inhale, thinking through the events of the last few days, the man whose face keeps appearing in my mind. "I've been working all this time to get close to Bevin. To get him to trust me. But today, I ruined it all. I've lost his trust, and I don't know how I'll get it back again."

"It can't be that bad." Toffer's voice is gentle. "What happened?"

"I lied to Bevin. He knew it. But the worst thing is, I don't regret it. I'd do it again."

"Why would you lie to him? You've never done that before."

"I have no idea." My tone is shrill. I'm so frustrated with myself. I suck in another deep breath, forcing myself to calm down. There's nothing I can do about it now. "A stranger—somebody I saw for the first time a week ago and barely know—told me to lie. And I did. It makes no sense."

"What stranger?" When I don't answer right away, Toffer lays a hand on my arm. "Sifa, what stranger?"

"I don't know his name," I explain. "I don't know anything about him. But we're connected in the weirdest way possible."

"What do you mean?" Toffer's face is twisted in confusion.

"I'm sorry," I exclaim. "I'm being so cryptic." I pause, gathering my thoughts. "You know that I can sense people, right?"

Toffer bobs his chin for a moment, his gaze never leaving mine.

"Well, this man, for some reason, puts my senses on high alert. I can feel him coming. And I'm convinced he can feel me. But it's more than that." I lean back and take a sip of my wine, letting myself remember the emotions he triggers in me. "When he gets close, my feelings go to war with each other. At the same time, I am both completely enticed by him and thoroughly repelled."

"Is he handsome?" Toffer looks at the cat and then back at me. "Thor wants to know," he explains.

"Since when do you serve as an interpreter for me and Thor?"

"He was nicer to me when you were gone. We're trying to get along."

That finally lightens my mood, just a bit. I've been waiting years for them to learn to like each other.

"And now I want to know too. Do you like the way he looks?"

"Gods help me, I do," I respond with a laugh. "He's a mean, rude man. But he's not bad on the eyes."

"And he asked you to lie to Bevin?"

"He told me to keep some things I learned secret. I knew I should have told Bevin when he asked, but I didn't. And Bevin can always taste a lie. It's how he got where he is. He knows what I did."

"But you'd do it again. Why?"

"That's the question, isn't it?" I sit with it for a minute, trying to figure out why. "He keeps showing up. The gods must have a reason for connecting us the way they did," I answer at last. "Even if I never see his miserable face again, I can't deny the link between us. Maybe it's there just so I'll listen to what he says."

"What are you going to do?"

"I'm going to try to earn back Bevin's faith. I don't like it, but I need him to trust me."

"And what if you see that man again?"

"That won't happen," I assure Toffer. "We've been in this town for years, and he's never crossed my path before. I'm done with Ulfhild, so I'm done with him."

Toffer gives me one of his crookedest smiles. "If you say so, Sifa."

"I've never been so positive about anything," I promise.

I'm not sure if I'm trying to convince him or me.

CHAPTER SEVEN

SIFA

WHY ARE YOU STALKING ME?

"**W**HY ARE WE STILL waiting for him?"

Bevin's man—Fhord—is late. Really late. I've been here more than thirty minutes, and he still hasn't arrived. I have no idea why Bevin puts up with this. I'd be looking for other work if I showed him such disrespect.

"Why do you care?" Bevin's irritated but not ready to send me on my own. Maybe this guy will never show up, and I won't have to deal with him at all.

"You're right. It doesn't matter. My time is yours. I'll wait if that's how you want me to spend it."

I should have tried to hide the sarcasm in my voice. Bevin glares as he watches me. His nostrils flare, and an angry grunt erupts. "Don't ever forget it."

We sit in silence a few more minutes, Bevin's eyes narrowing with his frustration.

And then he's back. I think he really is following me around. *The bastard.* That odd sensation that repeatedly has warned of his approach stalks toward us. I can't fully grasp his emotions, but somehow he feels even more ill-tempered than Bevin. When the door swings open, I don't need to look up to know who's there.

At least now I know his name. Fhord.

"Why have you summoned me?" he demands as he strides in the door. He must know I'm here. I'm sure he can sense me. Still, he doesn't even glance my way. No hint that he knows me.

Fhord also keeps secrets from Bevin. But I knew that already.

"Good of you to join us. At last. You were told to be here an hour after dawn."

"Thirty minutes ago," he bellows. "Your man dragged me out of bed just as I was about to..." And then he finally looks my way, a bit of red flowing into his cheeks.

I can't restrain my laugh. It bursts out of my belly, loud and sudden.

The red in Fhord's cheeks grows, but this time it's anger, not embarrassment.

"Tell us, Fhord," I ask sweetly. "What were you about to do? Do you need to go back to finish? Could you finish if you tried?" I have no idea why I need to irritate the man. I just do.

His eyes taper to two little lines, dark as the forest around the training grounds. Spinning his head, he peers at Bevin.

"Who is this female?" he demands.

"Sifa. She's one of my best spies. She'll go with you, help you retrieve it."

"You expect me to work with her?" His tone is bitter. "My Ætt will support me. I don't want or need her aid."

"She's good at what she does. She'll go with you."

"And what if I say no?"

Maybe Fhord isn't so bad after all. I might like a man who has the balls to put Bevin in his place.

"Then you'll no longer work with me. I need people who do what I ask. Without arguing." He glares at both of us as he adds the last two words.

Fhord stares at him for a surprising length of time. He seems to be carefully weighing his options. With a scale. That needs to be recalibrated. Twice.

Finally, he spins his head to look at me. "She'll do all I demand of her?"

"I will not..."

"She will."

Bevin and I speak over each other, but it doesn't matter. His word is law. He's promised I'll obey this bastard. Much as I hate it, losing whatever is left of Bevin's trust would be worse.

I may need to do what Fhord asks, but I don't have to make it pleasant for him.

He nods once. "We're leaving. Now."

I smile and stand. Not too quickly. Just fast enough to avoid angering Bevin any more.

"Can't wait," I say as I stroll toward the door.

When we're far enough away to be sure Bevin won't hear us, I spin to face him. He doesn't stop, so I reach out and grab his arm. His gaze drops to my hand and then lifts to hold mine.

He's not happy.

I don't care.

"What are you doing?" I demand, forcing my whisper to be flat, imposing. "Following me around while I was with Ulfhild's girls was one thing. This is a whole 'nother level of wrong. Why are you stalking me?"

"Foolish female. So, so dangerous."

By the gods, I already hate when he calls me that. I may be a lot of things, but foolish is not one of them. I open my mouth to tell him off, but before I can, he wrests his arm away and spins to continue stalking down the street. But now he's walking so fast I nearly need to jog to keep up with him.

"I'm not done talking to you. Why are you following me?"

"I would not follow you," he insists. "You keep showing up in places you don't belong. And now you've pissed off Bevin so much that he decided you need a caretaker. So I'm stuck with you." He stops abruptly, turning to inspect me. "I may have no choice now, but rest assured, we will finish this job for Bevin and then you will never see me again. I'm done trying to save you."

"I told you before, I don't need to be saved. And definitely not by you." When he doesn't start walking again, I look around, lifting my arm to gesture ahead. "I don't know where we're going," I remind him.

He watches me for another moment and then pivots abruptly, a spring released from a vise. Without a word, he's racing down the street again.

We travel halfway across Revalle without another word. His route takes us through the best neighborhoods and the worst. But even with the demanding pace, my ire at him doesn't waver. I don't want to spend another minute with this man. I'm not sure how I'll get through the next two weeks without killing him.

Finally, just as I'm starting to consider abandoning Fhord and returning to Bevin to plead with him to give me any other job, Fhord comes to an abrupt stop in front of what looks like an abandoned building. I glance up to see a faded sign barely hanging from rusty cords. "The Lucky Duck." I remember this place—a brothel that closed down after one too many clients came away with blue balls. It almost started an epidemic.

This day just gets worse and worse.

"Here?" I demand. "You do know what this place was, don't you?"

"Here," he tells me. He looks up and all around us before twisting the lock and opening the door to step through quickly. When I don't follow right away, he grips my arm and pulls me inside.

"Stop it." I yank my arm away from him, stepping back as he shuts the door behind us and turns the lock again. "Don't touch me."

"Then don't make me," he says. "Nobody can see us coming in here. We don't dawdle on the street."

"Just say something next time." I look up and am surprised to see light billowing down toward us. "Are there others here?"

"My people use this space when we're in Revalle. I need to gather supplies and let someone know he won't be joining me on this job."

"Why? Won't we be more effective if we have help? Maybe get this over with more quickly?"

He looks at me like I'm stupid.

By the gods, I hate this man.

"I will not have any of them spend time with you," he says as if it's the most obvious thing in the world. "I may have no choice. They do. They'll stay here while we do what Bevin asked."

"Sure. Because it's that horrible to spend time with me." I don't wait for an answer before finding the closest staircase and stomping up. I need to see what I've gotten myself into.

It's not at all what I expected. I find their haven on the third floor and it's wonderful. Cozy and warm. A big fire blazing in the corner. Comfortable couches with plenty of pillows. A large circular dining room table with chairs scattered all around it.

And people who don't want me here sitting in them. Four faces stare at me with varying degrees of surprise and distrust.

"Why is she with you?" The woman who led this group in the forest speaks first, standing abruptly as her right hand rests on the knife on her belt.

"Bevin stuck me with her. Wants her to help me on this new job he gave me. I've got no choice."

One of the men grunts. As I turn to look, his face settles into a grimace. He's enormous. A bear, with thick red hair and an even thicker beard. But his eyes capture my attention. They're brown and soft and kind.

"Does he know?" he asks in a muted tone.

"Quiet, Torsten," Fhord says.

"But does he know?" Torsten is serious. For some reason, this question is important.

"I don't think so," Fhord tells him as his gaze catches mine, glaring at me. "He doesn't trust Sifa, so he wants me to watch her. Make sure she's loyal."

"And he trusts you?" I demand. "You're the reason I lied to him."

"Maybe if you were a better liar, we wouldn't be stuck together." He twists his chin to look again at Torsten. "I'll go alone. I don't want you exposed to her for too long."

"I'm not contagious." Almost of their own accord, my hands find my hips and my back straightens. I didn't think I could hate this man more. But here we are. "I won't infect them."

"You have no idea how much danger you'd expose them to," Fhord spits out. "You put all of us at risk. We'll go alone."

Now it's the woman's turn to laugh. "Are you sure you can put up with her that long?"

"This is what must happen. I'll be fine. If she can just learn to hold her tongue," he adds as his eyes shoot daggers at me again.

"I said I'd go with you. I didn't say I'd put up with your nonsense. I'm not going to be treated like a child."

"Then stop acting like one." His voice is low, brittle.

"Enough," the woman interjects. "You're right," she tells Fhord. "You two can go alone. I don't think any of us could stand to be with you."

"As I said," he responds.

By the gods, I hate men who have to get in the last word. Who always need to be right.

"What are we waiting for then?" I demand. "I'm just as anxious to get this over with as you. Your friends know what they need. Let's go."

"Sit. Wait for me." He points a finger at one of the chairs. When I don't move, his finger wiggles a little, as if his ire could prompt me to move. Instead, I stroll over to the fireplace and lean against the hearth. Lifting my hand, I pick at a nail. And then I yawn.

"Insufferable female," he mutters as he stomps down a hall.

Fhord returns a few minutes later, dragging a pair of bags that look to be filled with an array of weapons. Well, at least he comes prepared.

"Which of those is for me?" I ask, hoping I'll get the ax peeking through the opening in one.

"Why would I give you weapons?" Fhord drops his load on the ground. "Get these on Sigurd."

I have no idea who he intended to ask, but his people seem to know. A tall, lanky man rises, his tawny skin and umber eyes rich and radiant in the soft light of the fire. He sways as he walks, like a young tree in a fierce storm. It's a wonder he can stay upright.

Fhord walks back down the hall and returns a few seconds later with a third bag. This one seems to hold clothes and other supplies. "Do we have enough food?"

Again, the others know exactly who he's talking to. This time, a woman responds. She's a beauty, with luscious blond hair braided down her back and bright purple eyes. But her breasts draw my eye. They're huge, a pair of watermelons sitting proudly on her chest. I'd have trouble walking with those things. She's got the hips to pull it off, but it's still good she's sitting down.

"You've got enough for two weeks. You'll need to get water after a few days."

"Fine." Fhord turns to me. "Come." And then he strides down the stairs.

I hate responding to his command, but I don't really have a choice. We need to leave, and unless I'm prepared to sit around and pout like a child, it's time to go. So I follow him.

We don't go through the front door this time. Instead, he leads me to a courtyard that's nearly as surprising as the building. It's lush, with green grass and plenty of shade trees, most of them rich with one fruit or another. It feels like one of the parks that Vanatians with power and wealth stroll through at night.

Except for the horses. They're dressed for the journey. I ignore the large stallion—Sigurd, I assume—because Fhord has somehow gotten possession of Hilde, the mare that carried me from the training grounds. She seems just as bitter as she did there. Until she sees me.

When I catch her eye and smile, she stills, letting the tall, thin man finish strapping a bag to her saddle. She paws at the ground twice, her nostrils flaring, and watches me from across the courtyard.

"Do you have any apples?" I ask Fhord.

"What?" he demands, his eyebrows slamming together.

"Apples. For the horse," I explain slowly. If *he* wants to act like a toddler, I'll treat him like one. "She likes apples, and I'd like to start this trip off on the right foot."

Fhord shakes his head, frustrated.

"Leif," he says after a moment. "Get Sifa some apples."

The thin man jerks his head and jogs off toward what looks like a stable along one side of the courtyard. As I'm moving slowly toward Hilde, my hand outstretched, he returns and gives a few slices to me.

"Thank you." He seems nice enough. No reason to be rude to Fhord's friends.

"You're welcome," he responds with a wink. "Anything to keep this one happy. She's got a bit of an attitude."

"Just a bit. But she's quite charming when you get to know her."

"So many things are," he says with a smirk this time. "I brought a few extra for your packs."

"Thank you, again. I appreciate it."

He steps to Hilde's side and lifts a flap, stowing his treasure, and then walks in my direction. "Be nice to Fhord," he tells me. "He's not nearly as miserable and mean as he'd like everyone to think."

"That I find hard to believe. We're destined to hate each other. At least we've only got a couple of weeks together."

"We'll see." Leif smiles again and spins to jog back into the stables.

Within a few minutes, we're sitting astride our horses, leaving through a gate I never would have found if I didn't know where to look. Turning after it closes behind us, I search for the latch, but it's disappeared too. I can't find any sign of it.

"I would never have guessed people live in that building. Or that there's an entrance on the back side."

"As intended."

"How long have you been living there?"

"Long enough." Fhord's brusque tone tells me he doesn't want to talk. But we'll be traveling together for a while, and I'll be damned if I'm going to do it in silence.

"Do you all live there?"

"No."

"Where do the others live?"

Fhord turns his head as slowly as he possibly can, frustration written in every line of his face. His arms drop the reins to fold across his chest as Sigurd finds his own way. And then he just stares while I hold his glare. Loosening my hands so they're gentle on Hilde's reins, I force my lips to tip up in the barest hint of a smile. I will not let him see the effect he has on me.

Finally, he speaks. "Do I look like I want to talk to you?"

My grin grows, which only deepens his scowl. "Do I look like I care what you want? We're stuck together. I'm gonna have questions. You may as well get used to it."

"I'm not here to educate you. Especially about my life. Keep your questions to yourself." He spins to face forward again.

"Well, at least tell me where we're going. That's something I need to know."

"You'll know when we get there."

Gods, this man is frustrating. "I need to know what to expect along the way. Whether we're likely to be attacked. I won't go into this blind and unprepared."

A long-suffering sigh erupts from Fhord. What a diva. It's just a question, not an inquisition.

"We'll go north," he answers at last. "The Nest holds something that belongs to Bevin. We'll find it and return it to him. Without being caught."

The Nest. Fuck. My heart jumps as a chill runs down my spine. Fhord twists his head at my sharp inhale, so I focus on controlling the things he can see or hear. Slowly, my hands stop shaking and my breathing returns to normal. I ride in silence as the cold spreads through me, even my fingers and toes tingling.

We're nowhere near the Nest, but I haven't been this terrified in years. I can almost feel the lashes across my back. The blade that takes little pieces of me, a bit at a time, while

Bolverkr and the others laugh and carve. The rack that holds me, splayed and naked, for days and days and days.

I haven't been back to the Nest since I escaped. I knew eventually I'd need to return, to try to figure out if it holds the keys to my path home. I've been preparing for years.

But I'm not ready. I didn't think it would come so soon.

I don't want to go.

I have no choice.

Finally, my voice is firm enough to speak. "It's been many years since I was there. How many days will it take?"

"Six if the weather doesn't turn on us." Fhord's words are clipped, angry.

"Do you travel this route often?"

He pauses, as if deciding whether to answer this question. "Usually I fly," he says at last. "My dragon was injured. The best healers are in the North. They care for her there."

The last thing I want is to feel any kind of emotion for this man. But I understand the connection between dragon and rider. I can hear it in his voice. His dragon's injury is hurting him more than he would ever admit. At least to me.

"What's her name? Your dragon."

He's quiet for a long time. I wonder if he'll even tell me. But then he speaks. "Tindera."

"It's a majestic name. Will she be okay?"

Fhord responds with a curt snap of his head. "As I said, she's getting the best care possible. They will heal her."

"It must be hard to be so far away from her."

Again, Fhord rides in silence instead of responding. When he turns to me, his eyes flash.

"I'm done speaking with you. I've told you what you need to know. I will not answer any more of your questions. And I will not talk to you about Tindera. Not now. Not ever."

I sneer as he spins his head to focus on the road ahead. He doesn't see it.

I don't know what I did to anger the gods so much.

This trip cannot go fast enough.

Chapter Eight

Fhord

She's Not Mine

Tʜɪs ɪs ᴡʜʏ I spent ten years trying to avoid her.

I felt her when she burst into this world. At first, I had no idea who—or even what—she was. But I knew something had arrived that could screw up everything. I knew I needed to keep her away from me.

I didn't know she'd be so fucking beautiful.

Or that she'd be such a pain in the ass.

Or that she would be my gods-damned mate.

Who I can never, ever claim as my own.

Not that I'd ever want to. Because she is a huge, fucking pain in my ass.

The gods have wicked senses of humor.

And they take too much pleasure in playing with our lives.

For ten years, it was easy to keep her away. She landed in the North, but her emotions were too heightened, overwhelmed. She never even noticed me. Never felt our bond.

I only learned later it was because she'd been tortured mercilessly as they tried to learn where she'd come from. How she'd gotten here. Why she'd come. What she planned to do. And more important than anything else, what or who had come with her and disappeared before it could be caught. The Dróttning sensed a third presence when Sifa and the troll erupted into this world, but it disappeared before her guards could get there.

Sifa never broke. Annoying as she is, I have to admit she earned my respect when I learned that.

She even managed to escape from a prison that had never lost a captive. She took control of a guard's thoughts, something nobody had done before. The Dróttning had a special device created for her—a manacle that will restrain Sifa's magic when she's caught again—because the Dróttning is determined to find her and get answers to her questions.

And then Sifa went south, away from her enemies in the North. Away from me. Those were good years. I could ignore her. Pretend she doesn't exist.

But the Dróttning decided to send me to Bevin. She wants me nearby. More than that, though, she wants me to prepare to usurp him. She's concluded I'm more trustworthy. Whether or not that's true, she's right about Bevin. He pretends to be loyal, but his allegiance is only to himself. He'd shove the Dróttning aside and rule this land if he could.

Sifa's getting closer to Bevin, but he won't hurt her. She's safer here than anywhere else in Vanatia. She has a home. She's even made friends. She isn't going anywhere.

So we have to share Revalle. And I have to keep her away from me, make sure she doesn't sense my presence or the pull of our mating bond. The first time our path crossed, I filled her with revulsion—made sure it would be stronger than whatever the mating bond would ignite in her. It took some effort, but I've had centuries to learn to control my magic. I can repel most people without them having any idea they're being manipulated.

And then the next gods-damned day, Bevin sent her to Ulfhild. And Ulfhild sent her to the training grounds. And she decided to get herself caught by my own people. I fill her with revulsion and anger every time she senses or sees me, but she just keeps showing up.

The gods are fucking with me. I'm sure of it.

I didn't even tell the Ætt about her at first. They didn't need to know. But when they found Ulfhild's girls in the forest outside the training grounds, I had to intervene. I couldn't let them—I couldn't let her—be taken to the Kastali. She'd never make it out alive. I made sure Jorunn and the rest of the Ætt let her go.

Now they know about my doomed mating. They think it's funny. *Pricks*.

I still tried to keep Sifa away. When I saw her splayed across a couch in the ballroom for all to see, the savage inside me reminded me she is our mate. I've never had to work so hard to control him. I almost shifted right then and there—which would have been totally fucked. But I held on. Then I stopped myself from killing the men who watched her a little too closely, bulges in their pants and lust in their eyes. It would have drawn attention she can't afford.

And she's not mine. She never can be. Because Tindera will be the one to suffer if I give in to this temptation. Probably my Ætt too. The Dróttning knows they're the best way to hurt me, and she will punish all of them for my weakness.

I warned Sifa about the Dróttning. Told her to leave. And then crossed paths with her again.

None of it worked. I can't get away from her. The gods must be laughing at the mess they've made.

Fucking Bevin. Forcing us to work together is one thing. Sending us on a job a week's travel away is something else entirely. I need to just get through this trip and make sure I never have to see her again.

In the meantime, she won't be quiet. I don't want to get to know her. I don't even like her, but it wouldn't matter if I did. We can't be together. It would cause too much pain.

"Fhord, I'm talking to you." Her hand wraps around my elbow as she tries to get my attention. "How much longer?"

Even her touch brings life to my old bones, sending little flames up and down my arm. I yank it away, though, and watch as her eyes fill with dismay, then turn to stone, as rigid as the chestnut they resemble. Mine stay hard. Cold. Let her think I can't stand her touch. It's better for both of us.

"I need some personal privacy. I can wait a little while, if we're going someplace with a privy. Otherwise, we should stop soon."

"We'll sleep in an inn tonight." After flicking my gaze up to the sky, I add, "We should be there within an hour."

"Good. It's been a while since I rode a horse. And Hilde's pace isn't as smooth as it probably once was. I'm a bit sore."

She looks down at the nag she rode from the training grounds, stroking its neck with a little smile. That animal should hate her like it hates everyone else. It doesn't, though. It seems to be fully committed to her already.

I still don't know what prompted me to get the horse from Ulfhild. Some pathetic part of me *needed* the beast that spent two days with Sifa's legs wrapped around her.

I'm so fucking weak.

Minutes pass in pleasant quiet before she speaks again.

"Are you going to talk to me at all, or are we going to ride in silence the whole way?"

"I enjoy the silence."

"I don't. And if I'm going to be stuck with you for days, you'll need to speak to me."

I steel my eyes before I turn to look at her. Reinforcing the barrier I've erected between us. Making sure my voice is cold, distant.

"No, I won't," I tell her at last. "We're not going to get to know each other. We're not going to talk about our lives or anything else. We will do this job for Bevin no closer to each other than we are now. Then we will go our separate ways. And we will never see each other again."

I expect to see a bit of hurt in her dark eyes, not the anger that flashes there.

"I don't want to get to know you, you arrogant ass," she flings at me, spite in every word. "But I'll be damned if I'm going to ride in silence *for days*. We're stuck together. You don't have to make it completely miserable."

"It is miserable. For both of us. A little chatter won't change that."

"Oh my gods, you're a bastard." Her head spins forward, and she kicks her heels to nudge Hilde forward. Away from me. When they're twenty or so feet in the lead, they settle into a walk, matching my speed to stay in front.

I smother the flames of emotion that start to stir inside. Regret that I have to cause her pain. Desire to comfort her, take away the angst and dislike of me that I've built inside of her. A wish we'd been born into a different time and place, that would let us explore our bond.

This is necessary, I remind myself. *It's the only way.*

I'm so relieved to see the inn when it appears in front of us. It's a slovenly place, but the kitchen will offer a hearty meal and the beds are clean. And I'll finally get away from her. Her smell of lavender with the smallest hint of rosemary. The dark skin that looks soft and firm in all the right places. The eyes that reveal bits of her soul. The curls I'm desperate to touch. The leather pants cupping a perfectly-shaped ass that I *need* to hold.

I'll be able to let go of my magic—the wall I must keep between us—while both of us are lost in sleep.

I let out a sigh of relief when the owner tells us they have two rooms.

"Thank the gods." Sifa echoes my feelings. She smiles at the handsome woman and lifts a hand to gesture to me. "This one's a miserable prick. I was dreading the thought of being stuck with him all night."

The woman's eyes narrow as she looks at me. "Happy to be of service," she says at last.

I resist the urge to defend myself. What do I care what either of them thinks of me? "Where are the stables?" I ask instead. "Our horses need to be rubbed down and fed."

"My men will take care of it," she assures us. "Just leave them out front."

I'd normally insist on doing it myself, but I need to get to my room.

I need to get away from Sifa.

She doesn't make it easy. "Are we going to eat together?" she asks as she follows me down the hall toward our rooms. They're too close together, but I can't do anything about it.

"No," I tell her. The fewer words between us, the better.

Reaching out, she takes my wrist, stopping me in my tracks. She places herself directly in front of me, inches between us, before speaking. I want to push her out of my way, but I don't know whether I can trust myself if I touch her.

"I don't know what this is about, why you hate me so, or why I can't stand to be around you. But I do know we have a job to do. You better not screw it up because you refuse to talk to me." She pauses, poking a finger into my chest as her gaze holds mine. "I don't want to be your friend. I don't want to be anything to you. But we need to learn to trust each other.

At least a little. In this, even if in nothing else. So get over yourself."

She spins to stalk down the hall, swinging her door open and slamming it behind her.

She's right. I know it. This job won't be easy. It'll be impossible if we don't figure out how to work together before we get there.

Tomorrow. I'll deal with that tomorrow. Tonight, I just want to pretend she's nowhere nearby and sleep.

I take a long bath, hoping it will give her time to eat before I go downstairs. But she seems to have done the same thing. She's sitting alone at a small table when I get there, no hint of food in front of her. She sees me as I enter the room and narrows her eyes. If she could throw a dagger at me she would. And then she turns away to look toward the kitchen.

Resisting the urge to go back upstairs and return in a half hour, I take the only small table still available in the full room. It's twenty feet from her, but it gives me a perfect view. I could spin the chair and stare at the wall instead, but I never give a full room my back. I'm stuck.

There are plenty of other people here. I can focus on them instead. But that's even worse, I realize after a few minutes. This inn is a favorite spot for the Dróttning's warriors. She's never been one to like Valkyries in her service so there are few. The men who protect her, fight for her, come here for drinks and bedmates. And Sifa looks to be the only female who doesn't charge for the pleasure she might bring.

It doesn't help that she's also the most stunning female in the room. By far.

She's so fucking dangerous.

Every man has noticed Sifa. I can almost feel their heartbeats increase when they steal a glance at her. Which they do way too much.

Fuck. I can't watch this.

I also can't leave. Because if I do, I'll spend the whole night wondering who Sifa chose.

Who's trying to please her with his scrawny little penis.

Whose hands are on the body that belongs to me.

Wishing they could satisfy her in the way only I can.

Because she's my gods-damned mate.

Even if I don't like her.

And I'll never have her.

I hate the gods right now, their cruel senses of humor. They're probably watching us. Laughing at the chaos they've created.

When my stew arrives, I dig into it like I haven't eaten in days, grateful for the distraction. My gaze keeps finding Sifa, eyeing the men who don't try to hide their interest in her. At least none of them join her.

I'm waiting for my second serving when a tall, wide man rises from his seat, staring at Sifa. He's not ugly, and I desperately wish he was. Sifa notices and gives him a small smile. His lips tip up at the encouragement, and he strides forward.

My blood pressure rises with every step. I can feel my savage struggling to break free, and I'm fighting again to rein him in.

This was my first lesson. The one beaten into me over and over again until I became flawless.

Always, always keep a short leash on that primal part of me.

But I've never been tested like this. The mating bond transcends everything. It is elemental and when it snaps into place, it is in control. Those old lessons, the power I learned to wield, to dominate, mean nothing.

By the time the bastard sits down, leaning forward to say a few words to her, my hands have clenched into fists. I focus on them, forcing my fingers to relax, then pushing that feeling up my arms and through my body.

She's not mine. I know that. I can't control who she chooses.

The savage, though, doesn't care about those niceties. He knows who Sifa is. That she's ours. And he's not willing to share.

When the stranger reaches over to take her hand and lift it toward his lips, I lose control. My magic slips out, slithering across the room to build a wall of disdain between them as I rise and stalk toward their table. Sifa leans back, flustered by the new feeling I've forced on her.

If I were a wise male, I'd leave well enough alone. Let my magic do what my body should not.

But I'm not wise. At least not where Sifa is concerned. I know that already.

"She doesn't want company," I say as I grab a chair from a nearby table and swing it to sit next to Sifa, straddling it with my arms on the back. I catch the male's gaze, letting my savage roar through mine. "You should leave now, while you can."

"What the fuck, Fhord?" Sifa's angry.

My savage doesn't care. "He's bothering you," I tell her as my gaze finds hers. "He needs to go," I add with a smile.

"No, you need to go. He's great. I was finally starting to enjoy myself on this trip."

"It's good I got here in time, then." I turn back to him. "She's with me. And I'm a dangerous male. This is your last chance to leave with all your teeth."

"The lady seems to want my company, not yours."

He's not prepared for the fist that flashes toward him, aimed at the teeth I warned him he'd lose. His head flings back, a spray of blood flying out to sprinkle a nearby table. When those men jump up, hands on their weapons, I do the same. My back is against the wall, sword in my hand, before the stranger reaches up to find his front teeth missing.

"What the actual fuck, Fhord?" Sifa stands too, ripping off a scarf to hand it to him, but I grab it before she can. She spins toward me, eyes filled with storms and shadows. "What are you doing?"

"He cannot have any piece of you."

"Why can't I give him a scarf? Why in the names of all the gods would you care? We don't like each other. At all. Remember?"

What can I say? She's right. We both know it. But I'll never be able to tell her why.

"We have a job to do," I finally offer as a feeble excuse. "Neither of us can be distracted."

"That is the most pathetic thing I've ever heard." She turns toward the male, an apology on her lips.

But he's done with her. "Get your man under control," he bellows before storming out.

And that's all it takes to smother every bit of lust in this room. They all turn their heads away from us. As attractive as she is, Sifa isn't worth the trouble to any of them.

My savage is howling, wallowing in his victory. *Settle down,* I tell him. *We'll pay dearly for this.*

He doesn't care.

Sifa snatches the scarf from my grip, spins on her heel, and stalks away. My savage wants to follow, but I'm in control again. Barely. I let her go, waiting long enough to be sure she's made it to her room before I find my own.

My mind, though, won't let go. Since the first time I saw her, I've been trying to strip her image from my fantasies. Sometimes I can. Usually, I can't. Tonight, it's impossible.

I didn't want to, but my eyes kept finding her as she rode. Now I've memorized every curve of her body. Her perky tits, ready to be licked and sucked. Her tight ass, shaped like a heart waiting to be held and caressed. Her full lips, made to be kissed.

Those images won't leave me. And I give in to them. At last.

Letting her fill my mind, I reach down and release the tie on my pants. I'm so fucking hard. Just the thought of her has me ready to explode.

I've never let myself do this with Sifa in my thoughts. I've always squelched the desire she triggers in me.

If I'm going to do it now, I want to savor it.

So I go slow, imagining her hands touching me. My dick twitches in response, anxious to feel her fingers wrap around it. I'm gentle as I reach for it. She'd start that way, I'm sure. Getting to know me. Exploring my cock as it grows for her.

In my dreams, I can feel her body too. My palms start on her breasts, holding them as I taste her for the first time. She's sweet, exactly as I knew she'd be. I take my time with her, kissing my way toward her center, watching as she opens up for me, invites me to suck that most intimate part of her. My name's on her tongue as two fingers reach inside to find the spot that will make her squeal.

Claim her as mine.

That's as far as I can go with any shred of control. When dreams of her cunt fill my mind, I lose it. My cock needs release. I stroke myself faster, her picture in my mind the whole time. The feel of my hand sliding up and down, sending little fires into every part of me as her face fills my thoughts, is unlike anything I've experienced before. The pressure builds in the most agonizing way. And then it releases in a rush. I actually shudder as waves of pleasure roll through me.

It's the best orgasm I've ever had, even with a female in my bed. Just the thought of Sifa—my stunning, infuriating, un-attainable mate—excites and satisfies me more than any lover ever has.

But it can never be any more than this.

She's not mine. She can't be.

The cost would be too high.

CHAPTER NINE

SIFA

I'M CLEARLY LOSING MY MIND

I'M WAITING FOR HIM. Again. After last night, you'd think he'd try to be on time.

I still can't believe what he did. That male only wanted to talk to me. Well, he probably wanted more, but he wasn't going to get it. Fhord attacked him for just sitting at my table. Broke his front teeth. Wouldn't even let me give him my scarf. Stood there staring at me like it was my fault. *Bastard.*

But by the gods, that was the sexiest thing I've ever seen. I hate myself for even thinking it, but part of me was so turned on by what he'd done. Turned on by Fhord. The crooked grin he gave me when he straddled that chair. The rumble of his voice when he told that male to go away. The flex of his tattoos when his arm lashed out, all power.

I've spent years trying to smother that little bit of me. It can't come out in Vanatia, ever. But it sparked to life when Fhord sat down, sending my stomach into cartwheels as chills rolled up and down my spine. I sat in a cold bathtub for a long time after I made it to my room.

I don't know why I reacted like that. I've always despised males like him, who act like females belong to them. Too many use violence to control their wives and girlfriends. And Fhord is so arrogant and irritating.

But I can't deny he's also gorgeous, or that my body responds to him in a way it never has, even to the most attractive males. When his gaze caught mine, jealousy sparking from his emerald eyes, I felt it in my core. I wanted him more than I've ever wanted anyone.

I need to get through this trip and get back home. Because I'm clearly losing my mind.

"Ready?" His voice is gruff, angry.

"That's what you have to say?" I demand, turning to stare at him. "Am I ready? Not, 'I'm sorry, Sifa. I screwed up'?" Even now, angry as I am, my heart jumps when I see him. *Bastard.*

He looks rested. Like attacking strangers helps him sleep. Maybe it does.

His eyes narrow as he spins away from me and strides toward the stables.

I stand there for a few seconds, stunned at his attitude. The apology he refuses to give. But I shouldn't be surprised. I know he's an asshole. I need to stop expecting anything else.

Sighing, I follow him to the horses, relieved when Hilde is happy to see me. Rubbing her neck, I reach into a bag and pull out a few slices of apple. And then I rest my head against her and breathe. "Today will be an adventure," I assure her.

At least it's gorgeous outside, I remind myself as we leave the town. We're still in the lush part of Vanatia, the trees rich with leaves the hue of emeralds, sparkling in the morning sun. The path we're following winds through the forest lazily, like a snake sunning itself on a summer day. Even the birds seem joyful, their song echoing around us as they warble their greetings to the morning.

We've traveled for hours in silence when a different sound floats toward us. Screams. But not just any screams. They're not human, and they are primal. Terrified. Desperate. I have no idea what beast is suffering so much.

I've heard cries like this before.

The fear they unleash nearly petrifies me.

In that instant, I'm back in the caves, trapped in a land I never knew existed. They know I'm an elf—my body betraying me as my terror strips my ability to control it—and use pain and fear to subdue me. To try and rip answers from me. To bend me to their will.

I'm not the only one being tortured. Other beings are here too. I recognize Toffer because he landed in this world with me. I ache when his cries reach me, feel his agony with him. When they drag him back to his hole, I try to comfort him with my words. Never my touch, because prisoners all are kept far apart. Only our torturers touch us in that place.

The wails that tear out my heart are the ones that reach us from outside the dungeon. They're not human or troll or elf or anything like us. A beast of some kind shrieks and howls in pain and horror I can't imagine. I could never learn the source. Even my probing questions to my captors didn't help. I just knew that my torment paled next to the torture those creatures suffered.

I shake my head, trying to bring my wandering thoughts back to the forest. Nobody will hurt me here, I remind myself. I'm suddenly grateful for Fhord's presence, the protection I don't want to need.

When I glance at him, a rock drops in my stomach. The color has drained from his face, and he's watching me with an emotion I've never seen him wear before. Compassion, maybe? Concern? He must have noticed my response, recognized my terror.

Breathing in once, and then again, I work to control the shivers that started when I heard the beast. I haven't shaken like this, unable to control it, since I escaped. No wonder Fhord reacted that way.

"I'm fine," I whisper, afraid to speak too loudly. Whatever it is doesn't sound close, but I don't want to take any chance of drawing it toward us.

Fhord raises a finger to his lips, echoing my caution. And then he drops from his horse, gentle enough to not make a sound, and gestures at me to do the same. I'm so relieved to have a battle horse beneath me. Her instincts seem to kick in as she stands motionless, waiting for me to dismount and lead her away.

We draw Sigurd and Hilde farther into the woods, away from the wailing. I haven't gotten the trembling under control—it seems to get worse with every shriek—but movement helps. Hiding will help more.

Fhord glances back occasionally, his eyes still shadowed in some emotion I don't want. I don't need his sympathy and can't stand the idea of him feeling pity for me. I won't let this male see me as weak or afraid, even though I'm both right now.

It only takes a few minutes to find cover. It feels so much longer. As we slowly sink down to our haunches, I focus again on my fractured response to this creature, whatever it is. I'm surprised to find a little relief. For all these years, I've wondered what made those sounds. Whether I was imagining them. Now I know they're real. Maybe Fhord can answer questions that have haunted me—if he'll finally start talking to me.

But I won't need to ask Fhord. Within a few minutes, the screaming moves in our direction. It's changing now, as the beast seems to give in to the demands of its torturer. Warbles erupt every few seconds, full of grief. Resigned. I can even hear the sharp inhales that follow its moans. As if it's crying.

I'm surprised when I see it. I shouldn't be. In this world, I'd never before heard a dragon do anything except growl or snarl. I knew they could make other sounds. The dragons in my world are expressive. They relay so much even without the mental bonds they share with their riders. These dragons look the same; I've always assumed they behave the same.

It's shocking, though, to see a dragon so afraid. Even from our distance, I can see that it's trembling more than me, and

I'm shaking like a leaf. I can see the hesitation in its steps. The fear in its eyes. The dragon's head hangs low, its gaze never straying from the male who walks in front of it. It seems defeated. Resigned. Hopeless.

My heart is breaking for the poor beast. Enormous as it is, perhaps seventy feet long, it acts small. Defenseless. I want nothing more than to protect it from the monster who inspires such fear in it.

Suddenly, I'm not afraid anymore. My hands are still, steady. I've lived for ten years terrified of these screams. Horrified by whatever beast they came from. By the madman who would cause such pain. Now I know what it was. I know that I don't have to fear it.

My breathing and heart rate slow, growing more measured with the dragon's approach. I'm aware of everything around me. The breeze that reaches me even in the midst of the bushes hiding us, a whisper across my skin; the hint of jasmine in the air, fresh and refreshing; the sun filtering through the leaves to surround us with a quilt of color.

I don't intend to send my thoughts toward the beast, but when I realize they're reaching out, I don't pull them back. I can feel his anguish and grief. He needs comfort, strength, hope. Maybe I can offer some.

He's confused at first, a hint of fear crossing his face. But in an instant, it's replaced with curiosity and then something close to peace. His head stays still even as his gaze spins to search for me, piercing through the leaves and branches to capture mine. And then he slowly, intentionally, blinks at me.

The only sign of thanks he dares to give. He felt my touch. He's grateful.

The dragon continues to warble, but I can tell it's for his captor's benefit. He fears for us. We shouldn't have seen his trauma. If he reveals our presence, we'll be condemned to death.

Fifteen minutes after they pass, Fhord stands, his hand dropping down to help me get up. I take it, grateful for a brief truce between us. We won't be friends, but maybe we don't need to be enemies.

"Are you okay, Sifa?" His tone is gentle, soothing.

"I am," I assure him, looking in the direction they left. "I've heard screams like that before but didn't know they came from a dragon. I was scared of them when it was some nameless creature. It helps to know the source."

"They're not supposed to be here. Nobody outside the Nests is supposed to know about this part of their training."

I spin to stare at him. "Training? This is part of dragon training?" I can feel a burn in the back of my throat as my heart rate again spins out of control. "You're kidding, right?"

"I'm not. I don't like it, but it's necessary." He holds up a hand as I open my mouth to respond. "We can talk about this later if you want, but I'd rather get away from here. If they discover us, learn what you've seen, they'll mark both of us for execution. Let's keep going. When we get set up for the night, I'll answer a few questions."

I watch him for a moment, willing my body to calm down. I don't know enough to be so angry. Yet. "Fine," I say at last.

Fhord leads us away at a fast pace. He must be more worried than he wants to admit. We ride for at least an hour, Hilde struggling to keep up with the younger stallion, before he slows down. But we don't stop yet.

Finally, hours after we started, I can't go on any longer. "Fhord," I yell out. He's more than two dragon's-lengths ahead of me, and Hilde needs a break.

Sigurd yanks to a halt, his rider spinning in his seat to look back. He watches for a few seconds as we approach and then dips his head. "Your mount needs to rest."

"Ya think?" I don't want my voice to hold as much disdain as it does, but I'm tired and hungry.

Fhord spins and points his chin at a nearby clearing. "We can stop there for lunch. There's a stream to water the horses."

He takes off again, our momentary proximity apparently too much for him to take. Shaking my head, I nudge Hilde to follow. She walks in their direction, in no bigger hurry than me. Smart horse.

Fhord can't avoid me at the creek. He's already removed Sigurd's harness and watered him. I do the same with Hilde, then follow him to a part of the meadow hidden in shadows. We tie the horses near a generous supply of grass then find boulders for our table. He's stuck with me while we eat.

"It's not much, but we'll have a better meal when we stop for the night," he says as he hands me jerky and some dried fruit and nuts.

"Will we be at another inn tonight?" I'm looking forward to a hot bath and a warm bed.

"No. Tonight we pitch a tent." Fhord's not even looking in my direction, like he can't bear the sight of me.

"A tent? As in one?" The gods cannot expect me to share a tent with this man.

"Yes, we carry only one tent."

They do. *The bastards.*

"You can't stand to be in the same room as me. How will you survive sharing a tent?"

Fhord turns his head slowly. His green eyes are as dark as the forest around us. "I'll manage."

I watch him for a moment. Fine. If this is what we need to do, we will. "I want to talk about what happened. Why that dragon was being tortured."

"Not now." Fhord's response is clipped, almost angry.

"You told me we'd talk about it."

"Tonight." He stands and starts to stalk toward Sigurd. "Finish your meal. We leave in five minutes."

The gods really must hate me, sticking me with this impossible man.

The afternoon passes quickly, with Fhord setting another fast pace. By the time we stop, Hilde is done. She hasn't worked this hard in a long time. I'm proud of her, though. I can feel the battle horse's resolve as she pushes herself to keep up with Sigurd.

Fhord works in silence to unpack the horses and erect the tent before gesturing at me to do something—I have no idea what—as he starts to build a fire.

"What?" I ask, confused and a little frustrated.

"Set up inside the tent," he explains, his voice low and slow, like he's talking to a two-year-old.

"Words, Fhord. Talk to me. I don't read minds."

He spins to stare at me, his eyes bright with … accusation. For a moment, I'm convinced he knows I can touch the thoughts and emotions of other beings. But then a mask drops over his face again. "You're old enough to know what to do," he explains.

I shake my head and crawl into the teeny tent, digging into the packs to lay out our bedding. We'll be sleeping nearly side by side. The gods definitely hate me.

Within a few minutes I'm crawling back out to join Fhord by the fire. He hands me a yam and a knife, then points at the pot simmering in front of him. We work in silence to prepare a dinner that turns out to be surprisingly good and satisfying. After we clean up, Fhord turns to me, ready to talk about dragons.

"I shouldn't tell you this." Fhord glances at me for a moment, then turns his eyes toward Sigurd. "Only those who ride dragons may know how their society works. But you already know more than you should. The damage is done. And it may help you hold your tongue if you know more about what you saw today."

"Because if I spoke about it, I'd be condemned to the penalty?"

"Yes." Fhord's silent for nearly a minute, staring out into the distance. "I don't like it," he says at last, his tone flat. "I wish there was another way. But there isn't. Sometimes dragons don't want to submit to the riders chosen for them. They rebel. They need to be punished. Controlled."

"Dragons don't choose their riders?" I'd suspected as much, but it still surprises me to have it confirmed.

"They don't." Fhord's voice holds no emotion. "Dragons cannot be ridden by peasants. That privilege must be earned. Only those who have built a place in Vanatia, who have proven their worth, deserve to claim such a mount."

"The wealthy? Even if their wealth is given, not earned?"

"Wealth, power, family, loyalty. Those are the factors that guide the Dróttning's decisions."

"What if the dragon doesn't want the rider chosen for it?"

"That's what you saw today. Dragons that rebel against the dictates of the Kastali are disciplined until they comply."

"Discipline? That's what you call it?"

Finally, Fhord looks at me. His nostrils flare as he bares his teeth. "*I* don't do anything. I didn't choose this. I wish there were another way. There isn't."

For some frustrating reason, I feel bad for Fhord. He hates this as much as I do. My hand wants to reach out and touch him, calm his rage. I don't understand the emotions this man inspires in me.

As I watch, his face softens, the anger dissipating. "That man hurt the dragon," I point out. "Badly. I felt his pain. He was completely hopeless. Discipline would not be so cruel. That's torture."

"They are stubborn beasts who hold great power. It sometimes takes ... some distress ... to force them to comply. The trainer must control them. Pain often works best."

"What did he do to cause such pain?" I'm not sure I want an answer. The question slips out before I can stop it.

"It is a punishment unique to dragons. You don't know enough about the beasts to understand."

He has no idea what I already know about dragons, but I can't tell him. Nobody except Toffer—and probably Thor—knows I don't belong here. That I know much more about dragons than I should.

We sit in silence a few more minutes, waiting. I don't want to sleep so close to him and I assume he feels the same. Eventually, though, I face the fact that I have no choice. I need rest.

He follows me into the tent a few minutes after I crawl in and snuggle under the covers, laying down without a word. My back is turned to him, but I can't ignore his presence. My senses focus on his breathing, steady but not yet sleeping. Having him so close is electric, setting my nerves on edge. My spine tingles, my brain sending signals to every part of me that he's here. He's close enough to touch. To hold. To caress.

To fuck.

Holy Helheim. I can't stand this man. I don't want him. At all. My rebellious body, though, doesn't agree. It's never wanted anyone as much as it wants him right now. Even without his touch, my core is hot, pulsing. If he weren't two feet from me, my hand would be in my pants, releasing some of the tension. The need.

It takes a long, long time to go to sleep.

Chapter Ten

Sifa

And Then I Notice Him

"**N**o! Let him go!"

"Sifa, wake up!" My eyes fly open. Fhord's hands are on my cheeks, his eyes wide as a vein pulses in his neck. He's terrified, for me.

I stare at him, confused. I was in the caves, watching as they dragged Toffer from his cell. His turn to be slashed and skinned in their endless search for answers he couldn't give. In the distance, the wails I'd come to expect from some beast being tortured continued. They'd started just after daybreak and seemed like they'd never stop, although our cells were growing dark.

But I'm not trapped below the Nest. I'm in a tent with Fhord. Shaking my head, I sit up. Fhord draws his hands away, but he doesn't move. He still watches me, but now he's concerned. Almost like he cares. Butterflies launch in my stomach as we sit there together, gazing at each other. Almost on its own, my tongue emerges to moisten my lips.

Fhord takes a sharp inhale, dropping onto his ass as his head spins away from me.

"I'm … sorry I … touched you. I shouldn't have. I was just worried. You were screaming." His hands are splayed out on his pants. They're still, as if he's trying to stop himself from wiping away the feel of my skin.

And then I notice him. And my heart really starts to race.

He sleeps without a shirt, giving me the view I've needed of his chest. His arms. His stomach.

As I suspected, there's not an inch of fat on him. His stomach muscles are clenched, creating ridges as they lead from his waist to his chest. The designs that cover him appear random at first—other than the golden dragon that emerges from his heart—but there's a harmony to them. They seem to have been drawn by the same hand, each telling a different part of a single story through dragons and beasts and blades. It's the scars that really catch my eye, though. They're everywhere and the artist used them as the foundation for the most intricate tattoos. As if to celebrate and revere them.

I lift my gaze to search for him. And my heart finds its beat.

Fhord is watching me with an expression I never expected to see on his face, a mix of longing and deep pain.

When he realizes I can see him, truly see him, his lips twitch up for a split second and he casts his eyes down. "I didn't have time to throw on a shirt," he says as he lifts to his knees and reaches to the foot of his bed. His blanket drops to reveal the tight shorts he sleeps in and a generous bulge at his groin, impressive even without any excitement to fill it. I bite back the groan that rumbles in my chest as my mind conjures thoughts of his hard dick resting between my thighs.

For the briefest moment, I want to stop him from covering himself. My hand almost moves, and I have to take control of my mind—a mind that's wholly occupied by his presence right now—to prevent it. A sigh escapes from me as his stomach flexes and a tunic drops over his shoulders to rest on his hips. He sits down again while I urge my galloping pulse to calm down. I'm afraid he can hear the effect he's had on me.

I'm a reckless elf. And I really need to get away from this man.

"Do you want to talk about it?" His tone is gentle. He's not the harsh, mean male I've come to know.

Yes. More than anything. But I can't. Because telling him about my time in the caves would reveal too much. He'd learn I'm an elf, and he's too close to the Kastali for me to ever risk that.

"It was just a nightmare." The words come in a whisper.

"Are you okay?" His voice is still soft, quiet.

No, I'm not. But I can't tell him that, either. "I'm fine."

"I'm going to try to sleep some more. I'm right here if you need me."

I dare to look at him again. His eyes still hold the worry I don't want to see from him. We need to trust each other, but that's as far as it can ever go. "Thank you."

He lays down, but this time he's facing me. He watches me a few moments, then closes his eyes and takes a deep inhale as I tuck myself back under my blanket. I can't relax, though.

I thought after seeing the dragon, finding the source of the wails that have haunted me for a decade, I'd finally escape that fear. It won't let me go. I wonder if it's part of me now, doomed to forever visit me in nightmares.

Gods, I hate that Fhord saw that side of me. Saw my weakness. My fear. And I hate even more that I saw a part of him I want to know better—a person full of compassion, who doesn't despise me. He's annoying and such an asshole sometimes. I wish we could travel together in peace. Still, it's better for both of us if he continues to push us apart.

I want him. I can't deny that after tonight. But I can never have him.

I can never have any man while I'm trapped here.

In my worlds, I learned to control my magic. I could hide my ears, look like a human. When I was young, my feelings would interfere. My ears would change, their sharp points emerging, whenever I lost myself in my emotions. By the time I entered Midgard, I had full control over my body. I never changed unless I wanted to.

Here, I can't fully harness that restraint. It's how they knew I was an elf when I landed in Vanatia. My fear revealed me, and I couldn't do shit about it. Since then, I've mastered the rest. My magic answers to me now in everything except this. This one thing refuses to be bound. Just like every reliable prick, my ears pop out, pointy and erect, when I get too aroused. When I lose myself to my body's demands. I've masturbated enough to know. There's no hiding who I am from a man who really excites me.

Which is why Fhord and I can never, ever be together.

I just wish he wasn't so gods-damned beautiful. And sexy. So fucking sexy.

I throw my pillow over my head as I stop fighting my magic and will myself to relax.

I desperately need my own tent.

He let me sleep in, I realize as my eyes pop open in the morning. The sun is peeking through the door, and I can smell something cooking outside. I'm hungry. Really hungry.

I dress quickly and step out of the tent. His back is turned and he doesn't sense me so I can watch him for a few seconds. He really is perfect. His broad shoulders lead down to a tight ass, then splay out just a bit to stretch into long legs. Short sleeves display the tattoos on his arms, and I inspect them. As I'd realized last night, they celebrate his injuries, as if he adds a tattoo with each mark to hold them in his memory.

He finally senses me and spins his head. But he doesn't smile. He's rebuilt the walls that disappeared with my nightmare. Instead, he nods, his eyes flat, and turns again to look at the meal he's cooking. Only then does he speak.

"We need a hot meal. Rabbit. It'll be done soon."

"Thank you. I'm starving."

He lifts his head to look in the direction of the nearby stream. "You have time to clean yourself before we eat."

"I'll do that." I duck back into the tent to grab my things and head over. It feels good to wash off some of the grime of the trip along with the sweat that covered me when I woke up screaming.

I dig into the rabbit when he sets a plate on the rock next to me. I haven't felt this hungry in a long time.

"We need to be alert today," Fhord tells me in between bites. "We'll be passing through a dangerous place. The Kastali has little authority over the rebels here."

"I didn't realize there was such a place. Why would the Kastali have trouble controlling these lands?"

He watches me for a moment in silence. "The Kastali is punishing the Meistari and Meistara who control this region," he explains. "The Nest has abandoned this territory for twelve moons. If the Kastali is satisfied with the penance offered, they may restore protection."

"We do need to be careful," I agree. Despite the sloth of many, dragon riders are key to keeping this land safe. I can't imagine life without them. I guess I'll soon find out.

We finish eating and pack quickly. With Fhord's warning, I'm as anxious as him to get through today.

The morning is calm and bright, and I like the ride more than I should. Mainly because I'm following Fhord, and he is magnificent.

I hadn't let myself look at him—really look—before last night. And maybe I shouldn't now. I can't be with him, but I can appreciate him. I can enjoy watching him. The dark, short but wavy hair, a hint of auburn catching the morning rays. The wide shoulders that turn into thick arms, covered with tales of his battles. The strong lines of his back, leading down to his firm ass.

Fuck me. Not literally. At least, that's what I tell myself.

As the sun is reaching today's zenith, Fhord turns. One side of his mouth lifts up when he sees me watching him. "We'll stop here for lunch."

Heat fills my cheeks. I need to keep my gaze away. I cannot let this annoying man know I'm attracted to him.

We're eating another cold meal of jerky with fruit and nuts when we hear their voices. Fhord notices first, sitting up straight as he brings a finger to his lips. His head spins slowly while he searches for their source. When he turns to me, worry brightens his eyes.

Standing, we scoop our things into our bags as quickly and quietly as we can. Within a minute, we're untying the horses and drawing them slowly to a nearby bramble, thick enough to hide all of us as they pass by.

We barely make it. Just as Hilde's rear slips behind the bushes, they appear. More than two dozen of them. They're not soldiers. These males are rough, crude, and loud. It's no wonder Fhord heard them from as far away as he did. They're laughing and bellowing at each other, rehashing some fight from the night before. I let myself relax a bit as they move past us.

But then one of the men looks up to see the clearing. "I'm hungry. Let's eat here."

"We've a long way to go today," another responds. "Let's go another viku before we stop."

The first male spins in his saddle, his eyes angry. "I'm hungry," he spits out. "We'll eat here."

"If you're gonna be a dick about it, fine." The second one yanks on his mount's reins and gives him a harsh kick, sending him straight toward us.

Fhord's arm wraps around my waist as one finger lifts to rest in front of my lips. Insufferable man. *Of course I'm going to be quiet*, I tell myself as I try to drag my thoughts away from the butterflies his touch launched in my stomach. I suppress the inhale my lungs crave as his hand drops to join the other on my stomach.

This is better and so, so much worse. We can't fight so many males. They'll kill us—after they rape me—if they see us. But all my reckless, traitorous body cares about is the heat that started just below his hands and is spilling into me. I have to stop myself from taking in the deep breath I desperately need right now. By the gods, I'm pathetic.

Fhord tugs gently, pulling me down with him to the ground below, both arms still tight around me. And then he looks at Sigurd as one of his hands releases me and flicks his wrist. The horse responds quickly, kneeling down behind us. Hilde does the same, her battle training apparently kicking in. We're as hidden as we can be. Hopefully it's enough.

I shouldn't be surprised when Fhord's hand returns to my stomach, tugging my back into his chest. But I am. He hates me. I know that. Still, he seems to be as drawn to me as I am to him.

We lay there motionless, Fhord filling my thoughts, his scent, full of coriander and cloves, wafting over me. I can feel the beat of Fhord's heart, his breath on my neck, hot and steady. Without even thinking about it, my heart rate and breathing slow to match his. And as terrified as I am, I feel content for the first time in years.

Fhord, though, is not completely motionless. Part of him blossoms behind me, growing impossibly large as it fills up the space between us. And gods help me, my body responds. The fire that started when Fhord's hands wrapped around me flares into an inferno, consuming every part of me. I can think about only one thing: the enormous dick digging into my ass.

And I can't move. If I do, my hands will be unleashed, taking his and leading them down. At this moment, I don't care who's nearby, what might happen. I need him to touch me. To possess me.

It takes every ounce of my willpower to stay still. To not give in to my body's reckless demands.

We lie there for a long, long time, and he stays hard. Unbelievably hard. Breathtakingly hard. The entire time. The heat that seems like it will never leave dries my mouth, making me empty and desperate for ... something I can't have. But his hands stay where they are too. He's as motionless as me.

Finally, thankfully, the males start to pack up and leave. We lie there another five or ten minutes, giving them all the time they might need to get far away from us. When Fhord lifts one of his arms, I turn to look at him, a hundred questions running through my mind.

And then I'm dropped in a cold bath. Every bit of fire that had been strumming through my veins is extinguished at once. As if a vast bucket in the sky just dumped its load on us.

Because Fhord is angry, his eyes brittle sparks of agate, his mouth a thin, tight line. He glares at me until I sit up enough for him to move his other arm, which he promptly whips away from me.

"Leave," he barks at me. Like it's my fault he can't control his body. As if he wasn't the one who wrapped his arms around me and held me next to him the entire time.

My heart is in my throat, and I'm suddenly struggling to hold back my own anger. This man incites every wrong emotion in me.

So I let my gaze slowly move to his chest and then down to the parts I don't want to think about. The bulge in his pants is so rigid, I wonder if it hurts to be constrained so tightly, for so long. "I can see why you'd be embarrassed," I tell him with a smug look as I find his eyes again. "Not that I'm interested. But I'm flattered you feel that way."

"My cock would rise for any woman who rests her ass next to it for such a long time," he bites out. "No matter how unappealing she might be. But it won't lead me to do something as foolish as bed you."

Oh my gods, the arrogance of this man. "Well, at least we agree about that."

Fhord still doesn't move, as if he's pinned to the ground. And I'm not in any hurry to make this easy for him. At last, he huffs out, "Are you going to go?"

"Oh, do you need some privacy?" My smile is saccharine. I'm gonna have so much fun playing with this man, now that I know how to get a rise out of him—figuratively and literally.

"Yes." His eyes are bright, focused. "Now."

"I guess we could go get some water," I tell him as I stand and reach for the harnesses. "We'll be out here when you're done," I turn to throw one last smile at him and draw the horses out to the clearing.

CHAPTER ELEVEN

FHORD

I DIDN'T HAVE A CHOICE

WHAT THE FUCK WAS I thinking?

My dick twitches when she sneezes. Every single thing she does turns me on. I'm in a constant battle to stop my savage from declaring his *need* for her. From claiming her as mine. From finally satisfying our fucked-up mating bond.

Fuck yes, I was going to burst when I pulled her next to me. When I tucked Sifa's tight, beautiful ass right next to the most demanding part of me. That has been demanding her since our eyes first met.

And there's no way my savage could relax once her breaths, her heartbeat, synched with mine. When we laid there together, not an inch of space between us.

I didn't have a choice—they would have seen us if I hadn't pulled her to the ground—but I didn't think I'd lose it as fast as I did. I thought I'd have some control over my cock.

Nope. Sifa is my weakness. Even if she drives me absolutely crazy.

I shouldn't have snapped at her when she sat up. But she looked so fucking good, the sun throwing speckles on her skin, her eyes bright and full of questions. I was about to lose it. Pull her down, and take her then and there. I needed her away from me before I abandoned everything I know is right. And wrong.

She knows what I did when she left. But what else could I do? If I hadn't, I'd have been trapped in that clearing until I did. Thinking about the feel of her ass riding my cock the whole time. About what it would be like to be inside her, to fill her up as I claim her as mine.

Gods. I need to get my shit together.

She smiled when I made it out of the brush, and I couldn't figure out if I wanted to strangle her or go jack off one more time for good measure. I didn't do either. Instead, I bit her head off again. I can't stay away from her, so I need to keep her away from me. Now she's pissed, but that's better than us getting along. Because I can't trust myself when she's nearby.

The gods-damned problem is that now I've touched her. And with a mating bond, that changes everything. The draw to be together is stronger, our resistance weaker, after our bodies have connected. My resolve cracked when she woke me with her screams last night, but this could shatter it. It'll be so much tougher now to push away from each other, especially with my savage demanding more of our mate's touch. I don't know if we'll be able to.

"I need to bathe." I almost jump in my saddle as her voice pulls me out of my thoughts. She's snuck up on me somehow. I *really* need to get my shit together.

"We're traveling," I remind her as I drag a hand through my hair. "We don't take baths."

"Not an actual bath. A lake; maybe a river or stream. Even a creek. I'm sweaty and sticky, and I stink."

I have to share a tent with her tonight.

Not that the smell would discourage anything. It might make it harder. Everything would be harder.

I need a cold bath too.

"There's a lake ahead. I'd hoped to get past it today, but we can stop there for the night."

"Will we risk being found?"

"I know where to go for privacy. We'll be safe." I make the mistake of turning to glance at her and am not surprised when my heart pauses for a beat. And my cock lurches. Traitorous things.

The sun is dropping toward the horizon as we near the final bend before the lake. I want nothing more than to watch Sifa's face when she sees the lake for the first time. I've been here before, and I carry its image with me. The deep sapphire water, rippling with life. The meadows that surround so much of it, their emerald and sage grass dancing with the breeze. The trees that stand tall and proud all around.

I don't stop myself. As we near the turn, I glance at Sifa. Her look is everything I'd hoped for. She tugs on Hilde's reins, drawing her to a stop. And she sits there, barely breathing, as she takes it all in, a hint of a smile on her face. I wish I could see her eyes. But then she'd know that I'd rather look at her than the prettiest lake in all of Vanatia.

As if reading my mind, though, she turns, her grin growing wider. Her eyes are rich with emotion. And my fucking cock twitches again. Bastard. I'm just gonna ignore all its random little outbursts.

"It's enchanting. I've never seen a prettier lake."

"I also have never seen anything prettier." The words spill out before I can stop them, my gaze still holding hers. "My little rabbit," slips out to join my treacherous blathering, filling the air between us as I try—and fail—to wrest my eyes away.

Gods. I am so fucking weak.

Sifa's eyebrow cocks up, a silent request for an explanation.

"It was our first meal together in relative peace," I remind her, giving in for a moment to the *need* to get closer to her. When the question remains in her eyes, I add, "You are soft but not weak, and as quirky, cute and smart as the bunnies I raised as a child." The corners of my lips lift as I consider the real reason: just being near her makes me want to fuck like rabbits. Everywhere. All the time. And she'd be so fucking delicious, wet and slick under my tongue.

Not that I'll ever find out.

I sigh as I admit one more thing to myself.

As fucked up as this mating bond is, the fates are right.

It's only been a few days, but I already know that my little rabbit is my mate for life. My perfect match.

It will always be her.

Only ever her.

She watches me for a moment, quiet and solemn. And then she shakes her head, a teasing smile tipping up her lips. "You're an odd man, Fhord. I don't know what to think about you sometimes."

I wrest some semblance of control back from the savage. "Best if you don't think of me at all," I force out, my voice as flat as I can make it. "You clean up first. I'll set up the tent."

"Thank the gods. I didn't want to have to fight you for it."

And then the savage takes over again. Because my control sits on a thin ledge, being constantly tugged between my brain and my boner. "The next time our bodies touch, *rabbit*, it won't be to fight."

I can't hold back the grin as her lips tip up at the edges and she shakes her head again. "So, so odd," she says as she nudges Hilde into a trot and leads the way toward the lake.

"So, so dangerous," I whisper, dragging my eyes away from the ass that tempts me far more than it should.

As I start unpacking our gear, my mind replays the day. The feel of Sifa next to me. I cannot keep my thoughts away from the fact that Sifa is bathing. Naked. Her body dropping into the lake, soap in her hands moving over every part of her, touching the places that should be mine. I imagine myself stripping down to join her, taking the bar from her hand and worshiping her body.

I'm not surprised at all when my legs carry me to the water. I do have the presence of mind to stop before I get too close. To hide from her as my eyes search. To slow down my breaths so she doesn't hear my excitement. My need.

When I find her, I'm relieved. She's fully submerged, only her head above the water. If I'd actually seen her nude skin, the breasts that have dominated my dreams since the first time I saw her, I might not have been able to stop myself. *And we don't want to do that to her*, I remind my savage. She's not ours. She can't be.

"I know you're there, Fhord." Sifa's voice pulls me from my thoughts. She's laughing at me.

"I need to wash too," I remind her, struggling to keep emotion out of my words.

"It's a big lake. There's room for two of us." The teasing note in her voice draws me from my hiding spot.

Her eyes are on me as I emerge and walk toward the shore. I'm so close to giving in. Striding into the lake and letting her take my clothes off. Piece by piece. And then fucking her so hard she'd never be the same again.

But I'd never be the same again either. I'd lose too much.

I can't do this.

"Hurry up," I choke out, my voice tight. "I don't want to be out here when the sun sets."

Seconds pass as Sifa watches me, wordless. And then she lifts her hands to run them through her hair, a smile tipping up the edges of her lips. "Sure, Fhord," she says at last. She drops fully into the water then rises enough to reveal part of her breasts, her nipples teasingly just under the surface. I can't stop the sharp inhale she prompts. Or the erection.

"Just ... hurry," I snarl as I spin and almost run back to the tent, her giggle following me.

Now I really need a cold bath.

She strides into the camp a few minutes later. "Your turn," she says as she strolls past me to sit by the fire. Her gaze finds the bulge in my pants, and a grin erupts as she looks up at me. "Take your time," she adds with a smirk.

She's really trying to drive me nuts, I decide a few minutes later as my hand moves up and down my engorged cock. The cold water didn't do a thing to the demanding bastard. It wasn't going to rest until it got some relief. I'm angry but so fucking turned on by Sifa's teasing and taunting. She knows exactly what she's doing and is having too much fun with it.

When I finally make it back to the tent, all of me relaxed at last, she's digging through our supplies. She still wears an infuriating smile when she looks up at me. "What are you doing?" My voice is rougher than I'd like but gods-damned, she's insufferable.

"I thought I'd get dinner started, but I can't find a thing in here." She drops the flap of the bag she's rummaging through and steps back. "It's all yours."

"You're looking in the wrong place." I step toward her and immediately know I've fucked up. Again. Her scent washes over me. I never knew lavender and rosemary could be so sexy. It's all I can do to keep my cock from rising again. Damn thing needs to settle the fuck down.

I'd intended to pull out what we'll eat myself, but I need to focus on other things. I flick my wrist at her. "Food's in there.

We'll rehydrate some mutton in a stew, then add some yams and beans I can forage nearby."

She's smiling again, her gaze dropping to my groin. "Trying to hold on there?"

"Only since you don't want to," I grunt at her.

Her laugh erupts from nowhere, whispering through me and somehow lifting my spirits. "So odd," she repeats as she drops down and searches for the meat. She nods when she finds it, grabs a pan and takes off for the lake. The saunter is probably for my benefit, I realize, because of the perverse joy she's taking in tormenting me. I try to ignore it as I stalk off in search of beans. And relief for the cock that's demanding attention. Again.

This is going to be such a long trip.

At least she can cook. Dinner is better than I expected and I eat more than I should have. I lean back, staring up as I watch the stars and think about the next few days.

"Are you ready to stop pushing me away?" Sifa's voice is light but layered with questions she doesn't want to ask. At least, not yet.

I don't look at her. Instead, I stare at the sky, focusing on the stars above. "We can't be friends. Ever. You know that."

"I don't want your friendship. I hope I never see you again after this little adventure Bevin has sent us on. But you know as well as I do that we'll have a better chance if we don't hate each other."

I sit for a long time, lost in the sky. The silence drags on but she's patient, waiting for me to speak.

The thing is, I know she's right. We'll fail if we can't rely on each other. Sighing, I drop my eyes toward hers. "I've been an ass."

"Such an ass," she affirms with another laugh that lightens my soul.

"If you knew why, you'd understand."

"But you can't tell me?" One of her eyebrows quirks in the most charming expression I've seen.

"I can't." I'm sure my smile reflects my regret as much as my eyes. "I would, though, if I could."

"I have secrets too," she points out. "We don't have to get into those, now or ever. We just need to know enough to trust each other, at least a little." One side of her lips tips up. "And stop being assholes."

"I can't promise anything. But I can try." I lean forward. "Why did Bevin send you with me? What does he think you'll provide?" I don't think he knows about Sifa's past—her time in the Nest when she landed in Vanatia—but I wouldn't put anything past that wily, power-hungry bastard.

"First you've got to tell me what we're doing. I know nothing right now."

"Right," I agree as my thoughts bounce through the things I can tell her, and those I can't.

"What are we going to get?" she prompts.

"Not what. Who."

Sifa's eyes grow wide and then narrow dangerously. She's angry. Really angry. "We're going after a person? At the Nest?" she demands, her voice a whisper.

"Yes. We go to retrieve one of Bevin's people. She got too close to someone and exposed herself as one of his spies. He wants her back."

"Thyra? Bevin sent us to rescue Thyra?" Sifa was angry before. Now she's furious. About to erupt.

"Yes, Thyra. Why are you so upset?"

"Why am I upset? How can you ask that? Thyra's being held in the dragon Nest. Bevin expects us to break in and free her. And you don't see anything wrong with that?"

"I didn't say it would be easy."

Sifa's chest is heaving, her eyes starting to water. She shuts them and drops her chin, forcing her breaths to slow, her heart to calm. More than a minute passes as she sits motionless, regaining control of her emotions. Finally, she looks up, her eyes bright with the tears she refuses to shed.

"I don't know if I can go there," she whispers in a voice that quivers. Her hands flatten out on her pants and move up and down, perhaps trying to calm the knees that have started bouncing. "Bevin sent the wrong person."

I should have known. I can't tell her why I understand but I do. They tortured her for weeks. Who wouldn't be afraid to go back?

"I can get us in and out without being caught. It's why Bevin asked me to do this. You're here to help get her out of the cage."

"I know enough about the Nest to know how difficult it will be," she scoffs. "I don't think we can do this without being caught." She leans forward, her gaze holding mine. "I can't be found there." Her words are sharp, intense.

"I won't let them get you, Sifa." Now I'm moving closer, reaching for her hand, my resolve to stay away shattered. Her skin is soft, comforting. "I can get us there and back without being caught."

She doesn't pull her hand from mine. I think the touch centers her as much as it does me. "We both know you can't promise that."

"I've done it twice," I assure her. "I'll get us into the Nest. I just don't know if I can get Thyra out of her cage."

Sifa takes a deep breath, her eyes never leaving mine. Finally, she dips her chin. "Tell me how you can be sure you'll get us there safely."

"Tindera was hatched in that Nest. She was ... precocious." I can't hold back my smile. "When dragons fully bond with their riders, they share memories. I can see what a troublemaker she was." I wink as I add, "Nearly as bad as my little rabbit."

Sifa's lips twitch up for a split second just before she drops her gaze to the ground. When she looks up, her eyes are a little clearer. "What would you do without a few females around to keep you on your toes?"

"Sleep a little better," I respond with a laugh. "But you do make life more interesting."

"I think you'd rather have interesting than sleep any day." Her fingers squeeze mine. I know I should pull my hand away, but I can't bring myself to do it.

"She often strayed from the Nest, curious about the caves they'd set aside for the hatchlings. She wanted to see the sky, but dragons aren't allowed such freedom until they're fledg-lings."

"Why?" Sifa shakes her head, her expression shifting to one of confusion.

"That's a story for another day." I don't add the real reason—that it's not something riders can share with those outside of dragon society. "Tindera spent a lot of time alone, searching for the stars. One night, she found a tunnel that carried her to them. It's hidden well, and she never saw another soul use it."

Sifa nods, knowledge filling her eyes. Maybe she used that tunnel for her own escape. It still doesn't explain how she got out of her cage, but it's one piece of information. "You're sure we can get in and out through the tunnel?"

"Positive." That much I know.

"But you may need help inside, diverting the guards, picking the lock?" Sifa's head tilts to the side as she asks the question, a small smile playing on her lips.

"Yes, I'm hoping that's why Bevin sent you. That your spying skills can get us through the guards and the door."

"I may have a way to get Thyra out. If we get lucky. And what will you be doing while I'm taking care of that?"

"Beating the shit out of anyone who threatens you." My tone is harsher than I intend.

"I don't need you to protect me, Fhord." Her voice is as soft as her eyes. Warm. Inviting.

This is why I pushed her away—why I manipulated her emotions when our paths first crossed, planting danger and a warning about me in her psyche. I know what a mating bond does. How hard it is to resist. We have to hate each other. There's no other way.

Right now, though, I can't hate Sifa. After we're done, I'll find those feelings again. Sitting here with her, the tension that's been building within me since we met is finally starting to go away. My heartbeat is calm, measured. My savage is soothed. I need a few minutes of peace with my mate.

"I know you don't." I rub my thumb along the fingers I still hold. "I'm going to do it anyway."

"Stubborn male." I don't miss the emotion in her tone. It washes over me in a wave, further settling the savage that craves this connection.

"You have no idea. The Ætt could tell you stories of the trouble my obstinacy has gotten us into over the years."

"Not that I'll ever see them again," she reminds me. "Because we hate each other, and we're going our separate ways when this is done?" It's a question, not a statement.

There's only one answer I can give.

"Maybe not hate. Not anymore. But we are going our separate ways when we're done."

Sifa pulls her hand from mine and lifts it to rest against my cheek. "I'm sorry I'll never know your stories, Fhord."

My hand moves up to cover hers. I wish I could hold it there forever. "I am too, Sifa." I pause, resisting the urge to taste her lips. "I am too," I add after a moment.

"Good night, Fhord."

She stands, facing me as she stretches her back, lifting her arms high into the sky—because she's not going to stop taunting me—and then smiles before she strolls toward the tent.

While I head into the forest to jack off.

CHAPTER TWELVE

SIFA

WORSE THAN THE LAST ONE?

"WE'LL PASS THROUGH AN unusual, maybe dangerous, area today," Fhord tells me over breakfast.

"Worse than the last one?"

"Different. In Vanatia's early days, this place held thousands of people and many went there for trade. You'll see signs of it as we reach the sun's zenith."

"Not too bad so far," I observe. "We can handle a few ruins."

"I wouldn't warn you about ruins," Fhord says before looking up in the direction we'll ride. "A battle took place here three hundred years ago," he continues, little wrinkles forming between and above his eyes as he draws his brows together. "Many died, some of them important. They held secrets the gods believed they might need, which they couldn't risk losing."

"The gods walked with humans then?"

"They did."

It's so different from my worlds. There, the gods walk freely, although before Ragnarök, they'd been hiding their presence in Midgard for more than fifteen hundred years. "What did the gods do?"

"They turned to the dark arts," Fhord mutters. His voice is brittle, as if it would shatter if someone struck it. "Such sorcery is powerful when humans use it. When gods use it, nothing is out of their reach. The gods fed their desperation into necromancy. They wanted to be able to question the dead, extract the secrets they would have taken with them to their grave."

"They raised the dead? And gave them the ability to think, answer questions?" I stretch out my fingers, which tingle at the thought of skeletons wandering around for eternity.

"They did." Fhord's eyes are calm, unconcerned. The walking zombies can't be too dangerous.

"And those ... whatever they are ... walk this world?" I've never been to Helheim, but I've heard tales of the souls sent to Hel's realm, who forever wear the injuries that killed them. A shiver rolls down my spine as I wonder whether these beings are anything like the specters that wander there.

"We call them draugrs. And they do still exist. Their bodies no longer decay the way humans do. They're forever trapped in whatever state the gods found them in when they decided to bind them here—injuries, rot and all. The gods keep them in this small area between the Nests. They can't leave. They're available to any who need their knowledge. And can convince them to share it."

"Do many people know about this place?"

"Almost nobody. It's spelled to push people away when they get close. A few books mention it, but none disclose where it is."

"How do you know about it?"

A half-smile glances across Fhord's lips then disappears. "That's a story for another day."

I watch him, wondering how many secrets like this he possesses. Whether he could help me find my way home. But I can't trust him with those questions. "How many are there?" I ask after a moment.

"Only a couple dozen. The gods restored those they believed might hold secrets they would want."

"If the gods questioned them, why do they still keep them here, trapped between life and death?"

"They may need them one day. The gods don't know what other mysteries they may hold."

"Can we go around them? There must be paths that avoid this area."

Fhord pauses for a moment as he watches me. "I need to question one of them," he answers at last. "It's not for Bevin's job. The Ætt and I have been trying to get here for weeks. I can't pass this area without taking advantage of the chance."

"Can I just meet you on the other side?" I suggest with a smirk.

"Afraid of a little necromancy?" Fhord responds with a laugh.

"I mean, why chase trouble? If I don't have to face walking and talking corpses, why should I?"

"I could use your help. It's really a two-person job."

"That's why you're being so nice to me? I knew there had to be a reason."

"You caught me." Fhord runs his fingers through his hair as he leans back, lifting his head to look at the sky above us. A muscle ticks along his jaw. "We'll go back to normal after I convince you to do this," he says in a flat tone. "All the fighting and hating each other."

"Not quite yet," I remind him. "First we finish Bevin's job. Then we can go back to hating each other."

Now Fhord's serious, his gaze dropping to find mine. "Will you help me, rabbit?"

I return his stare, trying to understand what he's asking of me. How dangerous it will be. But then I realize it doesn't matter. Fhord's not someone who likes asking favors. This matters to him.

"Sure," I agree with a little smile. "But you'll owe me. I'll let you know what I want when we're done."

"That sounds ... dangerous. For me. Am I going to regret this?"

"So, so much. But I don't think you have a choice." I stand to start pulling together our packs. "Time to go, before you change your mind."

The sun hovers to our right as we leave the camp, casting long shadows in our path. It feels so much like Midgard, I don't know if I want to laugh or cry. The jungles I called home for years—where I first saw signs that Ragnarök approached—hover in my memories. Tall trees, heavy with large emerald leaves sparkling with morning dew, a floor that looks like green felt splattered with red, yellow, and orange fronds, birds in a rainbow of colors swooping around us, all remind me of home. It's been too long.

We ride for hours before Fhord speaks again. "We'll enter the forbidden land when we cross this creek," he says as Sigurd draws beside Hilde. "They'll sense that we're there, but just stay close to me."

He reaches for Hilde's reins, drawing me to a stop. "You cannot end any of them." His voice is firm, unbending. "They shouldn't threaten us. But if any of them does, cut off whatever limb attacks but never their heads. The gods have spelled this place to harm anyone who takes one of the draugr from them." His eyes narrow into emerald slits. "No matter what, do not behead any of them. We'll both pay the price if you do."

"I love a good challenge," I respond with a smile and a quick dip of my chin. "This should be an interesting day."

Fhord nods, releasing my reins as he sits up straight in his saddle. "Stay right behind me. Don't let them separate us. If we're allowed to question one of them, they should let us leave unharmed."

"And if not?"

"Then we run. As fast as Hilde will go."

I feel it as we approach the creek, a gentle push that makes me want to turn a different direction. If I hadn't known what was here, I'd have believed it was just my own good sense encouraging me to avoid an unknown area. It's dark and dank, and I can see why travelers would stay away. The unease increases the closer we get, twisting my stomach and sending a chill up and down my spine.

It goes away, though, as soon as our horses trudge through the water, replaced by something worse. I can feel the draugrs' presence. All of them. It's as if their psyches are no longer attached to their bodies and float freely in this place. They are restless and lost, searching for some way to escape the purgatory in which the gods have trapped them. Now my mouth is dry, my heart racing in my need to do ... something. I'm overcome with a desire to help them escape their miserable existence. To put them out of their misery.

"Remember, rabbit, you can't end any of them. No matter what."

"How did you know I was thinking that?"

"I've been here before. I know how desperately they want to be released from this place. I feel it too. Everyone who comes here does. But you can't give in to it."

"It's horrible what the gods have done to them."

Fhord laughs, a cold, bitter snort. "The gods have done this and worse. Many times over. It isn't our place to question or challenge them." His voice suggests he doesn't believe his own words. Turning in the saddle, Fhord captures my gaze. "I've seen what happens to someone who ends a draugr's existence. Don't let it happen to you." Then he spins to face ahead again. "Follow me."

We're both silent as Fhord takes a meandering path, slowly leading me through this strange place. The grief and desperation I felt when we crossed the creek have only gotten worse, and I'm struggling to keep tears from rolling down my cheeks. My need to help these beings increases with each step, and I have no idea if I'll be able to resist when the time comes, regardless of Fhord's warnings.

The stench hits me first. I've lived through more battles than I'd like to remember, and this smell always lingers in the days that follow. Human flesh decaying in the hot sun, scavengers and vermin releasing the scent of death as they feast in the endless cycle of life. My breaths grow shallow as I fight the nausea that rolls through me, stop the retching that tries to erupt. This will pass, I remind myself.

When I see them, I'm horrified and fascinated. We've entered a clearing, and I realize as I look around that they've surrounded us. All of them. They look even worse than they smell. Although they're more than a dragon's-length away from us, I can see the causes of their death—holes in their heads or chests or guts that have turned green and yellow with their decay. Some carry so many injuries it's hard to see how they can still move. Hard to imagine that even the gods have the power needed to rouse these bags of bones and decayed flesh.

Fhord pauses to search the specters around us. He nods when he finds the one he seeks. "Follow me," he says quietly as he turns our horses in the direction of an enormous being who spent his life in battle and should have died there. The hole in his chest, exposing a spindly, decaying rib cage and the atrophied organs it once protected, suggests a slow, painful death.

The others don't follow yet. I don't let myself hope they won't. They can't catch us off guard.

"You may not be here." The words aren't spoken. They don't breach the air around us. Instead, they appear in my thoughts, as if they came from me. But they're guttural, desperate. This being has no hope. Nothing to lose.

Fhord speaks his response, disturbing the unusual silence that had settled around us. I realize for the first time that even the birds have abandoned this place. Nothing lives here. It exists only for these undead, perpetually trapped beings.

"I need knowledge you possess. We will leave when you give it to me." His voice is steady, calm. Quiet and compelling.

"Why should I help you? You will not release me from my pain."

"Not today. But I hope to find a way to release you. I will return if I do."

The warrior stills, though others start to move. It's almost as if they want to hear Fhord's words.

"The gods would not permit it," the draugr says dismissively, his voice angry. He steps forward but pauses when Fhord holds up a hand. The others do as well, as if all of them respond to Fhord's silent command.

"This world has changed since you walked its shores. The gods have changed. What once was impossible may come to pass at last."

The being scoffs, a surprisingly human response. I hadn't expected the emotion that arises within me with his dismissal of Fhord's words. "Nothing changes. Ever. The gods will not let it. The world you walk today is the world you will walk in a thousand years. As will we."

"Maybe so," Fhord concedes. "Still, hope echoes through this land. You don't feel it here because the gods control this place. But I tell you it is out there. I can see a path to a new existence. If we succeed, I will return and take this pain from you. On my oath, it shall be."

My skin tingles with my surprise at Fhord's traitorous words. Nobody may take or harm something that belongs to the gods. I wish I could see his face. I have no idea why he's decided I can hear whatever plans he's hatched. I don't know what he's doing, but I know it would get him killed if anyone ever learned of it.

The seconds drag by as the warrior watches Fhord in silence. A slight tilt of his head signals his decision. "What information do you seek?"

Fhord inclines his head in response. When he speaks, it's almost as if time itself echoes in his words. They carry a weight, a power, I've never heard before, even from the most powerful beings in my worlds.

I'll have many questions for Fhord when we leave this place.

"Tell us of your death."

I feel the draugr's response. He's angry at Fhord. Betrayed. Hurt. "Why would I share that story with you?"

"Do you not wish to speak of it?" Fhord hasn't moved. I suspect he also felt the warrior's emotions but decided to plow forward.

"I would not give you that power over me. You are of two hearts. I cannot trust one of them."

"Tell her, then," Fhord urges as his arm stretches out and he gestures me forward.

No eyes grace the specter's face, but it still feels as if he looks at me. Recognizes something in me he didn't find in Fhord. His emotions shift. Wonder, curiosity, peace now dominate.

"What is your name, female?"

"I'm Sifa."

"You came far to reach these lands. Have you found your way home?"

"I haven't. I'm still looking."

"That is the path you must take. Yet, you have much to do here, and your time to leave may never come."

My stomach drops, his warning echoing within me. But my desperation to get home is tempered for the first time since I landed here. Fhord's image ripples through my mind, some ridiculous part of me wondering if I would really leave the world that holds him. I shove that aside, though. I don't even like the male. I would never choose him over going home. "I hope you're wrong," I declare, ignoring that errant thought. "I want to go home."

"Be patient. You will learn much in time." The draugr pauses, unmoving. "Would you like to hear of my death, Sifa?"

I try to catch Fhord's eye, but he's not looking at me. Instead, his gaze scans the surrounding forest, watching the others as they linger in the nearby trees.

"I would," I affirm. Fhord must have a reason for asking this.

"And you will keep it from this man who travels with you?"

"Why must I keep it from him?"

Fhord spins as I ask my question, his eyebrows slamming together. "Assure him you won't share his story with me."

"But, why?"

"Get his story, Sifa," Fhord urges, his face softening. "You'll understand when you do."

I'm sure he can see my confusion, but he offers no explanation. "Okay," I say as I turn back to the specter. "I promise I won't tell Fhord."

The warrior nods. "Know you Nerthus? Does she still hold power in your lands?"

"Dróttning Nerthus?" Now, my response is in my mind. I'm not sure how I know, but I realize this conversation needs to be completely between us, with no words spoken out loud.

"Dróttning? I should not be surprised she would hold such a title. And yet I am." He steps closer, his vacant eye sockets focused only on me. "Nerthus once was an ally to the elves. Your companion knows well what that friendship produced. But her support did not last."

"You lived when the elves were free?"

"I died in the war for their freedom."

"Did you fight for the elves?"

"I did, little elf."

I spin to look at Fhord, but he's still paying us no attention. "You're sure he can't hear us? His mind is powerful."

"These words are only for you. His words will follow."

"Why did Nerthus turn on the elves?" I feel as if my entire existence will depend on his answer to this question.

"Nerthus craved the power held by the dragons. She wanted to lead them without challenge or opposition. But the dragons ever were aligned with the elves. Nerthus could not let that stand."

"The elves are all imprisoned, and Nerthus controls the dragons now. Do you know how?"

"Those events followed my death. The stories have not reached me here." He paused, watching me for a moment. "But it does not surprise me. Elves are powerful, as you know. Nerthus would need to constrain them, lest they rise again and retake their rightful place in these lands."

"Why does Fhord want me to know how you died?"

The draugr's face shifts slightly to glance at Fhord, and then turns to me again. "That he must answer. But I will share my story if you wish."

"Will you tell me your name first?"

"I am Konungr Erik. I ruled in the Far North until my death."

I lean forward, dropping my chin to my chest in a respectful bow. Now I really have questions. I've lived here for ten years and have only heard rumors of the Far North. Those willing to acknowledge its existence say the Dróttning has had people killed for discussing it.

After a few moments I lift my head and smile. "Thank you for telling me your name. Please tell me of your death."

"Know first that the dragons rejected Nerthus, although she craved that bond more than any other. More even than a mating bond. She held great power and was presented as a candidate at many hatchings. Never, though, was she chosen." Erik's head pops up as one of his hands lifts in a dismissive gesture. I spin to watch another of the draugr back away into the forest, then turn my gaze back to the dead king.

"Nerthus waged war to wrest control of the dragons from the elves. She fought dragons, elves, gods, and humans in her quest, but many stood by her side. Too many. None knew who would prevail. And then the fates brought us here. Where we would meet our doom." The ache in his voice echoes through me, leaving a gaping hole in my gut. His pain feels as stark and fresh as the day he received his death wound.

"What happened?"

"I know not how, but as our swords clashed, the land seemed to come alive, sucking away every elf who fought by my side. Half of my army disappeared, all of their dragons with them. Gone, as if they never existed."

"Elves and their dragons? Nobody else?"

"Only the elves and their dragons."

"How?" I'm not breathing, my need for his answer stilling every part of me. This is everything.

"Our books hold stories of those who can journey to another place or time. I had always dismissed it as myth, lacking substance. But I have come to believe those stories hold deep truths. That some unknown magic that day, in this place, took our fighters from us." Erik raises his head, almost as if he's sniffing at something, and then shifts his attention to me again.

"We have not much time, and I still must answer your companion's questions. My death came quickly after that, at Nerthus's hand. Without the elves or the dragons on our side, we were defenseless."

"And then the gods did this to you. Why?"

"Nerthus beseeched them, and they complied. She holds us here and could release us if she chose."

"Do you know why only elves and their dragons disappeared? And if they really went somewhere else?"

"One returned." Erik's voice is full of satisfaction. He can sense how much this matters to me. "I do not know how much time had passed, but many years after my death, one of the lost elves entered this land. He spoke of a different world, one in which the sun never shone. A people known as the jötnar lived there. Massive beings, who held great hate for elves. This elf searched for a path home for many years. He believed that emotion and an iron will opened the door between the worlds."

"Emotion? That seems ... impossible."

"Magic is not so simple. I suspect many things must coalesce for such travel to be possible. But I do know—because I have seen it—that it can be done." Erik is silent for a moment, letting me digest all he's told me. "Now I must answer your comrade's questions. He may not speak to you of what he learns, just as you may not share my answers with him."

"Thank you, Konungr. You've helped me more than you know."

I watch in silence as Erik shares more secrets with Fhord, my head spinning the entire time. It's possible to get home. I don't understand what he's told me, but he mentioned old myths. I need to keep searching.

Perhaps ten minutes after Erik turned his attention to Fhord, I hear his voice again.

"I wish you well, little elf."

And then he spins and lumbers back into the forest. The rest of the draugrs do the same as I follow Fhord out of this odd, enchanted place.

Chapter Thirteen

Sifa

Do You Like What You See?

T HE SUN IS STARTING to peek over the horizon when I wake up, bringing a dim light to one side of the tent. Fhord's still here, his breaths slow and steady. I've come to love the scent that always hovers around him, a mix of coriander and cloves. I think I liked his smell before I liked him.

But I do like him now. Most of the time. I roll over to see him facing me in his sleep. Not back-to-back like the first night. He's not so resolved to push me away. And I'm not as eager to get away. The repulsion I felt when we first met is gone. Now, our connection is more positive. It feels right.

Not that I can let myself get close to him. I know better than that. We can't be lovers, but we could be friends. We don't have to have sex. Even if I can't think of anything I want more.

Almost as much as he seems to want me. I almost laugh out loud as I remember just how much he wants me. He's spent most of our trip either fighting an erection or giving in and taking care of it himself. He's worse than any adolescent elf I've ever known. How could I not tease him? I think he enjoys it as much as I do.

Fhord shifts, his hand lifting from under the blanket to run through his hair, ink mixing with the dark strands. It's thick and silky and full of life. I'm dying to run my hands through it—one more thing I'll never have.

And then his eyes open. I watch as he seems to fight a smile before giving in. His face is brighter than the sun.

"Are you watching me, little rabbit?"

"You wish," I assure him with an exaggerated yawn. "I'm looking generally in your direction. You just happen to be in the way. Nothing particularly interesting over there."

"Do you like what you see?" The smile has reached his eyes, which crinkle with a laugh he hasn't released yet.

"I don't dare answer that, and risk building up your already oversized ego."

"So, yes, you do like what you see?" Now he laughs, a chortle that makes the tent lighter, more joyful. "Drink your fill," he adds after a moment, glancing down at his bulging blanket. "I'm not going anywhere yet."

"Good. Because we need to talk about what happened yesterday."

He groans. I'm guessing his mind is elsewhere. "You heard Erik," he says at last. "We're not to share his words with each other. Ever."

"That's not what I meant." I watch him for a moment, unsure how to ask without revealing things about me he can't know. "Why did you want him to tell me about his death?"

"Did he give you information that will help you?" Fhord's serious now, his eyes bright and clear.

"He did. But how did you know I would want that information?"

"I feel our connection too," he responds in a quiet tone, as if he's afraid to give voice to his words. "I can sense your emotions, as you can sense mine. When I let you," he adds with a wink. "We both have secrets, things we can never tell each other. But I know you search for something." Fhord sits up, holding my gaze. "The battle I mentioned was waged on the eve of the Downfall."

"When elves became prisoners in this land?"

"Yes. I don't know what, but something happened in that battle, or at the same time, that changed everything. I believe, or maybe just hope, that Erik holds the key to you finding what you seek."

I watch him for a long time, thinking about what he's said. His gaze never strays from me. "Why are we connected, Fhord?" I ask at last.

"That is a question for another day. Or maybe never. We'll have to see."

I narrow my eyes, pushing down the frustration that rises within me at his answer. He knows and it's annoying as fuck that he won't give me a simple answer. "Why can't you tell me what draws us together?"

"Because we both know we can't *be* together. No matter what. Even if a demanding part of me might want it," he adds with a glance down at his still engorged groin. "It'll be easier for both of us if we don't go down that path."

I don't follow his gaze because Fhord's morning hard-on is the last thing I need to think about right now. "I'll find out, you know," I declare. "Probably soon. This thing between us, whatever it is, is going to demand more than either of us can give."

"That's why we have to fight it. For both of our sakes. For everyone and everything we care about."

I watch him another moment. But it's time to go. "I'm going to clean up," I tell him as I dig out some clothes. I need to clear my head. Cold water will help. I hope.

We have far to go today and both overslept, so we don't dally. Fhord apparently relieved himself quickly; he's up and breaking down the tent when I get back. I pull together a quick breakfast, and we're on the road within a half hour. It's a long day, and we're both exhausted by the time we decide to stop. After another fast meal, we're asleep just after the sun sets.

I'm alone when I wake up but not surprised. It's light outside, probably an hour or so after sunrise. I can't hear anything—Fhord must be foraging or hunting—but I know we'll have another busy day. Throwing on some clothes, I toss open the tent door.

I see him first. A gag in his mouth, his arms and legs bound together behind his back, Fhord's lying on the ground with fire sparking from his eyes. Four males sit nearby, their smiles nearly as wide as the legs stretched out in front of them. My gaze is drawn to the male Fhord attacked at the Inn, his grin intentional as he displays the missing teeth that surely drove the bastards to track us down.

I'm positive the fear shows on my face when I see them. I can feel the hair rise on the back of my neck and up and down my arms. My stomach clenches as my heart skips a beat, and then another. But fear is the last thing these males need to see. So I do my best to shift my expression as I think through my options.

I can't use my magic. Fhord had a reason for taking me to Konungr Erik and asking about the Downfall. If he already suspects I'm an elf, I can't risk exposing myself to someone who might be close enough to the Dróttning to have some of her power, and recognize mine. These males don't sit or move like warriors, so I'd probably have a decent chance of taking them down, but I don't have a sword or even a knife in my hand. That's the last time I wander around without my weapons.

I don't have much choice. I'll need to earn their trust before I can do anything. Suddenly, I'm grateful Fhord was such an ass to me in that Inn.

"Oh, thank the gods," I announce as I let my shoulders relax and force out a long, relieved sigh as I gesture at Fhord. "I didn't think I'd ever get away from him." I smile, becoming the rescued seductress they'll want to see, and turn sultry eyes toward the toothless male who seems to be in charge.

Fhord's eyes are blazing now. It's a wonder he doesn't combust as he lies there.

"Did you come to save me?" I saunter over, dropping onto the log next to the male who lost his teeth to Fhord's jealousy, nearly close enough to touch. When I look up into his face, my gaze reflects relief, gratitude. And then I steel myself and let a desire for Fhord I've been denying for too long fill my eyes.

"I couldn't let this asshole hold you any longer," he affirms as he turns toward me and places a hand on my leg, then gives it a little squeeze.

It takes everything I have to hold my expression in place, not flinch in disgust at this male. I can feel the edges of his emotions. The damaged pride that carried him here. The anger at Fhord, so strong it sends shivers through his muscles. And now the rising desire for me. He's already starting to think of what he'll demand in payment for my rescue. This is an ugly, cruel male and I don't want to be anywhere near him.

But I don't let the growing repulsion show in my face. Instead, I grin, lifting my hand to place it on his chest. I can feel his heart thundering beneath my fingers. He'll be hard soon. And then he'll be mine. "My hero," I say in a breathless whisper. "Thank you."

His hand moves farther up my thigh. He's not wasting any time in telling me what he wants. But I need him to slow down. He has to get comfortable enough with me to let down his guard. That won't happen right away.

"Let me make you breakfast. To show you how grateful I am."

"I have something else in mind." His voice is low, guttural. He looks toward the tent and then back at me, reaching for my hand.

"I'm hungry," another male interjects. "Let the bitch feed us."

"Later," the leader responds. "I've got something to do first."

"No, Olan," a different one says, his voice almost pleading. Olan looks up, his eyes flashing. "We're all hungry. We'll give you all the time you want, but we came all the way out here for you. Let us eat."

"Maybe she could do it naked," the fourth male proposes, a note of lust in his words. I turn to stare, struggling to keep the terror from showing on my face. My thoughts drag me back to the Nest, the times they left me bound to a rack alone, legs and arms spread for all to see. "You can have her first, but I'd like to see what we're waiting for."

Now Fhord's pissed. He's struggling against his ropes, his grunts angry. I can feel the violence rippling off him, the blood rushing through his veins in wave after wave of hate. He'd rip these men to shreds if he could.

Olan turns back toward me, a grin erupting as he reaches out to lift my chin. "This one's mine," he says as his thumb swipes across my lips before pulling down the bottom one and pushing through my teeth, just a bit, while I fight the urge to bite him. My skin crawls where he touches me, and it's a struggle to keep my expression from displaying my disgust. "We'll find other women for you," Olan adds. "I'm going to save her for myself."

"That wasn't what we agreed," the fourth male spits out. "You said she'd be ours."

Olan's head snaps toward his comrade, and in an instant, he's on his feet, a knife at the other male's throat. "I changed my mind." His words are venomous. "I decided to keep her for myself."

Olan's definitely in charge now. The other male drops his eyes, his shoulders drooping. "Take her," he says after a moment. "I don't care."

Olan relaxes, re-sheathing his knife, and turns to me. "Cook. We'll eat first."

I smile and rise. He needs to believe I'm grateful. I close the distance between us and lean forward to kiss his lips lightly. "I knew you were my hero." Dropping my voice to a whisper, I lean toward his ear. "I'll thank you properly later."

I move slowly, seductively, as I gather supplies and start to cook. I can still feel the vibrations coming from Fhord, a hatred so pure it feels tangible. Like it could take form and strangle these males as they sit. Beneath that anger, though, is fear. A dread for me, or maybe about me. The rational part of him must know I'm working these males, but a small part of him may be terrified my act is real. That I'm actually grateful for the rescue.

And I'm kind of pissed. Fhord hasn't learned a thing about me in the days we've been together. But I shove that emotion deep inside too. These males can only see relief, gratitude. That's what will pull Olan's defenses all the way down.

We eat in silence, Fhord straining against his ropes the entire time. I want to tell him to relax and save his energy, but it wouldn't do a bit of good. Fhord's a stubborn male.

I can sense when Olan's mood shifts. He sets the plate down and looks up at me, wiping his chin on the back of his hand. "It's time for you to pay your debt," he says as his hand moves toward his groin. It's already bulging, I think. He doesn't have much to brag about.

I better get this right, I think to myself as I let anticipation blossom on my face. I do not want that little prick anywhere near me. "You've waited long enough," I agree as I rise and reach out a hand.

He stands, taking mine and letting me lead him into the tent. I suppress the shiver of disgust that tries to run down my spine as his friends offer a few lewd suggestions for what we should do.

"I'll be a while," Olan says as I reach out to drop the flap behind him. And then he lays down to watch me as I tie them in place. "Wouldn't want an audience," he adds, his voice raspy.

"I'm all yours," I assure him as I spin to face him.

He's still got his blades on him, but if I try to take them now, he'll yell and I'll be overpowered. I need to kill him quietly and leave this tent with weapons ready. That'll take some work. But then I'll have a chance.

He's rubbing himself as his gaze roves up and down my body. "Take off your clothes," he demands. "Not all of them. I want to see you in your skivvies."

I watch him for a moment, repressing the shudder when a bit of drool trickles down his chin. A vise has bound my stomach, making me feel like I need to puke. My heart is already galloping inside my chest as I fight against my need to get away, try to keep the bile from rising into my throat. I wonder if he can see the sweat that's coating my skin.

But he doesn't want me naked yet. This will give me a little time to fight back.

I need him pliable, so I decide to give him a show. Get him as excited—and irrational—as I can. Moving slowly, my hips swaying to a beat I dredge up from my memories, I untie my pants and shimmy them down to the ground. Stepping out of them with a wink, I take the hem of my tunic and move it up my torso. Grazing my ribs and then the band wrapped around my breasts, my hands lift over my head to pull my top up and toss it away.

And then I turn, letting him see my near-naked form. When I face him again, he's ready. His dick is probably as big as it's going to get—still nothing to brag about but a little more respectable—and his hand can't work it fast enough. "Now me," he orders. "Take off my pants first."

Thank fuck. This is the chance I need. I drop down next to him and release the twine that holds up his trousers. Letting one hand scrape along his crotch, I drag them down his legs, the other hand whisking away one of his blades while his thoughts focus on my touch. He's so wrapped up in his lust he doesn't even notice. The other knife comes loose, and I let him see me put it down.

But now his patience is gone. He pulls off his own shirt and lays back down, naked and erect. A skinny little pole greets me, quivering a bit as his gaze moves to my breasts. "I want to feel those next to me," he says, his hand dropping down again to work his little stick of a dick.

I move quickly, hiding the knife behind my arm as I drop it to the ground to lay down next to him. And then I cover his mouth with one hand while the other swipes the blade across this throat.

Olan's muffled cries fill the tent. They're too loud, too distressed. His men will know it's not sex driving his grunts and groans. My spine prickles when someone moves on the other side of the flap. I'm not ready to defend myself yet. But I can't move my hand from his lips until I'm sure he won't scream.

Long seconds pass as we lay there, his eyes shifting from an anger so intense it feels like it will burn me to fear and then resignation. I watch as he accepts the death that's inevitable.

I don't feel an ounce of guilt. Not yet. Maybe never. But I'll worry about that later.

The conversation outside the tent has shifted. They know something's wrong. Wiping the blade on his discarded shirt, I look away from the flap for a moment as I reach for the other knife. I'm still nearly naked but can't risk the distraction of dressing.

And then I crouch and wait. Fhord is still alive—I can feel the anger and dread that ripples off him—so I'm pretty sure he's safe for now. If they have to come in here, they'll need to do it one by one. I can take them that way.

"Olan." The first man speaks first, a tinge of nerves in his voice. "Done yet?"

I count twelve heartbeats as they wait for a response.

"Olan? Talk to us." That sounds like the third male, the one who wanted me to cook naked. I'll enjoy killing him.

Eight heartbeats this time. They'll be coming in soon. I focus on my hands, will away the trembling. These males won't see my fear.

When the flap lifts, I see his eyes first. It's exactly who I'd hoped. One of my daggers flips through the air, landing in the middle of his throat. He drops to the ground, the cloth drooping onto his back as I lurch forward to take the knife, twist it and then pull it back toward me. It's done its job.

"Fuck." The first man's voice floats toward me. But they won't make this male's mistake. I'll need to go out to them. At least the odds are better now.

Fhord's emotions shift as I hear his growl. He's worried now. They're threatening him.

"We'll kill him if you don't come out," the first man yells out. "Now."

We're going to regret this, I know—because we only have one tent—but I can't use the door. Spinning, my knives split the canvas that was behind me, moving through it like soft butter to create another opening. At least Olan's knives are sharp. I step outside and slip around the tent, watching with satisfaction when they turn their gazes toward me.

And then my knives are spinning through the air. The males don't have time to react before they land—one in a throat and the other in a chest. Fhord pushes up and away, rolling to put distance between them as the males grasp for the knives and pull them out. It won't matter. My aim was true.

When Fhord's movement stops, his head spins to find me. He smiles as he slowly looks down my barely-clad body, taking his time as he finds my breasts, nipples pushing through my bandeau, and the flat stomach that leads toward the parts that drive him mad. And then his eyes are focused on mine again. I see gratitude, respect. And some lust.

Now it's my turn to inspect his body. I can't suppress the grin, or the laugh that follows.

Fhord's hard. Again.

CHAPTER FOURTEEN

FHORD

I'LL PROTECT YOU

HOLY FUCK. THAT WAS the sexiest thing I've ever seen.

I'd have been turned on if my little rabbit had killed those men dressed in a potato sack. That devious mind of hers knew exactly what she had to do to save us. She played them like fiddles, giving the bastard Olan what he needed to trust her. He thought she was helpless. He died knowing how fucking stupid and gullible he was. And how brilliant she is.

But she's not wearing a sack. I can't drag my gaze from her bare skin. The little layer of sweat that sparkled in the sun as she flung her blades at them. Her powerful body, with curves where they should be, muscles where she needs them. The thin fabric covering her breasts, that can't hide nipples screaming her excitement. The smile that tells me she's got the courage to kill when she must.

My savage is roaring at me, demanding I take her now. I'm hard as fuck, but I don't care. Sifa knows what she does to me. I gave up trying to hide it. I like being teased by her, watching her eyes shine as she sees the rise she gets out of me. She's having fun and I'm here for it. Every single part of me is on board for whatever my rabbit wants to do.

My resolve is slipping and I need to care.

I cannot let myself get close to her. It would cause so much pain.

Tindera and my Ætt—they'll be the ones punished for my weakness.

But *fuck*, this is hard.

Everything is so hard.

She finally stops laughing and turns toward the tent. My grunt stops her, and I use my head to gesture to the ropes. She needs to untie me.

"I should throw on some clothes first," she says with a gesture at her curves.

I lay there helpless as she ducks into the tent and then comes back out fully dressed in tight leather pants and a corset that hugs her perfect tits. My savage is wide awake, trying to figure out what we have to do to see Sifa's skin again. To feel her next to us.

I need to calm the fuck down.

When she unties me, my hands find her cheeks. "You're so fucking dangerous," I breathe. "That was magnificent."

And then I leave. Because if I stay, I won't be able to stop myself. I'm by the creek for a long time, wresting control back. Finally, with every part of me a little more relaxed, I make my way back to the tent.

Sifa's dragged the men away and is trying to brush over the blood stains they left. She looks at me, her eyes crinkling with a broad grin.

"I thought you'd never come back. I need to wash their grime off, but we can pack up and leave as soon as you get a little food."

I pause, holding her gaze. "Thank you, my brave, selfless rabbit. I owe you."

She rolls her eyes at me. "We're traveling together. We do what we must to survive."

But I don't want to blow this off. "You exposed yourself—in every way possible," I add with a lopsided smile—"to save me. You could have escaped alone. Hilde would have carried you away. But you risked everything to protect me. Thank you."

Sifa's eyes start to glitter, and I watch as a swallow moves down her throat. "What else could I have done?" she asks in a quiet voice, full of emotion. Then she smirks. "At least until you answer a few of my questions."

"I knew there was a reason," I tell her with a laugh. "I still appreciate it."

"But you do owe me. We're agreed?"

"Definitely," I assure her. I'm stunned by how comforted I am to have this promise between us, as if any commitment soothes the savage that demands a closer connection. I can't put her behind me until this debt is paid.

We move quickly to pack and leave. Too much of the day already has passed, and we have far to go. The next two days are surprisingly smooth, making me nervous. It shouldn't be this easy to approach the Nest. Sifa seems to notice it too. We're both on high alert, our eyes constantly searching for any hint of a threat as we draw close.

Sifa's also growing more nervous by the hour. She's quiet on the final morning, her eyes distant, little wrinkles forming at their corners and across her brow every time she lets herself look toward our destination. I know why, but I can't tell her that. Still, it might help her to talk about it. We both need her at her best over the next two days.

"Rabbit? Are you okay?" I make sure my voice is gentle, soothing.

The world—my world—looks back at me as she lifts her eyes to find mine. And then I feel her emotions shift, from the anxiety tinged with fear I sensed when we woke, to resolve. Defiance. Resistance.

"I've heard a lot about this place," she tells me in a flat voice. "This will be dangerous."

"I'll protect you," I assure her, "from anything, anyone, we may find in there."

Sifa scoffs but I feel her comfort at my words. "Maybe it'll be me protecting you," she suggests.

"We'll protect each other." I hold her stare for a moment, letting her see the savage that will not let any harm come to our mate. Letting her sense my resolve, as strong as hers. She nods, and I feel her relax, just a bit.

We'll do this. Together. And then we'll get away from each other. Forever.

"Today we'll enter the caves," I tell her. "We'll need to be alert, but we should be safe there. I don't have any reason to believe they've been found."

"How would you know if they had?"

"Tindera's here," I remind her. "She still spends time in the caves. She likes being alone." My feelings for my mount wash over me, stilling my tongue for a moment. It's been too long this time. I can't wait to see her again.

"It's tough to communicate over large distances," I say after a minute, "but we're close enough for me to feel her presence, and for her to feel mine. She knows what I plan. If we were walking into a trap, she'd tell me, despite the risk."

Sifa quirks a single eyebrow, a silent question.

"The Dróttning can listen in on conversations between dragons and riders, and even capture the substance of the dragon's recent memories. She needs to be close enough and focused on the particular dragon to do that, so it's possible to speak without her eavesdropping. But she holds control in part by wielding knowledge."

I pause for a moment, lifting my gaze toward the massive peak ahead of us. "I'm told she's coming to the Nest soon," I tell my little rabbit after a moment, "and I'm not supposed to be here. I can chance a few words with Tindera but no more."

"How does your communication with her work?" Sifa's eyes light up with her question. She's eager to talk about dragons and my bond with Tindera.

"The closer we are, the easier it is." I pause, thinking through the limits on what I can say.

"If it helps, I know there are some barriers that can't be breached. They stop any communication between dragon and rider. And I know that includes the entrances to the caves."

"You're not supposed to know any of that," I point out. I don't agree with all the Dróttning's mandates, but this one makes sense. Enemies of the Kastali can't know the limits of the dragon-rider bond.

"I do, though. I can't tell you how—it's one of those secrets we're going to keep from each other," she adds with a smile—"but it might help us both for me to know what will stand in the way of you getting information from Tindera."

"You're right. It helps. I can tell you most of the rest. If Tindera's deep in the caves, I'll only be able to connect with her while I'm there too. I won't be able to reach her when I'm in the caves and she's not. Outside of those limits, distance is everything. When I'm in the South and she's here, we have only the bond that formed when we embraced our pairing, telling the other we still live. It's too far. As we get closer, I sense her and that feeling grows."

I pause, mentally stroking my link with my dragon. I can almost hear her purr—or, what passes for purring in dragons. "She and I first started to sense each other yesterday evening. It's part of the reason I pushed us so hard. I wanted to go to sleep with Tindera's touch. We can share emotions at this distance easily. If we needed to, we could exchange words, but we won't risk saying much. She'd let me know if we had something to fear."

"Is that why you slept so well?" Sifa's smile is soft, friendly.

"That and the female by my side to protect me."

Gods help me. I'm so fucking feeble. The words came out before I could stop them. I have to resist the urge to stroke Sifa's cheek. My savage fights to take over when she looks at me like that. But being this close to Tindera will bolster my resolve. The cost of giving in to my savage, of claiming Sifa as my own, would be too high.

"At your service," Sifa responds as she stands and gives me a playful bow. "We should go."

I'm grateful for the shift, reaching out again to Tindera to remind myself where my loyalties lie as I stand and follow Sifa to the horses. We ride in silence for a few hours, but we both know that won't last. We'll run into sentries soon. And as expected, we're eating a quick midday meal, hidden in some bushes near a creek, when we hear hints of danger.

"There's nothing out here," one of them complains, his voice bordering on a whine. "It was a trick of the light. Nobody comes this close to the Nest."

"I know what I saw," another mutters, angry. "You may not want to be here, but here you are. We will do our job, find any who would enter these grounds unbidden."

"But nobody does that. It's suicide. I've been here more than a year, and not a single soul has tried to come here without the Dróttning's consent."

Their voices are getting closer. If they're searching for us, we may have no choice but to kill them. Which I don't want to do.

"Because we do our job well. All know what they risk."

The males go silent, the only sound their horses' hooves crunching over the pebble-strewn ground. It seems that even Sigurd and Hilde hold their breath, waiting for this threat to pass. I chose these mounts for a reason. Even as slow as Hilde has become, she still outsmarts most of the others in the stables. Except Sigurd.

Perhaps the gods are smiling on them, because the males don't approach the bushes that protect us. We wait long enough to ensure they're gone and then start to pick our way toward the cave entrance. Four more times we hide to evade patrols—the Dróttning has pulled her forces closer to the Nest for some reason—but we make it by the end of the day.

I hear Sifa's long inhale as we break through the trees, giving us our first view of the range that harbors the Nest. Even from the side, our only safe approach, it's equal measures intimidating and awe-inspiring, Vanatia's largest array of mountains with its highest peak. The crags that shoot into the sky look like bursts of lava frozen in place, their shapes random and unpredictable. Black sand and rock have been covered over the millennia by trees and bushes but haven't disappeared fully beneath nature's blanket.

The dragons chose this place at the dawn of time, expanding to the southern Nest only when their numbers had grown so large they had no choice. Tindera has told me of the dragons' love for its untamed and savage landscape. Although dragon myth does not acknowledge it, I suspect their choice was more practical. A vast cave system winds beneath the entire chain, a river connecting each spike to the others, creating abundant pools along the way.

Greens and golds spread out to our right, a feigned invitation to any who might make it this far. The paths created by grass and bush lead to the front, where those who are welcome enter. We take the rocky trail, going left and toward the back. After a tedious trip picking our way across the slopes, hiding in shadows when we must, we finally make it to the outer cave.

"We'll wait here until Tindera comes. She knows when to meet us. It won't be long."

Sifa's eyes widen, delight glimmering in them for a moment before she blinks and quells her response. Still, I can't suppress my own pleasure. The rational side of me doesn't want them to like each other—no good would come of it—but I can't deny desperately hoping they do.

"She's here," I tell Sifa after a few minutes. And then she is.

I'm always awed when I see Tindera after a long separation. She's the most majestic dragon in the Nest, bar none. The gold and black feathers that cover her sparkle in the late sun, as if the dwarfs themselves wrought each on their forge. They create a shifting pattern over most of her body, enough of the black mixed in to highlight and contrast with the glittering plumes that dominate. As they lead to her legs the blacks take over, the massive claws hidden under feathers as dark as a cloudy night.

It's her eyes, though, that I love the most. They're the blue of the sea in my favorite lagoon, warm like the water there and every bit as fluid. Deeper and darker if Tindera's emotions ride high, they shift to a relaxed, crystalline azul when she's comfortable and happy.

I watch as they do just that after she rolls a massive boulder away from the cave and pops her head out of the opening she's created. And then I walk over and rest my forehead on her snout for a moment, letting go of the tension that's been building in me since this trip began. Tindera will settle me. She'll help me stay focused on what matters. And what I cannot allow to matter.

Home, Tindera tells me, using the shorthand of her species, which always relays more information than that single word. Like me, she's empty when I'm gone. Only when we're together does she feel like she's at home.

I'm not as concerned as I was about speaking with Tindera. Now that I'm in the caves, I'm positive the Dróttning's not here, so she can't overhear our words. Still, I talk out loud for Sifa's benefit. I remember how frustrating it was, before Tindera and I bonded, to watch a dragon and rider converse without including me. I've made it a habit to not do that with Tindera unless I must.

"It's been too long," I tell her, my heart in my throat. "Are you healing well?"

Strong, she assures me, heaving a breath to emphasize her point. The damage had been to a lung, and she wouldn't have been able to do even that a few weeks ago. *Soon.*

Relief washes over me, worries I didn't realize I'd been harboring lifting away and leaving me feeling light and free. I stroke her nose for a minute, savoring this reunion, and then stand.

"We should get inside before I introduce you."

Tindera nods and steps back, making space for us and the horses to enter. She pauses while I light a torch, then rolls the rock nearly back into place. She won't be with us when we return, so she allows enough room for us to leave without her. She'll come back later—when she can be sure she won't be found and possibly suspected—and close it completely.

As soon as she's done, Tindera drops her chin onto the ground, taking the least aggressive stance possible for a beast this large. Her eyes find my little rabbit and gaze at her for a long time, measuring this female she knows is my unwanted mate.

Kind, Tindera tells me. Dragons can sense character, a necessary part of their bonds with riders in the early days, when they were given a choice about who would ride them.

I huff out a laugh as I nod. She's right. I hate to admit anything about Sifa that might draw us closer, but I can't deny she's kind.

Elf, Tindera says, a deep despair embedded in that single word. I've been too far away to tell her, but now she realizes why this bond is so utterly fucked up. She knows how much danger we'd all be in—especially her—if I took this elf into my bed or my home.

The Dróttning never told me about Sifa, but I know she's spent the last decade searching for the first elf to escape the Nest. She never saw my little rabbit, thank fuck, but too many guards would recognize her. Even without that, though, the Dróttning would sense my bond with Sifa as soon as I embraced it. It would change me, and I'd never be able to construct a shield strong enough to hide such a fundamental part of me from the Dróttning.

Elf, I affirm in Tindera's thoughts. *Hidden*, I reiterate. Not even Sifa can know that our mating bond lets me sense her true self. Just knowing an elf walks free in Vanatia is a death sentence. Even for me, loath as the Dróttning would be to have me killed.

Tindera blinks her eyes once, shuttering the sorrow she'd let creep in, and then turns back to Sifa.

Grateful. She wants me to help her speak with Sifa.

"Tindera knows you saved my life," I explain. "She asked me to relay her thanks."

Sifa's responding smile is almost brighter than the torch I hold. "Can Tindera understand my words if I speak directly to her?"

"She can," I affirm.

Sifa turns to Tindera, focusing on a single eye like so many riders do. She acts as if she's spent time around dragons in the past and knows how to interact with them.

"You're welcome, but I don't need thanks for protecting him. We're in this together. I'll do all I can to keep him safe, just as I know he will me."

Strong, Tindera tells me, her scrutiny never straying from Sifa.

"She is that," I say out loud for Sifa's benefit. "Tindera has seen into your heart, found your strength of will."

Dangerous, Tindera adds. And I know exactly what she means. Sifa doesn't threaten us physically. Her danger lies in her appeal. In the fact that she's my mate, and I'm more attached to my little rabbit already than I ever wanted to be.

My response to Tindera is in my thoughts this time. *I'll keep her away from me*, I promise. *I won't let myself get drawn into something that would threaten all of us.*

I feel Tindera's conflict. She wants me to have this, knows the emptiness I'll carry for the rest of my life if I don't. But she understands better than anyone what would happen if I gave in. *Quandary*, she says after a moment.

No, I respond, my thoughts sharper than I'd like. *This isn't some challenge we'll work through. I can never have Sifa.* I pause to make sure she can see my resolve. *I will never let myself have her*, I insist.

Quandary, Tindera repeats, her thoughts emphatic.

Willful creature, I say as I pat her snout. And then she turns to lead us deeper into the cave.

Chapter Fifteen

Sifa

A Foolish, Foolish Elf

I KNEW I WOULDN'T be able to sleep, much as I need to.

I can't yet smell the Nest, but my thoughts keep dredging up the scents I lived with for weeks. Some were constant—the reek of the dung they threw into the prisons; the sulfur of the brackish water that had accrued over centuries; the tang of blood, as one prisoner or another was returned from the ever-present torture sessions; the shit and piss we all lived in. I dread the stench more than anything, I think.

Odors always trigger my memories, my emotions, faster than any other sense.

Twice I drift off, only to jerk awake in the midst of one terror or another.

And then I feel, rather than see, Tindera. She'd disappeared overnight, perhaps returning to the Nest so she wouldn't be missed. Now she's returned. She moves slowly, cautiously, as though she doesn't want to alarm me. Despite her bulk, she manages to creep closer to me without disturbing anyone else, even Fhord's light snores continuing to echo through the chamber. When she gets close enough, she lays her head next to mine, letting me decide whether to touch her or not. I shift just enough to place her long snout against my back. And sleep finally takes me.

I can feel Fhord's stare when I wake up. His gaze stirs the hairs on the back of my neck, drawing me from my dream of him. When I open my eyes, he's watching me, an arm's length between us. He looks down quickly, as if he's loath to be discovered.

"Why are you watching me, Fhord?"

Then his gaze is on me again, his teeth appearing ever so briefly as the edges of his lips lift. "You've stolen my dragon from me, rabbit."

Tindera's still next to me, her snout giving me the comfort I needed to sleep. I can feel the side of her mouth lift, as if she's smiling at Fhord's remark.

"I see she doesn't mind," he adds after a moment. "Are you okay?"

"I am," I assure him. Sitting, I reach over to stroke Tindera's snout. "I wasn't sleeping well, and she helped me."

"She's a very good backrest when she wants to be," Fhord responds with a smile. "She likes you."

The comfort that blossoms within me at his words surprises me. Suddenly, I'm back in Midgard, riding Lia's dragon, Zaria. I feel protected, safer than I thought would be possible this close to the Nest.

"She's a remarkable dragon." I drag my hands along her snout, standing to reach up and scratch behind her horn, wondering if she'll respond as the dragons on Midgard did.

I can't suppress the grin when she does. A loud purr rumbles from her chest, echoing through our chamber. The horses shuffle their feet for a few seconds then settle down. The only sound in the chamber is Tindera's hum as she leans into my hands, letting my nails find their way beneath feathers to the sensitive skin below.

"By the gods, she's yours now for sure," Fhord says with another smile. "My nails can't do what yours can."

Tindera grunts, staring at Fhord. After a moment he returns the grunt, the tips of his lips dropping down as his eyes flare. "You should go," he says abruptly. He turns to me, his words clipped. "Tindera shouldn't have come back to us. She needs to return to the Nest before she's missed. We can't take a chance they'll connect her to what we're going to do."

I nod as I watch him, wondering what words they exchanged. But it doesn't matter. We both know this odd relationship will end when we're done. The less I know about him and Tindera, the better.

Pulling back my hands, I rub her snout one more time, then step back while Fhord gives her a quick pat and sends her on her way. I turn to our packs to pull out food while Fhord stores our blankets. Within twenty minutes of waking, we've eaten and are following Tindera into the cavern.

Fhord's torch brightens enough of the cave to dredge up memories of my last time here. My heart is skipping in my chest, beating faster the farther we go, and I have to struggle to keep down the cold breakfast I ate before we left. Each step takes me deeper into my thoughts, my senses responding by amplifying every sound, sight, and smell. When I hear the water rushing through a tunnel above us, I know we're close. And I'm not sure if I'll be able to do this.

When they held me here before, I spent weeks wriggling into the thoughts of one of my captors, finally persuading him to release me and then Toffer. He'd been one of our crueler guards, so I had little regret for the price he'd pay when they found him. I had no idea how we'd escape, but Toffer's a troll and can sense changes in cave systems. I'd traveled through enough hidden doors in caves in my worlds to find an escape where Toffer told me to search.

Still, it was the most terrifying journey of my life. I'm still not sure how we got out alive.

And now I'm willingly entering these same caves.

I am a foolish, foolish elf. I'd laugh at myself if my stomach wasn't so twisted in knots.

When we stop for lunch, Fhord sits close enough for me to feel the warmth of his skin. I hate that he can sense my emotions, knows how terrified I am. The last thing I want is for him to see me as weak.

"I'm frightened," I tell him as we finish eating, my voice matter-of-fact. "This place has a bad reputation. But I'll be fine. Stop worrying about me."

The torch throws shadows across his face, hiding his eyes. Still, I can see the corners of his lips tick up.

"Does that make you happy?" I demand.

"No, rabbit," he responds as he turns to catch my gaze. "I'm impressed. I can feel your fear. And yet you go on."

"We have to do this," I remind him, my voice still cold. "I won't let any jitters interfere."

"I know," he tells me, letting the smile crease his cheeks. "I trust you."

"Good. That'll make this easier." I watch him for a moment, willing my heart to slow even more. "What happens next?" I ask at last.

"We'll be at the entrance soon. Tindera will be close enough to sense if anyone is nearby."

"And if it's clear?"

"The horses will wait here while we go into the prison alone."

"And this is where I come in? I'm going to traipse in there, find and free Thyra, and leave?"

"That's the plan." Now Fhord's smile is forced. I can sense his unease too. "Bevin sent you for a reason," he reminds me. "He said we're the perfect team for this."

The torch flickers all around us, throwing dancing shadows on the cavern's walls, drawing me back into the weeks I spent here. My breathing is accelerating, and I can't do anything about it.

"I don't want to just sit here," I explain as I stand abruptly. "We need to go and get this over with." I throw our things into a sack, tie it to Hilde, and then start to pace. Fhord still hasn't stood up. "What?" My tone is anxious.

"Rabbit, look at me." He's much calmer than he should be as he rises and places his hands on my cheeks. "We can do this."

"I know." I pause, inhaling deeply twice, and then three times. "I know," I say again, my words a bit more measured.

He drops his arms to his sides but doesn't step back. "Tindera will be in the same realm. Between the two of us, we should be able to sense if any guards or dragons are nearby."

Sucking in one more breath, I force myself to nod. "Once we're inside, I'll find someone who can help us," I respond. "It may take a while. If she's being held deep in the prison, where they keep their most important captives, we might not be able to do this today. Those guards are well-trained and not as easily controlled as some others." I pause, realizing I've said more than I should. "At least, that's what I've heard," I add after a moment.

"She's not a high-value prisoner. Bevin got her status from someone who should know."

Taking in one more calming breath, I nod. "I'm ready."

Fhord steps away, and I feel the loss of his presence. It's strange how quickly we've grown connected. He centers me, helps me find my calm.

He grunts once and leads us toward the entrance to the prisons. Sooner than I'd wanted, he's reaching out a hand to wriggle a thin knife into an opening I might have missed to our right. He pauses when it clicks then starts to pull it slowly, I assume searching for any nearby guards. When it's open no more than a hand's length, he stops and waits.

And then it really hits me. All the emotions weaving through these caverns crash into me—fear and fury and desperation, searching for some respite from the agony that beats on them every minute of every hour of every day. I scrabble through my fluttering thoughts for the blanket I'd erected when I lived among them, a barrier between my horror and theirs. I need to keep my senses open and alert without absorbing their pain.

Slowing my breaths, I center myself, drawing on the lessons that carried me through more challenges than I can recall. I let my eyes search the cave around me, focusing on details I would otherwise have ignored: the burgundy that weaves through the rock, like a glass of wine spilled, running in rivulets across its surface; the mild scent of decay hiding beneath the mildew and musk, evidence that something alive has been here before; the slight drip of water nearby, maybe a pool leaching into the cavern below it, one drop at a time.

I can do this.

I will do this.

Finally, I focus on my surroundings again. Fhord's pulled the door closed, leaving the barest gap—just enough to throw light in a narrow line on the other side of the tunnel. We're both still and silent as a guard passes near enough to trigger my senses.

After another minute or more, Fhord touches my arm, drawing me from my inspection of the ceiling far above us. "It's time," he mouths. Opening the door just wide enough to allow us through, he leads me into the prison.

The calm that always precedes a challenge washes over me, just as it did when I finally found my escape from this place. I count my steps, expanding my psyche as I notice everything around me without letting the despair weigh me down. Twice, we disappear in shadows just in time to miss an approaching guard. I calm down even more, trusting in Fhord's senses to keep us hidden and letting fear hone my focus.

When my probing thoughts find the guard that might help us, I almost laugh. It's the same male who freed me all those years ago. I was sure he'd be dead, but he survived somehow. I wonder if his mind is as weak now as I left it when I escaped. Or if his punishment led to walls I won't be able to surmount.

Placing my hand on Fhord's arm, I draw him to a stop and gesture for him to stay. He nods, his eyes as dark as the forest at dusk, and I turn to stride into the cavern. When I'm far enough away to hide *how* I plan to retrieve Thyra, I fully free my mind from the chains that hold it in place, letting it wriggle out and into my mark. I'll know soon enough if he'll do my bidding.

I hate what I find in this ugly, cruel man. He's worse now than he was then, his entire personality a cauldron of aggrievement and anger. They'd punished him mercilessly, but he survived. And then he clawed his way back into the ranks of the guards, although never trusted as much as he was then. These days, other prisoners suffer at his hands for my escape all those years ago.

But his brain still gives way to my push, opening a path for me to enter. I can use him again. And this time, I won't leave him alive.

My memories of this guard come rushing back in, allowing me to start now in the same place I left him. Slowly, carefully, I find images of his commander, a male he both despises and fears. My thrall has had any resistance beaten out of him. He'll follow this order without question. Then I create the memory that will direct him to free Thyra and bring her to me, dropping it into his thoughts.

He responds exactly as I'd hoped. The frustration at the unexpected order washes over him first. His loathing for every superior who barks commands at him starts as a rumble in his ears that grows into a roar, drawing his teeth into a tight clench as his jaws grind together. If he could kill them all, he would, dancing through their blood as it splashes all around him, decorating the floors and walls with his vengeance.

His survival instinct, though, is stronger. The time isn't right yet. For now, he's their drudge. For now.

Spinning, the guard stalks toward the prisoner he's been told to move. Soon, I lose my connection with him, forced to trust that the memory I constructed will continue to propel his steps. And I wait.

My sense of time in these caves is no better now than it was all those years ago. Although I try to measure it, my count keeps getting lost in my search for the guard's return. After a half-dozen stops and starts, I give up. It doesn't matter. He'll return or he won't. We'll succeed or we'll fail. Nothing I can do now will change that.

I almost breathe a sigh of relief when I feel him return, stopping myself just in time. He's even more angry than he was

before, rankled by the impertinence of the male who guard-
ed this prisoner. They don't know who he is. What he's
capable of. Someday soon, he's thinking, he'll show them
all.

But he's brought Thyra with him. This has been easier
than I could have hoped.

Until it's not.

I sense someone else approaching and shrink farther into
the shadows, stilling my breaths. This male doesn't notice
me as he stalks past, his mind elsewhere.

"Where are you taking her?" His voice is angry, impatient.

"Ivar commanded me to bring her to him. Fuck if I know
why."

"Nobody told me. She's mine. Ivar can't have her." The
lust that trickles through his thoughts threatens to pull up
memories of my own time here, but I shove them down. I
will not let those males harm me any more than they did.

My drudge wavers in his resolve, and I realize how lucky
we are that they encountered each other here, instead of
closer to the cages. I carefully bolster him, drawing up
memories of Ivar's temper and cruelty when he's dis-
obeyed. The effect is immediate.

"Ivar can do anything he wants," my mark reminds the
other guard. "He's your drott just as he is mine." He pauses
before his next words, which erupt in an angry warning.
"He'll punish you, not me, if you stop me from bringing
this prisoner to him."

And now it's the other guard's turn to waver. He fears Ivar too. "Fine," he spits out. "But you will return her to me. She's mine."

"I'll do as Ivar commands. If he wants her returned, she will be."

Neither speaks again as footsteps carry the second guard away from me. Moments later, Thyra appears.

She's stumbling in the chains that hobble her steps, her arms barely strong enough to hold up the cuffs around her wrists. The Valkyrie that disappeared is now a wretch, broken and barely alive. I search for a spark in her eyes but find none.

And again, I have to smother the memories that threaten to overwhelm me. I looked so much like this when the fates let me find my escape.

I survived. She can too.

My thoughts spear out for another search of the cavern. When I'm convinced nobody else is near enough to interfere, I step forward. I can't suppress my smile when the guard sees me. His eyes find mine and glare in an anger that's been building for the last decade.

He takes a step forward, too focused on me to recognize the danger he's in. And then my blade is in his throat, severing his vocal chords before he can utter a sound. He'd abandoned any chance of warning others—maybe saving himself—in the drive for vengeance that consumed him when he saw me. *Idiot.*

Part of me wants him to die more slowly, blood dripping from every inch of skin. My fingers itch as they wrap around a knife at my belt. Almost of its own accord, my mind is feeding his thoughts with images of the death I'd give him if I let myself. His eyes grow wide as a wicked grin splits my cheeks. When the smell of his shit spills out around us and his pants grow dark at the crotch, I sneer, expanding on the vision that's driving his terror.

But this is how he needs to die. Quietly and quickly. Much as I want it, I can't let my craving for revenge take over with this guard. I embrace the calm I need to let my knife finish its job alone, relaxing as a sense of serenity enters through the soles of my feet and whispers up and through me. By the time his eyes are permanently open, I'm ready to let go of him and my urge to shred his skin the way they shredded mine.

Exhaling one last time, I turn to Thyra. Her eyes shimmer as peace seems to wash over her too. And then she collapses into the dirt just as Fhord turns a corner, his gaze landing on the dead guard.

"I had to kill him." My words are a whisper. Anything louder would shatter the stillness Thyra and I need.

Fhord dips his chin once and bends to start rustling through the guard's clothes, searching for the key that will unlock Thyra's cuffs. Within a minute, he's tossing them away, freeing her arms and legs.

I pull Thyra into my arms, wrapping myself around her. This is what I'd craved, almost more than food or sunlight, when Toffer and I escaped. For months after, we spent every night holding each other. Even now, when nightmares find one of us, we'll escape our terror in the other's arms.

Thyra's breathing grows steadier as I hold her, the rhythm slowing as she finds comfort she probably relinquished weeks ago. When her eyes open, I'm grateful Bevin sent me here with Fhord. I needed this as much as her.

Now we just have to escape.

Chapter Sixteen

Sifa

I Need to End Him

F HORD CARRIES THYRA AS I drag the guard along with us, stopping every few feet to backtrack and wipe sand back over the path we've scraped clear. It's slow going, but Thyra's too fragile for anything else.

Four different times, Fhord or I sense a nearby guard and barely make it into the shadows, or down a nearby cavern. I can feel the blanket Fhord throws around us with his mind, protecting us from anyone who shares our gifts. Once, we're seconds away from being caught, ducking into an alcove a moment before a guard comes striding down the hall.

I'm prepared to leave the Nest with Fhord and Thyra. To abandon my own goals for now—my need to find something that will help me better understand what I must do to get back to my worlds. I know how to get in now. I'll go back home with them and return alone. Soon.

We're nearly there—a few male's-heights from the door we'll use to escape—when I feel *him* stalking toward us. Bolverkr. The guard in charge of my torture.

Sweat erupts on my neck as my palms grow slick. My breath catches in my throat, memories of his depravity consuming my thoughts. I almost can feel the knife as it slices my skin, carving off little bits at a time while he laughs and demands answers I won't give him. My thighs clench, as if I have any hope of keeping out the objects he shoves into me while I'm spread on the rack. Or the men who take me, one after another.

The phantom pains that stayed with me for months after my escape return, tearing into me while they remind me that these caves took a part of me I'll never get back.

That *he* took something from me I'll never get back.

I force myself to inhale and exhale, one shaky breath at a time. *I'm safe. He has no control over me. He won't hurt me again.* Finally, I find the calm I need to finish this job. To go back to Toffer and Thor.

But then my memories shift to the vengeance I knew I'd find one day, my pulse quickening as that compulsion seeps into my thoughts. Suddenly, I'm sitting in my cell carefully constructing my retribution, holding on to that thin anchor for my sanity. My fingers flex, skimming the knife along Bolverkr's flesh before I shove it up his ass, twisting the blade while he screams and begs. And then they're wrapped around his neck, watching as he accepts my punishment. As I remove his evil existence from this world.

I take a deep breath, dragging my mind back to this cave. To here and now.

I try. I really do. I know I need to push those thoughts away—to stay with Fhord and Thyra and leave this place with them—but my urge to destroy Bolverkr is too deeply ingrained. It became a part of who I am. I could sooner staunch its control over me than I could stop breathing.

Inhaling deeply, my jaw shifts as my teeth grind against each other and my gaze flits around the cavern. I let the truth settle within me.

I may never get this chance again. I know what I have to do to put Bolverkr behind me. I need to hurt him. And then I need to end him. Maybe if he no longer walks this world, he'll no longer haunt my dreams.

My eyes find Fhord, who's staring at me in horror. He can feel my emotions. He realizes I'm about to do something reckless.

It doesn't matter. I can't let my tormentor go.

"I'm sorry," I tell him, dropping the guard's shoulder and racing to find Bolverkr. Fhord won't be able to follow right away. We're close enough to the cavern for him to get Thyra and the guard there. He'll do that before he comes after me.

Still, I almost stop when his emotions chase me down the dark hall. I feel his disappointment. The hint of anger that grows the farther away I get. As I pause, though, something else rises in him. Acknowledgment. Acceptance. He may not know why, but he knows I need to do this.

My steps slow as Bolverkr approaches. For a moment, I feel like I'll collapse, the weight of my wrath nearly pulling me to the ground. My hands tremble as I unsheathe two of my blades and I have to shift my attention to my breathing, slowing it down with each inhale and exhale.

Dredging up the shields I learned to construct to hide my mind from him, I focus on my steps, testing every movement forward before I commit. I'm terrified that a pebble will alert him and take my vengeance from me. Desperate to be done with this—done with him—and leave this place behind me.

In less than a minute, as I huddle in a splash of shadow along the wall, he appears. Just as he always did, he strides through the cavern as if nobody and nothing could hurt him. As if he has nothing to fear.

This moment makes it all worthwhile. I savor the taste of revenge, drowning out my memories of the coppery taste of my own blood in my mouth, the brackish semen they spilled down my throat, hands around my neck to make sure I took everything they forced into me. I might keep his puny little penis as my prize tonight. A reminder that I'm strong enough to take this from him.

I cast my thoughts out one more time to make sure he's alone—that nobody's close enough to hear his screams—and then step into the light. His eyes grow wide and then narrow, recognition floating through the air toward me. My smile is vicious as I cast my first knife and take out his right hand. He's not nearly as adept with his left. The next blade carves into his cock, drawing out the squeal I need to hear as his red uniform darkens at the groin.

By the gods, this is every bit as satisfying as I hoped it would be. I don't even try to hold back the laugh that erupts from me, throaty and *malicious as fuck*. He needs to know how much I'm going to enjoy this.

"You." Even with his injuries, his voice is as strong as I remembered, a commander dripping with authority. He pulls the knife from his balls with his left hand, shoving it into his belt before grasping the one in his right hand to yank it out. His gaze never leaves mine. My stomach flutters a bit as I watch the pain pass through him.

I nod as I halve the distance between us. His eyes remain sharp, his shoulders thrown back despite the agony that must be rippling through him. He's still a dangerous man.

"I knew this day would come," I tell him, my fingers pinched on the tips of the blades that will take his life. "It's here sooner than I'd expected," I admit, my smile somehow growing even wider. "Today's a good day. For me."

"You still can get away," he spits out, his fingers clutching the handle of my weapon. "If you leave now, you'll take your life with you."

"Not before I take yours." My next knife flips through the air to pierce one of his lungs. I hear the whoosh as his breath gusts out and he leans forward. I have to admire his restraint. No scream this time.

"Bitch," he snarls. "I told them we needed to end you. Fucking idiots."

"Why didn't they? What did they think I would give them?" I never figured out how much they know about what landed in this world with me. If he can tell me, it'll be worth an extra minute or two in this cavern.

His head rolls up, dark eyes finding mine. This is the moment I've been craving since I left this place. He knows he'll die today.

"Fuck you," he whispers, a harsh wheeze emerging with his malice. "You may have taken my life but you'll take nothing else from me."

I kick out my foot, finding the hand that holds my blade to wrench it free. He reaches for the knife in his chest but my other foot finds it first, twisting it before it tugs free to drop to the ground. A wave of pain rolls through him, and I wonder if I've ever seen anything more satisfying. The rock that formed in my stomach when I lived here sheds layers, lightening the heaviness I've carried all these years.

I breathe in, laughing again when I realize he shit his pants. About time.

My next blade impales his left hand, slicing through the tendons that would let him grasp a weapon. At last, he sinks to his knees, dropping his eyes to stare at the ground before they lift to find mine again. He knows his life belongs to me. But he still hasn't let go of the anger, the need for someone else's pain.

"You won't leave here alive," he whispers with a chilling grin. And then I feel the sweep of his psyche across mine, followed by the response of a half-dozen other guards, now alert to the attack.

Fuck. Fuck, fuck. I'd hoped to have more time to savor his death, but I need to escape more. I can't be trapped here again.

Two steps carry me to him, his knees still on the ground, his neck arched so he can shoot spite at me while he still breathes. My spite, though, has a life of its own. It laughs at his pathetic attempt to intimidate me.

This is the memory I'll drag up when my thoughts carry me back here. When I wake at night screaming, thrashing against the cords he wrapped around my wrists and ankles. When I can't take the pain any longer and find some relief in my drifting mind.

I grab his hair and pull his head back, exposing the scarless neck. "I wish I'd had more time with you," I breathe as my blade opens his jugular. I hold him there and watch the life leave his eyes. A puddle forms around my boots, thick and pungent, and I smile again. Fitting that his blood will leave here with me.

The relief that follows his death cleanses me in a way I couldn't have expected. My gaze strays toward the ceiling as I inhale and exhale, in and out. I feel freer—lighter—than I have in years. As if this one act, a single swipe of my knife, removed an anchor I'd been dragging around since then.

I wish I could stay here and enjoy this moment. But I feel others approaching. If I don't leave now, I'll be forced to take risks I can't afford.

After one last look at the man who deserved so much more pain, I gather my blades then spin and race down the hall toward Fhord and Thyra. I'm dreading his anger, but it doesn't matter. We've rescued Thyra. We'll be enemies again soon anyway.

I sense the guards barreling toward me—between me and my exit—before I see them. Six approach me, called by the man I just killed. They won't have found Bolverkr yet since he's lying in a puddle of his own blood in the opposite direction, but they'll know I killed him. He should be here instead of me.

Even from this distance, I can tell that nobody has the talent they need to find my thoughts. But that won't matter. They'll know to search the shadows for me.

My body responds, the urge to fight overwhelming any thought of flight. The adrenaline that already flooded my system races through me, pushing me on as my vision focuses. I flit my eyes around the cavern, searching for some advantage against guards who'll be every bit as skilled in combat as me. When I see the ledge a dozen feet away, I sigh in relief. That's my best hope.

I take my time crawling up. If a single stone drops, they'll know to look up. I can't give up whatever surprise I'll have up here.

They stride into the cavern seconds after I perch on the ledge, slowing as they search for me. I can feel their anger and resolve. They know I'm dangerous. They know they won't find their comrade alive. And they're determined to make me pay.

But I'm determined too.

My first two blades flip from my hands at the same time, piercing the throat of one guard and the temple of another.

They crumple to the ground, not even a cry escaping their lips. The rest turn, finding me just as another two knives spin toward them. One finds its mark, dropping a third guard to bleed with his brothers.

These are better odds.

I drop to the ground ... and twist my fucking ankle. My foot plunges into a hole I hadn't noticed before and I nearly topple over. That's all it takes to shift the odds again. Gritting my teeth, I breathe through the daggers that shoot up my leg when I put weight on it.

And then I grin. Because fuck them. They won't see my pain.

They attack as one, flinging fists and legs at me. I'm outnumbered and nearly overwhelmed. All I can do is defend, spinning and ducking and scampering away more than once. My mind trips over itself, searching for an opening to do something other than respond to their assault. But they're too fast, too well trained.

Once, almost by accident, I land a punch to the jaw. He drops back, shaking his head for a moment, giving me the smallest window to charge the others. Before I can step into my next punch, though, he drops his head and rams into me, tossing me into the wall a few feet away.

The air whooshes out of me as my lungs expand like a balloon and then constrict. I'm struggling to take a breath, even as I force myself to roll away because if I don't, I'll be dead. The stabbing pain in my side tells me I've broken a rib, or worse. *Fuck*. This will take a couple of hours to heal.

"What did you do with Bolverkr?" one of them demands, his voice harsh and guttural.

"Fuck you." I'm scrambling away from them as they stalk me, searching for some escape I haven't seen.

"Is he dead?" This guard's hands punctuate his words, stretching out and then clenching into fists as if they want nothing more than to wrap around my throat. And then he stomps forward, giving in to their demand as he reaches out to grab my neck before I can get away.

He stands, pulling me up with him, his eyes narrowing.

My mind stills and slows, pushing out every sense, focusing on the fingers around my neck.

It's not over yet, I remind myself as I lift my legs to kick away the guard. But another one stalks up to jerk my wrists behind me, yanking them up and away, nearly as high as my shoulders. For just a moment, I forget about the hands around my neck, focusing on the sharp pain that shoots up my arms, the throb in my ankle. Then the first guard's fingers tighten, cutting off the last of my airflow.

Maybe today is the day I'll die.

A wave of sadness washes over me, not for my life, but for Toffer's and Thor's. All the others who've filled my days in this world. I don't want to disappear, leaving them wondering if I'll ever return. And then for some strange reason, Fhord's image erupts in my mind. I think he'll grieve my death. I wish I could have known him better.

"Is he dead?" the guard repeats, squeezing tighter with every word before releasing his grip enough to let me speak.

"Fuck yes, he's dead," I croak as a cough forces its way out of my throat, bringing a new and different burn with it. I'm still trying to find any leverage to push the guard away, but my body won't move the way I want.

I should have lied. Told him something to buy more time. But Bolverkr's death matters too much for lies. Even if it costs me my life, I need these men to know he went to Helheim before me, and that I sent him there.

The guard in front of me squeezes again, his fingers compressing so much they nearly meet at my spine.

It won't be long now. My mind is drifting, ready to let go.

At least I killed Bolverkr first.

When the guard's hands drop, his eyes wide and a blade sticking out of his forehead, I stumble to the ground, wresting my wrists free. At first, I can't wrap my mind around the change. It feels like I've died and landed in Hel's realm of chaos. The guard drops to his knees and then falls forward—barely missing me as I shove myself away—the sword pushing up just a bit when its tip meets the hard rock below us.

Fhord's standing behind him, his eyes flashing as his gaze finds me and then spins toward the man who held my wrists. He dies just as quickly, one of Fhord's knives splitting his heart. I can only watch as he turns toward the remaining guard and they grapple for a few seconds. But that man's no match for the ferocious dragon rider who came to save me. Before I can lift myself from the ground, he's dead too.

And then Fhord's turning toward me, his eyes haunted. "Why did you leave me, Sifa?" Fhord's voice trembles as if he'd actually feared for me.

I stare at him for a moment, still too stunned to speak.

"Why the fuck did you leave me?"

Before I can move, Fhord's in front of me, dropping to his knees to pull me to him. And our mouths collide.

Fhord's kiss is frantic, desperate. His lips capture mine, his tongue stroking into my mouth to claim me. His hands are on my hips, holding me so tight it feels like he'll never let go. An ache erupts in my center, spilling down to my core as every part of my body responds to him.

And gods help me, I kiss him back. My tongue joins with his, exploring his mouth as he takes mine, and my hands dig into his hair. Nothing has ever felt so right.

"You are so dangerous," Fhord rasps as he drags his lips from mine. He watches me for a moment, his eyes dark and hungry, before he stands and strides away, turning his back to me. "We have to go," he tells me, his voice tight.

"Fhord, I'm sorry. I thought I'd be okay."

When he spins around, his eyes are full of torment. Desperate. He sighs, lifting a hand to run it through his hair, the other splayed out, holding tightly to his thigh.

"Nothing's okay," he says at last. "Nothing will ever be okay again."

He turns and trudges into the cavern. I have no idea what to say to him—how to explain what I've done or why. So I push myself up and limp along behind him in silence.

Chapter Seventeen

Fhord

I Can't Do This

I can't do this.

I don't know why the fuck I ever thought I could.

I knew it when I felt Sifa's conflict—her recognition of *someone* and need for revenge. When she turned and whispered her apology to me, I was pissed. But just for a moment. I can't blame her. This place took something precious from her. I'd want to kill them all if I had the chance.

I let her chase her retribution, taking Thyra to the horses and hiding the guard before I went after my little rabbit. She's strong and fast. I thought she'd be safe.

And then I felt her, barely breathing. My savage roared to life, desperate to protect our mate.

I was moments away from shifting—something I learned to control centuries ago—panic rippling through me. Because when I shift, the magic is like a gods-damned horn, blaring my location to the Dróttning, no matter how far away she is. And I'm not supposed to be anywhere near the Nest right now.

It's been a long fucking time since I was so close to losing it.

My savage will always respond that way. If Sifa is in my life, the need to shelter her—to save her from any who would do her harm—will transcend everything. Maybe even my bond with Tindera.

I need to get the fuck away from her.

I need to keep my gods-damned priorities straight.

If I give in to my *need* for Sifa, Tindera and the Ætt will pay the price.

I almost wish we'd found someone else on our march back to the cavern, that I could have killed more of these guards. They're fucking evil and the world would be better off without them. Maybe it would calm down my savage to take out some of the humans who caused Sifa so much pain. He's thrashing within me, demanding sex or death. And sex is out of the question. I can never let myself get that close to my rabbit.

But we make it back without finding anyone else. She turns to me when we reach the cave, her eyes glistening with regret. Her hand reaches out to rest on my chest.

"I'm sorry. I can't explain why I left, but it was important. I had to do what I did."

"It doesn't matter." My voice is harsher than I want, and I regret the flinch it prompts from her.

Then I pull my shit together. If she cares for me at all, I'm going to hurt her. I need to destroy every last one of those feelings. It's the only option.

Twisting, I start to walk in the direction of Thyra and the waiting horses. "We've done what Bevin wanted. We'll stay together long enough to get out of danger. Then we'll go our separate ways. I'll get Thyra back to Bevin." My voice is flat, empty.

Hers, though, drips with emotion. I can hear her heart in her words. "I understand. I wouldn't want to travel with me after what I did, either." She pauses and I resist the *need* to turn and look at her. "I'll leave you when we get away from the Nest."

I nod, keeping my eyes straight, away from her. It's the only way this will work. The only hope I have of calming my savage enough to let her go when the time comes.

Thyra's waiting for us next to Sigurd, ready to leave this place. She managed to change while we were gone, replacing the scraps prisoners wear with the soft, comfortable tunic and leggings I dragged from a pack before chasing after Sifa. I help her mount then pull myself up behind her, nudging Sigurd into a walk as I resist the urge to help my rabbit. But when I glance back, she's hesitant to mount Hilde, looking down at one of her ankles. Guilt spills into my guts as I realize she's hurt.

"What happened?"

Her gaze lifts and I see a hint of tears in her eyes. "It's nothing," she mutters. "I sprained my ankle. And may have broken a rib. I'll heal soon."

Dropping back to the ground, I dig through my pack for a bandage. "Let me help you."

"It's not a big deal, but I should probably wrap it before we go."

"I'm going to help you, Sifa," I tell her as I stride over. "Can I lift you onto Hilde without hurting you?"

Her lips tip up in a sad smile. "Just don't grab me here," she responds as she pats a spot on her side.

I reach for Sifa—wishing my gods-damned cock didn't twitch from just being close to her—and set her in her saddle, then remove her boot and push up her pants. Her ankle's swollen and discolored, but it doesn't look broken. After wrapping it carefully, I draw her pants back down and shove her boot into one of her packs. "What about the rib?"

"It'll just have to heal. It won't take long." She smiles—the same sad look as before—and runs a finger down my cheek. "Thank you for taking care of me, Fhord."

I grunt and turn away because I cannot let her see the emotion her touch triggers in me. Mounting Sigurd again, I yank the reins and nudge him toward the cave's entrance.

We ride in silence for the first hour or so, Thyra's head resting on my chest, as if she doesn't have the strength to hold herself up. Finally, though, she straightens her neck and asks the question she's probably been pondering since we started.

"What's up with you two?"

Sifa's close enough for me to see her stiffen in her saddle, but she doesn't answer Thyra. She probably knows, like me, that Thyra can't know what Sifa did. Bevin would punish her. And then he'd start asking questions.

"Nothing," I assure Thyra. "Something unexpected came up, and Sifa handled it."

"Then why are you so angry at each other?"

"We're not angry," Sifa says quietly. "We don't work well together. But we got you out. That's what matters."

Thyra scoffs. "I've been reading people long enough to know what this is," she declares. "Don't tell me if you don't want to," she adds after a moment. "I'm just grateful to be free. You can keep your secrets."

The rest of the trip is silent. And heavy, the weight between Sifa and me increasing with every step. I'm aching to see the sky, let the emotions that seem to be trapped in the space around us find someone else to haunt. I'm aching to get away from Sifa.

Finally, a splash of sunshine appears in front of us. Thyra sees it at the same time and gusts out a sigh of relief.

"I didn't think we'd make it, that I'd ever feel the sun on my skin again."

"I wasn't so sure either," Sifa says from behind me. "Fhord's done the impossible, it seems."

"We've done the impossible." She probably was more important than me in getting Thyra out. Which I'll let Bevin know.

"How long until we can leave here?" Sifa whispers this question, as if she didn't want to ask it.

"We'll wait in this cavern until it's dark," I respond, looking anywhere except at her. "They'll have doubled the sentries, at least, by now. It'll be easier to get away when the sun's down. From here, it's about a six-hour ride to a safe place we can hide, if we move fast."

"I'll leave you both there," Sifa says.

"Why?" Thyra spins in the saddle to find Sifa's eyes.

I keep mine straight ahead, where they belong.

"Like I said, Fhord and I don't get along well." She pauses a moment. "And you'll have a better chance without me. I'm pretty sure they think a woman acting alone helped you escape. They'll be looking for two females traveling together."

Fuck if my next words don't come out before I can stop them. "We should go a little farther together," I say, contrary to all my best intentions. My savage can't let go. He needs to keep Sifa safe. Overprotective, meddling bastard. "We'll be safer if we stay together until we get to a town."

Sifa's silent for so long, I nearly spin my head to find her. Finally, she speaks. "It's a bad idea, Fhord."

"Just until the first town. One night," I insist as I give in and turn toward her. "You and Thyra can sleep. I'll stay outside and keep watch," I add for good measure. My savage rewards me with a grumble of approval.

I'm so fucking pathetic.

"Okay," she says at last. "One night." Pausing, she glances down and I realize she needs help.

"Wait there," I tell her, my voice soft as I dismount. "Let me help you."

"I can do it, Fhord. It's not a big deal."

But I need to do this for her. As angry as I am—as resolved as I am to push her away—she's still my little rabbit. I can't just let her hurt. So I help her down from Hilde and turn away.

Being close to her calms me.

And that is so fucking dangerous.

I cannot let myself find calm and comfort in Sifa's presence.

I gather a few supplies for Thyra—water and food she should be able to keep down—then find a spot as far from Sifa as possible, where even her scent won't reach me. When I lie down, my face to the wall, I will myself to relax. I don't think I'll be able to sleep but I need to at least try.

We wait in another silence so thick it seems to drip down the surrounding walls. Somehow, I manage to drop off for an hour or two. My eyes fly open as the cave starts to dim, flipping over to search for Sifa before I'm fully awake. When I find her, something inside me relaxes. She's sleeping, peaceful. I wish I could capture this moment and hold it forever.

When Sifa moves, I shift to stare at the rocks above us. I need to keep all these feelings to myself. Sifa can't know how fucking hard it will be to watch her ride away.

"We should go," she says as she sits up, stretching her arms above her head. And then I feel her gaze on me and I turn to look at her. "I'm ready for this to be over," she whispers, her voice sad and distant.

"I know. I understand." Standing, I pull together our things and stow them on the horses, then help Thyra mount Sigurd. I turn as Sifa does the same—her body healing quickly, as elves do—smiling despite myself at the nag Sifa somehow brought back to life for this journey.

She has that effect on everything she touches. Especially me.

Sighing, I mount Sigurd and jostle his reins to lead us into the night.

The first few hours are treacherous. Every fifteen or twenty minutes, we're forced into hiding, sliding off our horses to crouch behind a rock or bush and wait, our hearts in our throats the entire time. Thyra's exhausted within the first hour, her body so depleted she can barely hold herself up on the horse. More than once, I have to tighten my arms around her and keep her in place, her head dropping back to lay against my chest.

Three different times, I'm certain we're going to be caught. The first group of soldiers gets too gods-damned close, and I can't see an escape. My savage is roaring inside me to protect Sifa, but when I turn to her, I don't see fear. She's watching me, her brow furrowed as if she's weighing a heavy decision. Just as I'm about to risk everything by using my magic when I sure as fuck should not—hoping I can kill our pursuers fast enough to stop them from sending a message to the Dróttning—they move away.

The second time, I understand. I shift my head to glance at Sifa after we've dropped to the ground behind a bush. Her face is twisted in concentration, eyes distant. She's watching the guards approaching us, mouthing words I can't discern. When they're so close I know they'll find us this time, her eyebrows draw together, her forehead furrowing as she whispers through firm lips, her jaw tight.

Even if I wanted to, I wouldn't be able to look away from this stunning female. The knowledge that she trusts me enough to risk using her magic sends sparks up and down my spine. Every part of me wants to claim her right now. *Mine,* my savage rumbles, dragging himself toward the surface as he tries to take advantage of my need for our mate. Fucker.

Finally, they start to move away. Sifa nodding as her silent chant grows a bit less frantic, smooth and calm. When they abandon their search and turn from us, she relaxes, watching them ride away with a satisfied look.

"Holy fuck." My voice is so low, I wonder if she'll hear me. She does, spinning her gaze toward mine. "You're so fucking incredible. I've never met another female like you."

"And you never will," Sifa responds with a wink. "Time to go."

After we're nearly caught for a third time, Sifa starts to wilt, the concentration required to send so many searchers away draining her energy. I wish I could take this from her, carry some of her burden. But I can't do anything like this and we both know it's necessary. The gods are with us, though. We've gotten far enough away from the Nest and haven't run into anyone else.

By the time we find the cave that will shelter us, Sifa's drooping. She and Thyra can do nothing but watch as I start pulling together a quick meal—a soup that will nourish us all—then prepare their beds. Thyra's too weak to feed herself, so she and I work together to get a meal into her before I carry her to her blankets and tuck her in. She'll be better after a good night's sleep.

Sifa's head is drooping when I return to the fire, but I'm relieved to see she's finished her soup.

"What you did today," I start, but before I can finish, her gaze is whipping up to find me. She's wide awake now.

"What I did today is between us and Thyra," she hisses, her nostrils flaring as her fingers stretch out and then curl into a fist. "We've both learned things about each other that would doom us." She pauses, her eyes growing wide as she sees my surprise. And regret. Taking a deep breath, and then another, Sifa's face softens.

"I will keep your secrets, to my grave," I assure Sifa as I hold her stare, willing her to see my resolve.

"And I'll keep yours." Pausing again, she inhales and exhales one more time. "Sorry," she says after a moment. "I've spent a lot of years hiding what I can do. You've seen more in our time together than anyone else in this world. I've put everything at risk being so exposed."

"I know. I've done the same." I reach out to take her hand, hoping the contact will help put her fears to rest. Peace washes over me as I feel my mate's touch, perhaps for the last time. "This thing between us can never be," I remind her—or myself—my thumb stroking the back of her hand. "We both have our reasons. But know this, my rabbit. I value your life as much as my own. I will never do anything to put you at risk. I swear it."

"Sweet talker," Sifa responds with a sad smile. "You know just what to tell a girl." And then her face grows serious, her eyebrows moving together in the most charming expression ever. "I trust you," she says at last. "And you can trust me."

"I know."

She watches me for a moment, then her chin dips as a sigh escapes. "Thank you, Fhord," she whispers as she stands. "Sleep well."

"You too, Sifa."

The wailing wakes me. We stopped too close to the training grounds, I realize as my stomach clenches. I wonder if there's any chance Sifa will sleep through this. After everything that happened yesterday, it's the last thing she needs.

She doesn't, of course. Within a minute, she emerges from the cave, fully dressed. Her eyes find mine and I can see the purpose in them. She's going after the dragon.

"You can't do this, Sifa. Nobody is allowed to interfere with training. Even other riders."

"I just need to see the dragon. Maybe I can help comfort it, like I did before. I'll stay hidden."

I shake my head, standing as she strides in the direction of the screams. "It's too dangerous. And we're still hunted. You'll risk everything." Reaching out, I wrap my hands around her arms, turning her toward me. "This is part of dragon life. It's necessary."

She scoffs. "Necessary? That's bullshit. Don't give me the official line just because you ride a dragon. You know it's wrong."

"I don't like it any more than you do. But you can't change the world. Especially not now. Let's finish this job, get Thyra back to Bevin. Then if you want to comfort a few dragons, you can come back alone." My voice is cold, mean, but I can't let myself care. She has no idea how much danger she's courting.

"I don't answer to you, Fhord," she spits out. Then she pauses, her eyes starting to glisten. Lifting her hands to rest them on my chest she gives me a small smile, full of apology. "I can't explain why—I don't even know why, myself—but I know this is something I have to do. This dragon is calling to me. I must answer his call."

"It's the same dragon, isn't it?"

"Yes. And he needs me. I have to go to him."

"Fine," I declare, lifting my hands in frustration. She's so fucking stubborn. It's a good thing we can't be together. She'd drive me to an early grave. "But you're not going alone," I add, against every bit of my better judgment. "Tell Thyra what we're doing while I throw some clothes on."

Within ten minutes, we're crouched behind a bush, watching the dragon and trainer approach. She was right. It's the same red beast as before, and he's every bit as traumatized as the last time we saw him. The trainer's different—the Nest's leaders will sometimes change a trainer if a dragon won't submit to the Dróttning's demands—but he seems just as cruel as the last.

The most stubborn dragons experience the greatest trauma as the punishments grow more and more extreme. This one looks to be as headstrong as the female by my side. The device holding back his wings is one of the worst I've seen. Every rider knows where the dragons' most vulnerable spots can be found.

This ... abomination ... is designed to carve into every spot on the wings—the dragons' most sensitive area—shifting and tightening with each step.

I glance at Sifa. Her face has twisted as if she's experiencing the dragon's pain. She's concentrating, all her focus on the beast and his trainer.

When the dragon turns his head, recognition sparks in his eyes. The trainer is striding ahead of him, the chain that binds the dragon's powers dragging on the ground between them. Arrogant and cruel. He knows the dragon can't break free and can't imagine anyone interfering with his work.

Sifa's going to do just that. I sense the shift in her emotions, the resolve that grows as she makes her decision. I turn to glance at her and my suspicion's confirmed. Her muscles are tight, eyes alert, and lips set in a thin line. She turns to me and I recognize the apology in her expression.

Shaking my head, I mouth "no". She doesn't care. She already decided.

Sifa anticipates my reach, spinning away in the soft grass. Rising to her knees, her hands on her hips, she turns to look at me. "I have to do this," she whispers. And then she's by my side, her words low in my ear. "I don't know why, but I have no choice. I must save him." She pauses just for a moment, leaning her head back as her gaze finds mine. "They've nearly run out of patience with him. He'll die soon. I can't let that happen."

"You must," I tell her, my lips finding her ear. "This is the way of dragons." I wrap my hands around her arms again, ready to hold her down if I must.

And then Tindera's voice echoes through me. *Stop*. A pause, followed by, *Mine*. There's no room for debate or disagreement. Those words were a command.

So I stop. Tindera has claimed this dragon that Sifa seems determined to save. He's her drake—the dragon destined to be her mate—and the only being in this world who might matter more to her than I do.

I can watch or I can help. Tindera's left me no other choice.

I sigh, a rock dropping into my gut as I decide to join Sifa in committing high treason against the Kastali.

CHAPTER EIGHTEEN

SIFA

I WILL FREE HIM

H E'S CALLING TO ME.

I have no idea how I know it, but I do. While I slept, he found me and started whispering in my dreams. I woke up with his image in my thoughts—the terrible, majestic, tortured dragon I saw earlier in the trip. When I heard his screams, I realized what I had to do.

Fhord tried to stop me. What else would he do? We're both painfully aware what a bad idea this is. How easily it could go wrong. That even if I succeed, the dragon and I will be outcasts, forever hiding in a land that won't be nearly big enough. But I couldn't have stopped myself if I tried. And I didn't see any reason to try. This is bigger than anything else in my life. Bigger, even, than going home.

When Fhord and I hide behind the bush, I reach out to the beast, caressing him with my thoughts. His response is everything. Relief sits highest atop his emotions, his weary spirit desperate for an end to his torment. Shimmering just below that, though, is anger. Hate. Spite.

Vengeance.

He's so fucking strong. They've tried—the gods know how cruelly and sadistically they've tried—but they've never broken his will.

I will free him. And then I'll join him in serving retribution on everyone who harmed him. All those who hold dragons in their grip, taking but never giving back.

I was born for this. It's why I was drawn to this world. The next few minutes will set my fate or end me.

My thoughts stretch out again, gently probing at the trainer's mind. I'm on edge, ready to yank them back if I get any hint he realizes I'm here. He doesn't, as far as I can tell, but my search fails. He's built walls of steel around his psyche. I can't find a way in.

Freeing the dragon won't be easy. The trainer is powerful, and I have no idea if I can beat him.

Slowly, a plan takes form in my mind. I'm turning toward Fhord when I feel his breath in my ear.

"Can you come up with a distraction?" He asks. I find his eyes, dark and solemn. He shifts a bit to again whisper directly into my ear. "I can attack while his focus is on you."

My lips find his ear, mimicking his caution. "I need to do this Fhord. I'm not sure how I know, but I have to be the one who takes the guard's life."

Pulling my head back, I watch as he wrestles with my decision. I have no idea what this is between us, but I do know

Fhord is driven to protect me. It pains him when I expose myself to risk. He has to fight to control some urge to smother me and keep me safe. Eventually, though, the rational side of him prevails. He nods his head.

"I'll provide the distraction." His voice is resigned, echoing with fear and doubt. My chest swells with the knowledge of what this male will risk for me. How important he's become to me, despite our efforts to push each other away.

And then his lips are on mine. This kiss is different from the first one. It's gentle, probing. He's asking me to open to him, to trust him with this part of me. When I respond, parting my lips and letting my tongue taste him, he doesn't pull back. He leans into the embrace, wrapping his arms around my back to pull me closer.

Every single part of my body responds. My stomach flutters, launching a kaleidoscope of butterflies to the tips of my toes. I burn for him, like I never have for a male before. In that moment, I want nothing more than to open myself, letting him see every part of me.

When I feel the dragon purr in my thoughts, I pull away. I can't get this close to Fhord. Ever.

Fhord holds my gaze for a moment, his face a chaos of emotions. "This is why I can't be with you," he rasps in a low voice. "If you are in my life, my little rabbit, I can't see past you. I can't see anything but you. Too many will suffer if I let myself lose sight of them." His lips find mine, more reckless this time. Desperate. "But know this," he adds as he pulls himself away. "If not for Tindera—everything she would endure for my happiness—I would choose you. Even if it doomed everyone else."

Fhord stands abruptly, backing away as he watches me. His eyes flare, a war of emotions reflected in their depths. "Be safe, my rabbit," he whispers before spinning to slip away from me.

I can't move. I can barely think. He's so fucking dangerous. To me. To everything that matters to me.

Because I realize he may matter more than anyone or anything else.

Shaking my head to dispel the lunacy creeping through it, I focus again on the dragon and the brute holding his chain. *Soon*, I assure the beast. *Be prepared*.

Within less than a minute, Fhord's diversion echoes through the valley around us. The trainer whips his head up, his eyes alert and searching. Turning, he whispers a command of some kind to the dragon, then stalks to a bag strapped to the saddle and pulls out a thick metal pole. I feel a hint of power as he stabs it through a link in the chain and into the ground, pulling the beast's chin down.

The dragon's pain in this position drowns out every other sense. His wings are drawn tight, the contraption that holds them digging even more deeply into every pressure point. He can't move. He can barely think. Which is exactly the intent. The dragon can't do anything until the trainer returns and frees him.

The trainer strides off in search of whatever has dared enter this area, and I slip from behind the bush toward the dragon. Resting my hands on his snout, I whisper my apology for leaving him in such agony. I can't free him yet. The trainer can't know I'm here until he gets close enough to kill.

The dragon's response soothes my guilt. He knows. And he's patient. He'll suffer what he must to escape this chain and the torture instrument at his back. My heart rate slows as an unexpected calm washes over me. My fingers are loose as they reach for the knives at my belt. I'm exactly where I should be, doing what I must.

I don't have to wait long. Within a few minutes, the trainer is stomping back toward us, angry at the interruption he couldn't identify. I back away to hide on the dragon's side, waiting until the male is close enough to attack. Inhaling slowly and silently, I check the blanket I've erected around my psyche, making sure no hint of my presence will seep out.

He turns his back to me as he reaches for the rod holding the dragon's chain. And I smile. My knife is around his throat before he knows I'm here, its edge drawing a trickle of blood.

But this male is not so easy to kill.

Throwing his head back directly into my nose—the pain echoing through me—he flings himself away, breaking free of my hold. I sense the initial push of his psyche as he calls for help, but before he can send out more than a word or two, my blade is at his throat.

He focuses again on the physical threat, reaching for my wrist to try to whip me around and into his back. Before he can, I spin away, wresting my arm free as I dance back a few feet.

"You dare to enter these grounds?" he demands in a harsh voice. "To interfere with my training? Your life is mine. Lay down your knife and your death will be quick."

"I'm here to take your life," I sneer at him. "This dragon has suffered too much. You'll pay for all you've done to him."

His eyes grow wide as he somehow senses the true me. "An elf," he whispers, his voice low and dangerous. "Now your death is certain. The Dróttning will reward me when I carry your lifeless body to her."

I feel his power shift, as if he knows my weaknesses. If I don't kill him now, he'll win. And the dragon will be bound forever. Already, though, my energy is draining from me. My thoughts can't reach him. My arms grow heavy, the knives I hold anchors weighing them down. I drop to my knees, defenseless against the unexpected power this man wields.

The trainer moves toward me, his lips tipping up in a grin full of malice and hate. When I see the medallion he holds, pinned to his coat—a design I recognize from the prisons—I understand. He's prepared to meet and subdue an elf, unlikely as it seems. He carries one of the amulets imbued by the Dróttning with the magic she uses to control elves. I never found a defense against them. They can cause pain or this weakness he's chosen to use on me. I steel myself for the agony that inevitably follows.

But then the dragon shifts, ever so slightly. I feel his torment as he breaks the trainer's grip on the medallion, the damage he causes his wings by that little movement nearly dropping him to the ground. It's what we both need to escape, though.

The trainer grasps for the amulet but it's too late. Before his fingers reach it, my knife is flying through the air toward his heart. It rips through the leather on his chest like a blade through butter. A heavy moan echoes around us as he drops to the ground, dead before he reaches it.

I turn to find the dragon's eyes full of anguish. "I'm so sorry," I tell him. "I moved too slowly. I should have taken his life the first time my knife touched his throat."

Lurching to my feet, I reach out for the rod pinned through his chain. It takes three yanks to pull it from the ground but I finally manage to wrestle it free. Tossing it aside, I turn to the metal wrapped around his wings.

"Gods," I whisper as his agony wraps around me. He's trying to hold it back, to protect me from his pain, but it grips him too tightly. He can't think past it. "I don't know how to get this off of you." My ribs constrict as a wave of helplessness washes over me.

But I can get the harness off, and that will help. Maybe he can relieve some of the pressure on his wings if he's not weighed down by the chain. My fingers are reaching for the links along his cheek when I feel Fhord's hands rest on mine.

"Let me help you with this," he tells me. "I know how to remove it."

"Thank the gods," I respond with a groan that's more a sob than anything else. "Because I have no idea what to do right now."

And then I turn to look at Fhord, my heart breaking at what I see. His features are blank, not a hint of light in his eyes. He's given up, resigned to the fact that this thing between us is even more impossible now.

I made myself an outcast, expanding the already insurmountable barrier between us.

But we both knew it would happen. This always was temporary.

That doesn't make it any less tragic.

We spend nearly ten minutes removing all the metal from the dragon's snout and wings. I can feel his torment with every tug, pull and push. He doesn't let out a single sound, though, as he suffers through it. Instead, he watches us with quiet gratitude, his gaze finding mine every chance he gets. The spark of life in his eyes grows with each inch of him we free.

Finally, Fhord and I fling the final piece of metal as far away from the dragon as we can. Our eyes meet for a moment, but nothing's changed. Resignation still wraps around every emotion. We'll get someplace safe and then we'll go our separate ways.

And so I shift my thoughts to the dragon and his relief. Bone-numbing, deep in his veins, dominating each sensation whispering or galloping through him. Overwhelming relief.

He's also achingly tired, this episode of torture having lasted long days without any sleep or food. But he'll follow us where he must before he collapses.

For a moment, I wonder how I know him so well. How I can understand his thoughts and emotions as thoroughly as I do. But that's a question for tomorrow. Today, we need to get far away from here.

I turn to start moving toward our camp but the dragon grunts lightly. Swinging his snout toward the trainer, my mind fills with his warning.

"We need to bury him," I tell Fhord. "Quickly."

"You're right." His voice is so flat, empty of any feeling. Already I miss the short time we've had together.

The dragon heaves himself toward the trees, where leaves and dried moss cover everything. We can hide the grave here, I realize. Even in his agony, his thoughts are sharper, more focused than mine.

Fhord and I can't do much, our hands no match for the claws that easily break into the ground. We drag the trainer and the remains of his torture device over to the grave the dragon is digging, and do our best to hide the blood spilled. Within a few minutes, we can drop his corpse and the chains into it. And then the dragon fills it, his snout and paws moving more dirt than we ever could. When he's done, Fhord and I cover it up and inspect our work.

If we can get away quickly, not draw attention to this area, we might be okay. We just need to get back to our camp and get Thyra and the horses before anyone realizes he's missing.

Thyra's surprisingly blasé about the dragon who follows us back to the camp. Which is probably why Bevin values her enough to send us to retrieve her. She takes everything in stride.

"I owe you my life," she assures me as we're packing the horses. "You were doing a job for Bevin, but I know better than most how risky it was. What you sacrificed to get me out. I'll keep your secret."

And that's that. I know her well enough to trust her word.

The rest of the day is brutal. So fucking brutal. I'm tired after too little sleep, but my fatigue pales next to the dragon's. He drags himself after us out of sheer willpower. The *training* has stripped him of muscle and fat, leaving him a shell of the beast he must be at full health. It's in his claws—the exposed skin scaly and patchy—and the featherless patches along his wings. And I feel it. He's beaten, almost defeated. But he's here, with us. And he'll follow us wherever we go, for as long as it takes.

Finally, hours after the sun sets, Fhord finds shelter for our group, a deep cave with enough growth in front to hide the fire we need to light. As the dragon and Thyra collapse, Fhord and I scout the surrounding foothills, looking for any hint of danger. When I feel Fhord's relief, I echo it in my thoughts, then turn back to the cave. We'll be safe here. At least tonight.

My heart settles when I stumble back inside and see the dragon sleeping near the fire, Fhord sitting on a log watching him from the other side. I feel complete, as if I could live and be happy in this strange world, even if my time will be brief. In a ridiculously short period, I've forged bonds with these two males. When I go, I'll leave part of me with them.

Tonight, though, I'm complete.

I sigh as I walk over to settle down next to the dragon. Nestling my back into his side as he shifts to make room for me, I close my eyes. And I sleep.

The cave is light when I wake up, the bushes outside not nearly enough of a barrier to keep out the sun. But I barely notice anything around me.

Instead, my thoughts, my very being, are filled with the dragon. His presence. His existence. His love.

His name.

Astarot. The Leading One, he shares with me. When he came into being, it was foreseen that he would lead his family out of their torment. He would be the first, but others would follow. He would be their leader. And so he was called Astarot.

I sit up, finding soft brown eyes, which watch me with patience. And love. The love I felt when I woke was for me.

Mine. The word drops into my mind, a wealth of meaning buried in that little syllable. I am his. He is mine.

"You gave me your name," I whisper, unable to keep the awe out of my words.

Mine, he repeats. This time, though, it's an explanation, not a declaration. I know enough about dragons in this world to realize that outside of dragon society, dragons share their names only with those they've claimed—the human (or long ago, elf) who becomes theirs. Who they bond with.

"I am yours. And you are mine."

His chin drops as his eyes hold my gaze. Yes, he's telling me. We belong to each other.

I can't keep the grin from my face. Or hold back the laugh that bubbles out of me.

"We're in so much trouble." My hand lifts to stroke the snout that drops to the ground to receive my touch. My grin grows even wider as he leans into my fingers, shifting so they'll find the sensitive space behind his horn. "They'll kill us for sure if they find us. We just have to make sure they don't."

His eyes blink closed once and then open to hold my attention. *Peace*, he tells me in a voice rich with satisfaction. He's more relaxed, lighter than I could have hoped. He believes he was born to change this world, to free the dragons of the Dróttning's bonds. So he's sure we'll live. That certainty carried him through his punishment, gave him the strength he needed to survive without bending.

Fate, he adds after a moment. Again, a single word tells me so much more. If Astarot had let himself be joined to another rider, he would have been stuck with that human. In almost every part of their existence, dragons must give in to their riders' demands. When they are tied to cruel humans, they manifest that cruelty. Even the most peaceful and solemn dragons become ugly, evil beasts when the Dróttning chooses ugly, evil riders for them.

Once that bond is formed, it can only be broken by the Dróttning, even if the dragon finds its destined rider. Too many dragons have been forced to kill the humans the fates intended for them because the Dróttning compelled them to give themselves to an unworthy rider. The fated bond between Fhord and Tindera is rare in this world.

Astarot refused the rider the Dróttning chose for him, a weak male who was rumored to prefer children to adults in his bed. He paid a heavy price for his defiance, but he has no regret. His pain is behind him. He would pay that price again to ensure he was unbound when he found me.

So that he could bind himself to me.

CHAPTER NINETEEN

SIFA

EVERYTHING'S CHANGED

"THYRA AND I WILL go alone, leave you here with Astarot. I'll come back after I drop her off and help you find your way out of here."

Fhord's on edge, anxious to put distance between us. The news that I bonded with Astarot rattled him more than I expected. He wants to get Thyra away from us. He'll take her to a tavern nearly two day's ride from here to hand her over to some of Bevin's people. And he insists my dragon and I should wait for him to return before we leave this cave.

"Just go," I demand, my voice growing more strident. I turn to him, frustrated and trying to ignore the pounding in my ears that started when Fhord insisted he'd come back after dropping off Thyra. "I don't know why we're even arguing about this. We're going our separate ways. We may as well start now."

"Everything's changed, Sifa. Surely you can see that." Fhord's tone touches something inside I want to ignore.

"We're so close to the training grounds," he continues. "They probably already realize the trainer's dead. The search will be thorough. I understand dragons and I've traveled every inch of these lands. I'm not sure I can get you out—I have no fucking idea if anybody could with a dragon who won't be able to fly anytime soon—but with me your chances are better."

I let him get too close to me, and now I need him out of my life. Astarot and I have huge targets on our backs, and the longer he's with us, the longer he's at risk. So I spit my next words at him.

"Why the fuck do you care?" My voice is harsh. It has to be if I'm going to push him away. "We're going our separate ways. You'll just make yourself and Tindera the Dróttning's enemies if you come back here. Astarot and I will face this alone when he's strong enough to move."

"And where the fuck do you plan to hide with a dragon?" Fhord's tone is cold, but his narrow eyes are full of fire.

"I have no idea, Fhord," I yell, my hands digging into the air above me. "We'll figure it out. Without putting you or Tindera in any more danger."

Draikana. Astarot's voice drops into my thoughts. Spinning as a chill rolls down my spine and reaches out to capture every finger and toe, I stare at my dragon. And then I snap closed the jaw that fell open with his word. Tindera and Astarot are bonded. She's the reason Fhord helped me save him.

"He told you, didn't he?" His words emerge with a sigh. He didn't want me to know.

Now my gaze finds Fhord's. Pain and a hint of fear have replaced the flame in his eyes. Our impossible situation has gotten even harder. "Why didn't you tell me?" I'm not angry. All I can feel is grief wrapping around my heart as a rock forms in my throat.

"We can't be together, rabbit. You know that as well as me. Even if Astarot and Tindera are destined to be."

"How is this going to work?" I don't know much about the mating bond between dragons—whether it will compel them to be together, or what it'll cost them if they're not.

"I have no gods-damned idea what's going to happen," Fhord snarls. "The gods are fucking with us all." He pauses, running his hands through his hair as he huffs out a breath. "Right now, though," he adds in a more measured tone, "I need to get Thyra to safety. I'm coming back. Just be here when I do."

"Fine. We'll wait for you." I don't think we have a choice anyway. Astarot's in bad shape. He'll need that time to recuperate.

"We'll take Hilde. We can travel faster if Sigurd isn't weighed down, and you don't need another mouth to feed while you're here. I'll leave most of the food with you and get more supplies when I drop off Thyra. You'll have to go hunting for Astarot. He must be able to move when we leave. Two animals a day. That'll rebuild his strength." Fhord strides over to start pulling food out of the bags. "I think I'll be gone three days."

Three days doesn't sound like nearly enough time, but Fhord knows more about dragons than me. I focus on the one thing I can do, because I can't deny I need his help in this. "Any idea where I'm most likely to find food for Astarot?"

"Head west," Fhord tells me as he starts strapping a few bags onto Sigurd. "There's a herd of sheep in a valley you'll find a couple of vikus from here. It's part of the Nest's food supply so make sure nobody's around. Take some of the carrots and the rope I'm leaving with you. They're tame, used to getting treats from humans, so you should be able to catch them. Dragons will only eat live prey." He catches my gaze, a hint of a smile ghosting across his lips. "And strong as you are, you don't want to drag a carcass all the way back here."

I nod, relaxing a bit as his mood shifts. "Be safe, Fhord."

"You too, rabbit." He watches me for a moment as if he's memorizing my face. "I'll see you soon," he adds as he turns toward the back of the cave to go wake Thyra.

They're gone within a few minutes, Thyra whispering her thanks to me as Fhord settles her on Hilde and hands her some dried meat and fruit for her breakfast. And then it's just me and Astarot. He's soon asleep, though, his body demanding rest as it recovers from the weeks of pain he endured.

Dragging myself up from my spot on the floor next to my dragon, I put some distance between us and then turn to look at him. I was so preoccupied with his trauma the first couple times I saw him, I didn't pay much attention to the details. Now I want to drink it all in, commit every part of him to memory.

He's large, even with all the weight he's lost. I suspect he'll stretch seventy feet from his snout to the tip of his tail and weigh a couple thousand pounds. His feathers are red like the cardinals from my world, with black interspersed throughout. The design seems random at first but as I look, I see the waves that will run across the backs of his wings when they're fully extended. The weeks of punishment cost him some feathers—patches mark the places the instruments dug into his skin—but he's still got a stunning, regal plumage.

Stepping closer to him, I stroke his snout for a few minutes, luxuriating in the feel of him.

And then I go hunting.

At first, I'm surprised how good it feels to be outside and alone. I hadn't realized how much I needed time to myself, to think through everything that's happened in just a couple of weeks. How much I've changed. How much Fhord—and now Astarot—have changed me.

My thoughts drift back to Halla's fateful words—that I should take a risk to save us all, and the warning that I'd soon be starting an unexpected journey. Maybe she really did see the future, predict this trip. If she did, was I destined to save Astarot? Was that the risk I was supposed to take? Or is something else coming?

Who knows? I wrest my thoughts away from those worries to focus on what I can do. I can find the herd and take food back to Astarot. I can help my dragon—*my* dragon, my brain reminds me with a wash of gratitude and pride—regain his strength. And then I can help him hide. Somewhere.

That last part is fuzzy, but we'll work on that together. With Toffer. He'll be ecstatic when he learns I've bonded with a dragon. I can't hold back the smile that emerges at the thought. I wonder if Astarot will give him a ride. I'll never hear the end of it if he does.

My good mood, buoyed by the morning sun and the beauty around me, carries me through my search. Twice I have to hide from a dragon flying overhead, but nobody gets close enough to find me. Barely an hour after leaving the cave, I find the massive herd Fhord mentioned. So far, so good.

I lay in the grass to watch the area around me, breathing in and out slowly to calm the heart that has started to beat more quickly. This could go awry at a moment's notice.

It doesn't, though. I wait until a dragon patrol flies overhead, giving it a chance to get far away as I cast my mind out, searching for anyone else in the area. When I find no mortal thoughts, I stand and approach the sheep, choosing an enormous male who stares at me for a moment. The carrot draws him close enough to rope his neck and I trap another. We're all trotting back to the cave in a few minutes.

Astarot's reaction when I return with two large sheep is everything. He hasn't had fresh meat in weeks. His gratitude fills me with peace and, somehow, even more love. I tug the beasts farther into the cave and remove the rope from the larger one, stepping to the side to give Astarot more room.

Before I reach the entrance, though, I hear a short squeal and turn around to see an enormous lump sliding down the dragon's throat.

"Did you swallow him whole?" I'd expected him to at least taste the meal he's been waiting so long to enjoy.

Delicious, Astarot responds, his eyes sparkling at me. This is how dragons eat when they're hungry. Every part of the prey provides some nourishment, fur, bones and all. He needs any food he can get right now.

"Do you want the other?" I have no idea how long it will take to digest his meal.

Later. Astarot tells me he should eat two each day, as Fhord said. In this weakened state, desperate for nutrition, his body will digest his meals quickly.

"Okay," I agree. He settles down and I walk over to scratch him behind his horn. "Do you need to sleep again?" I'm hoping he's awake and we can get to know each other. I want to learn everything about him, good and bad.

Later, he repeats. Astarot wants the same thing as me—to talk and explore our lives from before. He can sense some things about me, but we both have much to share with the other.

And so we do. We spend the next three days learning about our lives. He's young by dragon standards, barely a hundred years old. He was connected to a rider earlier in his life, a cruel male whose death he celebrated. He'd expected a similar connection with his next rider. But then he sensed me and knew he had to wait, no matter what it cost him.

He was in this Nest when I landed in this world. He felt me appear, knew what I would mean to him. But he couldn't do anything to help me. Dragons have no such power in this place.

Pain, he tells me when we talk about those days. Dragons are more sensitive than elves, even before a bonding. He felt my pain and suffered with me, although I never felt him. Some of the wails I heard were his, as he lived through my torture with me.

"I'm so sorry to have put you through that." I stroke his nose as I watch his eyes reflect the agony we both felt. "But it helps to know I wasn't alone, that you were with me even then." Part of the weight I've been carrying for a decade lifts away, helping me find a bit more peace with what I experienced.

Sympathy. He's grateful for the pain and the connection to me it created. It gave him the strength he needed to withstand his own torture when they tried to offer him to a different rider.

"Tell me about that," I ask when his thoughts shift to the unworthy human they'd chosen for him.

Wicked. The Dróttning demanded that he bond with an evil man, unworthy of Astarot. The dragons share stories about the humans in this world. They all know who's looking for a beast to bond and what to expect from that rider. They'd warned each other about this human's request for a mount and what it would mean.

"You refused. And they tortured you."

Yes. It's been two months since he rejected the rider, he relays to me with that simple word. Two months of agony, growing more extreme every week. Three different trainers tried to break him, the last one the most cruel. He'd spent only a few days with this male and had already come close to giving in.

"When did you realize you were connected to Tindera?"

I sense his joy and a love so intense, it's hard to believe it could exist. It's my first experience with the bond between mated dragons, and it renders me breathless. We both sit in silence for a moment as he lets that emotion settle within me, now a permanent part of my being.

Draikana, he tells me, wonder in his voice. For whatever reason, their paths never crossed until Tindera was brought to this Nest for her injury. He first sensed her the next morning as she said goodbye to Fhord. Her grief at his departure, combined with the pain of her damaged lung, overwhelmed him even as he suffered his own abuse. He suspected they were bonded, but wasn't sure of their connection until she found him.

She tracked him down as he rested after a particularly grueling torture session, arriving just when he needed her most. It had been so long since he sensed my presence—the ten years I'd been in the southern part of this world—and he'd struggled to hold on to hope. Tindera renewed his resolve, gave him something to live for. Since she got here, she's spent as much time with him as she could without getting caught.

Tindera helped him hold on long enough. And then forced Fhord to accept her choice. And mine.

When Fhord returns, I'm snuggled next to Astarot as he sleeps, luxuriating in the peace of his presence. I'm so focused on my dragon that I don't notice his approach, looking up to find him staring at me, eyes wide and full of some emotion I can't let myself acknowledge. And my heart twists. He's so fucking beautiful. I wish to all the gods he could be mine.

We watch each other for long seconds before he glances up at Astarot. "He looks stronger. I think we can move him. We'll find you someplace safe to hide and then I'll leave. Give us both the space we need to forget about each other."

"Not forget, Fhord. Never that," I whisper as I stand up, afraid of losing this part of him—the memories of the time we've spent together. "But we'll let go. We have to."

"Tindera and Astarot can keep their distance. They know what it means to be mated to a dragon not chosen for them by the Dróttning. They need to hide their connection. Too." The last word is a whisper that barely reaches me.

"Astarot told me the same thing. Dragons are patient, he said. He can wait as long as he must to make sure they're safe when they fully bond." I catch Fhord's gaze, holding it as I add, "Their relationship is every bit as fucked up as ours."

He nods, dropping his chin for a moment and then looking up at me again. "I'm going to miss you, my little rabbit." Fhord steps forward to place his hands on my cheeks, his thumbs catching the tears I can't seem to hold back. "I wish we'd been born into a different world. That we didn't have these secrets that keep us apart."

I lean into him, standing on my tiptoes to kiss him lightly, and then step away. Because if I don't leave now, I might give in to the part of me that wants nothing more than to open myself completely to this man.

"Don't go yet, little rabbit. We can't have tomorrow. But that doesn't mean we have to give up today."

Something inside me sparks to life with his words. I know as well as he does this is a bad idea. That we shouldn't let ourselves explore this thing between us. But I want it. I want him.

He watches me for a few seconds and then takes a single step, dropping his head toward me. Hovering there, barely any space between our lips, he pauses, letting me decide if we go any further.

When I kiss him, Fhord is unleashed. His hands sweep out to pull me closer as his mouth opens and his tongue reaches into me. I burn everywhere he touches—the lips and the tongue that tangles with mine; the hands in my hair and on my back, holding me like he'll never let go; the strong chest underneath my hands, which want nothing more than to feel his skin.

And the erection. Gods, the erection. It grew as soon as our bodies touched, declaring its need for me. I am desperate to caress Fhord's length, and then feel him inside of me.

When Fhord's hand drops to my ass, the other reaching around to stroke one of my breasts, a sigh slips from my lips. My core is erupting, demanding his touch. I have never needed anyone more than I need Fhord now. One of my hands leaves his chest, dragging down his stomach to find his erection and squeeze, drawing out a long moan from him.

"Fuck," he gasps out, his lips finding my earlobe and then whispering down my neck. "You are so fucking dangerous. I need you, my little rabbit. I've been trying to deny it, to push you away. I can't. I need you. Even if it's only once."

And then my ears respond. The tingle tells me I've lost control of my body and they'll be emerging soon. But I'm ready. To share this secret with him. Our dragons are mates. He needs to know this about me. To know what I am.

I step back, dropping my head to wrest back control of my body. My limbs are shaking, and I don't know if it's fear or passion. I do know, though, that I have to tell him. He can't find out when my body responds to him. He needs to hear it from me first.

Fhord's gaze is haunted. "I'm sorry." He spins around, his hands spearing through his hair. "You're right. We know we can't do this." Turning to look at me again, his heart in his eyes, Fhord lifts a hand but lets it drop before it reaches me. "It's just … when I saw you with Astarot … I forgot. For a minute, this fucked-up world disappeared, and it was just you and me. The sun and the moon that will always revolve around you—the only light or heat I could ever want." He inhales again, his eyes shuttering. "It won't happen again," he murmurs.

I watch him for a moment, his shoulders tense even as his head droops in front of him. And my heart cracks. "I kissed you, Fhord," I breathe out. "This is as much my fault as yours. We've let this thing grow between us. But that's not why I stopped." I pause, a rock forming in my stomach to replace the fire Fhord had launched in me.

His gaze finds me again. And he waits.

"You have to know something first. I need you to hear it from me before you see it." My fingers are trembling. I can't believe I'm about to do this. But I trust him.

Stepping closer, erasing the distance between us, I reach for his hand. And then I stare at the floor. I'm about to bare myself to this man I've known for a couple of weeks. Somehow, I trust him.

"Nobody but the Dróttning and a few of her guards knows this about me," I whisper. "And Toffer," I add with a smile he probably can't see. Looking up again, I find Fhord's eyes. "If the Dróttning knew where to find me, she'd have me killed. Or imprisoned. With the rest of the elves."

Fhord doesn't speak. He doesn't move, the hand that holds mine motionless. My heart beats a dozen times as I wait. And then his grip on my hand tightens as the other rises to rest on my cheek.

Danger. Astarot's warning drops into my thoughts. Searchers are coming. We need to hide.

My stomach clenches.

I just exposed myself completely to this male I met barely two weeks ago.

I know nothing about him, other than what he's chosen to show me.

But it can't be a coincidence they've arrived on his heels.

The pain and desperation I escaped a decade ago fill me, dragging me back to those wretched days and the handful of soldiers who used deception to try and reach me. They pretended to be allies, only to betray me when I tested their lies.

The realities of this world—the agonizing lessons I learned in the Nest—wash over me.

Everybody bows to the Dróttning.

I shouldn't have trusted him.

Chapter Twenty

Fhord

I'll Miss You

"**P**eople are coming this way," Sifa hisses at me. "Did you bring them here?"

My mind spins as I watch her eyes narrow in accusation, and then grow wide, the pain stark in their depths. Her back stiffens as she turns to look at Astarot. When she turns to me again, she droops, as if the air's been sucked out of her.

She thinks I've betrayed her, just as she trusted me with her greatest secret. The secret that could get her killed.

She knows as well as I do they must have followed me. There's no way they could have found us on their own, showing up minutes after I arrived. They must have seen me on my trip back, leading a saddled horse with no fucking rider. Like a gods-damned idiot. I was so wrapped up in my thoughts about Sifa, I didn't even think about how that would look. I let my guard down and led them here.

Tindera's going to kill me. If Sifa doesn't kill me first. Or Astarot.

I need to get them the fuck out of this.

"Not on purpose," I whisper, my hand reaching out as I watch her flinch away. "They must have tracked me."

"You?" she demands, her voice low but strident. Accusing. "You're a dragon rider, one of the Dróttning's chosen. You know this land, what to expect of her soldiers, better than I ever could." She pauses, her eyes flashing. "You *know* how to avoid them but let them follow you here." Now, Sifa sucks in a deep breath, her gaze flitting around the cave as she searches for ... something. There's only one escape, though.

"Let me get you out of this. They don't know you're here yet. I'll take Hilde and lead them away and then you and Astarot can escape." That's our only option. It needs to work.

Sifa spins to look at Astarot. She shakes her head once, and again. Finally, she nods. Reluctantly.

"Astarot thinks we need to trust you. You're right, we have no choice. This is your chance to prove you didn't betray us. They're half a viku north of here. Lead them away. And then stay away. We'll find someplace to hide." Turning, she starts to throw supplies into a bag.

"Look at me, rabbit."

"Don't call me that." Her voice is angry, defensive.

"Look at me, Sifa."

She stills for a moment, her hands hovering in front of her, before she lets out a deep sigh. Setting down the food she'd picked up, she wraps her arms around her stomach, inhales slowly, and turns toward me.

She's everything I need, all I'll ever want. My heart is cracking because I've broken hers. I need to make this right.

"I swear to you I didn't do this on purpose," I whisper, my heart in my words. "I would never hurt you intentionally. I care too much about you to do that."

Her shoulders soften as her hands unwind from around her and find her thighs. "I believe you," she whispers. "You feel this ... thing ... between us too. It doesn't matter, though. Even if we can get away from here, this just proves we can't be safe together. For both of our sakes, for our dragons' sakes, we need to stay away from each other."

She's right, and it kills me. My savage is roaring at me because he knows he's lost. She'll never be ours.

"Give me at least a half hour to draw them away ... or kill them," I tell her as I grab Hilde's reins and then stride toward Sigurd. "When you leave, head southeast, where the forest is deepest. You'll find cover and food there. You should be safe until Astarot's fully healed." Mounting, I pause to hold her eyes one last time. "I'll miss you, my little rabbit."

The look she gives me is deep with grief. "I'll miss you too, Fhord." She pauses, the corners of her lips ticking up as she watches me. "Maybe I'm a fool," she says after a moment, "but I have no regrets."

I nod, struggling to stop myself from dropping from the saddle and taking one last kiss from her. Tasting her lips one more time. And then I turn and go. Because if I touch her again, my savage may not let me leave.

Turning to the west—to approach them from a different direction than the cave—I push Sigurd and Hilde to run as fast as they can. I need to get far enough away to convince them I came from that direction and then intercept them before they get to the cave. I don't know if I'll make it.

I'm circling back in the direction of Sifa and Astarot when I sense two guards. They're riding slowly, as if they're following a trail they keep losing. The trail I left, fucking idiot that I am. I get close enough for our paths to cross and then lift my hood and slow down, trying my best to make our meeting look accidental. I don't want to be recognized, but I'll use my dragon's name if I must to get rid of them.

"What are you doing out here?" I demand in my most derisive tone when I catch sight of the guards. Spurring Sigurd forward, I plant myself in their path, forcing them to yank back on their horses' reins.

"We come on the Dróttning's business," the closest man exclaims, his right hand moving to his sword hilt. "Step aside."

I hate meeting the Dróttning's guards on horseback. If I were on Tindera, they'd show me the proper respect.

"Fools," I spit at them. "You're wasting my time. I'm on the Dróttning's business, searching for the prisoner and the traitor who helped her escape. I found this horse north of here"—beckoning with a dismissive wave of my hand—"and have been leading the old nag around for hours, hoping she might give me a clue about her master."

"How do we know you're not in league with them?" The larger guard is holding his ground, even as the other one tugs on his reins to pull his horse away from me.

He's brave. I'll give him that. Better men than him have withered under my gaze. But the last thing I need right now is a guard trying to make a name for himself. Tossing my hood back, I sneer at him. "Do you know who I am?" I demand, my words brittle.

He watches me for a moment before his eyes widen. "You ride Tindera."

"I do." I let the words sit between us.

"Where is your mount?" he asks after a few seconds of silence.

Fucker. Now I wish I could kill the inquisitive bastard. I let my anger twist my features and snarl out the next words. "If you truly are the Dróttning's guards, you know those who ride horses do not challenge dragon riders. Ever."

The big guy doesn't like my attitude, but I don't give a fuck. He's a peon. He doesn't get to question me. I don't really want to kill them, but I will if that's what it takes to protect Sifa and Astarot.

"Apologies, dragon rider," the smaller guard offers. "Shall we aid you in your search? We were just about to follow the footsteps in that direction." He lifts his hand and points his finger almost directly toward the cave holding Sifa and Astarot. Fuck.

"Is everyone in this Nest as simple as you two?" I bark at them, letting my frustration show. "Those footsteps are mine. I already looked there." Now it's my turn to point. "Go north," I tell them. "Scour the forest between here and the Nest."

The large guard isn't ready to give up yet, though. I watch his chest puff up as he prepares himself to challenge me. "We must search that area before we leave. The footsteps lead there."

"Of course they fucking do," I explode, "because I made them when I searched that area." Nudging Sigurd, I stalk forward, straightening my back so he'll be forced to look up. "My dragon recovers from an injury. But she'll be well soon. Shall I tell her you angered me?"

That does the trick. The guard swallows as his head spins to look in the direction I pointed. He nods then turns back to me. "We will head north as you wish," he concedes. "Good luck in your searches."

"For the Dróttning," I intone, inclining my head slightly. They'd expect the standard salutation if I were on the Dróttning's business.

"For the Dróttning," they respond.

I watch them for a few minutes before resigning myself to following. I want to go back to Sifa and Astarot. Convince them I didn't betray their trust. Make sure Sifa knows she could be a troll and I'd still want her in my bed. But that would be even worse than leading the guards here the first time. I need to confirm they're truly gone before I even consider following Sifa into the trees.

The forest is too quiet around me, even the animals holding back their chatter. Sigurd and Hilde play their part, their hooves barely disturbing the ground beneath us as we sneak after the guards. Only my thoughts, dark and angry, disturb my reverie.

Twice, I let myself get close to the guards, their bitter chatter breaking through the silence around me. The large guard is offended, more frustrated than he should be. I wonder if he came from a powerful family but was passed over as a hatchling candidate. He acts like someone who has wielded authority in his life. Being forced to ride horses when you crave the bond with a dragon has turned many a human bitter and cruel.

After two hours of trailing them, I'm comfortable they won't turn around. They're still complaining about me but say nothing to suggest they'll disobey my command that they travel north. So I let them go, turning the horses to retrace our steps. And find Sifa.

I can't leave while this accusation hangs between us. I need her to understand. To believe me. And then I'll disappear from her life, let her find safety with her dragon.

I let my thoughts run free for the first few hours, imagining a life with my little rabbit. Another world, where elves roam freely and we don't have to run away from our mating bond. Where dragons choose their riders and their mates.

Where the Dróttning doesn't exist.

I almost can see it. The land we'd claim to give Tindera and Astarot all the fields and streams and mountains they could want. And goats. Lots of goats for Tindera. She's always loved a fat goat.

Toffer's probably with us. Sifa's attachment to the troll grates on me, but I won't stand between them. We'll bring along the cat and any other strays Sifa may find. Because that's who she is, and I wouldn't change any part of her.

We're on our dragons returning from some trip or another and Sifa turns to smile at me as she catches sight of our home, the sun filtering through the trees to cast it in dancing shadows. Our children emerge as the dragons touch down, running toward us while Toffer watches from the door. They take after their mother, lucky bastards, nearly as beautiful as her.

My little rabbit takes them in her arms and then looks back at me, her eyes bright with love.

My savage is soothed, content for the first time in my long life.

But it's just a dream. I shake my head, breaking out of the fantasy I've wallowed in for too long.

I'm going to Sifa because I can't let her believe I would betray her. I need her to know I'm committed to her safety. Even though we can't be together. Because that hasn't changed. I would never ask Tindera to make the sacrifice it would require. Especially now that she's found Astarot. I won't exchange my suffering for hers.

The sun's nearly reached the horizon when I catch the first hints of her presence. Something within me calms, a flutter that started when Sifa left me finally finding rest.

My senses, which have spent hours searching for her, find other sounds and smells and sights to enjoy. The gurgle of a nearby creek, waves and splashes rising and falling as the water whispers past. The pine that tickles at my nose as I ride deeper into the trees, dredging up memories of winter nights as a child, playing in front of the fire. The shadows that reach all around me, hiding leaves and needles that cushion the ground.

Leaving the trees, I enter a clearing, dark granite mountains reaching into the sky ahead of me, and relax even more when I see her walking next to Astarot. He's come so far in just a few days. He'll be able to extend his wings and fly soon. He can take Sifa someplace safe. They'll figure out the rest later.

"I know you're there, Fhord," she says after a moment, spinning around to glare at me. "You were supposed to go away. And stay away. What if you've led the guards back to us?"

I tug on Sigurd's reins, keeping my distance as I drink in the view of her. Her hands rest on her hips, emphasizing their perfect shape, leading to long legs and a foot tapping her displeasure. I can't hold back my smile as my gaze follows her curves back up and finds her nipples stretching through the thin blouse she's wearing. With her head cocked to one side—her neck in exactly the right position to be nuzzled and teased—she's the sexiest female I've ever seen. I'm fucking hard just thinking about tasting her again.

And she's pissed. I'm gonna need to grovel. A lot.

"I got sloppy. I can't get you the fuck out of my mind. I wasn't paying attention because I see you everywhere I look. All the time. I fucked up."

Her foot stops tapping, but she's still clinging to her hips like she has to stop herself from stalking over and punching me. Or kissing me. I hope to fuck it's the latter.

"I was careful this time. I ordered them back to the Nest and followed to make sure they went. But I couldn't leave you like this. You need to know I'd never betray you. I would never hurt you."

My breath catches in my throat, a gods-damned vise holding it there as I wait for her response. I *need* her to forgive me. To trust me.

Finally, her arms drop to her sides. We exhale, a slow release, at the same time.

"We can't do this, Fhord. We have to stay away from each other. You're just making it harder."

I glance down at my raging erection and then lift my eyes again, my lips curling a bit. "You make everything harder, too," I rumble. My gaze drops to linger on her chest, those beautiful nipples punching through her thin shirt, and then drags up to watch her, making sure she sees my grin. "You missed me. You're glad I'm here."

Even from this distance, I can tell she's fighting her own smile. She wants this as much as me. But she can't give in yet.

"Arrogant as ever, I see."

"Confident." I nudge Sigurd into a slow walk toward her. "About you."

"What am I going to do with you?" She tries to inject frustration into her tone, but I can tell it's an act. She's struggling to keep the corners of her lips from tipping up even farther.

"What do you want to do with me, little rabbit? Or maybe the question is what am I going to do with you? I have my own ideas but I'm always open to suggestions. Or requests."

"Maybe Astarot should teach you a lesson," she suggests as I pull myself even with her dragon. He lets out a noncommittal grunt, probably unwilling to anger his draikana this early in their bond.

I drop from Sigurd, halving the distance between Sifa and me. "I'd suggest that Tindera teach you a lesson, but I want that honor for myself. Should I spank you first?"

"Only if you want to be gutted." Sifa's whisper winds its way inside me, sparking flares everywhere it touches. My cock responds like it always does, twitching as it tries to draw her attention. I have to stop myself from reaching for it.

Sifa roves her gaze down my chest, slowly, as she confirms how much control she wields over my body.

"Okay. No spanking ... yet," I rasp. "But you haven't told me what you want to do to me. Or, better yet, what you want me to do to you." One more step and I've closed the distance between us. My hand is on her cheek as she lifts her eyes to mine. Dropping my lips to her ear, I whisper, "What should I do to you, little rabbit?"

"Do you need instructions in every part of your life?" Sifa's husky chuckle sends another jolt of lust through me. "Or just the bedroom?"

"We'll experiment?" I muse. One of my thumbs drops to tug on her bottom lip as I savor the feel of her skin. "I can't wait to discover all the ways I can make you scream. And beg."

Sifa's fingers reach up to dig into my hair, pulling me down to her. And our lips meet. This kiss is hungry, desperate, searching for the connection we've denied ourselves too long. Her tongue sweeps in, tasting me as mine dances with hers. There is only us. The rest of the world stops as I let myself get lost in my mate.

Her hands drop to yank up my shirt, lifting it over my head. I suck in a breath as her lips find my chest, fluttering over my tattoos as she explores me for the first time. Inhaling her lavender and rosemary scent, my lips trail down her neck as my hands reach under her blouse to unhook the band around her breasts, dropping it to the ground. Her nipples press against my chest through her blouse and it takes all my restraint to stop myself from stripping her bare and sinking into her.

And then she's wrapping her arms around me to pull me close. My engorged cock literally trembles—the first time the bastard has done anything like that—as her hip grinds into it. Heat flows through me in waves, every part of my body hyper-sensitive. I reach for her breasts, rolling the nipples between my thumbs and fingers as she melts against me and sighs.

I've never heard a more beautiful sound in my life.

Astarot's roar rips through us, anger and pain and frustration echoing all around.

"I knew it." The large guard's voice floats toward me, bitter and cold. "Gods-damned dragon riders, always pushing us around. Not this time."

My gaze holds Sifa's for a moment as my thoughts splinter. She doesn't have to say the words. Astarot's yell, her expression, tell me everything. They've captured Astarot. Dragon hunters always carry the nets that give them control over rebellious beasts. The next one is aimed to trap Sifa and me. And then the Dróttning will execute Sifa. And the Ætt. And maybe our dragons.

She won't kill me—I think—but she'll fuck me up. Our relationship won't be enough to save me from the pain the Dróttning will rain down on me. It'll be months, maybe years, before I'm free again.

There's only one thing I can do.

"Fucking bitch," I growl as one of my hands reaches for Sifa's hair, the other wrapping around her throat. "If you hadn't put up such a fight, I'd have been done with you by now."

And then I turn to the guards, making sure they see my anger.

CHAPTER TWENTY-ONE

SIFA

SHE'LL RIDE WITH ME

FHORD YANKS MY HEAD back as his other hand grips my neck. The eyes that had sparked with lust—and something deeper, I'd thought a moment ago—now glare in anger.

"You're here a few minutes too early," Fhord snarls as he looks up at the guards who threw their trap over my dragon. "I'd almost finished with her." He rakes his gaze over the men as he leans over and spits my taste from his mouth. "Even traitors feel good on the cock," he adds as his hand squeezes my throat.

I gag, struggling to hold down the disgust that ripples through me. I'd trusted him with ... everything. Again. How fucking stupid could I be?

"You were about to capture her?" The bigger guard demands, his voice laced with skepticism. "We're supposed to believe that?"

His suspicion splashes cold water on my anger. My head spins before I can stop it, searching Fhord's face. He doesn't turn so I can only see his tight lips, the firm set of his jaw, the lift of his chin. If he's playing the guards, he's doing a gods-damned good job of it. He doesn't look like he gives one single fuck about me.

I doubted him in the few minutes after the guards found us the first time, my time in the dungeons filling me with dread and reminding me of the Dróttning's tight grip on everyone and everything in this world. But in the hours that followed, I pulled myself back from that edge. Too much has happened between us. I've seen his soul. He was sloppy, and that pissed me off, but I don't think he betrayed me.

I grasp onto that memory, desperate to believe this is a ruse. That Fhord hasn't fucked me over.

Fhord straightens, dropping the hand that held my neck. The other stays put, holding my hair tight but not enough to cause pain. He pins the guard with a look that would crumple the resolve of most humans, a scowl twisting his face.

"I don't give a fuck what you believe. We've got her and the dragon now. I'll fuck someone at the Nest since you couldn't wait long enough to let me finish here." He throws me a glance, his eyes empty and cold, before looking back up at the men.

My heart breaks a little at his look, not a hint of emotion in it. My chest collapses like a popped balloon as every part of me grows heavy, lead weights threatening to pull me to the ground. Staring down at the hands that haven't yet been thrown in cuffs, I fight to hold back the tears, clinging to the hope that Fhord hasn't betrayed me. That he's just trying to find a way to get both of us out of this mess.

He felt this thing between us. I know he did. This must be an act.

Calm. Astarot's voice drops into my thoughts, helping to center me. He's right. They'll have to remove the trap if they're going to get him to the Nest. He's strong enough to fight back. We might still have a chance.

Can you fly? I speak to him in his head for the first time, my mind finding the path I hadn't needed before. I haven't asked him yet about his wings, loath to push him and risk damaging one that's still healing. But we might have no choice.

Perhaps. Uncertainty fills my mind, sending rocks to drop into my gut. He doesn't think his wings are strong enough. But he's willing to try.

I cast my gaze at him, trying to fill it with hope. *I don't want you to hurt yourself. We'll figure something else out.*

Fhord jerks my hands forward, dragging me from my focus on Astarot. Before I can pull them away, he's retrieved a cord from his belt and is wrapping it around my wrists. It's snug but might leave some room to maneuver.

"She'll ride with me," he declares as he pulls me close and starts to drag me toward Sigurd.

"The fuck she will," the large guard responds, kicking his horse forward. "I know what I saw. You're not strangers." He brings his horse to within a few feet of Fhord, staring him down. "I don't trust you."

He's close enough for Fhord to grab his weapon and fight for us. Fight for me. When he doesn't, my stomach drops and I struggle to hold back the tears. A cold dread that these last couple of weeks have been an act—and I'm a gods-damned stupid elf—builds within me. But I push back the fear again, grasping onto memories of Fhord's fierce gaze and soft hands. He's just waiting for the right time and maybe that wasn't it. He could have seen some threat or risk I didn't.

"Like I said," Fhord responds in the low tone he uses before he resorts to violence, "I don't give a fuck what you think. She'll ride with me." He nudges me toward Sigurd before lifting me into the saddle and throwing his leg up to settle in behind me. I lean forward but there's no escaping contact with him here.

Others, Astarot tells me, and my stomach drops. I can feel the worry in his word. Three more riders approach. We may have lost our best hope of escaping. I look in the direction Astarot senses and a lump forms in my throat. Maybe we had a chance before. Not now.

Try. Astarot isn't ready to give up yet. When they lift the net, he'll attack. He's desperate to save us—I can feel the energy building within him—because he knows as well as I do what capture means. And I don't know whether to cry in relief that he's willing to try, or beg him to submit. He's as likely to get killed as he is to escape.

"How the fuck did you find them?" The first rider to reach us snarls the question as he approaches. His gaze touches on Fhord and me before it rests on Astarot. "I figured we'd never get 'em back."

"I subdued them," Fhord responds in a tone full of derision and … boredom.

My back straightens as I waver between desperation and a hope that's threatening to slip away. I want to believe he's acting. That he really cares for me. But he's so fucking convincing. With every word he mutters, I feel like my soul's being ripped apart. Like this strange connection between us is a living thing, buried in my chest and burning me from the inside out.

If he did betray me, I hope Tindera punishes him. My fingers grow cold as I let my thoughts rest on his dragon. How tough it will be on her. Her bond with Astarot is new and still weak, but she claimed my dragon. Fhord would piss her off as much as he did me. Maybe more.

I'll hold on to that knowledge like a blanket. Tindera is everything to him, and she'll be livid. That'll get me through the torture I'll be suffering soon.

But *fuck*, I don't know how I'm going to get through what they'll do to Astarot now.

Fhord nudges Sigurd, dragging my attention back to him.

"Hold the fuck on," the first guard yells before we've taken more than a few steps, urging his horse into our path. "Where do you think you're going?"

"I'm taking her back to the Nest," Fhord explains in a voice dripping with disdain. "You've got enough men for the dragon." He tugs on the reins to go around but this guard is stubborn, staying in Sigurd's path.

"I'm gonna let her ride with you," he snarls at Fhord, "but you go back with us. Like I said, I don't trust you."

"And like I said, I don't give a fuck what you think. I'm taking her back to the Nest now."

Astarot's roar interrupts their dick-measuring contest. They've pulled the net from him and this is his only chance to escape before he's bound again. He shakes off the remaining strands, his thoughts caressing me for a moment, and swats at a nearby guard. I watch as the male flies through the air, droplets of blood splattering on the rock where he lands.

For a moment, I think Astarot's going to make it. The path ahead of him is clear and he's able to extend his wings as he begins the short run that will help him launch.

Just for a moment.

The men who arrived came prepared for this.

The arrow that flies through the air pierces Astarot's side, barely missing his heart. But I can feel his pain. Doubling over in the saddle, my hands grasp for the hole in my side that feels like it must have appeared while I try to hold back the vomit pushing into my throat. I can't. Leaning to the right, I barely avoid my legs as my stomach empties. Again. And again.

As I struggle to breathe, sharp gasps filling the space in between my heaves, my mind finally wraps around the fact that this is Astarot's pain. He's already struggling to take it from me, to keep me from experiencing his agony. *Please*, I whisper to his thoughts. *Please stop trying to protect me from this. I'm okay. You need your strength to live. You must live.*

Sorrow. His devastation and grief echo through me, eclipsing the pain. He'd hoped to save us both and has only condemned us to death. Or worse. I can feel the weakness in his limbs, the pressure building in his chest, as his life drips out of him.

"You've subdued the dragon," Fhord bellows, malice and anger in every word. "Now save him. You have no authority to take his life."

"He would have escaped," the guard who shot Astarot declares. He's strident, but I can hear the tremble in his voice. If Astarot dies, he'll die with him. Even rebellious dragons are too valuable to be killed unless absolutely necessary. Guards can injure and subdue them. But they can never kill them. Sometimes it's too fine a line to walk. This guard couldn't do it.

"And now he won't." Fhord's words are a whisper laden with a threat. "Remove the arrow and stitch him up. He may still recover if you act quickly."

"How in all the gods' names am I supposed to do that?" Now the guard is afraid, his life tied inexorably to Astarot's. "I don't carry medical supplies."

"You left the Nest with a dragon bolt but no suture? Do you want to die?" I can feel the rumble in Fhord's chest as his anger takes hold. Young as their mating bond is, Astarot's death will hurt Tindera.

"I have no suture. And even if I did, I don't know how to sew up the beast."

"Fuck." Fhord swings his leg off Sigurd as he digs into one of his packs. "Hold her," he yells at one of the guards. "And don't fucking touch her. She must reach the Nest unscathed."

Another guard approaches and grabs my arm to pull me down from the saddle. I'm still struggling to control the pain in my side, wincing as he drops me on the ground. "Stay put," he demands, his hand resting on my shoulder. I concentrate on breathing, fighting to block out the pain like I did during my time in the Nest.

My gaze catches Fhord's as he finds what he needs and nods to himself. "You have to save him," I whisper. "Please."

Hints of what look like regret and sorrow rise in Fhord's face, darkening his eyes as he turns to me, and filling me with hope. But just for a moment. Scorn takes their place, and I'm thrown back into my terror that it's all been fake. That he's never felt anything for me and everything between us was a lie. I pray to all the gods I'm wrong, but the betrayal I felt again and again in the Nest rises inside me to splinter my faith, casting shards at my feet. Because *everyone* in Vanatia belongs to the Dróttning.

"'Dragon lives are precious and may not be forfeited without cause, and only on the order of the Dróttning,'" Fhord bites out, assaulting them with the mantra everyone in this land knows by heart. "If I'm able to save him, I will. For the Dróttning."

I can only watch as he stalks over to Astarot, examining the gaping hole the bolt made in his side. And then a cloth drops in front of my eyes as someone wraps a blindfold around my head.

"I need to see him," I cry out, raising my hands to pull at the fabric. A large hand smacks mine, the impact hard enough to shove me onto my side. I stretch out my arms to push myself up, but he grabs my shoulder to push me back down.

"You need nothing. You'll lay there until I let you up."

                    ROCHELLE L. WILCOX

He wants to hurt me. I've put all their lives at risk by helping Astarot escape. And even though Fhord seems to be the only one determined to get me to the Nest alive, I need him to focus on my dragon. I can't drag his attention away from saving Astarot.

So I lay there. Broken. And I wait.

I have no idea how much time has passed when I feel hands yank at my wrists, dragging me up to stand. And then he's shoving me ... somewhere. My side still ripples with Astarot's pain, and I'm struggling to stay upright as I stumble over the rocks and plants in our path. I have no fucking idea what's going on, and it's all I can do to keep from dropping back to the ground and wrapping myself into a fetal position.

Someone lifts my left leg, setting my foot into what feels like a stirrup. "Get up."

"What are you doing?" Fhord calls out, his voice angry as I lift myself into the saddle.

"I'm taking her to the Nest," a male snarls, little bits of spittle landing on my cheek when I turn toward Fhord's voice. My stomach clenches, a wave of nausea rolling through me, because I recognize the asshole's voice. It's the guard who started this mess when he found us, and he must realize that Fhord knows me. That he lied to him. *I'm so fucked.*

"She's my fucking prisoner, and I told you to hold her. I'll deliver her directly to the Dróttning. Why the fuck do you think you have the right to do anything with her?"

I can hear Fhord's frustration. He's stuck with Astarot and can't return me to the Nest himself. A smile emerges as I ponder the revenge I'll take on him if he really has betrayed me—a nugget of hope I cling to as it starts to take shape in my thoughts. I hold many of Fhord's secrets. He's right to fear what I can do to him.

"I. Don't. Fucking. Trust you." The guard screams each word as he lashes me to the saddle, strapping my hands to the pummel and an ankle to each stirrup. "And I don't answer to you. I'm taking her now. The rest of you help him get the dragon back when it's strong enough to travel." He pulls himself into the saddle behind me and I feel his heels shove into his horse's side as he yanks the reins. Then we're running. Fast.

I hold on to Astarot's pain as long as I can. It feels like it's ripping me apart physically, but that's nothing compared to the ache in my gut that forms when our connection starts to slip. Bit by bit, the distance between us grows too great, until only the shadows of his pain remain. My side still aches, but the rest of me is a cavern, empty and cold. I'm terrified that when I lose the fire of his wound, I'll never feel him again.

Perhaps an hour after I'm dragged away from my dragon's side, the pain holding us together fizzles down to nothing. Our connection's so new, or maybe Astarot's so weak, I can't even cling to the invisible string that ties dragons and riders. Casting out my thoughts, I search for Astarot, desperate to know he still lives. Instead, I find Fhord. My mind reels back from him—anger, pain and an overwhelming feeling of betrayal roaring to the surface—but I force it forward. If Fhord's still working on Astarot, I should be able to tell, even from this distance.

But he's got his walls up. His need to help Astarot—for Tindera, not for me—isn't important enough to occupy his full attention. He's rebuilt this barrier between us, holding me at bay and denying me this bit of knowledge about my dragon.

And I crumple. The hole that started in my gut has consumed me, a fire burning away any emotion I once thought I felt for Fhord. I am nothing but grief and pain and despair.

Because I'm returning to the Nest. As its prisoner. I know what's waiting for me and I'm terrified. Not of the torture. I learned to live with pain when they held me before. No, not just live with it. I learned to savor the agony, to hold on to it, like I clung to Astarot's torment when our connection frayed. Pain is life. When it disappears, life soon follows.

No, I fear the rack. Those hours and days will never leave me. The horror of being stretched out and displayed. The agony but worse, the violation of having little dicks and large instruments shoved into me—into every part of me—while men and women laugh at my panic. When I escaped, I didn't know if I'd ever be able to lay with a man. To trust someone enough to risk living through that again.

Now, Fhord's taken that from me too. I trusted him.

I can't hold back the tears as I realize that his betrayal hurts even more than everything I suffered in the Nest.

Shaking my head, I wrest my thoughts away from him. None of this matters, I realize, since they'll probably send me directly to an elven prison. Before, they were able to keep my presence in the Nest secret. Only the Dróttning and her chosen torturers and guards knew I'm an elf. But I told Fhord—a mistake that makes my stomach clench whenever I think of it—and he's got no reason to keep my secret. The Dróttning won't have a choice. Elves aren't held in human prisons.

That frightens me more than anything. At least I know what to expect in the Nest. The Vanatians are predictable, and I've faced their punishment before. I have no idea what faces me in an elven prison.

"Stop." A voice I don't recognize draws me from my malaise. "You don't have permission to be here."

"This is the bitch that freed the dragon," my captor sneers. "I'm turning her in."

"And where's the dragon?" This man likes the authority he wields, a hurdle to anyone seeking access to one of the most protected places in Vanatia.

"Injured, several vikus back. I left him to be handled by others while I take her to the commander."

"How do I know she is who you claim? She doesn't look strong enough to steal a dragon from a trainer."

"I don't know how the fuck she did it and I don't care. I found her with the dragon. And I'm taking her to the Nest. Do you want to be the man that stopped me from turning her in? You gonna send me back to my squad, maybe give her a chance to escape?"

The silence holds for a few seconds, as a burst of hope rises in me. If he takes me someplace else, I may be able to escape. Nothing other than the elven prisons are as secure as the Nest.

"All right," the guard agrees at last. "Proceed."

"Good fucking decision," my captor proclaims, belching in the direction of the voice. He nudges his horse and we're moving again.

But this touch of hope stays. I got lucky when I escaped the Nest before. I found a guard with a mind weak enough to manipulate. It was supposed to be impossible but I did it.

I escaped before. I'll do it again.

CHAPTER TWENTY-TWO

SIFA

TRAPPED IN MY CELL

"WHAT THE FUCK ARE you doing here?"

This questioner is different, more familiar, than the last guard we found. The man behind me knows him.

"Fuck if I didn't find the dragon and the female—a gods-damned female—who stole him." These words are full of defiant pride. I'm quite the catch, it seems.

"Are you shitting me? Can I see her?"

The blindfold rips away, dragging a good chunk of my hair with it. But I hold back my yelp of pain. These males won't get that satisfaction from me. Four soldiers on horses stare, different emotions on every face. One is amused; the others are varying degrees of curious and skeptical.

The Nest is behind them. I've only seen it from the outside a few times and never from the road we're on now. But there's no mistaking it—an enormous mountain cleaved by caverns large enough for dragons to pass. The range is remarkable for its size, but more remarkable for the desolation that surrounds these caves. Even the trees and grasses that blanket other peaks refuse to provide cover for the horrors that occur within this pile of rock.

Dread wraps around me as I acknowledge what I've known since I escaped a decade ago. It's always been my destiny to return here for my death.

"Gods-damned looker, that one," the new guard says, his gaze roaming up and down me before it rests on my chest. He's a large man, but that's not what catches my attention. It's the undertone of yellow flesh peeking out from his uniform. When he finally looks up, I see his eyes are the same. I wonder how much longer he has to live. "Can I have a go at her before you take her into the Nest?"

And just like that, he's joined the list of males I intend to kill. If he survives long enough for my vengeance.

"She's tricky," the guard behind me responds as one hand reaches out to grab my tit. Just because he can, the bastard. My skin crawls, and it's all I can do to keep myself from flinging my head back. But I'm badly outnumbered, and they'd as soon kill as capture me. He tweaks a nipple before dropping both hands to rest high on my thighs.

He's near the top of my list of males to kill. Fucker.

"What's she gonna do? There's five of us. It's not like she could get away."

"She killed a trainer and captured the dragon. And she seduced a gods-damned dragon rider who found her first, probably about to kill him. She's fuckin' tricky, and I'm not untying her until she's in the Nest." His voice is firm, threatening. He's not taking any chances with me. "This is my capture," he adds for good measure.

"Fine," the other guard grumbles. "Let 'em pass," he adds as he tugs on his reins to back his horse out of the way. The others do the same, opening a path for us to follow. Everyone spouts off the obligatory "For the Dróttning" and we're moving again in the wrong fucking direction.

I'm struggling to hold myself together as we approach the Nest. The dread that began when the guard took me from Astarot has grown into an invasive blight, roaming through my system to corrupt every part of me. Any hope I felt when we started is gone, forced out by the dread that I won't survive this torture again. My only prayer is being sent to one of the elven prisons right away. Where I'll wish I was dead.

"Maybe I should have fucked you when I had the chance," the guard whispers into my ear.

His breath is laden with the stench of rotten teeth, and I have no idea how I didn't notice it earlier. As I look around, though, I realize all my senses are more alert. The pommel under my hands is rougher, my fingers finding the ridges and grooves they'd missed this entire ride. The landscape around us is more defined, the hues richer, with emerald in the bushes and trees, and periwinkle and ruby in the flowers.

When I feel Tindera's touch, I understand. My eyes water and I fight to hold back the tears that want to roll down my cheeks. Regardless of Fhord's feelings, Tindera is here for me. Her bond to Astarot is strong, even from this distance, and his love for me radiates through her. She's helping me in her own way, giving me the advantage of her dragon senses as I enter the Nest and examine the cage they'll send me to.

The blindfold drops back into place as he ties it around my head. "Don't try anything," he snarls. "I've done my part and got you to the Nest alive. If you die here, it's not on me." He pauses a moment, his hands wrapping around my breasts again, my skin tightening everywhere he touches, trying to shrink away from him. "I just wish I could be the one to do it," he adds as he drops his hands and lifts himself from the saddle before untying and yanking me down with him.

"This one took the dragon," he declares, shoving me forward. "The beast was injured and needed to be sewn up. If he survives, they'll bring him here."

"The wound was deep," a strange voice responds. "The dragon probably won't live. You're lucky you weren't the one wielding the bolt. We've already dispatched of the man who took it upon himself to attack."

I crumple to the ground as my knees give out. My chest is caving in, holding on to each breath like it'll be my last. And maybe it will be. I've barely bonded with Astarot, but I know I won't survive his death. I wouldn't want to try. If my dragon goes, I'll follow him.

Alive. Tindera drops that single word into my mind. Unlike with Astarot, it doesn't carry a wealth of meaning with it. We don't have the kind of bond necessary for that. But it's something. I cling to it like a life raft. It may be the thing that salvages my sanity while I'm here.

"Take her below." An unknown voice orders me to the dungeon. "Wait," he adds after a moment. "Put the band on her first."

A knife slices through the thick cords Fhord used to bind my wrists and I feel them drop to the ground. Metal wraps around my neck, tight and cold, but I barely notice. My mind is trapped in my cell, ten years ago. It's dredging up every horror I'll soon be reliving. My skin itches, and for a moment, I can almost feel the knife slicing off parts of me, blood oozing out for hours after they were done.

Without warning, the guard yanks at something attached to the collar on my neck and starts to haul me ... somewhere. Twice, I stumble and lurch forward, prompting cursing. Finally, he rips away my blindfold, pulling out even more of my hair, then tugs on the chain he's using to lead me through the tunnels. *Bastard*. My kill list is growing by the minute.

"Keep up," he demands as he continues dragging me along. I can only scramble behind him, hoping he's taking me to a cell. I'm not ready yet for the other rooms they have down here.

"Where the fuck is she?" Fhord's voice rings through the hallway, and my treacherous, treasonous body responds before I can stop it. I literally get weak in the knees—to my eternal disgust—as a shiver rolls down my spine.

And then my heart skips a fucking beat. Because it forgot for a moment that he betrayed us. We hate him.

The guard doesn't stop. He may not even realize Fhord's after me. He'll know soon enough. Fhord must be terrified I'll betray his secrets to have gotten here so fast. I just hope he did all he could to help Astarot before he left. I'll kill him in this life or haunt him in the next if he didn't.

"You! Stop!" Fhord's voice rings down the corridor, echoing off the walls, and the guard finally realizes he's after us.

Turning, he eyes Fhord, who's nearly running down the hall. "Who are you?"

"I'm the dragon rider who captured that prisoner," Fhord explains in the voice that demands compliance, "and I'm here to make sure she's still alive when the Dróttning arrives."

"The Dróttning? Why would she come here? Or want to see this prisoner?"

"How fucking stupid are you?" Fhord demands, his tone dripping with derision. "This prisoner killed a guard and subdued a dragon. She may have been responsible for the freed prisoner. Of course the Dróttning will need to interrogate her. And this prisoner sure as fuck better be alive when she gets here."

The guard's eyes widen as the truth of Fhord's words settle into him.

And my stomach flips as they settle into me. I'll take the blame for everything. If I tried to point the finger at Fhord, it wouldn't matter. It would look like vengeance against the man who caught me. The Dróttning will do everything in her power to wring the truth out of me, even if it's really a lie. Because as much as I hate him, exposing Fhord means exposing Tindera. I can't do that.

The guard's throat expands and settles twice as he thinks about his choices. "I am commanded to take her to the rack," he says after a moment.

Fhord's eyes flash to mine as what looks like … fear, or maybe worry … erupts in them. In a beat, though, it's gone, replaced by a cold disgust. "She deserves the rack," he utters, his fists curling into balls as anger breaks through his emotions. Turning back to the guard, he wrests back control, his features dropping into a menacing calm as he releases his fingers to splay them across his thighs. "But that must wait. Hold her in a cell, ensure she's fed and kept safe until the Dróttning arrives."

"Those aren't my orders," the guard croaks. He's terrified of the position Fhord's placing him in.

"They are now." Fhord watches him for a moment, then strides forward to wrest the chain from the guard's hands. "I'll take her. If anyone asks, tell them to take it up with Tindera's rider."

Without waiting for a response, Fhord turns back toward the entrance, pulling me with him. His pace slows when we're out of the guard's sight and he walks close enough to whisper to me.

"I need you to trust me, Sifa," he breathes, sending a tingle down my unfaithful spine. It's supposed to toe the line. We hate Fhord. Instead, it's melting as it searches for the touch every part of me craves, even after what he did. A flicker of hope erupts in my gut, but I smother it. I won't let him destroy me with the betrayal I know is coming. "I can't get you out now, but I will. I promise."

"Where are you taking her?" A commander I don't recognize approaches from a corridor to the left. He wears his authority like a shield and a sword, protecting him as he attacks anyone who stands in his way.

"Did you order her to the racks?" Fhord's tone is belittling, dismissive.

"I did. You have no authority to belay my demand."

"Perhaps you don't know who I am." Fhord drops the chain as he adopts his warrior stance. He's all threats and intimidation as he stalks forward. "I ride Tindera. I hold authority where dragon matters are concerned. This prisoner killed a trainer and stole a dragon. She will be held until the Dróttning can get here to question her."

"This prisoner appears to have helped another prisoner escape, and killed many of our guards. She belongs to me. She goes to the rack where we can find out who helped her."

"Would you challenge the Dróttning?" Fhord's voice is low and dangerous. The tension in this narrow passageway feels thick, like it's wrapped around me, draining the heat from my body. Few humans can stand up to Fhord when he's in this mood.

This commander, though, doesn't give up easily. He straightens his back and takes one step, placing himself in Fhord's space. "I don't believe the Dróttning would give one little shit about this prisoner," he proclaims, his arm gesturing toward me in a move that nearly smacks Fhord.

Fhord's eyes flick down to the errant limb, and I wonder how hard he's fighting to keep himself from killing the man.

"Then you're just as stupid as your guard. The Dróttning controls the dragons and this prison. Nobody threatens or challenges that control. I will say it again. This female"—with an angry, contemptuous glare toward me—"was able to kill a trainer and then take control of a powerful dragon. She may have done what nobody has for years, breaking into the Nest to help a prisoner escape."

Fhord pauses for a moment before leaning in to snarl his next words. "The Dróttning will need to know how. She will come here herself to question the prisoner. And the prisoner sure as fuck better be alive and healthy enough to withstand the Dróttning's interrogation when she gets here."

At last, a hint of doubt sneaks into the commander's stance. Because I do sound pretty powerful when you put it that way. His shoulders drop, and he takes a step back as he glances at me. "Where would you take her?"

"Where the fuck do you think?" Fhord demands. "She needs to go to a prison cell. A secure one that can't be compromised."

The man watches Fhord for another moment and then dips his chin sharply. "I agree," he declares, claiming Fhord's order as his own. "She must be held for the Dróttning. Follow me."

Spinning, he turns toward a hallway to the left. Fhord stalks back to grab my chain and drag me along behind him. He doesn't speak to me again, but I hadn't expected him to. He's said what he could to try to earn my trust back—as if I would believe he plans to help me—and can't risk talking to me in front of the commander.

We walk for a long time, entering a part of the prison I don't recognize. And I'd know. The memories of my time here are engraved on my psyche, an ever-present etching through which every part of my life must pass. But while I can't see anything I recall, the stench already has wriggled inside me to drag out emotions I never wanted to experience again. My insides crawl with every hint of rot and shit that slithers up my nostrils, and I struggle to hold back the retch that plays in my throat.

I'm almost relieved when we reach my cell. Almost. While I'm ready to get away from these males and try to find some semblance of calm amidst the horror that is the Nest, I'm overwhelmed by the realization that I'll suffer as I wait for the Dróttning. The smell here is somehow worse than I remember—dominated by the sulfur I'd grown to despise—and the cell itself is nothing more than an empty space with a hole in the ground. No cot or blankets or water source. But I shouldn't have expected any of that.

"Key." Fhord drags me closer and holds out his hand.

The commander watches for a moment then gestures toward my new abode. "She'll keep the band. She may have magic and that'll help control it."

I realize with his pronouncement what I've been missing since they wrapped the metal around my throat. I hadn't felt Fhord, but he's gotten good at shielding against me so that wasn't surprising.

I don't feel Tindera at all. I haven't heard anything, although she comforted me before.

Worse, I can't cast out my psyche to find any other mind. The splattering of thoughts that always sieges me is quiet. No fears respond to my own. No thirst for vengeance. No despair. No hope. No desire.

Nothing I can manipulate and control.

Nobody I can shape into my unwilling ally.

No way to escape.

And that's what finally breaks me. I stumble into the cell and slump to the ground, my fingers holding on to the shackle that will spell my doom. They've found a way to hold my mind. I have no idea how I'll get past this barrier they've created.

"Make sure she's fed and kept safe." Fhord's words echo through me, but I don't look up. I can't see his face again. His betrayal cuts me more sharply than the knowledge I have no way to escape. He won't see me collapse. He won't see what he's done to me.

The lock clanks, echoing through the corridor, and I hear them stride away, boots pounding on the stone floor.

Silence surrounds me, heavy like a thick cloak, and I lift my gaze and stop fighting. The tears start as a trickle, soon growing into an inferno as the grief burns through every bit of my skin and muscle and blood and sinew. For an hour, I let myself be consumed by fear and despair. But just for an hour.

Those emotions won't help me survive.

When I feel like my broken parts have started to mend again—and I can let go of Fhord and the ache of his treachery—I straighten my back, sucking in a deep breath.

Grief won't get me out of here. Anger. Resolve. Retribution. They are my most potent weapons. My need for vengeance—against Fhord, the Dróttning, and every single being who helped create this fucked up world—will be my salvation. Those are the emotions I'll need to escape and exact my revenge.

So those are the emotions I nurture.

I meditate on Fhord's betrayal, letting myself remember the game he played and how effectively he fooled me. I can't deny it any longer. He drew those guards to Astarot and me in the cave. My dragon must have been healthier than he expected, so he pretended to help us escape, only to ensure more guards would find and capture us.

He deserves to die, but I don't know if I can do that to Tindera. I'll find some way to hurt him as badly as he hurt me.

Then my fury turns toward the Dróttning and everything I've learned about her. The words of the dead king in the grove come back to me, and I wonder how I can use his information against her. Because she must pay. She's created a horrific world to feed her vast ego. Elves and dragons suffer the most, but they're not the only ones.

Maybe I'm here to tear it down.

And I'll need every bit of my strength if I'm going to do that.

CHAPTER TWENTY-THREE

FHORD

WE'VE MADE OUR DECISION

THAT GODS-DAMNED MANACLE AROUND Sifa's neck is going to fuck up everything.

I'd hoped it wouldn't work. The Dróttning had it developed after Sifa escaped and tested it on a lot of elves, but nobody as strong as my little rabbit. When they put it on her, I knew. I can't even sense her presence. It's smothering her magic.

A dark cloud is forming inside me, and I don't know how I'll ever get rid of it. Even my savage feels it, holding himself at bay to avoid feeding that storm. The storm that could consume me entirely.

I need to talk to Sifa. Need her to know I didn't betray her. That I'll get her out if it's the last thing I do.

But I can't risk going to her. Not unless I have no other choice. If they capture me, I won't be able to help either of us. And they'll punish Sifa *and* Tindera for my sins. For my weakness.

I can't let that happen. My only choice is to get rid of the gods-damned shackle around her throat. The problem is I have no fucking idea how to do that. She's in a part of the prison I can't control. Any influence I wield at the Nest ends with those cages. They're outside of the reach of the dragon riders. They placed her there intentionally because they don't trust me.

That fucking know-it-all guard will pay for how badly he's fucked it all up.

He'll experience everything Sifa does. Every pain forced on her. Every bit of shame. Every moment of despair.

After I figure out how to get Sifa out.

At least Tindera's healed. She's terrified for Astarot, who's still trapped in the blood-stained meadow where everything went to Helheim. I've gotten an update and am anxious to assure her he's recovering.

They're resolved to fly together, at least once. And she can't wait to share her favorite field with him. He's somehow never tasted goat before. Tindera spends a lot of time—a *lot* of time—thinking about their first meal together. Feeding Astarot her own memories of her favorite food. She's always been a little food-obsessed.

I'm heading to my voracious dragon now. I need to be with her. We're connected while I'm in the Nest, but it's never as good as sitting by her side. Hearing her heart pound in her chest. Feeling her breath as it wisps over me. It calms me like nothing else can other than Sifa. And I need some fucking calm right now.

I also need to talk to Tindera. The Dróttning is expected at any moment, and I can't risk her overhearing our conversation. When she's close, it's easy for her to eavesdrop on any words shared between dragon and rider. There are no secrets. It's one of the reasons she's so dangerous.

So I'm heading into the lair to be with mine. A rock lifts from my gut when I see her, sprawled out in front of a vast underground lake the dragons claimed for their own. I've tried to get in the water more than once but never succeeded. No riders allowed. A smile emerges against my will as I think about Tindera's response the last time—how much fun we had racing around the cave as she held me at bay.

The Dróttning has taken too much from the Thunder. She stole their independence and freedom. Forces them to accept unworthy riders. Takes private thoughts from what should be a sacred bond. Tortures any who defy her. But she's allowed them this. A scrap that costs her nothing. It's theirs, and nobody, not even their riders, will take it from them.

Tindera looks up from her nap, stretching as she watches me approach. By the gods, she's beautiful. Even in this low light, her feathers sparkle, enough dappled sunlight filtering through to catch the gold and cast an umber glow all around. She's one of the few gold dragons. *Mine.*

Mine, she echoes, her eyes bright. I can't deny that. I'm hers, just as she is mine.

Leave? Tindera's ready to go. She's been stuck here in the Nest for weeks. We're waiting for the final okay from the Dróttning, which should come any day now, maybe today. We won't head to Revalle yet—we need to stay close to Astarot until he's fully healed—but we'll be out of here.

And while she doesn't know this yet, I can't leave until Sifa's free. I hope she understands. That she agrees.

"Walk with me," I urge as I reach out to stroke her snout.

She holds my gaze for a moment then drops her chin. Standing, she stretches again before leading me away from the pool. We roam deeper into the caves, searching for a place I can speak without fear. She takes me down a passage I don't recognize, our feet disturbing a sandy ground untouched by any footsteps. Finally, perhaps fifteen minutes after we left, Tindera settles in the middle of a large cavern, dropping her head to give me access to her horn—the place she loves to be scratched.

"The Dróttning will be here soon," I say as I lean against my dragon and dig my fingers under her feathers. She rumbles at me when I find her favorite spot. "We know things she cannot. Things that would get both of us killed. Get Astarot and Sifa killed."

Tindera rumbles again, this one a warning. She doesn't like it when I tell her things she already knows. Another smile emerges of its own will as my hand wriggles farther under her plumage. "I know. I'm sorry. Just making sure we're both agreed about the stakes."

Her unblinking eyes watch me, unamused. Finally, she relents and gives me a single drop of her eyelids.

"I did everything I could with Astarot," I assure her. I've felt her angst. She's tried to hide it—the Dróttning cannot learn that Tindera bonded with Astarot—so we haven't spoken about him at all.

"The wound was deep, but he's strong. Stronger than he should be after just a few days of rest. When his body is healed and he can fly free, he'll be nearly as impressive as you."

Tindera snorts, pride rippling through her. She's one of the most magnificent beasts in all of Vanatia. She would not bond with a lesser dragon.

"He'll heal. I promise. This wound won't kill him."

She watches me, measuring my sincerity. Like every dragon, she can see all of me. I can't hide a thing from her. When she assures herself that I believe Astarot will fully heal, she blinks her eyes again. She's ready to talk about home.

"I want to go back home as badly as you. We've been gone too long. But Sifa's being held someplace I can't reach. No dragon riders are allowed in that part of the prison. They're using the iron manacle around her throat, so I can't speak with her either. I can't leave her there."

Tindera's pause this time is even longer. Finally, a single word drops into my thoughts. It comes alone, unlike her usual messages. But I don't need an explanation. It can only mean one thing.

Save.

I exhale a sigh of relief. Tindera agrees we need to help Sifa.

"It puts us both at risk. If I'm caught, she'll condemn you too. We'll both suffer for a very long time."

It's Tindera's turn to sigh in her dragony way. She huffs out a breath, exasperation layered with resolve. Her eyes are unblinking, solemn.

Quandary.

The laugh bubbles out of me unprompted. My hand reaches even deeper under her feathers, scratching at her favorite spot. She claimed Sifa in the caves when they first met. Even before Sifa and Astarot bonded, Tindera knew we would face tough choices as my dragon's interests diverged from my mate's.

As I was forced to choose to place one at risk to protect the other.

It is a gods-damned, mother fucking quandary.

But we've made our decision.

I spend the next hour with Tindera, just being together. We don't talk much. She tells me about her recovery and assures me she's fully healed. I talk about our journey and tell her more about her drake and my short time with him. We settle our souls.

As we walk back, my gaze catches on footsteps I don't recall from earlier. In a few places, it looks like more than one dragon has passed through these tunnels, and I search my memories for images of the ground before. I thought we were in a system that had been untouched.

Neither of us felt another dragon's presence. We would have known if we were followed. Shaking my head, I cast out my fears of phantoms. They must have been here before, and I missed it.

Leaving Tindera back at the pool, I return to my chamber and settle in for the afternoon. Before I went to see Tindera, I visited the library to research the manacle they're using on Sifa, sneaking out a book that looks promising. It was developed from restraints used long ago, when elves walked freely in this world. Maybe I'll find something helpful.

Less than a day later, the Dróttning appears, the energy in the Nest changing as soon as she arrives. Without even feeling her presence—which only happens when I search for her—I know she's here. The corridors outside my rooms grow busier, occasionally verging on frantic. Whispered voices pass by the door, the sound but not the words reaching my ears. Even shouts rumble down the hall occasionally.

She'll want to see me, and I need to meet with her. I'm not ready yet. I have to figure out a way to convince her to hold off on torturing Sifa without suggesting I care. But she's perceptive as fuck. Especially with me. I have a hard time keeping secrets from her.

Her summon surprises me. I hadn't expected her to call for me so soon. Within an hour of her arrival, a knock stirs me from my book. Tucking it behind the displaced stone I use to hide things, I open the door to find her favorite messenger.

"The Dróttning calls for you."

"Hello Ældit," I answer with a humorless smile. "How are you?"

"Fhord," he intones with a sharp drop of his chin. His voice is as terse as normal. He's good at his job. "My state is irrelevant. The Dróttning would speak with you. Follow me."

"Happily," I tell him, stepping into the corridor as I close and lock my door. "I welcome her return."

Ældit spins on his heel and strides away, his heels clapping on the stone beneath us.

The Dróttning waits for me in her chamber, a vast space comprised of several interlocking rooms, that sits empty most of the time. It's as dry and cold as she is. The furniture is sufficient for its purposes but bland, devoid of any color other than gray, black and white. Three couches, a dozen chairs and a large table surrounded by more chairs occupy the largest room, into which I'm led. I've spent enough time here to know the feel of each by heart. They're comfortable enough, except the one she chose because she's a cruel bitch, which I always avoid. If the bedrooms haven't changed—and after all these years, I'm certain they haven't—they'll look the same.

The Dróttning is not one for change. Or sentiment. Or anything soft.

"As requested, I have brought Tindera's rider." Ældit's voice is as flat and dull as the room around us.

"Leave us." The Dróttning's gaze finds mine as her words dismiss her messenger and my stomach plunges into my gods-damned toes. Her eyes are shards of glass. She's pissed at me and my plans for protecting Sifa just fucked right off. Dread for my rabbit grips every bone in my body, twisting them the way the Dróttning's gods-damned medallions torture elves.

But I shut that shit right down. I can't let her sense my fear. If she has even a trifling of doubt about my allegiance to her, she'll destroy everyone and everything that might have come between us. So I plaster on the lazy smile I always give her when she calls me and hold her frozen gaze.

Ældit responds to the Dróttning's dismissal with a crisp "My liege" before stalking from the room.

When he's gone, her eyes narrow. "I expected you to come for me when you knew I'd arrived."

Striding over to sit in a nearby chair, I stretch my legs out in front of me and turn to examine the weapons hung all around the room—the only adornment the Dróttning tolerates in her space. She hates my informality around her, even when we're alone, but I've never cared before. I can't start now.

Finally, I look back at her. "I knew Ældit would find me when you were ready to see me. As he did."

"You also know," she reminds me in words as sharp as the blades around us, "that *you* are to find *me* when I arrive at the Nest. I should not have to seek you out."

I sigh, then continue my inspection of a nearby wall before rising to get a closer look at an ax I don't recognize. "Is this one new?" I ask as my finger reaches out to test its edge, drawing a drop of blood. It's every bit as sharp as it looks.

The responding sigh is tinged with anger. But she also expects this. It's been many years since I cared what she thought about me. Or wanted anything from her. She'll tolerate this and more and it'll help convince her I don't care much about the request I need to make.

"Sit," she demands, frustration echoing in her voice.

I turn to see a finger pointed peremptorily at the chair I vacated, her back straight. Nodding, I stroll back toward her, plopping down to extend my legs again.

"You know you can have no secrets from me? Here or anywhere." It's phrased as a question but we both know it's a statement.

"I would not keep a secret from you. I have nothing to hide." Lifting an ankle to drop it over the other one, I stretch my arms to link my hands behind my head.

"You didn't think I would care about your ... tryst ... with the elf?" She gets right to the point, as always.

"Why would you care? I found the rogue elf who'd managed to kill a trainer and subdue one of our most powerful—and stubborn—dragons. I've never had an elf before." My shoulders shrug, the height of indifference. "I decided to fuck her before I turned her in."

The Dróttning's lips curve down, her distaste at my declaration drawing a sneer.

"How is an elf walking this world?" I add in a tone tinged with curiosity. It's what she'd expect me to ask, even if she'd rather discuss other things.

She takes a deep breath, making an effort to hold her temper with me. She hates how quickly I can draw her ire. For a woman known for her stoic behavior, the Dróttning's always been surprisingly emotional about me.

"We don't know," she says at last, her eyes looking past me toward the shackles Sifa wore when she arrived. They're unlike anything we have in Vanatia, proof of another world—where this odd metal exists—that the Dróttning hides from her subjects. Only her most trusted soldiers enter these rooms, so she's displayed them here for the past decade.

"Those cuffs," she tells me, "bound an elf who appeared ten years ago with a troll and something else." She rises to wander in that direction as if they're drawing her toward them.

"She's been here that long? Where has she been? And where's the troll ... and the something else?"

The Dróttning laughs, a dry sound that has nothing to do with humor. "So many questions. Perhaps you should have asked the elf before you tried to *fuck* her."

She's angry. She doesn't often cuss, but when she does, she's ready to draw blood from someone. I wonder if this time it'll be me after all.

"I've never been one for talking first," I respond, rising to stand next to her. My physical presence calms her. It will help me navigate this rope I need to walk. "I did intend to ask her a few questions, but we were interrupted, as I assume you've learned."

Turning, her eyes sear into mine, fury sparking at me. "I shouldn't have learned this from anyone but you. This is why you must come to me when I arrive here or anywhere. I wasn't prepared to learn what I did." Pausing, she places a hand on my arm, her gaze softening. "I can't protect you if you're not honest with me."

I nod, resting my hand on hers for a moment before they drop away and to our sides. Physical contact is strange and uncomfortable for both of us. I've never been able to tolerate her touch for long.

"I apologize," I intone at last. "I didn't think it would cause problems for you."

"Perhaps if this were any other elf, but this one is different. She's dangerous."

"Different, how?" This may be the opening I need to protect Sifa long enough to save her.

The Dróttning looks again at the shackles as she seems to ponder her response. "Ten years ago, the elf and troll arrived with some vast power source that disappeared within seconds, leaving them behind. They just appeared in an empty room. They'd been tortured—badly from what we can tell—but were alive and strong."

"Where did they come from?"

"That we do not know. We held them for weeks and they tolerated ... intense questioning ... but they gave us no answers. The troll was not as defiant as the elf, but he knew nothing. The elf alone could give us information that she refused to share."

"Why is she alive and free?"

"You recall hearing of the escape a decade ago?"

"Of course." Until the recent one, a single prisoner had escaped from these caves. She'd expect me to remember that. "Was that the elf?"

"Yes. The elf controlled a guard's mind, convinced him to release her and the troll."

"That's an unusual power for an elf." I know Sifa's powers well, but the Dróttning can't realize that.

"Not so unusual," she tells me, spinning to return to the couch. I follow and lounge across from her again. "Some of their mental abilities are quite pronounced. It's one of the reasons elves may not walk freely in Vanatia. They're dangerous."

"This one certainly seems to be."

"And yet, you would have *fucked* her before bringing her to the Nest?"

I shrug again. "As I said, I've never had an elf before. And this one is quite beautiful. I didn't want to pass up the chance." Fortunately, I've spent enough time in women's beds to convince the Dróttning that I would indeed pause in the midst of capturing a dangerous enemy if I found her attractive enough.

A single eyebrow lifts as she watches me, tests my words for the lie. When it drops, I know my reputation has given her the explanation she needs. "It won't happen again."

"She's in a cell, out of my reach. Even if I wanted to, it wouldn't happen again."

"What did you say to each other before you were found? We hope to learn where she's been. How she could hide from us for all this time. And we still must get answers to the questions we asked ten years ago."

"We spoke very little," I explain. "A mutual attraction and desperate circumstances led us to seize the moment fairly quickly."

"You didn't talk to each other? She opened her legs to you without persuasion?"

"I didn't say she was completely willing," I respond, my steady gaze holding hers. "I was tenacious enough to drag a response from her body." I've never forced a female, but I've nurtured a reputation that would satisfy the Dróttning's demand for cruelty in all who serve her. She believes me to be a mercurial ... and persistent ... lover. It's not a leap for the Dróttning to believe I'd raped females in the past and would again.

"Why did the dragon not stop you?"

"I don't know why he would care. She's a random elf and I ride Tindera. The dragon—Astarot, was it?—has been in the Nest long enough to recognize me as a dragon rider."

This time she watches me for a very long time, measuring my words. When she speaks, anger and disappointment echo through hers. "I'd like to believe you, Fhord. You know the penalty for aiding elves. And you know I would have no choice but to punish you if you committed such a heinous crime."

"Of course," I concede. "I would expect nothing else."

"I can't protect you if you continue with this reckless behavior. I have sacrificed much to keep your secret," she reminds me.

"Our secret," I interject. "Yours as much as mine."

Her eyes grow hard, little bits of agate. She doesn't like being interrupted. "Quite so," she bites out. "If you're exposed, we'll be condemned together. I won't let that happen. Even for you."

"My apologies. I'll be more careful." I need to calm her down if I'm going to push her at all about Sifa's punishment. Ensure, if I can, that Sifa won't be tortured before I can get to her.

"If I must punish you, I will," she adds, a note of warning entering her voice. "I would not tolerate your death well, but I would wrest Tindera from you and bind her to another if you betray my trust. After she spends time with the trainer to remind her where her allegiance lies."

"I've known since I bonded with Tindera that any punishment you wield against me would fall on her. I would not risk that. Ever."

She dips her chin once. "Good." Curiosity rises in her face for a moment. "What did Tindera ask you to save?"

I struggle to maintain a flat, bored expression in response to her change of subjects. "What?"

"I've heard very little from Tindera today. She's not very talkative. Earlier, though, she asked you to save something ... or someone. What does she want you to save?"

I let understanding wash over my features. "You misunderstand. It was a question, not a request. She heard about my attempt to repair the dragon's injury and wondered if I'd saved him."

"Why would she care about one rebellious dragon?"

"You know dragons better than me," I remind her. "They're nosy creatures, always looking for information about others in the Thunder. She wondered if this one still lived or if he'd been killed for his stubborn nature."

Again, the Dróttning watches me for a moment, measuring my response. And again, she seems convinced enough to accept my assurances. Finally, she nods, her eyes lighting with what looks like an idea. "I need your help with the elf."

"Anything." I hope my twinge of excitement doesn't appear in my eyes or voice.

"She didn't respond to our questions before and we have no reason to believe she will now. We'll try a different approach."

"You're not going to torture her?" I don't have to pretend for my tone to reflect my surprise.

"Oh, we will. She must be punished for her crimes. My people would not tolerate a weak hand. But not yet. We'll let her simmer in her fear. After a week or so, you'll emerge and protect her. Or so she'll believe. You were able to persuade her to respond to you physically. Perhaps you could be persuasive in other ways."

I watch the Dróttning, weighing my options. It feels like she's telling the truth. She's lied to me before, but I don't think she is now. And if I agree to this, they won't kill Sifa. They won't even torture her. I'll get access to her and an excuse to save her from their hands. It'll be the best opportunity I'll have. Even if it means I have to stay away for a week. Let her suffer in her cell while I roam through these caves, free and unharmed, pretending not to care. I couldn't risk exposing myself and squandering this opportunity.

Or maybe I could use the time in a different way. It could be exactly the opportunity I need.

"You want me to romance her?" I ask with a tilt of my lips that I hope comes across as blasé.

"I want you to do anything you must to get answers from her. Anything."

I pause, careful not to appear eager. "As you wish," I agree at last. I can't hold back the smile this time but I don't try, shifting it a bit to appear devious. Let her see my approval of her plans. She's given me a better gift than I ever could have requested.

Now I have to figure out how to save Sifa, hopefully without exposing Tindera to the Dróttning's wrath.

CHAPTER TWENTY-FOUR

SIFA

AND I WAIT

I'VE MADE SOME TERRIBLE decisions in my long life. The series of choices that landed me back in the gods-damned Nest might be the worst yet.

But I can't bring myself to regret them.

I will. I know I will. My time here before nearly broke me. This will be worse. And I probably won't be able to escape. This thing around my neck is designed to keep me in. But even without it, the Dróttning won't allow the same weaknesses as last time. My guards will have strong minds and be changed regularly enough to defeat any manipulation. She won't make the same mistakes.

Today, though, as I sit waiting for the torture to begin, I'm grateful to have bonded with Astarot. I've received the most precious gift any elf could get. My connection with my dragon completes me in a way I never knew I needed. I found our thread—a thin link, different from the pain I clung to as the guard carried me away—and I can feel his presence again. It gives me strength. But even if he dies, a thought that guts me, I wouldn't regret saving him.

And as much as I really, truly hate admitting it to myself, I'm grateful to have known Fhord. Despite his betrayal, I can't deny that our connection brought a part of me to life that I thought had died. I haven't felt lust—because that's all it was, I remind myself—since I left Midgard.

But I don't want to think about Fhord. It hurts. A fog billows through me, deadening all my senses, whenever I let myself remember him. How he made me feel. The lies he fed me. My chest grows heavy, an anchor weighing down my heart, when my mind dredges up his face as he turned me over to the guards.

Soon, the pain will outweigh any gratitude I feel for having known him. And then I can push him out of my thoughts entirely.

Shaking my head, I stand to wander around the small cell. I still have enough strength to exercise, so I do. Dropping to the floor, I do push-ups until my arms feel like they can't hold me up any longer. And then I do ten more. Lunges and squats follow before I finish by running in place. Perhaps ninety minutes after I started, I collapse on the floor, gulping in air while my gaze searches the ceiling above me.

"I did that too when they threw me in this hole." The male voice that floats toward me is weak, like all the life has been wrung from it. A bitter laugh follows. "For a while."

"How long have you been here?"

"Seven hundred and eighty-four days."

A wave of pity for this faceless comrade ripples through me. I don't think I'd be able to endure that much torture, and can tell from his voice he may be nearing his end. "How have you survived more than two years of this?"

"I am ridiculously difficult to kill." This laugh is more genuine, as if he's pondered his mortality long enough to find it amusing they still haven't succeeded in taking his life.

"A blessing and a curse."

"More of a curse at the moment, although it's been a blessing in the past." He sighs, a bone-weary exhale filling the space between us. "I'm ready to die. I just can't find a way to do it."

"What would it take?"

"When my head is separated from my body, I will rest."

"Nothing else will end your life?"

"Nothing. I'll grow weak, but I won't die. After my first year here, I stopped eating for seventy-two days. The pain of starvation turned into a numb nothingness. I thought perhaps it would kill me, but it didn't. Eventually I gave up. It's been several months since I resigned myself to this existence."

"Will they hold you here forever?"

"Eventually they'll take my head," he explains, a note of hope entering his voice. "They must know by now that I won't give them anything they seek. I don't know why they haven't done it yet."

"What do they hope to get from you?"

"The identities of the rebels in Revalle." His tone is matter-of-fact, as if he long ago gave up trying to hide his connection to the rebellion. An unexpected thrill rolls through me as

I realize this connection might be even more important than the link to the Dróttning I've been pursuing. They're my best hope for finding a place for Astarot and me to hide. If we can get out of this place.

"Yes, that's something the Dróttning would desperately want," I agree. "You're strong, to deny them information that might give you the death you crave."

He sighs again, the weariness sneaking back into his exhale. "I have no choice. My mate joined me in the rebellion. If I gave up any of them, he would suffer, and it would be worse than anything I've experienced here. I would spend a thousand days on the rack before I would do that to him."

"You have a mate? I didn't think those bonds really existed." I've heard references to mates in this world but only in whispers. I saw these bonds between elves in my worlds, but here, it feels like myth. Stories told long ago that have evolved over the years to describe an unattainable love.

"Our mating bond snapped into place when we saw each other. For more than two hundred years, it has been the reason we live. Dragging him into my misery would cause me more pain than the Dróttning could ever inflict."

We sit in silence for a moment, my thoughts whirling. "Is that what it means to be mated to someone?" I ask at last. I don't know why, but I need to better understand the mating bond. Maybe it will help me in my connection with Astarot.

"That is part of it," he responds, his words trembling with emotion. "We are fortunate. With most of the elves trapped in the Dróttning's prisons, few mates find each other. We somehow both evaded the Dróttning's personal Helheim in the prisons, and then landed in each other's arms. We've had more than most."

"How many elves live freely here?" I've never met any, other than Bevin, if I'm right that he's an elf. But I wouldn't know if I had. I'd need to develop a friendship with another elf that would last long enough to break through the shields that protect our minds. Only then could I discern their nature.

It's part of the reason my connection with Fhord is so confusing. Even if he were part elf—although he doesn't *feel* like an elf—my mind seemed to recognize his when I first encountered him. I've never experienced that kind of link with someone I didn't know.

"A few dozen," he says. "But not freely. Their location is another secret the Dróttning would like to wring from me but hasn't." His voice is layered with pride.

"What's your name?" I ask at last. "I suspect we'll be good friends before our time here is done."

"I am Joralf. And what is your name?"

"Sifa. I'm an elf too—which I've now admitted twice in a week, more than in all of the years I've lived in Revalle. Not a good sign," I add with a laugh.

"I suspected you might be," Joralf tells me. "The air shifted when you arrived. Your power must be great, to occupy so much space in these caves."

"Maybe," I concede. "I have no idea how to measure it here."

The boots slapping on the floor in our direction draw our attention, ending any conversation. In a few seconds, two guards stop in front of my cell.

"The Dróttning requires your presence," one snarls as my stomach drops. He pauses, a key just shy of the lock on my door, to sneer at me. "I'm not allowed to kill you, but I can cause you pain. As much as I need to get you to her alive. You don't plan to fight me, do you?"

I drop my head and then hold still for a moment, letting the emotions wash through me. The dread I felt when they stopped at my cell has tempered, a flash of thrill taking its place. My pulse quickens, and I have to hold back a smile as their words settle.

I'm going to meet the Dróttning. Whatever I may suffer at her hands will be worth it because she holds all the answers in this place. Every bit of knowledge I can gather about or from her will help me find my way home. Or at least help me find a way home for Toffer, if I can't bring myself to leave Astarot behind.

But they can't know I want to meet her, so I don't move right away, forcing them to speak again. "Are you gonna come willingly?"

I grasp on to sorrow and fear, pulling up my memories of Astarot being shot, to make sure that when I lift my eyes, they'll reflect those emotions. "I will," I tell them, dragging myself to my feet. When I shuffle toward the door, shoulders drooping and back curved, my gaze drops to the floor. They scrape open the door, grasp the chain still attached to my throat, and drag me out of my cell and down the hall.

The corridors wind endlessly and dread returns with the realization that we're going deeper into the caves—toward the rooms they use to punish prisoners. After a dozen turns, I abandon any hope of remembering our path. I'll never escape from the rack anyway. They'll lead my broken body back to my cell when they're done with it. Instead, memories of my weeks here fill my thoughts. It feels like my throat will close completely, the bile that's started to rise from my stomach the only thing that will pass.

Fuck me. We turn into a hallway I recognize, right outside the room that holds the rack, and I'm deep in my dread. My emotions whip through me as I come to terms with what comes next. My stomach is tied in knots and I wonder if I'll be able to keep myself from vomiting.

I don't want them to hurt me again.

I know the cave they take me to, too well. The rack that waits for me. I fought them the first few times they tied me to its frame, thinking I could change or avoid anything they tried to do to me. It only made it worse. I always ended up trapped here—every single time—but when I fought, I did it with broken bones. Forcing myself to move, aligning my bones to make sure they healed properly while I hung here, was the most painful thing I've ever experienced. I won't do it again.

When they lead me in, I let them strip me naked, spread my arms and legs, and tie me to the cold wood. Then I wait for the Dróttning to arrive. For the punishment to begin.

And I wait. And wait. And fucking wait.

Bitch.

But I won't let despair suck me into its inferno this time. I choose anger. Erecting my strongest shields around my thoughts—because I will not let that bitch see any part of me—my mind replays everything the Dróttning has done to this world. Everything she's done to me. It's a never-ending loop that I refuse to stop. My pulse races and my heart pounds out its beat, the blood of my ancestors preparing me for anything she may bring.

Twice, Fhord's betrayal dances into my mind, but I push it away. This is about the Dróttning. She's coming, and I will be ready to spit in her face when she does. She will not see fear or anguish. Only fury. Hate. Resolve.

Guards occasionally traipse in to leer at my nudity. Some even touch me, fondling my breasts and poking their grubby fingers inside me. Laughing at my horror and degradation as I refuse to give them the satisfaction of screams or tears. Skin crawling, my mind occasionally shutting down when the assault goes too far, I deny them any response. I hold my body still because I will not shrink away from their depravity.

And I wait.

Twice, someone other than the Dróttning appears to give me pain. They beat me, leaving dark bruises all along my body and face. But I've suffered pain before. This will heal, and I know it's only the beginning. So I hold on to my malice.

And I wait.

Finally, hours after they strapped me here, my head drooping in a sleep I desperately need already, I feel a pulse of energy moving toward me. It's similar to Fhord's but colder somehow. A winter storm driving forward to destroy everything in its path. If I can feel it, even through the manacle, it must be the Dróttning. Only her power could be so strong.

It won't destroy me.

She won't destroy me.

She's pretty, in a frigid sort of way. I knew she aged slowly—she's been alive a very long time—but I'm still surprised by how young she looks. Perhaps she's like the Vanir and Æsir in my worlds, and will live forever.

Or until I kill her.

I suspect she and I are nearly the same height, but I'm taller than most humans. Her long, straight hair is black as a starless night, a stark contrast to the pale skin it frames. With strong bones and full lips that are painted so dark, they nearly match her hair, she looks like a witch from children's nightmares on Midgard. The red dress she wears hugs the few curves she has in an otherwise stick-thin frame. Only the knives in her belt interrupt the look of blood from neck to toe.

She strolls in, her eyes dancing, and shoves two fingers inside of me, the longer fingernails scraping my walls to pull blood with them when she draws them away. As I'm gasping, struggling to control the agony that erupts in my core, her tongue reaches out to taste my pain, before sucking her fingers into her mouth.

"I've always enjoyed the taste of elf blood," she purrs as she takes a knife from her belt and rests its edge against my bare skin. My flesh puckers where she touches, flinching away despite my resolve to stay still. And then she slices a thin strip of my skin, her gaze holding mine the entire time.

I can't stop the shudder that washes over me. Closing my eyes, sucking in deep breaths as I work through the agony throbbing through me, I cling to the mountain of hate I built while I hung here.

She will not break me. Ever.

"Remove her manacle," she directs one of the guards. Turning to me, her lips lift in a sneer that tries to mimic a smile. "I want to be able to touch your mind while we do this. It's so much more fun when I can taste your pain." She pauses as a man with a rough hand does her bidding, then backs away.

Twisting my neck to stare at the wall instead of her, I hold back the sigh that wants to escape as the blanket lifts from my thoughts. If the Dróttning knew me better—if I'd given in and revealed myself to my captors all those years ago—she'd have kept me bound. She knows I'm strong but not how strong.

"Look at me." The Dróttning's demand echoes through me, persuasion layered through her words. She's trying to control my mind, but I'm more powerful than anyone else I've encountered in Vanatia other than Fhord, perhaps. She won't take this from me.

"Look at me," she repeats, anger entering her tone.

But I hold on. Because she will not control my mind.

"If you don't look at me, I will slice off your tits. Now, before we've even had a chance to talk. I know your body heals itself, but I also know it will be a slow, painful process. I don't have to do that. We may never get there, if you're smarter this time and give me what I want."

I turn my head and show her my anger and defiance. She may compel me with threats, but we both know it's not what she wants. She wants to wield my thoughts. She wants my secret. I refuse to give her that.

"Never." Holding her stare, I let venom fill me, twisting every feature. "I will never give you what you want. You failed before and you will fail now."

"Why?" Curiosity fills this word. I think she's legitimately confused about why I would defy her, deny her access to my thoughts and memories

"You've always chosen yourself over everyone else," I hiss. "You can't understand any other choice because your dominance in this world matters more to you than anything. Or anyone. But I see how small and empty you are. How fucking alone you are. Because you choose yourself."

Pausing, I let her seethe in her anger at my words for a few seconds. And then I spit out the rest.

"My fear, my greatest fear, is that I would become like you. That I would sacrifice others to my own needs or wants. I will never let myself drop so low, become so depraved, as to be anything like you. I will suffer any pain, tolerate any humiliation, before I will give in to your demands."

"Then you shall." She drags her fingernails across the wound that still seeps blood, knives digging in to wrench more agony from me, before lifting them to her lips. A slow smile twists her features as she sucks away little bits of my life. "Bring a chalice of this elf's blood to my room within an hour," she orders, her gaze still holding mine.

Spinning, she strolls away, her words echoing through the chamber along with the staccato of her heels. "Leave the manacle off so I can relish her torment. Every drip that fills my cup must cause her pain. I want her to suffer as you extract her sacrifice. She'll heal quickly, but you're to ensure she bleeds through the night. Do anything you must. Or anything you'd like. Just don't kill her. I'll check back in tomorrow."

My head drops as I prepare for the hours ahead.

They are everything I feared when they threw me in the cell. The pain that began in a single wound, its fire already filling me with an agony that ties up my lungs and fills my stomach with rocks, grows with every slice. Every cut. Every puncture and stab and twist. Every laugh and jeer and grope.

So I go away. The Dróttning will punish them if they kill me. My body will be alive when I return. Right now, at this moment, I need to protect my mind. I need to rebuild the walls inside that helped me get through the agony of their questioning without going mad. It will take time, even though the walls I forged before never fully came down.

My mind casts out, escaping the blades that hope to strip away my soul, as it searches. I don't want to seek him, but I have none of the control I'd found when they held me here before.

That will come in time. Today, my scrambling mind needs its anchor. It needs Fhord.

Tomorrow, I'll build the new barriers I need to protect myself from him.

But he's not here.

After only a couple of weeks, I know his essence better than my own. I've become attuned enough to sense him at the far reaches of the Nest. Even if he was shielding from me, I'd recognize his presence, at least.

He's not here.

Finally, after my desperate mind has searched everywhere it can reach, it leaves the Nest. I can send it a few vikus away and still reel it back to me. That's where I find him—perhaps two vikus from the caves. He's blocked me, of course, as he races south alone on Sigurd. He didn't even wait for Tindera to be released and must have left soon after the Dróttning entered this cavern. As she sliced my flesh away and tasted my blood.

That's what breaks me. Not the punishment I'll face alone, the pain I'll endure at the hands of the Dróttning and her guards. Not the humiliation of being displayed for leches to see and touch. Not even the despair of knowing I probably can't escape this time. They won't make the same mistakes they did before. This is my life until they give up and send me to a prison.

Fhord destroys me, in a way the Dróttning didn't and never could. I saw his face when he betrayed me and the rational side of me knew. He chose his duty, himself, over a chance of saving me. He gave me up because he would suffer for helping an elf.

Anyone would. Survival is the most important instinct in this world.

I still hoped.

I wanted to believe it was an act. That this thing between us was more than lust. It was for me, I know now. I fell for Fhord. I didn't want to. I should have pushed him away. I should have refused Bevin's demand, forced him to choose someone else, even if it meant losing all the progress I'd made. I knew when I saw Fhord that he would threaten everything. And I let myself get close to him anyway.

I wanted to believe he cared about me too. But now I know he didn't. Because if he did, he would have saved me from this fate. This pain.

If Fhord felt the way I do, he would have moved mountains to rescue me.

But he's not fucking here.

SIFA

ENOUGH FOR NOW

T HE MINUTES AND THEN hours flow into each other on the rack.

My mind returns, heartbroken, when I realize Fhord is running away from me. My body is still displayed and tortured. And I hurt so fucking bad. Everywhere I look, my skin is shredded. These guards did exactly what the Dróttning demanded, making sure I would feel each drop of blood they take from me.

The night drags on and I don't leave my body again. I experience all of it. Every slice of a knife. Every puncture where it will cause the most pain. Every scrape on an open wound. It is pain and pain and more pain. Three times, I nearly leave to find an escape in the clouds. To hide from the agony for a time.

Instead, I stay. Because in the clouds, I would only think of *him*. And that pain is even worse.

So I let the physical pain fuel my anger and resolve. I'll need every one of those dark emotions when I'm free. The path in front of me shimmers with the vengeance I'll take against the Dróttning and all who serve her. Every man and woman who acts out her cruel demands. Every person who inflicts pain on another, usually because they take pleasure from it just as the Dróttning does.

Finally, too many hours after they tied me up here, the Dróttning returns. I'm asleep, my body demanding rest even now, when I hear the *click-clack* of her heels strolling toward us. Her presence floats into the room, a wave of ice-cold air preparing the way for her. Then she's here, her face a mask of cold cruelty.

"Well done," she declares as her hands lift into a mocking clap. "She looks exactly as I'd hoped she would." Letting her feet carry her toward me, blood seeping into the hem of her dress as it sweeps across the floor, the Dróttning reaches out a hand and swipes it through a wound her guard just opened. Agony follows her long fingernails as they trigger nerves all along their path. She again lifts her fingers to her lips and tastes my torture. "Almost as sweet as your pain."

"It won't matter, you know," I whisper, the words barely passing through my mutilated throat. "I won't ever give in to you. You'll never get what you want from me."

"Maybe not," she concedes, her lips twisting into a smile of pure malice. "But we'll have fun trying." She lifts a hand to cup my cheek, then turns to the closest guard. "Enough for now. I want flawless, unbroken skin the next time I take my knife to her. Replace the manacle and return her to her cell. When she comes back to me, she'll be bathed and pure."

She spins to stride away, her hips swaying as her dress leaves a trail through my blood.

Flinching away from the hands that wrap around my naked form, I try and fail to hold back the shudder of relief when they release me. My knees clatter to the ground as I collapse, barely holding myself in a kneeling position.

"Up," a stocky, sweaty man barks as he wraps the metal around my throat again. A tremble rolls through me when I feel it stifle my mind, trapping me fully in this body. I hate this sensation, but at least now I don't have to fight to keep my thoughts here. To prevent them from searching for Fhord.

I barely notice the trek back to my cell. Hints of an occasional sharp, stabbing pain break through my stupor as I stumble along the winding corridors, but my mind is dazed, my blood loss too great to stay alert. A wave of relief washes over me as I realize I'm being dragged back to the same little cage. They toss me in, the door clanging behind me, and then I'm gone, my body demanding the sleep it needs to heal.

It's dark when I wake up, a heaviness hovering in the prison, as if the air itself needs light in order to drift around me unencumbered. For just a moment, I'm in the caves adjacent to the Nest, Fhord's comforting presence a few feet away as we hold a needed distance between us. I can hear his steady breathing, almost but not quite mimicking the sleep we both should be chasing. His scent of coriander and cloves fills the space.

Just for a moment.

Too soon, my eyes open and I look around, a chill wafting into every part of me.

I'm in the Nest.

Again.

Forever.

"How are you, Sifa?" Joralf's voice floats toward me, concern layered through each word.

The groan erupts before I can stop it. *How am I?* I have no idea.

Looking down, I can see my wounds are healing. A little blood still seeps out of the worst of them, but very little. The pain pounds through me—every severed or damaged nerve ending reminding me what it suffered—but it's not as overwhelming as when I collapsed. Soon, the pain will give way to an unbearable itch. I'm grateful to not be there quite yet.

"I've been better," I answer with a laugh after a few moments. "I'm alive. So there's that."

"You are alive," Joralf echoes. "For now, that's a good thing."

"It does feel like a blessing right now. I guess when I've been here nearly eight hundred days, it will feel like a curse. And I'll wish for death like you do."

"Perhaps," Joralf concedes. "Or perhaps not. Every elf responds differently to challenges such as these."

"Challenges," I ponder. "That's what this is? A challenge?"

"What else would it be?" Joralf's tone matches my mood—dark and pensive. "The gods have wicked senses of humor. We are their toys. They delight in watching us struggle."

"Do you really believe that?" The gods in my worlds—at least the ones who controlled things—did not savor misery as the gods seem to do here.

Joralf doesn't answer right away. When his words float to me, they hold so much sadness, it almost brings a tear to my eyes. "I can find no other reason for their actions, the games they play with our lives, the pain they relish, drawing it from us in all its varieties and nuances. I've come to conclude the gods grew bored with all the good this world has to offer and found that wickedness, depravity, sorrow, better filled their days. And their nights."

"That's a very depressing outlook." My words barely made it out of my corner of this dungeon. "But I can't deny its truth in this world we call home."

"Most certainly, my dear little elf. Most certainly." Joralf sucks in a deep breath, as if he can draw away all the horror that hovers between us. "Still, we need not wallow in the misery they would hoist upon us. We are elves. We write our own stories, even when others would try to filch our quill."

"And what story should we write today?" I can feel my mood lighten with Joralf's shift. I need the distraction he's offered me. "What's your mate's name?" I ask after a moment.

"That I cannot tell you. The Dróttning cannot know how to find any of us. She has not been able to wring that knowledge from me. And she will not."

"Can you tell me about him? Something that doesn't risk exposing him?"

I can almost feel the smile in Joralf's voice when he responds. "It's been a very long time since I've been asked about him. Thank you." He pauses for a moment and I can hear him shuffle around in his room, as if he's settled in to share his tale. "Shall we call him Bjorn? It's not his name, but it shall do."

"Bjorn's a great name. Full of strength."

"It suits him, I think. He is the strongest elf I've ever known." Joralf is quiet for a long time. When he speaks, his love echoes through every word. "I first saw him across the dining room in an inn just outside the town. He sat with a group of others who shared his trade. He was the center of their conversation, laughing and drawing mirth from all. That's what attracted me to him at first. His laugh. When our eyes met, I felt something shift inside me. I soon learned he did as well."

"Is that how all mating bonds work? You know right away when it exists?" I don't know why I'm so curious, but I am.

"Not all," Joralf tells me. "As I understand it, you both must be ready for a mate, willing to acknowledge the bond. If either mate is resistant, the bond will resist too. But it happens so rarely in this world, I don't know how it might feel for others."

"What happened after you saw each other?"

"I couldn't move," Joralf responds with a deprecatory laugh. "Even if I'd been brave enough to stand and walk across the room, my knees wouldn't have carried me there." He laughs again, a snort of pure joy. "He's the most stunning male I've ever seen. He held everyone around him in the palm of his hand. Yet he somehow belongs to me."

"Bjorn came to you?"

"He didn't say a word to anyone at his table. Just stood, holding my gaze the entire time, and strode toward me. When he extended his hand, I took it. We spent the night in his room, just talking at first. And then we explored each other in different ways." Now Joralf is definitely smiling. I have no idea what he looks like, but I almost can see the wicked grin on his face.

"How long did it take to commit to each other?"

"How long does it take a mother to love her child? A bird to treasure its eggs? The sun to share its light with the world? It was not a choice. It merely was. As he crossed the room to me, I knew I belonged to him. At our first touch, I realized he was mine as well. Bjorn and I did not 'commit' to each other. We simply were, because we always had been. We just didn't know it yet."

Joralf is quiet for a long time after that and I wait for him, letting him enjoy his memories without my interruption. When he speaks, his tone holds hints of sadness, but joy dominates. "I didn't yet live in Revalle, but nothing bound me to my home. Bjorn had a job he couldn't leave. I moved to him. We spent nearly two centuries together. The happiest of my life. And his, I'm sure."

"Can you tell me what he did?"

"What can I share without risking his freedom?" Joralf muses. "Nothing," he says at last. "Revalle, despite its size, is too small. I would risk Bjorn if I told you more."

"Thank you for sharing with me what you did. It's nice to hear a love story."

"Have you no love?"

My traitorous mind pulls up an image of Fhord.

Oh, fuck no.

"Nope," I announce, perhaps a bit too quickly. "I've never been in love."

"Ah." Joralf's response hangs between us, heavy and thick.

"Not 'ah.'" Gods, I wish my voice wasn't so shrill. "There's no 'ah' here," I add in a more measured tone.

"Do you know why the Dróttning imprisons elves?"

I shake my head, surprised by the change in topics. "A bit," I say after a moment.

"What do you know?"

"It has to do with dragons, and the connection between dragons and elves. The Dróttning coveted that kind of bond and found a way to do it. She imprisons the elves so they can't threaten her control of the dragons."

"You understand more than most."

"Which is hardly anything."

"Do you know why elves and dragons bond so readily?"

"I don't." Pondering his question for a few seconds, I add, "I've never thought about it."

"It's because we have mates. The ties between dragons and riders are much like mating bonds."

"And you're telling me this, why?"

"I don't know who you love," Joralf tells me in a voice full of emotion, "or whether that person is your mate. And I don't know why you're denying your love. But I do know that things in this world rarely are simple. Dragons sometimes are forced to kill the riders the fates intend for them so the Dróttning may bind them to another. Because she controls all they do."

Joralf pauses, perhaps choosing his next words carefully. "Things are not always as they seem in this place. The Dróttning's command skews everything. Even the ties the fates intend. Do not dismiss your love so readily. It's a rare gift that few may experience in this cruel place."

My silly heart responds to his words, a glimmer of desire spiraling from deep in my gut to fill me, for a moment, with hope. But I'd be a fool to wish for anything from Fhord. I know where his allegiance lies. It's not with me.

"How does she do it?" I ask, eager for a change of subjects. "Control the dragons, I mean."

Joralf's laugh floats through the cold air. "I saw my dragon once," he tells me. "From a distance, but we both knew. It was so much like when I met Bjorn, it couldn't be anything but the bond the fates intended."

"But you're still alive. Obviously," I add with a smirk at myself.

"I heard her surprise when she saw me. It washed through me, coated in love. All dragons know, though, what happens when they are called to someone other than the Dróttning's choice. And she is a very smart creature," he adds with so much delight, it nearly brings a tear to my eye. "She blinked her eyes once. And then she swung her head toward her rider, letting him feel the wash of emotion. She never looked at me again."

"What did she look like?"

"The moon," Joralf responds, his voice bright and simmering with adoration. "She is silver and black. Small but mighty. I wish I could know her better."

"I wish that for you as well. In a different world, a different life, perhaps."

"Or perhaps in this one. The Dróttning's control is not absolute. Even in this hole, I have learned of the brave dragon who defies her. The one who refuses to accept the rider chosen for him."

Pride rushes in, washing over me as I think about *my* dragon. Brave, determined Astarot. I wish I could see him again. "What could one dragon do? Even if he withstood her torture and survived somehow?"

"The Dróttning realized during the war with the elves that the dragons' links to this world are tenuous. That they can be severed under the right circumstances."

"The disappearance of the dragons and elves during the battle with the Far North?"

"Again, you know more than most. You are an enigma, Sifa."

"I learned a lot on the trip that brought me here," I explain dismissively.

"I should not know that story," Joralf continues. "But I am descended from the elf who returned to this world. His secrets live within me."

My stomach tightens and then expands as a hint of hope fills me. Perhaps the fates do have me in their hands.

"You know of the world he traveled to? Of the jötnar he discovered?"

"I do. But that is not why I tell you this." He pauses, breathing in deeply once, and then again. "I've only found hints of the source of the Dróttning's power over the dragons. I've wondered if it grows from an overwhelming fear the dragons hold that she can end their lives by cutting their links to this world. My grandfather's dragon did not join him in the other world he discovered. He did not survive the journey from this one."

"You think there's some portal or path that elves can traverse but dragons can't?"

"I'm certain of it. I also know something in this world—perhaps some substance—is the reason. Control of that would destroy her stranglehold on the dragons."

"Because the dragons need it?"

"Exactly," Joralf exclaims, a hint of pride in the word.

"What could possibly give the Dróttning such power?"

"That I cannot tell you," Joralf tells me with a laugh. "The Dróttning suspects we've discovered her secret. She's desperate to learn what we know. I have no doubt I'm still here, instead of in an elven prison, for that reason. She may be listening now, hoping I give you information I've never given her. Or the walls could have ears. I can't risk her hearing anything I may say to you."

"But you, maybe others, think you know what it is?"

"We do. We've yet to learn exactly where it rests, but we will. And when that time comes, we'll bring the Dróttning's tyranny to an end. We'll restore this world to what it once was. When elves roamed free and dragons chose their mates."

We both sit in silence after that. I'm too caught up in my own thoughts and hopes to speak further. It feels like an impossible dream, but I've lived long enough to know that all things are possible. Maybe this is, too.

CHAPTER TWENTY-SIX

FHORD

NOW, SHE'S EVERYTHING

THEY HAVEN'T RELEASED TINDERA yet—the Dróttning is probably using her to control me again—so I have no choice. Sigurd and I left without my dragon the morning after the Dróttning dismissed me.

Sifa will be okay, I assure myself as we race away from the Nest. The Dróttning told me she doesn't plan to torture her right away. She doesn't know about Sifa and me, has no reason to lie about something like this.

I wish I could cast out my thoughts to find my rabbit—make sure she's not suffering. But if I let down my shield to search for her, the Dróttning would have a path into my mind. I can't risk that. I have to trust that the Dróttning told me the truth. That she doesn't plan to torture Sifa right away.

Still, it kills me. My mind keeps dredging up the agony I felt when Sifa first entered this world. Before I knew her. When I could ignore her pain because she meant nothing to me.

Now, she's everything. My commitment to the Ætt, even my bond with Tindera, feel empty next to the mating bond with my little rabbit. Much as I love them—much as I resisted this—I love Sifa more. I *need* her more. And I will risk everything to save her.

I hope it doesn't come to that. That I don't expose Tindera and the Ætt to the Dróttning's wrath with this decision. But I know now that I have no choice. I must free Sifa. I won't be able to live with myself if she's sent to a prison where I'll never be able to reach her. Or, just as likely, if the Dróttning kills her. I'll follow her to Helheim if that's my only option.

So Sigurd and I are headed south. We'll find Astarot first and do what we must to save him. I'm desperately hoping he can protect himself, even attack, if I free him. His wound was severe, but he also isn't in the Nest, where the Dróttning controls even the rate at which a dragon heals. His body can recover as all dragon bodies do from an injury. As quickly as me, or a god or elf.

Then we'll return to Revalle and get help. Not the Ætt yet. They don't have the skills I'll need for this escape attempt. Leif can set some things up—make sure we have a refuge when I free Sifa—without exposing himself to risk. The others will just stay away. Go into hiding. If I can keep them at a distance, they may not suffer if we fail. I might be able to protect them.

Instead, I'll find Sifa's troll. He could make a difference.

I'm not sure what it will take to convince him to trust me, but I'm sure as fuck gonna try.

As far as I can tell, Astarot hasn't moved yet, but he's nearly ready. He should be healed enough by now to walk. Hopefully fly.

If not, we're all fucked.

I recognize Astarot and seven guards when I'm a viku or so away. More than I'd hoped—they've added a few since I left the dragon—but I'll have the element of surprise. I wish I could free my savage. They wouldn't stand a chance. But she'd hear my shift, recognize this attack as mine. I can't let that happen.

Slowing Sigurd, I swing off, stretching out my senses around me, searching. The scents of the forest greet me, mildewed plants and moss mixing with fresher leaves and the sap of trees to create a familiar earthy, musty fragrance. Birds swoop and cry overhead, some beckoning and others warning in their shrill notes. In the distance, I can hear the yips and cries of a pack of wolves, the adults watching over and playing with their pups.

And the soldiers. They're brash and arrogant, assured of their safety in these woods. Because none but Sifa would defy the Dróttning, and she's trapped far away. They're cruel, too. I can sense their delight at Astarot's pain. His suffering. They have no idea what they'll soon face.

Strengthening my shield, I creep toward the group, not letting any hint of my presence reach them. When I get close enough to attack, I pause. With this many, I'll need them distracted or unfocused when I emerge, or I'll risk getting hurt. One of them could get in a lucky shot. Fortunately, I'm gods-damned good at providing distractions. Not as good as

Sifa—I've never been able to plant false memories into minds the way she does—but I can stir up emotions and create conflict.

Holding my shield in place, I spear out with a portion of my mind. Just enough to touch a few minds without revealing myself. I'm searching for the weakest one—the angry idiot who perpetually carries the kindling of conflict, ready to explode from the smallest flame.

My mind brushes three of the males, caressing their thoughts as it searches for what I need. They are just as depraved as I'd expected, chosen because they won't shrink from the need to cause this dragon pain if necessary. Even from this little contact, I know how much they savor that part of their job. But they're not as unstable as I need them to be.

The next mind I touch, the only woman, gives me what I want. She's not an idiot, but she's fighting to control emotions that seem to have a life of their own, desperate to lash out at the others. It's not just her anger I can exploit—although there's plenty of that—but also her need for revenge. I can't read her thoughts but the sharp edges of her feelings tell me everything I need to know. One of the men in this group attacked her. Probably on this trip. And she either didn't report it, or she did and her complaint was ignored.

Her wound is open and festering. It wraps around her, placing every nerve on edge. Waiting to erupt.

I can give her the vengeance she needs. And then maybe I could even avoid killing her. She wants an escape from this life.

I take another breath, gathering my thoughts, and then reach out with my mind. Focusing just on her, I let myself recall all the times the Dróttning and her drudges have harmed Tindera or one of the Ætt to get back at me. Her attacks never are direct, because she knows I've felt pain before and would weather it again without complaint. Instead, she aims her ire at the places where it truly hurts. Those I love.

Anger, wrath, and bitterness engulf me before flowing into the woman. Not all at once. She would suspect my intervention if I did that. Instead, I let it seep into her, helping to draw up the memories of the attack. When her gaze lifts, anger in her eyes as they rest on him, I open the path between us a bit wider. Then I add more.

This time, my thoughts take me to Sifa and the morning of our attack. I'm still furious at myself for letting those males bind me. I'd been so preoccupied with thoughts of her—how it felt waking up in the same tent, how fucking hard my cock had been just because of her scent—I hadn't even noticed them creeping up. They'd caught me on the edge of release, all my thoughts on my rabbit and what I wanted to do to her. I was hog-tied and helpless being dragged back to the camp almost before my dick went limp.

I'd been so fucking angry. At myself, but even more, at them. What they planned to do to Sifa. If they'd actually threatened her, I'd have used my magic no matter the cost. But she didn't need my help. She's so fucking smart, stronger than any female I've ever known.

Now, I feed my rage into the soldier, a steady trickle of hate and horror. And I wait and watch.

"I still can't fucking believe you let him get away with it," the woman spits out as she turns toward a different man, probably the commander. "I told you what he did to me. But there he sits."

"None of us gives a fuck, Gertha," he responds with a shrug. "Take it up with his drott when we get back to the Nest." Turning, he throws a little smile at the attacker. "We've all thought about taking what you've been offering since you joined this squad. He's the only one with the balls to do something about it."

Gertha's face falls for a moment, pain and disappointment dragging everything down. I hope I can save her, I realize as she responds exactly as I need from one of them. Drawing a knife from her belt, she throws herself at the man who forced himself on her.

He takes the choice from me. Quicker than I would have expected, his blade is at Gertha's throat. When she doesn't back down, twisting as her knife lunges toward his heart, he swipes his dagger across her throat and tosses her to the ground.

"Ungrateful bitch," he snarls as he kicks at her.

Fuck. He's dying tonight. I just wish I had time to give him the slow death he deserves.

My sword slides from its sheath as I toss myself into the furor I ignited.

Three guards fall quickly, their collapse easier than I'd hoped. But the fourth, the man who attacked Gertha, is a fighter. He's joined by the other two who still live, and they push me to my limits. I'm barely avoiding the swipes of their swords and jabs of their blades. Twice, I don't, my skin flaying open as I let them get too close. Close enough to kill me.

I'll be gods-damned before I let these drudges best me. On my worst day, I'm better than them.

Swinging, I take the head from one of them, barely noticing as it drops a few feet away and rolls toward Astarot. The others pause a moment, aware for the first time they're in trouble. I can see the fear in their eyes as they glance at their headless comrade and then back at me.

They don't delay long. This attack seems coordinated, and I realize they've fought together before. They're both too fuck-ing good to be stuck with dragon guarding duty. But it's As-tarot. The Dróttning doesn't want to chance losing him again.

This fight lasts longer than it should, and they manage to cut me open three more times. They're little slashes, nothing life-threatening, but they're annoying as fuck. One's on my sword hand and it makes it gods-damned hard to hold on to the blade that's getting slicker and slicker with each pulse of my blood.

Finally, the man who attacked Gertha falters, his foot slip-ping on the gunk we're splashing through. His sword arm lifts a bit as he tries to find his balance, and I shove my blade into him. I watch as his eyes grow wide and then all the light leaves them. I must have struck his heart. Good. Fucker.

The final soldier doesn't give up, but he's got no hope. Maybe he had a shot with the help of the others. Not now. It only takes a few seconds to disarm him and take his head from his neck.

Sucking in a deep breath, I look down at myself. I'm fucking filthy. I need to clean myself off before I even consider riding Astarot. I won't sully Sifa's dragon with the blood of these worthless creatures. That is, if he's strong enough to carry a rider.

And then I look up at the dragon I've saved. Again. His eyes are solemn as he watches me. We'll be able to communicate a bit—his bond with Tindera gives us a shallow connection—but he hasn't chosen to speak with me yet. Maybe he's as angry as Sifa. I wouldn't blame him if he were.

Mate? he says at last. I'm not sure whose mate he's asking about. Whether he knows Sifa is mine as well as his.

"Your draikana?" I ask, holding my position for now. I'll release him soon. First, I want to make sure we understand each other. That he won't turn on me for what I did to Sifa.

Yours, he tells me. He knows, which means ...

"Did you tell Sifa that she's my mate?"

No. He must have heard it from Tindera and, for whatever reason, hadn't yet shared it with Sifa.

Smart dragon.

"Sifa's okay," I assure him. "The Dróttning doesn't plan to torture her right away."

Astarot's eyes narrow as a puff of flame bursts from his nostrils. *Liar.*

"I know we can't trust the Dróttning," I concede, "but I think she told the truth about this. It made sense, what she planned."

Liar, Astarot insists, the fire erupting from his mouth this time too.

My stomach plummets to the ground as I watch Sifa's dragon. "She started?" My mind fills with memories of Sifa's pain from years ago. Of the torture I've seen—and inflicted—in those caves. Astarot's word settles into my gut, a chunk of ice ready to shatter and take me with it. "But she told me she wouldn't." My words come out as a hoarse whisper as guilt starts to consume me.

Liar, Astarot repeats, this time with disdain.

He's angry at me for believing her. And he's gods-damned right to be.

What the fuck have I done? A chill creeps up my spine, stretching through me to drag a numbness all the way to my fingers and toes. I was so eager to accept the Dróttning's assurances, so anxious to believe Sifa wouldn't be harmed, I took her word at face value. But I should fucking know better.

"Is she okay?" My voice nearly breaks on the last word.

Pain. Astarot's bond to Sifa is strong enough to feel her pain, even this far away. He's experienced everything she did.

"Is she still on the rack?" I don't know if I want to hear his answer.

No.

My chin drops as my thoughts skitter through the options. The idea of exposing Sifa to more torment kills me. It's all I can do to keep myself from freeing Astarot and then mounting Sigurd to race back to the Nest. Which would do no fucking good. I can't help her alone. I know that.

I realize now what Astarot was asking. Not whether Sifa's okay. He knows better than me what she's going through—what the Dróttning did to her and will do again. Astarot needs to know what the fuck I'm gonna do about it. How I'm going to free his rider.

First things first. "I have a plan for Sifa," I assure him, taking a step forward. "Right now, though, I'm going to release you. Okay?"

Astarot's eyes blink, and he watches my approach. I start with the stake that holds him to the ground, trapped in the same agonizing position as when we freed him from the trainer. The soldiers had kept him bound like this the entire time, I realize with a lurch in my stomach. I can't imagine the pain he's endured, just with this torture device.

A deep groan escapes the dragon when I pull out the rod, giving him some freedom to move and release the pressure on his wings. I can almost feel his relief as I remove the harness and, at last, the metal contraption that keeps his wings bound to his sides. When he's free, he stands on legs that tremble and shakes himself, crimson and black feathers finding the wind he creates.

His snout spins and nudges me, a gentle thanks. "You're welcome," I tell him as my hand reaches out to rub his nose, and then the space behind his horn that Tindera always loves.

"I'm not sure what to do here," I tell him as I scratch. "I don't want to leave Sifa there—I can't stand the idea of her suffering—but I need help if I'm going to free her. I can't do it alone."

Astarot watches me, his eyes unblinking. He's waiting for me to explain what I have in mind.

"Sifa's best friend is a troll," I tell him, my voice still warbling with guilt. "I think he can help us. My plan was to get you, then go to Revalle and convince him to join us. We might not be able to get her free, but it's our best hope." I pause, Sifa's pain as we chase help filtering through my thoughts. "We'd have to leave her there a few more days. And she'll suffer if the Dróttning starts to torture her again."

Again, Astarot watches me without speaking. I have no idea what he's thinking. Whether he trusts me despite what I did to Sifa. I doubt he and Tindera have spoken and risked the Dróttning learning about their mating bond. All he knows is what he saw, the hurt and anger Sifa felt when I betrayed her. Or appeared to.

Troll, he says at last.

I suck in a breath, grateful to have the decision taken from me. He's right, I know. But the savage in me would have ridden Astarot back to the Nest and killed everyone we found if the dragon had suggested it. Even though I know we'd have died—or worse—and Sifa would still be trapped.

My savage is a gods-damned idiot sometimes.

Thank fuck Astarot's more rational than I am right now.

"Can you fly?"

Astarot's eyes never leave mine as he stands—steadier this time—and spreads his wings. They're glorious, the sun reflecting off them to cast scarlet and ruby and hints of cherry into the air around us. For a moment, my mind draws up an image of Tindera and I can almost see them flying together in the sky above.

Yes, Astarot tells me at last. He can get us to Revalle.

"I'll leave Sigurd here and send someone for him," I tell Astarot. "It would be too much for you to carry him. We'll go high, so nobody can see us. We should be able to reach Revalle in a day and a half, maybe two, resting for a few hours tonight. When we get there, we'll stop in a field a few vikus north of town. There's a cave there you can hide in. I'll get a message to my people. Then I'll get the troll and meet you back there."

Astarot's chin drops, his agreement with my plan. It's half-assed, but it's as good as I've got. He's trusting me to get Sifa out without tossing Tindera into the Dróttning's clutches.

I have no idea if I can do it. But I'm sure as fuck gonna try.

CHAPTER TWENTY-SEVEN

SIFA

IT'S NOT TIME YET

I T MAKES ABSOLUTELY NO sense—because I'm in a hopeless situation—but for some reason, I have hope. Hope that I can survive and even get home.

I'm not sure if I would go, though. If Joralf's right and dragons can't pass through whatever portal between worlds brought me here, I'd have to leave Astarot behind. I don't think I can do that. Even if it means I'll age and die as a human would in this world.

And then there's Fhord. Whatever he is to me. I don't want to think about him.

I could find a way to send Toffer home. He doesn't have to stay here just because I may choose to.

Of course, none of this matters if I can't get out of here. Which seems impossible.

Five days pass while I wait for the guards to come back and get me. My wounds have closed, but they're still pink and angry, not healed enough to give the Dróttning the unblemished skin she demands for some reason. I should have another day, perhaps more, before she takes her knife to me.

So I'm surprised when the guards show up early one morning and open my cell, the shrill squeal of little-used hinges waking me from a restless sleep.

"Stand." The demand echoes around me as I roll over and look at the four guards she's sent this time. My bones ache with the effort, days of sleeping on concrete amplifying the agony of the Dróttning's abuse.

"It's not time yet," I whisper, dread coiling in my stomach. "The Dróttning wants unblemished skin." The cold around me seeps deeper into my joints, triggering nerves up and down my spine that had calmed for a time. I've barely moved and I'm already miserable.

"We're not gonna play with you yet," the guard insists, his gaze turning toward Joralf's cell. And then his door is screeching as another guard's voice, low and menacing, floats toward me. "We'll see how you like his punishment."

Fuck. Images of Toffer rise in my thoughts. I'd come to hate his torture more than my own. Once we became friends—when our friendship turned into love—they started using us against each other. That's why they put us close enough to talk. Captives form strong bonds, and they used everything they could to pressure us to comply.

"I don't give a fuck what you do to him," I declare, disdain in my voice as I hear Joralf stumble to his feet. "You're just wasting your time."

"Lucky for you we have nothing else to do." His eyes narrow, and he takes a step into the cell. "I'm not allowed to mar your skin, but I have many other ways to hurt you. Stand up. Now."

I bite back the groan that threatens to flow from my gut into my throat. Joralf stumbles toward the guards waiting outside my cell, his gaze meeting mine. He's as broken down as I'd expected, but his back is straight, even after so many months of torture. He'd stand a full head taller than me, and hints of blonde hair lie hidden beneath the grunge and dirt that covers every part of him. With a narrow face, wide eyes and full lips, I can see the beautiful and alluring elf his mate fell in love with. It's the color of his eyes, though, that draws me in. This place hasn't dimmed their light. They're as blue as the sea, warm and bright. Despite everything, they're smiling at me.

I nod as the corners of my lips lift, just a touch. We had more of a reprieve than I'd hoped. The first time I was here, every day brought new and different pain.

Joralf and I have been through this before. We'll survive today too.

We trudge toward the dungeon, our steps as slow as the guards will allow. I'm shoved twice, nearly toppling to the ground, with a snide remark about my pace. I can't bring myself to go faster, though. I cling to every second of delay like it's a lifeline.

Too soon, we step into the cavern I dread. My eyes grow wide as I glance around to find another rack facing the original. They are a dozen feet apart, giving both of us a clear view of the other. They didn't do this when Toffer and I were here.

Then, one of us just curled into a ball as far away as possible, trembling as we watched the other suffer, helpless to do anything to stop it. The guards soon forgot about us in their glee at finding new and different ways to cause pain to whoever was being tormented that day.

The Dróttning's torture has grown more sophisticated. Lucky us.

They bind Joralf to the rack that's absorbed so much blood it's turned crimson. Unbidden, a shiver rumbles through me, my mind dragging up the feel of the wood on my bare skin. The dread that always settles in me when I'm stretched across its planks, deep and cold, finds its place again in my gut. My bones feel like ice that will never melt, holding me perpetually in a Helheim that's somehow achingly frigid.

Like me, Joralf doesn't fight the ropes that twist around his wrists and ankles, securing him in place.

And then I'm shackled across from him, his face all I let myself see. As I did with Toffer when he suffered, my eyes hold Joralf's, mirroring his agony in my expression, never shrinking away from his pain. I make sure he knows I'm here with him, every step of the way.

"This one's my favorite," one of the men proclaims, his knife shaving off one of Joralf's nipples and tossing it to the side.

My friend's face twists as he fights to hold in the scream. I watch, impotent, as his body shudders through the anguish. For ten seconds, maybe more, he holds his breath, struggling to control his reaction. And then he smiles.

"Yup," the guard says, a self-satisfied grin turning his face even more grotesque. "This is why I like this elf. It's been, what"—he looks up at another guard—"five months since I made him scream. It's a challenge. And I love a good challenge."

The blade rips up from its place near Joralf's groin, removing skin all along the path to Joralf's other nipple, which is tossed aside too. Again, Joralf seems to battle the *need* to scream and cry and rage, every part of him shaking as if a gust of wind rushed into this room to dance around and with him. His eyes close and he sucks in a breath, and then another. A cruel smile follows as he lifts his lids and glares at his tormentor.

The abuse continues for what must be hours, although I have no way to judge the passage of time so deep in Vanatia's bowels. Twice, I let my gaze drop from Joralf's as his face reflects the torment they're inflicting and he glances down at his maimed body. I can't see a bit of skin, the blood and gore so thick it seems impossible that Joralf is the only source. When he looks up, I do the same. And I hold him the only way I can.

I'm numb, and I'm sure Joralf is too. We've both learned this lesson. Every emotion, save one, is dangerous. We can allow ourselves rage alone here. But that takes energy that drips from open wounds, red and black. The only thing to do at this point is shut down. Endure the pain. Wait.

Occasionally, the guard laughs, a wicked gurgle that erupts from his belly devoid of any joy. Hate drives him. "I fucking love this," he bellows as he looks around the room, smirking at each of the guards in turn before he glances back at Joralf.

Spinning to face me, he adds in a low voice, "You're next. But I'll be tasting those nipples—and the rest of you—before I take them as trophies. You're as sweet as they come."

"Fuck. You." The anger that pours out of me is cleansing. I grasp onto it like a life raft, clinging to the knowledge that he and the rest of them will deserve every ounce of pain I can inflict. And then I spit, a measly amount of saliva all I can muster, but enough to reach him.

His finger rises to his cheek. He wipes off the spittle and then, with a leer, licks it clean. "Like I said. Fucking tasty. I can't wait until the Dróttning gives you back to me."

"But wait you will," she says as she strides into the cavern. The guard backs away from us, and I spin my head, my thoughts scattering as I realize I didn't even hear her approach. Glancing around, I can see that nobody else did either. They're surprised, but they've experienced this before. She has some way to conceal the sound of the heels that now click-clack across the stone. She's a snake, hiding when she wants to better attack her prey.

She stops just in front of Joralf, her hand lifting to drag a sharp nail around the mess of tissue that used to surround his belly button. "Such good work," she purrs with a nod toward the guard. "He'll feel your torment for days." She straightens, licking the blood off her finger. "Take his cock next, then return him to his cell," she demands in a dismissive tone, her hand waving as if Joralf's presence offends her.

"No." The word escapes before I can stop it. A tremor rolling through me, I straighten my spine and say it again. "No. It's my turn. Just send him back to his cell."

"Not yet, elf," the Dróttning responds in a cold whisper. "We have much to do before you'll be ready to share your secrets with me. You and I will have fun while we prepare." Her hand snakes out to rub along my bare skin, skimming my thigh before lifting up to graze my stomach and ribs, landing on the swell of a breast. "So much fun," she adds as her thumb caresses my nipple.

Revulsion ripples through me, my flesh crawling, desperate to escape her touch.

"Not yet, though," she repeats, taking a step back. "Her skin is nearly ready. It must be clear, none of this pink remaining." She lifts her arm, waving at me with a little grimace. "I don't like to work with blemished skin."

"We won't touch her," one of the women declares, her voice firm. "She'll be ready for you."

"Good. After you return the male to his cell, bring this one to my rooms." Turning, she strides away, the sound of her steps echoing through the room as she goes. Before she walks out, she pauses and spins, her gaze meeting mine. "I'll tell her what she can expect," she adds before giving us her back and strutting out the door.

Silence hangs around us for a moment, broken by the lead guard's laugh. "My favorite part," he sneers, lifting his blade as he stalks toward Joralf.

This time, Joralf can't hold in his scream. As the knife slices through the tissue and muscle hanging between his legs, his lips split and he emits the most anguished sound I've ever heard. He pants through the agony, his eyelids tight as he struggles to find his control. Finally, a minute or more after the guard attacked him, his breathing slows. And he smiles.

"It always grows back bigger," he gasps out, his eyes hard as they focus on the man who's caused both of us so much pain. "When I take yours, it won't grow back. And mark my words. I will carve your cock from you and shove it directly into your gut before I leave this world. You will know every bit of the pain you've given me."

"Yeah, yeah, yeah," the guard responds, flicking Joralf's penis toward the rest of the skin and tissue he's stripped off while we've been in here. "Big fucking words from an elf who'll never be free again." He rubs his hand on his grimy pants. "Take them where the Dróttning wants," he directs as he strides out of the cavern.

I can only watch as they free Joralf, their hands causing even more pain everywhere they touch. He collapses, sucking in breath until someone kicks him. "Stand up. We ain't gonna carry you back to your cell."

"I'll stand when I'm ready." Joralf's voice is firmer and more controlled than mine would be. He waits a few more seconds before lifting himself to his feet. "Be strong, Sifa," he murmurs before turning to walk away, his back straight and shoulders pushed back.

A male and a female remain, waiting by the entrance for someone to return to take me to the Dróttning's rooms. I desperately want to let my mind wander—to search for Fhord, much as I hate to admit it to myself—but I can't. Even if I weren't wearing the manacle, the Dróttning could exploit any opening in the shield I'd create around my mind. I can only keep her out if I hold an impenetrable barrier whenever she's around.

They finally come to retrieve me, laughing as I drop to my knees after so many hours stretched out on the rack. I want nothing more than to pause on the floor, let my body rest even for a minute. But before I'm ready, a hand grasps my hair to pull me to my feet.

"We can't keep the Dróttning waiting," a guard snarls in my ear as he pushes me forward.

They don't give me clothes, but I hadn't expected they would. This place stripped me of the shame of a naked body a decade ago. I lift my chin and take a deep breath before I stride into the caves. Anger swirls through me as leers and taunts follow me down the hall, but I refuse to let myself care. The disgrace they should bear for being part of this is so much greater than any I've ever known.

I'm surprised when we reach a door that must belong to the Dróttning. For some reason, I hadn't thought they'd really bring me here, despite her command. I spent weeks in this place last time and never saw her, barely felt her presence. She's apparently decided to take a special interest in me now.

The guard swings open the door, and I struggle to hide my disgust. The Dróttning wears the only color in the room, a robe as red as the blood she craves. Gray and black furniture is scattered throughout to create different sitting areas, but it all looks uncomfortable. Her rooms are as sterile and cold as her, weapons adorning the walls but nothing else. My gaze lands with surprise on shackles I wore when I came from Midgard. I'd nearly forgotten about them—although I'll never forget which bones my captors broke to squeeze my hands through the cuffs they couldn't unlock.

"Leave us," she commands the guard who shoves me into the room. Her head cocks to the side as she looks at me, a puzzle she's never been able to solve. "Sit," she says after a moment, waving her hand at a couch in the center of the room.

I return her gaze, examining her as she just did me. And then I smile and stroll toward her, plopping down on the cushion. The material feels like burlap, rough and dry against my bare skin. I glance around and my smile grows more broad as I realize she's placed me on the only piece of furniture covered with such an uncomfortable material. She's petty and cruel even in the little things.

"Why am I here?"

The corners of her lips lift in a curious sneer. My heart beats a dozen times before she responds, while I focus on keeping my hands still. I won't let them shake in her presence.

"We didn't meet when you were here before," she reminds me at last.

"We did not."

"Do you know why I kept you here? Instead of sending you to one of the camps that holds your kind?"

"Camps? Is that what you call the prisons?"

Her expression shifts to frustration for a moment, a flicker of anger rising before she smothers it. "Answer me."

I watch her in silence, wondering why a simple question would draw such ire. When she seems like she's ready to ask again—or perhaps strike me—I respond. "I have no idea."

"Let's have no lies between us," she snarls. "We both know you've been hiding something—or someone—since you landed in this world. I need to know where I'll find it. Or her."

The fear that trickles down my spine doesn't surprise me. I hope she can't hear my heart, which is growing frantic in my chest. For ten years, I've barely let myself even think about this secret. I may have been the one who broke out of this prison, but I've become convinced that something about her brought us here from our worlds, then carried her away from the Nest before the Dróttning could find and imprison her. If I'm right, she'll be key to us returning when I find the path.

Nobody knows. Not even Toffer. It's why I won't let myself break now. The Dróttning can't have her.

"I don't know what you're talking about," I declare, my voice as steady as I can make it.

The Dróttning shakes her head, adopting an expression that's supposed to look like disappointment but doesn't hide the anger in her eyes. "I already know more than you think," she says, her voice growing low. "If you want to save her life—yes, I know it's a girl," she adds as she sees the reaction

I can't hide—"you'll tell me where you've hidden her. Don't make me take it from you."

A knock interrupts whatever she's about to say. Smiling again, she turns toward the door. "Come."

And then Fhord walks in, a sneer on his perfect lips. My breath catches in my throat, my chest expanding as my body responds on its own to his presence. He's so achingly beautiful. I can't believe I thought for a moment he might be mine.

He turns his eyes directly toward me. I see something that looks like alarm or fear in them before he shutters that emotion. A leer emerges, his eyes softening as he looks over my naked body, pausing at my breasts and the tips of my thighs, then roving back up. Slowly.

And of course, my gods-damned nipples stand to alert like Fhord's their fucking commander calling them to salute. My center grows hot, the flames spilling out in a wash of desire as Fhord fucks me with his eyes. Even here in one of the coldest rooms in these caves, my body responds to Fhord with a heat I've never felt before.

His gaze moves back to my nipples, still poking out like they're saying "hello" to him, and stays there. "I'm happy to see you too, little elf," he growls at me. His hand reaches down to caress his groin, which has bulged out of his pants in the few seconds since he saw me. "I'd hoped to be the one to remove your clothes the first time I saw you naked, but this'll do. I'll make sure we're alone next time."

"Fuck. You." I spit out the words, struggling to stop the tremble threatening to consume me.

"Soon," Fhord responds with a wink. Turning toward the Dróttning, he gestures at me, one eyebrow quirking up. "What is this?" he asks in a voice that holds curiosity but nothing else.

"A gift," she purrs. "I heard you were interested in her. I thought you might like to finish what you started in the forest when you should have been capturing the dragon."

He nods, grinning like the shit-eating bastard he is, and looks back at me. "A generous gift, indeed. To what do I owe this ... pleasure?"

"Consider it a gesture of my goodwill. You may do with her what you want. When she's returned, I expect her skin to look like this. As you know, I do not like to play with scarred skin."

"I thank you," Fhord declares as he drops into a deep bow. "I'll have fun with her." He spins toward the door, striding over to call in a guard before stalking toward me. "Take her back to her cell. Give her clothes and food and leave her alone. Let it be known she's mine. Nobody else may see—or touch—what belongs to me."

His hand reaches out to caress my cheek and despair flares inside me, only to be pushed out by humiliation. Fighting back tears as my throat constricts, I let myself glance at him, see the firm set of his jaw, his flat, empty eyes, and a cruel smirk. But the pain of his betrayal lasts just a moment. Anger takes its place, dragging me back to my time in the caves when I wanted nothing more than vengeance. With quivering muscles and a heartbeat that's poised to fight, I lift my hand and smack his away.

Fhord smiles and stretches out his arm, beckoning me toward the guard.

"Go, little elf," Fhord whispers when I don't move. "Before I carry you back to the cell myself. Or maybe you'd like my arms wrapped around your naked body."

The room blurs as reality sinks in. The shame I felt before is nothing compared to what I'll feel in Fhord's hold, knowing I'm just a toy for him to play with. Even though I'd wanted to be so much more to him.

But I won't let Fhord see me cry. Standing, I stride out the door. Somehow, I hold back the tears through the caverns and corridors we follow back to the prison. Only when I'm in my cell, dressed and huddling in a corner, do I release the firm grip I've held on my emotions.

And I grieve.

Chapter Twenty-Eight

Sifa

Who Are You, Fhord?

"**S**ifa, wake up."

It's just his voice, I realize as I lay there on the concrete facing the wall. He hasn't touched me. He probably knows I'd take his hand off if I could.

Memories bounce through my thoughts. Joralf being tortured in front of me. All the blood and pain and hatred while I just hung there, helpless. Watching his agony.

The Dróttning appearing and ordering the guards to trot me through the caverns, naked, to her rooms, where she confirmed she knows my secret. She may not know everything—I don't think she has any idea where to find what I've spent years trying to hide—but it's enough to terrify me.

Fhord, appearing in her gods-damned rooms, like he's a regular visitor. Eye-fucking me while my traitorous body responds to his leer. Then him accepting the *gift* from the Dróttning—the chance to rape me at his leisure for as long as he wants. Somehow, that's the worst part. I'll be his plaything, and there's nothing I can do about it.

"We need to talk, and we don't have much time. Please wake up, my little rabbit." He's whispering—probably afraid Joralf will hear him—but a hint of desperation warbles in his voice.

"Don't call me that. Ever." I don't move. I don't want to see him. I also don't whisper because I trust Joralf more than Fhord. But I do respond. I need him to know he's nothing to me. And he never will be.

"I'm sorry. I know you don't believe me. But I promise you, I only did what I thought I had to for you to survive." Fhord's still speaking barely loud enough for me to hear him.

"Then you left me here in this prison. And she tortured me."

"She told me she wasn't going to hurt you. Not yet. I thought I had time. I believed her and it's killing me how badly I fucked up. That I let her hurt you."

Those are the words that drag me up. I want to look him in the eye when he lies to me. So I sit—every part of me aching from the long hours of hanging on the rack yesterday—and turn toward him. "You believed her? Why the fuck would you believe the Dróttning?"

"I can usually tell when she's lying. And she doesn't lie to me often."

"What is she to you?" I pause, my eyes searching his. "Who are you, Fhord?"

"I'll tell you. I promise. Right now, though, we don't have time."

My responding laugh is bitter. Angry. "Look around, Fhord," I snarl, waving my arm at my little hole. "I have all the time in the world."

"The guards are changing, Sifa. The next one will be here soon. I'm sure the Dróttning has them watching us, listening to what we say. She doesn't trust me yet to be alone with you. We need to talk before he gets here."

I hold his gaze for a long time, too tired, too defeated, to spin away from him again. But I make sure he sees my pain. My anger. My hatred. Because he betrayed me, again and again.

Fhord's voice drops even further as he leans toward me. "Astarot is healed and hiding just outside the Nest. He'll help us get you free."

"He's healed? And close?" Fhord knows how to reach me, thaw my cold heart just a bit.

"He is," Fhord assures me. He lifts his hand, the thumb stretching out as if it wants to reach across the cell and stroke my cheek. But he lets it drop when he sees my eyes narrow. "I freed him and got some other help. We can get you out."

"What other help?"

"Toffer. We needed a troll, so I went to Revalle and convinced him to come." The corners of his lips curve up in the smallest smile. "He's … something else. Also completely devoted to you. And excited to tell you about his ride on Astarot." Now his grin is genuine, reaching his eyes. My treacherous heart thaws a little more.

I sit back, willing ice into my veins to freeze him out again. He's shown me more than once that I can't trust him. This could all be a trick. "Why should I believe you?"

He pauses for a moment, his lips tipping up as he whispers, "You've been so fucking dangerous to me since the first time I laid eyes on you." And then he takes a deep breath, dark green eyes smoldering as he watches me. "It's gonna make our lives impossible, and we could cause so much harm. But I can't deny it any longer. You own me, my little rabbit." Another pause as his gaze searches mine. "My life's been dark and cold for such a long time, I forgot what the sun felt like. You are my sun, the other half of my soul."

His eyes are bright as the sun. Solemn as a prayer. Like he really does care.

My gods-damned heart responds to those words as if they're true. They can't be, though. He wouldn't have left me here to be tortured if they were.

"I don't believe you, Fhord." Standing, I stalk toward the bars, placing my hands on them as I look out into the hall. "How can I possibly believe you?"

"I'm asking a lot. Fuck, Sifa. I know that. But it's the only way I can help you. Just be ready. When the time comes—and I promise you'll know it—open your thoughts to Astarot. To me. Do what we ask. Let us guide you out of here, take you to safety."

"I have no magic," I remind him, my hands reaching up to touch my manacle. "And even if I did, if I let down my shields, the Dróttning could find things I don't want her to have. She's searching. I can't give her that chance." My stomach clench-es as a rock settles in my chest. I turn, my gaze searching his. "I guess that's why you're here. You were in her rooms. She trusts you. She's using you to get to me. This is how. Getting me to drop my shields so she can find my secret."

Fhord holds my gaze, not trying to hide the hurt that flows into his eyes at my words. Or maybe it's all a ruse. Maybe he's that good of an actor. I can't know. So I can't trust him. "I deserve that. I know I do." His voice is sad but resolute. "I should have protected you. I'll never forgive myself for letting you suffer at her hands again. And I swear I will make her pay. But I'm here now. We can get you out if you trust me, just enough for that. When you're free, you and Astarot and Toffer can leave. Never see me again. If that's what you want."

His head lifts as a door opens down the hall and footsteps move toward us.

"Go, Fhord." My voice is hard. Cold.

He nods, his eyes searching mine. And then a mask drops, a leer taking over his features. "I'll see you soon, little elf," he tells me. Now, his voice is loud enough to be heard.

The guard stalks up, anger flaring from his eyes as he blocks Fhord's path. "What are you doing here?"

"I'm checking on my gift from the Dróttning," Fhord drawls, his hand reaching through the bars to caress my ass as a sneer emerges. I step away, drawing a slow smile as he continues to leer at me. But then Fhord turns toward the guard, the same arrogant, dismissive dragon rider I met in the forest. "You're keeping your fucking hands off her, right? Because she's mine. And nobody touches what's mine."

The guard's angry, but he must know Fhord's protected by the Dróttning. He drops his chin, just barely, and steps out of Fhord's way. "Ain't nobody put a finger on her. We follow the Dróttning's orders here."

"See that you do," Fhord barks, angry. "If I learn that anyone has so much as touched her, I will remove every body part that comes into contact with any part of her." He turns to look at me, sneering. "And she's too fucking skinny. I like my women with a little meat on their bones. Feed her. Well."

The guard's chin drops again, a little lower this time. "I'll make sure she's fed."

"Eat what they bring you," he says looking at me one last time. "Or we'll spend some private time together and I'll make you eat." A wicked smirk emerges, his eyes flaring as he reaches down to squeeze a cock that somehow has grown hard while we stood there. "I think you'll enjoy what I put in your mouth."

"Fuck. You."

I keep repeating myself, but seriously. Fuck him.

"Like I told you before, soon, little elf." He throws one last sneer at the guard, and spins to stride down the hall.

I drop to the ground as the guard turns to stalk away, emotions battling within me as my mind holds Fhord's image at the center of my thoughts. He's still the most stunning man I've ever known. This thing between us is more than that, though. I don't believe he really cares for me—and I know I can't trust him—but I also know I'm connected to him. Even now, my body is trembling just from his presence.

I hate the idea of being his toy, and hate even more the part of me that wants it. Wants Fhord, even if it wouldn't mean anything to him. At least I'd have that time with him.

I am so gods-awful pathetic.

"Are you okay, Sifa?" Joralf's voice floats toward me, concern in every word.

"I should be asking you that," I snort. "I'm not the one who got carved up yesterday. Are you okay?"

"I've been better," Joralf responds with a shallow laugh. "It's always a bad day of torture when they take my cock from me. Although it really does get bigger with each new growth." This laugh is more genuine. "Bjorn will be a satisfied elf when I return to him."

"That he will," I concur, my voice light with relief that he can joke about yesterday's events. "I'm sorry I couldn't do anything to help you," I add after a few moments.

"You were there with me, my friend," Joralf responds, his voice eternally kind. "You helped me more than you know." When he speaks again, his tone is tentative. "What did he tell you?"

"You didn't hear?"

"No. He hid his words well."

"He claims he can help me get out." I don't try to hide the scorn in my voice.

"Do you believe him? That he'll help you escape?"

My eyes fill with tears, the ache of betrayal spiraling through me again. "I want to, but I don't know if I can."

"Perhaps you'll know when the time comes." His voice is soft.

My heart swells as I realize Joralf's trying to comfort me, when I should be the one comforting him.

We fall into a silence that lasts a long time. I want to talk to Joralf, help him find peace with what just happened, but he's been through this before. He sounds better than me right now. And I need to think about Fhord and everything he told me. I need to decide whether to trust him and open my mind to Astarot if I can—and maybe Fhord and the Dróttning—when the time comes.

I let my mind take me where it will. It focuses on Fhord, dragging me through all my memories of him and the time we spent together. His face when we met and he tried to push me away, anger and threats exploding from his delicious lips. His gentle words when he woke me from a nightmare—and then the bare skin and tattoos I'd been desperate to see without realizing it. His eyes staring at me with an emotion I couldn't deny after I killed the men who'd tried to attack us.

His kiss, which always felt like a starving man desperate for the food and water he'd been denied. Like I was the most important being in the world and he would never let me go.

What if he was telling the truth, and he did what he felt he needed to do to protect us? To protect me? What would I have done in his shoes?

I want to believe him. What we experienced felt genuine. The emotions felt real.

But he left me to be tortured. Every time I think I might be close to accepting what he told me, this simple fact creeps back in. If he cared for me the way he claims, he wouldn't have let me suffer. He would have moved Valhalla and Helheim to protect me.

Food comes and I eat, wishing there was some way to share with Joralf. But he's too far away to pass anything, and they've given me nothing I could throw. I swallow it all, too buried by guilt to enjoy it.

Finally, hours after Fhord came to me, I fall into a restless sleep. And again, Fhord occupies my thoughts, my mind vacillating between dreams of finally being with him and nightmares of losing him. In each one, though, a feeling washes over me as I wake—a need so deep it has no bottom—before sleep drags me back down.

It's Joralf's voice that wakes me this time. His whispers wriggle into my dreams and drag me from Fhord's arms. "Sifa, something's happening."

Shaking my head, I try to focus on his words. I can't feel anything except a bone-deep sorrow at losing Fhord's touch.

"Sifa, you need to wake up." There's fear in his voice now, but I can't tell if he dreads what I'll find when I wake or me missing it.

The pulse that rolls through me destroys all the exhaustion and despair that had been sucking me back into sleep. It's a warning or a call. I'm not sure which. But it's desperate to get my attention.

"Sifa, wake up. Please." Now Joralf is exhausted. Whatever he did drained reserves he needs to heal.

"I'm sorry," I whisper, finally paying attention to the world around me.

"I can feel them." Joralf's voice is low, as though he fears being heard. He's never tried to hide his words from the guards before. "They're close, searching for you."

This is what Fhord told me to expect, I realize. I'm still terrified that he really did betray me, and this is a ploy. But I can't let this chance pass me by. I take the risk I didn't think I would, releasing part of my shield to search for my dragon. And for Fhord.

When I find Astarot racing beside Fhord toward the Nest, a warmth spills into my soul. Somehow, my bond with my dragon is stronger than the manacle. Even this metal around my neck—the Dróttning's chain on my psyche—can't suppress our connection. I can sense the truth of Fhord's words through Astarot. They've come to free me. I need to trust them for this to work.

I've missed you, my beautiful beast. My thoughts caress Astarot, searching for the remnants of his injury.

Healed, he tells me, gratitude for Fhord wrapping around his thoughts to share hints of all that's happened. Fhord saved him, stitching up his wound but also sharing magic to help him heal. Astarot was ready to fly when Fhord got back only because Fhord had drained nearly all his magic to help the dragon.

When he returned, Fhord killed the guards who held Astarot. And then they went together to Revalle to retrieve the most annoying troll my dragon had ever encountered.

I can't hold back the laugh as I see Toffer through my dragon's eyes, his fascination with the beasts so strong he's never left Astarot's side. Question after question after question—worse than a hatchling trying to understand a world they just entered—has plagued Astarot as he traveled north with an enthusiastic Toffer.

Still, in a ridiculously short period of time—and as much as my dragon hates to admit it—he's come to care for the troll who's been the most important part of my life for the last decade. The warmth blossoms even more, filling me with a love so complete, I can't believe I ever survived without it.

Control. Astarot tells me he needs my help to escape—and that I can help him, even with the manacle. He explains that the Dróttning has no idea I'm bound to a dragon. If she knew, she'd have done more to subdue my magic. Because when elves and dragons find each other, their abilities grow exponentially with the strength of their bond. They can access each other's power if their bodies are close enough, as ours are now.

Strong. Astarot says he and I already have a link that rivals any between a human and a dragon. When he's close enough for me to draw from his deep reservoir, I have magic that can overcome even the manacle.

My limbs tingle with the knowledge that I can access magic, even wearing this collar. Spreading out my thoughts, I find the closest guard and spear into his mind. He's oblivious to the angry dragon he'll face if I can't get out of here. I sift through his memories as quickly as I can, using the same technique I always do. The commander he hates and fears the most will get me free.

This one's a woman, which really pisses off the guard. Everything she does reminds him why he prefers little girls, who won't talk back to him. They do whatever he wants. And they know he's in charge. He hates uppity bitches, who think they have the right to tell *him* what to do.

I can't hold back the smile that erupts when I understand the kind of man this guard is. It's always nice to destroy the life of someone who deserves it. He deserves it.

As quickly as I can, I shuffle through his memories of her, letting them create a complete picture of who she is, from her surprisingly high voice to her odd mannerisms when she speaks—twists of the lips that sometimes are at odds with the words coming out—and the haughty stride as she walks the halls. When I've gathered enough to create a memory, I do, dropping it into his thoughts.

The guard turns, afraid, as he realizes he hasn't yet transferred the prisoners. *Fuck. She'll have me whipped again if I don't get them down to the Dróttning's caves. It's already been too long. She'll be pissed when I get there.*

Sucking my mind back in, I erect my shield and slump down against the wall. When his baton slaps against the door, I jump in surprise. Just like I do every other time.

"Stand, both of you. Time to go."

"It's not time yet," Joralf pleads, his voice shivering with fear. "I haven't healed yet. They never take me until I'm whole again."

"Well, they changed their fucking minds, I guess," the guard spits back. "Just hurry the fuck up. I need to get you down there."

A loud click echoes down the hall and Joralf's door squeals open, followed by footsteps coming toward me.

"Please," I whisper when they're both standing in front of me. "Leave me here. I don't want to go down there again."

"I don't give a fuck what you want, elf," he snarls. "Just get up and get moving."

I drag myself from the floor, desperation and fear in every movement. As I force my legs to move forward, he unlocks my door and swings it wide. "Hands," he commands when I join him in the corridor. But then his eyebrows slam into his hairline, and he spins his head to glance back at Joralf, who isn't wearing cuffs.

The command already is screwing up his responses, and the memory I created will conflict with reality too soon. He can't come with us. So I spin, one foot landing on his chin and the other in the center of his chest as I kick him toward the cell. He's dazed enough to control if we move quickly.

"Help me." I'm whispering, although I'm not sure why. If anyone can hear me, we're already lost.

Joralf's focus is better than mine. He's on top of the guard as soon as I ask, pulling his arms around his back as he gestures for the cuffs the guard had been about to place on me. He's starting to struggle—my kick not enough to knock him out—so Joralf and I have to fight to get them on his wrists.

We do, holding the guard splayed on his stomach as we snap them on. He's spewing out curses and threats now but it doesn't matter. I yank the keys from his belt and we're out the door, swinging it closed with a *clang* that echoes through the cavern.

"Where do you think you're going?" The voice that floats toward us sends a chill down my spine.

She's not supposed to be here.

She's never been down here before.

But it could only be her. She knows, and she's here to stop us.

Turning, my stomach drops, terror sending my heart racing and the blood crashing through my veins. The walls close in around me as my hopes of escape disappear. The Dróttning, surrounded by a half dozen guards, is staring at us with a wide grin and cruel eyes. She lifts a hand and crooks a finger, calling me to her.

We are so fucked.

CHAPTER TWENTY-NINE

FHORD

I WILL ALWAYS FIND YOU

IT'S NOT HER, SIFA. I cast my thoughts at my little rabbit, desperate for her to understand. It's dangerous. The Dróttning will catch my words if she's searching for me, and it's taking more energy than I can afford to speak to Sifa this way. But I have no other choice. I don't have time to relay this through the dragons.

Of course it's her. I feel Sifa's confusion. Her fear. I'm glad her thoughts are scattered. I wouldn't have been able to reach her if her shields went up when she saw what she thought was the Dróttning and her guards. But she'll need to be focused if we have any hope of getting her out. And soon.

Rabbit, listen to me. It's an illusion. I make sure my voice is calm, soothing.

Trust. Astarot's message spears out, dropping into my thoughts at the same time as he does Sifa's. I don't get anything more than the word and an echo of emotion, but I know what he's telling her.

He believes Sifa can rely on me. I can almost feel her centering herself before sending her words to me. *How do you know it's an illusion?*

I'm connected to her. I will tell her everything but not right now. I've already risked too much just by speaking to Sifa this way. The Dróttning gave us a short window when she left the Nest to chase down ... me, although she doesn't know it yet. The guards haven't been able to find a trace of whoever freed Astarot so the Dróttning headed south to bring the inspiration only she can. Fear is a potent motivator.

There's no time, so I put off giving Sifa the truth about me. Again. *I'll tell you more when we're together*, I promise her. *For now, just take a chance. Trust me. Walk toward them and really look at them. You'll see it when you do.*

I almost laugh with relief when I hear her surprised gasp. *How is she doing this?*

It doesn't matter. Go through them. Follow Astarot's instructions because I won't be able to speak with you again. He'll lead you to me. To safety.

Her delight echoes through our bond as she strides down the hall, probably passing right through the spell the Dróttning cast to emerge any time a prisoner stands outside their cage without a guard by their side.

If the Dróttning didn't know before that Sifa's escaping, she does now. She'll have felt the shift in her magic, and I have no doubt she's already racing back here and sending guards to secure the area. Sifa won't be alone for long. Astarot knows he needs to move her along quickly.

"Sif-Sif says she's safe?" Toffer's staring at me, his legs bouncing beneath him, massive eyebrows drawn together. I think he can speak normally—I sure as fuck hope so—but apparently, when he's nervous, he does this. Or frightened. Or excited. Basically, any strong emotion has him talking like a gods-damned minstrel. And the little bastard's been nervous since we left Revalle. Lucky me. "Sifa's surfacing soon?"

"I had to stop talking to her so we don't get caught. Astarot's getting her here," I assure him. "He'll let us know if anything goes wrong."

"Speedy status to your sidekick?"

And fuck if I don't already understand the troll's odd questions. I place a hand on his shoulder, trying to instill a confidence I don't feel as I force my lips into a smile. "I promise you'll know as soon as I do."

The next five minutes are the longest of my life. I don't like being helpless. Waiting. But for this part of the plan to work, I need to be quiet, let Astarot take the lead. So that's what I do. My skin itches with my need to go kill someone and drag Sifa away with me, but I reel in my emotions. I can't let myself screw this up because I feel like a heart-broken hatchling.

Toffer's even worse. I realized when I found him in Sifa's apartment that he holds a tight leash on his emotions, constantly fighting his baser urges. But he loves Sifa. He's holding it together for her. The only sign of his impending mania is his constant motion—usually a bouncing leg or fingers tapping through a never-ending rhythm.

I feel her before I see her. Even with both of our shields up, her presence caresses me like a long-lost lover. It's the most intimate feeling I've ever experienced and fills me with a hope I'd nearly lost when I learned the Dróttning tortured her while I was gone.

When she finally rounds a corner, eyes wide as she scans the cavern holding Toffer and me—with another prisoner on her heels—I can barely breathe. Her gaze finds mine, and for a moment I'm not sure what emotion I'll see. I'm terrified that distrust or hatred will glare back at me. Instead, her eyes soften and the corners of her lips tip up just a bit. She's giving me a chance, I realize as the breath I'd been holding huffs out.

"Rabbit," I whisper, stopping myself from striding forward to wrap my arms around her. My savage needs to feel her skin again. To reassure himself she's real and here. But he needs to calm the fuck down. The only thing that matters is what Sifa needs. And she has to work through this on her own terms. To come to me, if she chooses.

Her lips tip up just a bit more, but she doesn't respond, turning instead to look at the troll. Now, her smile's broad and unrestrained. Striding forward, she throws herself into his arms, my guts twisting with an odd kind of jealousy. I understand why. Still, it hurts more than I could have expected to watch her go to him first.

We have to get out of this cavern, but they both need this moment so I wait, forcing myself to count out the half-minute I'm going to give them. When I hit thirty, I grunt. "We need to go."

Sifa's arms tighten around Toffer with one hard squeeze before she steps back. "You're right." She looks down at the troll, her face still lit up with her joy at seeing him. "Gratitude to my gallant guardian," she says quietly as one hand caresses his cheek.

"Relief for my rescued roomy," he responds with a shy grin. "Me missed my mate." Pausing as a hand reaches up to wipe his wet cheeks, he adds, "Thor, too. Home and hearth hearken."

"I've missed you both so much," she tells him with a shaky laugh. Turning toward me, she adds in a soft voice, "Thank you for finding me."

"I will always find you," I breathe. "I'm sorry it took me so long. That you went through so much while I was gone. I didn't know." My hands curl at my sides as anger—at myself, the Dróttning, this whole fucked-up world—rises within me. "I would have stayed. I would have done anything to stop her if I'd known."

She inhales deeply, her eyes closing as she seems to let my words calm and settle her. "You're here now, and you brought help." Finally, she turns toward the male that came with her. "Joralf, this is Fhord and Toffer." Looking at me again, she adds, "Joralf helped me get through this. He's coming with us."

My chin drops in assent. Whatever Sifa needs. "Toffer got us here through a cave I didn't know existed. I don't think anyone does because it's too small for dragons. It's tight in a couple of places, but it can get us out too."

"Let's go." Sifa's all business now. It's time to escape.

Toffer responds with the grin of a child whose mother has just given him permission to lead them through the forest. He starts to stalk deeper into the caves, following the innate sense all trolls have for caverns and passages through rock. I'd have gotten lost already if it weren't for him.

This time, though, we can't follow the same path. We've walked for less than five minutes when we hear the first group of soldiers looking for us. They're angry, the Dróttning's punishments harsh when she's failed. Every one of them will suffer if they don't capture us.

"They won't be here," a male voice proclaims, his voice angry. "Nobody even knows about this area."

They're so gods-damned close, a turn or two away from finding us. My gaze scatters, searching for someplace to hide or escape.

"We know," a female responds, her tone dripping with disdain. "If we're here, they could be too."

"They're probably already gone. We're all fucked because Gunnar let that elf control him."

"She's stronger than she looks." I think I hear a hint of respect in her words. "And they can't have gotten out yet. There hasn't been enough time."

We're going to need to kill them. They'll pass by here, and this cave doesn't have any place we can hide. But then Toffer's massive hand is on my shoulder as he gestures toward a shadow in the corner. "Go," he mouths.

Nodding, I follow his directions, careful that my steps don't reveal our location. My gut is a rock, every sense alert to any shift in the space around us. I'm about to face two fucked-up choices.

If the guards realize we're here, we'll have seconds, if that, to take them down. Every guard here knows me. The Dróttning's in the Nest and will catch any thought thrown her way. I don't know if we can stop them before the message lashes out telling her what I've done.

I could use my magic to kill them before they see us, but I alone can wield the power I'd need and the Dróttning will recognize it when it echoes through the caves. My magic is like a horn to her. It always tells her exactly where she can find me.

Either way, we're fucked. The Dróttning will learn I'm helping Sifa escape, and she'll take Tindera from me. Maybe kill her. I don't know if I'd survive that, even with Sifa by my side.

We huddle together—my savage taking my thoughts in the wrong fucking direction when Sifa's thigh rubs against mine and my gods-damned cock twitches. Because I can't control the bastard when I'm around her. The soldiers pass by slowly, still bickering about their decision to search this part of the caves. They're nearly out of our sight when one of them stops, his head spinning in our direction.

"Did someone check that area?" A finger lifts to point directly at us.

And my pulse races. If they take a few steps toward us, I'll have no choice.

I'm sweating, my skin tingling as my magic rises to the surface, ready to lash out.

"There's nothing there," another says, his glare roving the area around us.

"I saw something move," the first one insists. "Go check it out."

"You're seeing ghosts. You go. I'm heading back to the base."

Now my stomach is twisting, the power I've gathered demanding release. I won't be able to hold it much longer.

"Alright," the first one agrees after a moment as he watches the other guards walk away. "Like you said. There's not shit in these caves."

We stay there, hunched down and still, for a minute or more. I think we're all afraid to move and risk drawing them back. Finally, though, Joralf stands. "They're gone," he says, reaching out a hand to pull up Toffer. "Let's get out of here."

We're not so lucky the second time I sense others moving our direction. I'd recognize her presence anywhere. The being that's governed and manipulated my life since it began. The Dróttning is striding toward us, her thoughts chaotic and furious. If she finds us, I won't be able to defeat her. Even as strong as my magic is when I unleash it, it is no match for hers. Yet.

Toffer spins, touching a nearby wall as he inhales deeply. He points and trots down a new cavern, his feet surprisingly light for his bulk. The others follow and I take the rear, ready to do whatever I can to give them time to escape.

We turn a dozen times as we try to find a path away from the Dróttning, Toffer pausing occasionally to place a hand or two on the rock and breathe in whatever scent he's following. Time slows to nearly a stand-still as we barely stay ahead of our pursuers. Every time I think we've found an escape route, they turn or backtrack, chasing us once again. My mind is screaming at me to get away, dragging up image after image of Sifa in her cell. Imagining my little rabbit on the rack. Feeling her pain as I did when she first arrived.

We won't be able to lose the Dróttning. That reality settles within me, a truth I can't avoid. I'm as familiar to her as she is to me. She's following us as if she already knows every turn we'll make. She must recognize my presence. It's the only explanation. Which means they won't get away if I stay with them.

My hand reaches out to take Sifa's arm, pulling her toward me. The others notice and slow down, pausing a dozen feet away. Sifa looks up at me, her eyebrows rising in her silent question. My savage is roaring, loath to leave her, but I push him down. We need to separate if she's going to get out.

"Go ahead without me," I breathe as I lean into her. "I'll divert the Dróttning and her guards. I'll catch up."

Sifa's shaking her head, grabbing my arm to pull me farther into the cavern. "We're not leaving you."

She's so fucking beautiful. My heart cracks with her resolve to keep me close. I can't give in to this, though. We won't get away from the Dróttning this way.

"She can sense all of us, but she knows me," I hiss in Sifa's ear. "I don't think she's certain it's me, but she won't give up the chance to find out. She'll follow me, not you or the others. I can get away from her. If she's not leading the chase, you'll be able to evade whoever she sends after you. Let me send her in another direction and then I'll catch up to you."

The seconds tick by slowly as Sifa watches me. Finally, her chin dips for a second before her gaze rises and holds mine. "You will find us," she demands in a husky voice, full of emotions I can't let myself consider yet. "This thing between us isn't finished. And I have questions for you."

I lift one hand to her cheek, the other grasping her waist to pull her close. "I told you already, my little rabbit. I will always find you."

When my lips find hers, the world makes sense, Sifa at its center. But that's all we can have. I pull away, caressing her cheek one last time. "Go," I urge her.

She nods and turns to follow Toffer and Joralf deeper into the cave.

I spin and start to backtrack, leading the Dróttning as far away from them as I can. For a moment, I think it's not going to work. That the Dróttning decided to follow Sifa and I've abandoned them to her wrath.

My chest lightens when she trails me, though. I wind through the caves with her on my heels, abandoning any hope of finding my way back to where I left Sifa and the others. Toffer will lead them to Astarot and the horses, and they'll get away. That's the only thing that matters.

Perhaps ten minutes after I split from Sifa and the others, I lead my pursuers into a cavern with no exit, my heart dropping into my feet when I realize it.

Fuck. Me.

It's deep enough for me to have some time to try to fix this, but not much. They're on my heels, and I have a minute, if that. I have no choice but to use my magic—which the Dróttning will recognize, because my power alone in this land will echo through the entire cave system. She may only *believe* right now that it's me she's following. This will remove any doubt. And Tindera will be fully fucked.

Because I fucked this up so badly.

Reaching out, I lay my palms against the rock, searching for the best path. If this works at all, it will take every ounce of my magic. When I sense another cavern, perhaps a male's-height away, I slow my breathing. And I push. The rock is stubborn. It's been here for a long time. I'm more stubborn.

Too gods-damned slowly, the rock starts to move under my touch. I'm trembling, the mix of anxiety and exertion reaching into every part of me, but my hands are solid and the rock is responding. A tunnel. That's all I need. But I have to move a shit-ton of rock to do that, pushing most of it into surrounding stone to force the density to increase, while rock along the edges can shift out and add to the surface area.

Long seconds pass while I create a path I can take, expanding its size from a pinhole to a space large enough for a mouse, then a child, and finally an adult. I'm sucking in air by now, barely able to get enough, but I think I'll be able to get through.

Just in time. The Dróttning's soldiers are racing toward me, their leader fast on their heels. I shove into the hole I've opened, finding crevices and cracks to pull my body in and forward. My head is nearly through the other side when a hand wraps around my ankle, tugging me back. Grasping the edge, I try to turn—give myself a better angle to kick this bastard away—but I can't. I can go backward or forward. That's it.

My heart is pounding in my ears, my stomach twisting into a tight knot. If the Dróttning captures me, I'll never be able to help Tindera escape. And I cannot let my dragon pay an even higher price than she's already condemned to suffer because of my fucked-up mating bond.

Inhaling deeply to try to calm myself enough for another burst of magic, I let go of the edge with my right hand, placing my palm on the rock as far down my body as I can. And I shove, forcing more stone to give way. Finally, I have the space I need to spin. One more push—gasping as I dig deep to find more power—and I open the tunnel enough to kick at the bastard holding my leg.

I can't hold back the smile as I hear the satisfying crunch of bone. He lets go and I spin again, yanking at the tunnel's edge and barely shielding my head as I tumble to the cave floor. Scrambling to my feet, I splay my palms inside the tunnel and pull up the last dregs of my magic to fill part of the tunnel. A smirk tips my lips as the soldier with the broken nose is trapped in the rock, his skull crushing under its weight.

And then I collapse to the ground, thanking the gods for finally giving me a gods-damned break.

I'm rising to my feet, wondering how I'll find my way out of here, when the Dróttning's voice drifts toward me, frustration and anger in every word. "I'm done with this game, Fhord. I know you're responsible for the elf escaping. I knew you were lying to me when you sat in my rooms, trying to convince me there's nothing between you. You can't hide that kind of secret from me. You're more of a fool than I realized.

"So go. Leave these caves. But know this. Unless you bring the elf to me—alive or not, I no longer care—you may never return. You are dead to me." She pauses a moment, a laugh gusting out of her. "And to your dragon. She's mine now. You won't see her again."

Every part of me deflates as the Dróttning's words sink in, and I feel her move away from me.

Tindera will pay the price. As I always knew she would.

I only hope her words didn't reach Sifa. My little rabbit can't know what her freedom has cost me. She can't know what a risk I'll be taking when I come back here to try to free Tindera. Because I have to try. I won't be able to live with myself if I abandon my dragon to the Dróttning's punishments for my sins.

I can't move. For a minute or more, I stand there motionless, my mind skipping through my options, dismissing each. I want to race back now, try to free Tindera before I follow Sifa from the Nest. But I've used every bit of my magic.

It wouldn't matter anyway. In this, the Dróttning holds all the power. Tindera can't go until the Dróttning releases her. Nobody leaves here without our dear leader's permission. If I know the Dróttning—and I do, at least where her wrath is concerned—Tindera's already imprisoned.

My stomach clenches, my last meal threatening to push its way up and out. I'm helpless to protect my dragon. And I don't know how in the fuck I'll ever find Sifa and the others.

Toffer's hand on my shoulder pulls me from my desperate thoughts. "Sifa summons her savior." His voice is low and solemn. "Salvation," he adds as he points down one of the many caverns leading from this one.

Fuck, am I glad I went and got the troll.

Nodding, I let him lead me into the tunnel, twisting and turning down a path I never would've found. When we enter a large cave with a pool at its center, I can only stare at the splendor around me. I've never been here—had no idea this place even existed—and it's the most marvelous thing I've ever seen.

Reds, oranges, and yellows dominate the walls, light from some unknowable source casting its glow all around to reveal stones of ruby, citrine and topaz. But they can't compare to the water that sparkles in soft luster. It's the deepest blue, the color of a jay spinning through the air as the sun casts its first rays on the day.

It also vibrates with magic. I feel as if I could touch the beginning and end of time just by swimming through its waters. All knowledge awaits me if I drink from its plenty. I want nothing more than to drop into it and never leave.

"The pool will prolong and protect." Toffer's shy smile accompanies a shove to my back. "Proceed."

The troll's strange words shouldn't make sense, but they do. Whatever is here almost feels sentient. It wants to sustain us. I can't fathom the possibility we would drown, no matter how long we were submerged.

I take a deep breath regardless, too aware of how easily magic can manipulate our minds. And then I drop into the pool and let myself sink down, following Toffer as he begins to kick deeper and deeper. We swim farther than we should be able to go without breathing, but I'm sure I could go farther still. My chest is light and full of air.

When Toffer leads us into a tube deep below the surface, I feel the magic shift. My lungs start to constrict as my brain registers that I've gone minutes without a breath. With every kick, darkness wraps around us and the pressure inside increases. Every part of me is screaming to breathe, even if the water would take my life. I have no idea how Sifa and Joralf could have made it so far, weak as they were.

When I see the light ahead of us—a disc of hope that brightens as I continue to rise—my soul lightens. I throw every bit of myself into this swim, watching as the surface grows closer and closer.

We emerge in a pond on the rear of the mountain, and I suck in a breath, marveling that I'm alive and free of the caves. Tindera's image floats into my mind, but I push it aside. Right now, I need to get Sifa away from here. I'll return for my dragon soon.

Toffer and I float on the water and fill our lungs. The moon rests high in the sky above us, bright and full, casting light and shadows on the surface. And then he starts to swim toward the nearby shore. My gaze follows him and a fist unclenches inside me when I find her. She's waiting, as Toffer said she would be.

Steeling myself for whatever Sifa may do or say to me, I follow Toffer to the shore, watching her as I step from the water, dripping wet but alive. When I'm a dozen feet away, I stop, letting her decide where we go from here. How, or if, we move forward.

She closes the distance between us. Striding forward, she places her hands on my chest, looking up at me with melancholy eyes.

"She hurt me," Sifa whispers, her voice so soft I can barely hear her words.

"I'm so, so sorry." What else can I say? I let this happen.

"You were supposed to be there. You left."

"I didn't know she would do that to you. She said she wouldn't, and I believed her. Then my thoughts couldn't get to you while you wore the manacle. I didn't feel your pain." I drop my forehead to rest against hers, my hands wrapping around her waist. "She'll never hurt you again. I swear it."

"I don't think you can promise that, Fhord." Her hand lifts to caress my cheek, her eyes searching mine. "Did you mean it?" she whispers with a glance down and then back up at me. "That I hold part of your soul?"

I place my hand on hers, the other reaching out to cup her cheek. "Before the dragons, the Dróttning and the draugrs," I tell her with a hint of a smile as I glance at Toffer, "before the gods breathed this world into being and gifted us the lifeblood that flows through us, before the mountains rose and the oceans formed, before magic filled this land and all its beings, there was you and me. We have always been and we always will be. You are the sunrise in my day, the air I breathe, the reason I exist. I didn't know what it was to live before you. There is no after. I don't want a life without you. Ever. Whatever the price to be with you, I will pay it."

The look she gives me is glorious. Her heart peers back at me, open and pure.

And my savage rejoices. I can feel him expanding out, ready to take over and take her.

Holy fuck. I need this. I need her. I tried to deny it, to push her away. I've lied to myself every single day since I met her. But I can't hide from it anymore.

"I want this, my little rabbit—I want you—more than I've ever wanted anything, anyone. But you have to know what this will mean. To me. To us."

Sifa cocks her head, her hands ghosting over my arms as the corners of her lips lift. She rises to brush those lips against mine. "What would this mean to you, Fhord?"

Something opens inside me, a dragon discovering the joy of flight, a wave flowing through the open sea, a star suspended in the sky, beaming its light across the universe. My savage soothes as I embrace the destiny he's demanded since I laid eyes on Sifa.

"When you're mine, there will be no other. I'm not a good male, rabbit. I will hunt ... I will destroy ... anyone and anything that would come between us, that would hurt you, or try to take you from me. When you give yourself to me, Sifa, you give it all to me. Every part of you. Everything you will ever do or be. You'll be mine. And I'll be yours. Forever."

Sifa doesn't shrink from me as I claim and open myself to her. Holding my gaze, her hands caress my chest and then lift to my cheeks as she pulls my lips down to hers. She doesn't respond with words. Maybe she's not ready yet to love me the way I love her, after everything she's been through. But it's enough for now.

Chapter Thirty

Sifa

Did I Please You, Rabbit?

I'm traveling north with Fhord. We'll find a place where Astarot can fully heal while Fhord goes back to the Nest to retrieve Tindera—if the Dróttning hasn't figured out yet that he was involved in my escape. The thought terrifies me, and I'll need to talk to Fhord about it soon. Not yet, though.

Toffer and I both cried when he and Joralf mounted Hilde to head south. I'm still amazed Fhord had her here waiting for us, but I shouldn't be. He knew what he had to do to get me out and made it happen. Joralf will take Toffer back home before he goes in search of his mate. Much as I want Toffer with me, his kill-first-ask-questions-later approach to life is too risky while we're moving through unknown lands. We'll get settled then I'll find a way to get him and Thor.

Now, I'm nestled into Fhord's chest as we ride Sigurd into forests that grow deeper with every step. Astarot's walking behind us while he can, before the forest blocks his path. We can't risk him being seen from the air and Fhord has promised he knows a cave we'll be able to hide in.

I have so many questions. So many thoughts. But I'm tired and hungry and having a hard time putting them into words. Those conversations will come. For now, I'm just savoring this time with Fhord.

"Are you ready to eat something, rabbit?" Fhord's soft voice breaks into my thoughts.

"I really should. I'm starving. I'm just not sure my stomach will hold anything while we're riding. Will we be at the cave soon?"

"Another hour, maybe a bit more. I'll be able to make a stew quickly with what I have waiting there."

"You planned everything." I don't try to keep the wonder and gratitude from my voice.

"I had help. When I went to get Toffer, I checked in with the Ætt. Leif came to get things set up while we went into the Nest. He's gonna go hide with the others until I can get back to them."

"I'll have to thank him, the next time I see him."

"It'll be a while, rabbit. We're not going south again anytime soon. We can't."

"I know." I take a deep inhale, realizing as I do that I'm not as worried about the future—and the drastic changes ahead—as I would have expected. "It's okay," I assure Fhord as a peace settles over me. "Did I tell you about my friend, Sagga, and her words for me before we met?"

"No, you didn't." Fhord's voice is so gentle.

"She's a seer. Always before, she saw little things and I didn't pay much attention to her predictions. But the last one. That was different. She predicted," I say as my hand lifts to gesture around us, "all of this. She knew my life was about to change, starting with some big journey, and said it's all necessary." I pause, thinking about her message and what it could mean. "Something big's about to happen, to change life here, and we're part of it."

Fhord's quiet for a long time. "Maybe it is. This world is broken in so many ways. It can't go on like this."

We fall into silence again, both lost in our own thoughts. Fhord's hands, though, are a constant comfort. He's just holding me, Sigurd's reins loose as he follows a path he must know well. He's keeping me centered, even hopeful, in the wake of the chaos I just escaped.

Finally, hours after we separated from Toffer and Joralf, Fhord leads us toward a mountain that doesn't look like it might have an opening big enough for us. As before, though, we find a cave that's so well hidden, it could only be found by someone who knows it's here. It's exactly what we need.

Astarot shuffles in after us and I can feel his surprise when he sees a sheep tied at the rear of the cave. He spins his head toward Fhord, eyes rich with gratitude, and drops his chin once.

Food, he tells me. He's as hungry as me and had no idea when he would eat next. He didn't want to ask and is relieved he didn't need to.

"Thank you," I whisper as I lean back into Fhord.

"You can thank Tindera when you see her next. She wanted a goat for Astarot but this was the best Leif could do."

"It's perfect. Astarot is grateful."

Fhord dismounts and helps me down. As I head to get the sheep for Astarot, he steps toward the fire pit to light the tinder that Leif must have prepared for us. When I get back, he's unpacking Sigurd and gathering supplies to make our meal.

"There's a hot spring farther into the cavern," he tells me, gesturing to an area behind the sheep. "Go bathe while I make us something to eat. You'll find what you need waiting for you there."

"You really thought of everything," I whisper, my heart expanding in my chest. "Thank you. Again."

"Anything ... everything ... for you, my little rabbit."

Nodding, I turn before he can see the tears that formed in my eyes. As I walk around a corner I hadn't noticed before, I see the pond waiting for me, steam drifting up from the surface. Soap and a towel sit by the edge, and I can see a change of clothes farther in. I shrug out of the dirty rags I wore from the prison, tossing them aside as I step into the water.

It's a glorious feeling to drop into its warmth and let it cover me, start to wash away the grime and filth of my cage. My mind tries to take me back there but I push those thoughts away. Today is about moving forward with Fhord. Tomorrow I can come to terms with the past week, all that happened.

A big part of me wants to soak here forever, never leave to face the demons waiting outside of this cave. But Fhord's just around the corner making a meal for me. Taking care of me. An even bigger part wants to be with him.

I scrub myself as quickly as I can, washing out my hair as I rid myself of every hint of the Nest and its depravity. Toweling off, I don the clothes Fhord brought—soft night clothes from my own drawer in Revalle—and slide the slippers onto my feet. And then I go to him.

His back is to me as he feeds herbs of some kind into a pot simmering above the fire. I could watch him forever, I realize as I stare, stunned, at this male who's risking everything for me. He's all I could want in a man. Perfect. Perfect for me.

He must feel my eyes on him, turning to cast a devious smile. "I'd planned to give you time to recover," he whispers, his voice deep. "But if you keep looking at me like that, I can't be responsible for my actions. There's a big part of me that's been very impatient as I forced it to wait for you."

Suddenly, food is the last thing on my mind. "How long, Fhord?" I breathe, my heart racing as I feel the weight of his look in my core. I'm burning hotter than the fire already. "How long have you waited for me? For this?"

"I think I've waited my entire life for you, my rabbit. When I felt you enter this world, I knew you would change everything. I didn't realize then how much I needed that change. Now I do. I need you."

"Then what are we waiting for? Because I need you too. I want you, Fhord."

Fhord hesitates just a moment, his expression a conflict between protecting me after everything I've been through, and giving in to the invitation I can see he desperately wants to accept. "Are you sure, rabbit?"

"I've never been more sure about anything."

I take the first step but Fhord doesn't wait any longer. He's striding forward as if released from a spell, scooping me into his arms to carry me toward the bed he apparently set up right after lighting the fire.

Always prepared, this male.

My gaze finds his and I lift my hand to cup his cheek. "You wanted to be ready?" I ask with a laugh.

"For you to rest," he assures me, his voice light. And then he responds with a smile that lights the cave around us. "Or for this," he admits with a chuckle. "My savage insisted. He's not a patient beast. He'd have been pissed if I made him wait even longer while I dug out and threw down some blankets."

And then his lips take mine, and the world stops. Nothing exists but us and this moment.

He is gentle, letting me set the pace for us to discover each other. But I don't want gentle. I need him as badly as he needs me. My hands weave through his hair, and I pull him toward me, my lips parting as they explore this male who means more to me than I want to admit.

Too soon, he breaks the kiss as he lays me down on the blankets, his lips caressing an earlobe before they feather along my jaw, drawing shivers up and down my spine as his light touch starts fires in every part of me. I reach for his shirt, desperate to see and touch this body that's been kept from me too long, but he takes my hand, holding it as he lifts it to his lips.

"Not yet, rabbit. Let me savor you a bit more. I want this, our first time, to last. I need you to know, I need you to feel in every part of you, how much you mean to me."

"I know, Fhord." My hands caress his cheeks as I lift my head to kiss him lightly. "I know."

"Let me show you anyway," he asks, his green eyes as bright as a field of grass on a spring day.

Nodding, I lay my head back down, holding his stare.

"Close your eyes, Astarot," Fhord directs with a laugh as he glances at my dragon. "This is between Sifa and me."

Elves, Astarot responds with a harrumph, offended at the thought he might want to watch this. His head swings away from us to face the wall as sleep tugs at him.

"It's just you and me," I assure Fhord.

"Forever," he promises.

His hands rest on my hips as he leans forward to kiss one eye and then the other, moving slowly over my cheekbones to my jaw. When he reaches my neck he pauses there, licking and nipping at me, drawing trembles with every touch. Finally, one of his hands moves up, fluttering over my stomach as he reaches for my breast.

My body responds of its own volition, arching into him as his thumb circles my nipple, his fingers massaging the skin that tingles with his every move.

"I've been waiting for them," Fhord breathes as the elf in me emerges, the points in my ears revealing the secret I finally gave to Fhord, after hiding it for so long. His hand lifts and fingers caress this evidence of his effect on me, triggering emotions I've kept buried since I landed in this world. "My little elf," he whispers, his teeth nipping gently at each tip.

And then he's kissing me again. This time, Fhord's hungry. His lips are more demanding, his tongue parting mine to taste me. His hands, though. They tell me Fhord is starting to lose control.

Thank the gods.

First one and then the other palm reaches under my shirt to stroke my bare skin, moving up to my breasts. He cups them both, drawing them together as his thumbs work my nipples, his lips leaving mine to drop to my stomach. "You're right," he admits after a moment. "We have too many clothes on."

Standing, holding my gaze the entire time, he kicks off his boots and then draws his shirt over his head, smiling as my eyes grow wide at the bare chest, tattoos rising and falling with his deep breaths. His hands find the ties of his pants, loosening them so they can drop to the ground and release the large, hard dick that's waiting for me. My tongue reaches out to lick my lips as I imagine wrapping them around Fhord and drawing out his orgasm.

"I need you inside me," I breathe.

"Not yet, rabbit." He continues to stare, lids hooded, as he drops to his knees and unbuttons my top, pulling it off slowly. His gaze leaves mine only when I'm wearing nothing but pants and his lips drop again to my stomach. Slowly, oh so slowly, he tugs them down, his caress following as he grazes the skin he's exposed.

When I'm as naked as him, he starts to work his way back up, kissing along my ankles, then my calves and the insides of my thighs. Which are dripping wet.

I am trying, *the gods know I am trying*, to give this male the time he wants. And those same gods know I'm enjoying every bit of this too. But *fuck*. I *need* Fhord to touch me. I have never wanted anything more than his hands or his tongue on me—or better yet, in me—right now.

"Please, Fhord." My voice is so quiet, I'm not sure my words reach him.

"Fuck it turns me on to hear you beg, rabbit. Say it again." His tongue licks my thigh, his breath sparking little fires that I *need* to grow.

"Please." I reach down for his cheeks, drawing his eyes up to meet mine.

"You're so fucking beautiful," he whispers. "And you're mine," he adds as he finally—*finally*—touches me where I need.

His tongue reaches out to lash against my core, licking and nipping at me, and I can't hold back the groan. My hips buck against him, drawing a wicked laugh, as he reaches up to push them against the blankets and resume his luxurious plundering of my soul.

When he sucks at my clit—my back arching as I fight to break free of his grip and drag more from him—one of his fingers joins in the fun. He laughs again—the sexiest sound

I've ever heard—and then adds another. His fingers are going in and out of me, hitting that spot that makes me see stars every time he gets close, and all I can do is hold on as the pressure builds inside me, a fire burning itself free to consume every part of me.

And then I'm coming, the orgasm washing through me in wave after wave, Fhord's tongue and fingers pulling every bit of pleasure my body has to give.

But Fhord's not close to done.

He pauses a moment, watching the shivers ripple through me, and then starts again. His tongue reaches into me before he drags it up to lick my clit. I gasp in a breath as his lips start to suck, sending me spiraling again into a desperate need for Fhord. Finally, he starts to pull himself back up my body, biting and licking as he goes, to rest between my legs, his cock hard against my thigh.

"Fuck me, Fhord," I murmur as I dig my hands into his hair. "I need you to fuck me."

He shakes his head, a sultry smile lifting his lips. "I'm going to make love to you, rabbit," he rumbles, leaning forward to brush his lips against mine. "Later, I'll fuck you. The first time you come on my cock, though, you're going to feel my love with every breath you take, each beat of your heart, every flutter in your body."

A tremble rolls down my spine. "Please," I whisper—the only word I seem able to mutter tonight—as I wrap my arms and legs around him to drag him closer to me. "Please make love to me, Fhord."

Slowly, gently, Fhord pushes at my entrance, sliding into me as he lets my body adjust to his size. His gaze doesn't leave mine as he pulls out and enters me again. And again. I can feel him everywhere, the sensations building into another wave of pleasure that forms at my core and spills out to the rest of me. Our hips find a rhythm that is ours alone. We move together, slowly at first, but then with more urgency.

When Fhord kisses me, it's with a hunger I realize he's felt since our eyes met in the forest. I can feel his need for me as he lunges in and out, in and out, filling me with each plunge deeper into my core.

When my orgasm comes, it's nothing like I've ever experienced before. It consumes me, the world narrowing down to this cave, Fhord and me the only beings who will ever exist. I am whole, complete, in a way I never thought possible. Gasping into the waves that cascade through me, I smile as I realize Fhord fell over the cliff with me.

We lay there motionless, caressing and breathing in each other, for a long time. Fhord pulls away before I'm ready, lifting himself up to kiss me again and draw me into his broad chest. His thumb rubs circles on my arm as another hand rests on my hip.

"Well, that was ... everything I'd hoped it would be," I sigh. That doesn't come close to describing what Fhord just did to me, but *fuck*. I don't know how words could do it justice.

"Did I please you, rabbit?" Fhord's eyes twinkle at me, a wicked grin curving up the lips that just finished doing wicked things to me. "We've only just begun," he promises, his hand floating down to rub his thumb against my clit. His smile grows more broad as he lifts it to his lips and sucks gently.

"We may never leave this cave," I whisper, my core already heating again as I glance down. One little taste of me has Fhord ready to go again.

"We'll never want to," he agrees, leaning forward to place his lips on mine. "First, though, I should feed you. I have plans for you tonight and you'll need all the energy you can get."

"Promises, promises," I respond with a laugh, reaching down to caress the cock that's beckoning to me.

"None of that," Fhord insists, taking my wrist to lift it above my head. His lips drop to a nipple, sucking in for the most tantalizing moment, before he lifts himself away from me. "Food. Then you can have your way with me."

My stomach agrees, grumbling at the worst possible time. Fhord laughs and then pulls on his pants, throwing a wink at me before he saunters toward the pool.

Leaving me and my thoughts alone as I watch him prepare our meal. Wondering where we go from here, and how we can possibly survive the Dróttning's wrath we just unleashed.

Epilogue; Tindera

Then I Will Soar

I KNEW SHE'D COME for me.

I'd hoped to have more time. To fly with Astarot, my drake, just once. To swim with him in the crystal waves of my favorite pool. To share the joy of the fat goats.

To *be* with him, as a drakaina should be with her drake.

But I knew it would end. That the Dróttning would end it.

I don't regret it. I told my rider to choose the elf—to save her, even if it meant my doom.

He resisted, but he could do nothing else. It was the elf's life or my freedom. He could not have both.

And I would not want to be ridden by the husk of a male that would remain if the elf had been killed.

The elf will help my drake and my rider fill the emptiness from my capture. She is worthy. Of them both. She will lead them to their destiny.

If they return for me, if they can free me of the Dróttning's clutches, then I will soar with Astarot.

The End,

For Now ...

Sifa and Fhord are waiting for you in
Frenzied Fate, Book II of *Tales of the Vanir.*
Get your copy here.

Thank You

Thank you for reading *Sacred Struggle!*
I hope you're enjoying Sifa and Fhord's story so far,
and I would appreciate it so much if you could
take the time to leave a review on Amazon,
Goodreads, or wherever you review books!

Author's Note

I'M SO LUCKY TO be able to do what I love, supported by family and friends. Thanks to my hubby Al, our boys Albert and Stephen, and the amazing friends who have been cheering me along.

Thanks also to everyone who read *Sacred Struggle* and shared their thoughts with me, starting with my alpha reader Cynthia, who's read all my books and given me great feedback.

With this series, I relied heavily on beta feedback.
Many thanks to Cindy Ray Hale and Keele Publishing,
Kaitlin Slowik, Keeya Marquez, and Gemma Poulton
for all of their comments and suggestions.

And last but definitely not least, thanks to everyone who gave this book a try. I fell in love with this world and hope you do too. As an indie author, your support means everything. I'm grateful to everyone who talks about my books, through a review or on social media, and just as grateful to everyone who reads them. Thank you!

Also by Rochelle Wilcox

The Road to Ragnarök
(mostly closed-door portal romantic fantasy;
Heavy Heart has one spicy scene)

Fickle Fate
(the spicy prequel, available to subscribers
to my newsletter at RochelleWilcox.com)
Lost Long
Enemies Eternal
Alive Again
Heavy Heart

About the Author

Rochelle Wilcox is happily retired from practicing law, focused on writing what she loves to read. You can find Rochelle at rochellewilcox.com and at any of the social media sites below:

amazon.com/stores/Rochelle-Wilcox/author/B007PEWME6

goodreads.com/author/show/6951175.Rochelle_Wilcox

bookbub.com/authors/rochelle-l-wilcox

facebook.com/TheRoadToRagnarok

instagram.com/rochellewilcoxauthor/

tiktok.com/@rochellewilcoxauthor

www.ingramcontent.com/pod-product-compliance
Lightning Source LLC
Chambersburg PA
CBHW020324010826
48973CB00005B/1115